Praise for previous novels

'Utterly gorgeous ... so funny and relat[able] ... [Aisling] is one of the finest comic creations of a[ll time.'] ...

'Aisling has become that rare, precious thing: a fictional character you care about like a friend.' **LISA MCGEE, CREATOR AND WRITER OF** *DERRY GIRLS*

'My unofficial autobiography.' **AISLING BEA**

'A wholesome but modern heroine ... reading Aisling feels like a hug, the warm embrace of a safe world.' **LOUISE MCSHARRY**

'We all need a little Aisling in our lives.' **LOUISE O'NEILL**

'I laughed on every page ... Emer and Sarah are the funniest, smartest writers in the land.' **SOPHIE WHITE**

'Funny, sassy, smart ... Who doesn't love Aisling?' **MIRIAM O'CALLAGHAN**

'Emer and Sarah can look into their hearts and know exactly what the women of Ireland want ... It's really special to know a character so well but also feel like she knows you so well.' **ELLEN COYNE**

'One of the funniest books I've read in twenty years.' **PAUL HOWARD**

'I was expecting comedy and social satire but what I hadn't bargained for was the sheer humanity of the book that left me giggling at some pages and sobbing at others.' **SINÉAD CROWLEY**

'A publishing behemoth ... The literary equivalent of lightning in a bottle. Aisling is a tremendous creation: fun, warm, charming, kind ... an authentic, astute reflection of Irish womanhood.' **TANYA SWEENEY,** *IRISH INDEPENDENT*

'A tribute to the warmth, charm and resilience of modern Irish women, Aisling is well on her way to becoming one of the most beloved characters in Irish literature.' *IRISH INDEPENDENT*

'A cultural phenomenon.' **JAMES FENTON, LOVIN DUBLIN**

'Aisling is the best of us, the sort of person the world needs.' **LAURA KENNEDY,** *THE IRISH TIMES*

'Readers will get from this book what they came for: some laughter, some familiarity, some Aisling for the soul.' **NIAMH DONNELLY,** *THE IRISH TIMES*

Aisling Ever After

Emer McLysaght & Sarah Breen

Gill Books

Gill Books
Hume Avenue
Park West
Dublin 12
www.gillbooks.ie

Gill Books is an imprint of M.H. Gill & Co.

9781804580820

Edited by Emma Dunne
Printed and bound in Great Britain by Clays Ltd, Elcograf S.p.A.

The paper used in this book comes from the wood pulp of sustainably managed forests.

A CIP catalogue record for this book is available from the British Library.

5 4 3 2 1

In loving memory of Donie O'Brien, cherished husband
of Laura, and much-missed Aisling fan.

ABOUT THE AUTHORS

Emer McLysaght and Sarah Breen are co-authors of the *Aisling* series. *Oh My God, What a Complete Aisling* was the best-selling fiction title of 2017, and its sequel, *The Importance of Being Aisling*, won the award for best popular fiction book at the 2018 Irish Book Awards. The third book in the series, *Once, Twice, Three Times an Aisling*, won the same award the following year, and the fourth book in the series, *Aisling and the City*, won again in 2021. Combined, the Aisling books have sold over half a million copies to date.

Emer McLysaght has worked extensively in journalism and radio and is a columnist at *The Irish Times*. She knows the N7 like the back of her hand and lives in Dublin 8.

Sarah Breen began her career in magazines and now writes a parenting column for the *Sunday Times* Ireland. She lives in Dublin 7 and dreams of the day Oasis will reunite.

PROLOGUE

t's spring but it's still cold so I'm wearing the jigsaw jumper with the big polo neck that Granny Reilly knitted me and a pair of leggings with pink love heart shorts on over them. They're Majella's shorts, but she left them in my house after a sleepover, and I've been coveting them ever since her auntie took her up to Dublin and bought them for her in Clerys. If she finds out I'm wearing them to feed lambs she'll be bulling.

'Hold the bottle firm now, good girl, Aisling. These petties are hungry this morning and they'll pull off you if you're not ready.'

Daddy calls all the orphan lambs 'petties', and they come screaming down the field when he calls them every morning to be fed in the calving shed. He opens the pen and the first one runs over to me, tripping in the thick layer of straw that covers the floor, its little tail wagging excitedly. I proffer the warm MiWadi bottle full of milk to it, and it sucks hungrily on the pink teat, pure delighted. The straw scratches my legs through my leggings, and Daddy places another bottle into my free hand and releases another wriggly pet towards me to clamp down on the teat. I go down on my hunkers and rest my elbows on my knees, steadying myself with a shoulder against the gate. The lambs are so vigorous with their gulping that they'd easily have me pushed over otherwise.

Daddy gets two more bottles on with ease and smiles over at me. 'You're doing a fine job, so you are.'

'Sure, I'll make a great farmer just like you when I grow up, Daddy.'

'You will of course, if you want to.'

'And I'm going to feed all the lambs with a bottle, even the ones that have mammies.'

'You won't have much time for everything else so. It's hard work being a farmer, you know.'

'I can already drive the tractor. And Paul can help me.'

Daddy laughs. 'You're going to run it together, are ye? And no fighting?'

'I'll push him in the slurry pit if he annoys me.'

'Oh Jesus!' Daddy's laughing again.

My first lamb loses the teat and screams at me. 'Here it is, you eejit. Here!' He finds it again and his tail goes into overdrive once more.

'Paul wants to be a rally driver when he grows up, Aisling. I don't know if he'll have time for lambing and dosing. And I thought you told Mammy you might be a nurse like her?'

I *have* thought it would be cool to be a nurse. Mammy has her own stethoscope and always has good stories about people getting into the wrong bed or waking up from operations talking about their sister's husband's affair. I have to get my tonsils out next month, and I'm hoping I don't wake up telling stories about me and Majella rewinding the sweaty-car bit from *Titanic* over and over again.

'Sure, maybe I'll do both. Someone will have to do it when you're old and gummy like Granddad.'

Daddy draws his lips over his teeth and drops a bottle for a second to smoke an invisible pipe.

His lamb roars in protest and I raise my eyebrows. 'Now look who's a better farmer!'

Daddy chuckles and placates the lamb. 'Alright so, you're a brilliant farmer. And you'd be a brilliant nurse, or teacher, or astronaut, or –' He stops to think.

'Rally driver,' I offer.

He gives me a look. 'I mean, you can be whatever you want when you grow up. Sure, I'll be farming here until I'm ninety years old and poking calves into pens with my walking stick. And you'll have your own house and you might be bringing your children here to feed lambs.' He gives me a sideways look. 'And your husband.'

I wrinkle my nose in disgust. 'Ughhh, don't be gross, Daddy! I'm never leaving the farm.'

'Okay, well you might change your mind when you grow up. Or you might make this your home forever. It's up to you. Don't be worrying about it for the moment.'

'I'll always be here in Ballygobbard. Me and Majella want to have a DVD shop. I'm going to look after the money, and she's going to get Leonardo DiCaprio to come and open it for us.'

Daddy throws his eyes up to heaven. 'No better women. No better woman, Aisling.'

CHAPTER 1

My phone suddenly jumps to life in my hand, filling the apartment with the chorus of Westlife's 'Uptown Girl'. I bring it up to my ear on autopilot.

'I never thought I'd see the day, Ballygobbard on CNN International, if you don't mind! Did you manage to catch it, Aisling? We had a watch party here in the town hall. The whole place is gone berserk now that the Big Stink is finally behind us.'

Mammy is talking ninety to the dozen in my ear, but I can barely take in a word she's saying because I've just opened the door to John. He should be in Dubai, where he lives with his fiancée, but he's not. He's standing in my doorway here in New York, and it's knocked the wind right out of me.

'I thought Trevor came across very well, didn't you? His phone was beeping the whole way through the segment. Three texts from his daughters, all about how his tie was the wrong shade of burgundy. I made him promise not to tell them I picked it out. The last thing I need now is getting off on the wrong foot there. Did I tell you they have a podcast? What time is it in the Big Apple, love? Have you had your dinner?'

Across from me John mouths a silent 'hi', and I realise I haven't said a single word since I opened the door thirty seconds ago. I've just been gawping at him, stunned.

'Mammy, I'll have to go.'

'Did you think the Welcome to Ballygobbard sign looked a bit run-down in that montage of the village? Tessie Daly is saying …'

I hold up a hand to John, a signal to 'wait there a second', and I back into the apartment a bit, depositing my wine glass on the coffee table before sinking down onto the arm of the sofa while Mammy goes down the rabbit hole of Tessie's impossible standards for the Tidy Towns committee. I grab the remote and lower the volume on the blaring telly. The last time I communicated with John was on the phone the other night. We were both sick with worry about our friends back home in the midst of the Big Stink. We even managed to figure out that it was probably Mad Tom and his counterfeit pig feed that was the source of the mysterious smell that had descended on the village, making people sick. I missed John so much talking to him that night, but it felt safe missing each other with him in Dubai and me in New York. Now he's standing at my front door. I glance over and he's staring at his feet, looking sheepish. I can't just leave him there.

I stand up and interrupt Mammy, who's moved on to giving out about parking at the nursing home. 'Mammy? Mammy? I'll have to ring you tomorrow, Mammy.' She's still doing the customary fifteen 'bye bye byes' as I knock her off, shove the phone in my back pocket and go back to stand in front of him at the door. 'Hi.'

'Hi, again.' He smiles, just a tiny bit, and the whole world seems to narrow down to the two of us.

A rush of hot and then cold sweat shimmers over the surface of my body. I really take him in, going from his eyes down to his lips, across his shoulders and up to his hair, which is clinging on to quickly melting snowflakes. Back down to the soft edge of his collar and to the strap of the holdall across his chest. He's doing the same to me, searching me for some kind of reaction. My mouth is slightly open. In the silence, the telly informs us about the side effects of taking a drug for indigestion. Hallucinations and purplish bruising across the entire body does sound like a high price to pay for negating the effects of a lasagne and chips. I'm blessed with a high tolerance for most foods, but the gin does have me reaching for the Gaviscon.

The longer I stand staring the more the tension builds up. I can feel myself leaning forward infinitesimally. I can smell him, just about. A smell that buried itself in my memory after all those years together. A smell he took with him when he left for Dubai with Megan. That mixture of his deodorant and the good hair putty that I bought him in a salon for Christmas about six years ago and that he's been chipping away at, pea-sized amount by pea-sized amount. All mixed in with his innate John smell. I'd know it anywhere. It's like there's a tiny thread between us. I wonder can he smell me. I wonder does the American Herbal Essences Apple and Elderflower smell different. I've been using a sample of a Chloé perfume I got in Sephora. I wonder does he notice the absence of Clinique Happy. I've heard people talk about aching to hold someone, and for the first time I really get it. It's like when my legs go restless on a plane, except in my arms. I have nothing to say in this very moment, and it seems like he doesn't either. I just stare and that invisible thread pulls us closer to each other. I don't know what my body might do if we touch. I lick my lips ever so slightly. I have it done before I can stop myself. He notices and his lips twitch into the tiniest little smile, truly one of the most erotic things I've seen in my thirty-one years on the planet, and I've seen Westlife in Croke Park with Golden Circle tickets on the tour where they wore jeggings. This is absolutely mad. What am I doing? Oh God, I'm leaning. What am I doing?

THUD!

The door of number 43 crashes open. I shriek involuntarily and John jumps, clutching his holdall strap. My next-door neighbour Candice emerges, bringing with her the racket from her telly inside and its usual messaging about how Satan is coming for us all and particularly us sinners. She's clutching the biggest pizza box I've ever seen. I didn't have her and the husband down as pizza lovers.

She ignores John. 'Ass-ling. Can you get rid of this? I gotta watch Mo's franks.' She gestures back into the apartment where Mo is sitting in his armchair and certainly not watching his own franks. I gaze back at her, frozen once more. So she turns her attention to John instead, thrusting the pizza box at him. 'Hey, can you help me, please?'

He utters his first proper sentence. 'Sure. Yep, no problem. I'll just …'

I watch, helpless, as he manoeuvres the pizza box out of her hands, his wingspan barely able to take it on.

It's her turn now to stare at him, which she only does for

one and a half seconds before barking at him, 'The garbage. Put it in the garbage.'

As she returns to Mo's franks she thanks him by way of 'You're an angel' before slamming the door.

It's back to just the two of us. His fingers turn white trying to grip the vastness of the pizza box and I finally snap out of it.

'The garbage chute.' I point at it and feel instant mortification for saying 'garbage' in front of him. 'The rubbish chute,' I clarify, gesturing at the metal door in the wall at the end of the hall. 'Just pull the handle.'

He sidles over to the chute and drops the pizza box at his feet. I pad out after him in my slippers but quickly double back on myself to put the latch on the door. The last thing I need is to get locked out. I flip the latch and decide to reach for my keys from the little dish that also contains a bobbin and a book of matches from Shebeen. Better to be safe than sorry.

At the chute, John is trying to fit the colossal pizza box into the too-narrow opening.

'Have you never seen *Friends*?' I ask him, knowing right well he's seen every episode at least twice because he owns the box set. 'You're going to have to tear it up.'

He gives me a look. It's his patented 'You always get to the solution a millisecond before me, Aisling' look, and he laughs, pulling the box out and ripping the lid from the base, which I take up and start to tear into.

'John, this is insane. What are you doing here, ripping up a pizza box on my landing in Manhattan?'

He shrugs. 'I needed to see you. We've been talking so much, and I missed you and you said you missed me and I wasn't sure if I'd be able to get home with all that was going on …' His voice cracks and he trails off.

It has been such a stressful few weeks with the mysterious stench forcing BGB into lockdown. I know John was up to ninety over his sick friends and felt helpless being so far away from home. I was the same. 'I can't believe you're here. Like, the world is huge, and you were just on the other side of it, and now you're right in front of me.'

'Planes are mad that way, Ais.' He turns back to the chute, where he's making bits of the box, and I gaze at the back of his head. At the brown curls at his nape that mean he needs a haircut. At the tiny hole in his earlobe that's the result of a secondary-school bet he lost and ended up on antibiotics over.

Without turning around, he speaks again. 'I got to the end of *Sex and the City* anyway.' He'd been struggling to find a job in Dubai and had been watching the whole series from the start, sending me his thoughts along the way.

'Big surprises Carrie in Paris.' My eyes sting with tears.

Then John turns to look at me. He raises his eyebrows and does his best Miranda impression. 'Go get our girl.'

I laugh. I can't help it. 'You big fucking eejit.'

'Hey!' He pretends to be annoyed, taking the last of the pizza box out of my hands and stuffing it down the chute. 'Mr Big's name turns out to be … John. Just saying!'

'Yeah, and then he jilts her at the altar in the first film.'

'Spoilers, Ais!' Then he looks disappointed. 'Does he really?'

I look at him for maybe five seconds, feeling sick and excited and dread all at the same time. I move back towards the door. 'You know I'm not actually Carrie, don't you? I only have four pairs of shoes, and three of them are flat.'

He follows me, and we resume our places in front of my apartment.

'Yeah, but it's pretty romantic, though, isn't it? If I could have dramatically raced through the airport I would have. Although there was already an incident at Duty Free when a fight broke out between two influencers over a fancy handbag.'

'Oh my God, which influencers? Was one of them Molly-Mae? She's had the teeth done again and they're much better this time round.'

'I couldn't tell you now, to be honest. But, Ais, I came all this way for a reason. I really needed to see you.' He steps closer, decisively this time, closing the distance between us. 'This is going to make me sound like a sap, but I was aching for you.'

We close in further on each other, and I can see where the snowflake from his hair has dripped onto his shoulder, leaving a small, dark patch. I lift my hand, wanting to touch it. He takes a deep breath.

SLAM!

The door downstairs crashes open and then shut with one cacophonous noise and my heart jumps against my ribcage. Jeff! Shit! The sight of John pushed the guy I've been seeing completely out of my mind. Ten minutes ago we were watching CNN together – he only went to the bodega on the corner for more crisps. There's the sound of whistling as a person, unmistakably him, bounds up the stairs. I put my hand on John's shoulder and push him away, stepping back over the threshold into the apartment. I only have time to take in his puzzled face before Jeff rounds the banister onto my floor, a paper bag in each hand.

'They didn't have any Flamin' Hot Cheetos but' – he lifts up his arm – 'I got Ruffles.'

He steps around John, past me and into the apartment, deposits his goods and sticks his head back out. 'Hey, howya doing? Can I help ya?'

'No, no,' I croak. 'He was just wondering if I had time to talk about our Lord and Saviour Jesus Christ.'

John looks at me like I have two heads, but Jeff doesn't miss a beat. 'She's Irish Catholic, so we're all good, but you might have some luck next door. They are sure afraid of something. Maybe you can help them.'

He heads back into the kitchen while John gazes at me, baffled.

'I'm sorry,' I hiss, as I close the door.

CHAPTER 2

I feel like the world is collapsing in around me. Two worlds, actually: the one where John played the leading man for so long and this other one, my New York one, that was supposed to be a fresh start away from all that.

'I've an awful headache – it's just come on me,' I gasp at Jeff, lowering myself onto the couch dramatically. I need him to leave so I can try to make sense of things. I'm probably gone into shock. The same thing happened Majella when a lad she ghosted off Tinder showed up in her classroom as the *cigire* a few years ago. She could only speak in grunts for two days.

'You do look a bit pale,' Jeff says gently, sitting down beside me and placing a massive hand on my forehead. 'No fever. Maybe that wine?'

'Yeah, could be. Bad tannins or something.'

'You got any Advil?'

'There's some paracetamol – sorry, Tylenol – in the bathroom. Would you mind getting it for me?'

As soon as he leaves the room I snap back into action and grab my phone. There's a new message from John Dubai. I only get to read the first line – 'Ais??? Who was' – when I hear Jeff coming back and shove the phone under a cushion.

'You want me to stick around? Maybe you need some rest but I'm happy to play doctor.' He winks at me as he's putting the tablets on the coffee table, and I suddenly feel a bit suffocated.

'Ah, look, the snow is really starting to come down and I'll probably go to bed soon.'

He pulls a blanket up around me. 'Okay, you do that. And stay warm. I'm working tomorrow but I'll call you.' And then he adds pointedly: 'Maybe we can have that talk.'

The talk about our relationship. The talk I've been putting off for days. 'Yeah, definitely,' I say weakly, 'thanks a million.'

He starts gathering his bits and a wave of affection hits. He's such a good guy. The realisation that I'm so baldly lying to him makes me groan out loud.

He turns around, a look of concern etched on his handsome face. 'Hey, hey, you okay? I can stay if you like?'

I shake my head, the icy grip of guilt creeping upwards from my stomach into my chest. 'No, no. You better go before the weather turns. It's just with everything at home,' I gesture at the telly, where we'd been watching the report about the Big Stink, 'I think it's the relief that it's all over and everyone's going to be okay.'

He nods and heads for the door. 'Talk to ya tomorrow. Get some sleep – paramedic's orders.'

As soon as the door clicks behind him, I rifle through the couch cushions and find my phone.

'Ais??? Who was that? I knew I should have told you I was coming. I'm in the bar across the road. I'm going to wait a while. If you want me, you know where I am.'

I untangle myself from the blanket and scramble to the window, my eyes searching the dark street outside. The door of my building slams shut and I watch Jeff, his shoulders hunched against the cold, make his way down the street in the direction of the subway. Not two seconds later, the door of Dingo's opens and I see the unmistakable shape of John. The sure-footed stance. Those wide sloping shoulders. The outline of his beard, a bit longer now than when I saw him for the last time in BGB. It really is John. I'm still processing it. John is not in Dubai. He's come to see me. He raises his hand and steps forward under the Christmas lights that have sprung up like mushrooms all over the city in the past couple of days. He's staring up at me, fighting a smile.

I jump back and yank the cord, slamming the blind shut. And then, without thinking, I'm pulling on my runners and reaching for my parka and flying out the door and down, down, down the stairs and out into the frigid night. When I stumble over the front steps he's waiting there on the foot-path – sidewalk – to steady me.

'Thanks' is all I can manage to squeeze out.

'Your Lord and Saviour Jesus Christ?' He frowns. 'I'm not sure I want to know who that guy was. Why didn't you introduce me?'

I don't want to explain about Jeff right now. I can't, it's too complicated. 'He's just a friend, and in my defence, I was fairly shook! What are you doing here?' I croak.

'I told you, I had to see you. Look, Ais, I have things I've wanted to say to you for a long time now.'

I reach out and touch his chest just to be sure it's not all just a dream. He's wearing tracksuit bottoms and a Knock

Rangers half-zip. His travelling outfit. The fabric is soft under my fingers. And familiar, oh so familiar.

'John ...' I swallow.

But he interrupts me with a deep inhale and a flow of words. 'I've never stopped loving you, Aisling. Not for one minute. I need to explain to you how everything got out of hand.'

My heart is hammering so hard in my chest I'm sure he can hear it.

'I know I owe you that, and so much more.' He takes a breath. 'Megan ...'

His fiancée's name catches in his throat and I feel it in mine too. Did she know about all the emails and texts over the last while? That phone call the other night when me and John put two and two together and figured out what was causing the Big Stink? Where is she now? Does she even know he's here?

'Megan,' he continues, 'was offered the teaching job in Dubai and she was mad to go for it. The money is so good out there.'

'Tax free,' I say. It comes out sounding strangled.

'That's right.' He nods. 'She wanted me to go too, and I suppose I wanted to get away from BGB. I knew I still had feelings for you, and I thought a bit of distance would draw a line under us for once and for all. Out of sight, out of mind, you know? And you were with yer man James Matthews anyway, so what was the point in staying? There was nothing for me at home.'

It sounds like he's rehearsed this speech. Maybe he did on the flight over. I want to ask him if he's telling me the truth but I can't get any words out.

'So I told her I'd go. And then the school, well, they don't like women to be unmarried if they're living with a lad out there. It's a cultural thing. So she said we could tell them we're engaged. Loads of girls she knows have done it and it works so, yeah, that's what we did. But we shouldn't have. We were never going to get married. We both knew it.'

I think back to Majella's wedding – well, joint wedding with Hollywood couple Emilia Coburn and Ben Dixon, the new James Bond – and how I felt the moment John told me he was engaged. And leaving. I'd just finished things with James, lovely James Matthews, in the hope that me and John could rekindle what we once had. It felt like a punch to the gut. 'But you seemed so happy together.'

He reaches for my hand. It feels soft and warm despite the cold, and mine small and at home in it. 'Things between us were … grand. But when we got to Dubai it started really falling apart. I hated it there as much as she loved it. I was thinking about you all the time, so I was glad of it – I was glad to be away. And then everything happened with the Big Stink, and we were back talking, and I knew I couldn't live the rest of my days without being honest and telling you how I feel. Aisling, you're the one. It just took me a really long time to get here.'

'Stealing lines from Mr Big again?'

He smiles. 'I just wanted to come and rescue you.'

Now I'm the one who has to be honest. 'I don't need rescuing, John. I like it here. I'm happy. I have a good life. And what about Megan?'

'That's been over for ages. Well, not officially. That only happened in the last few days. It was mutual in the end.'

'Everyone says that. Áine Conatty said that when Packy Grady shifted Gillian McGrath in front of her after the 2016 county final.'

'It really was, I swear. We're going to stay friends. But I've left Dubai for good. I'm not going back. I didn't even have that much to pack. It was like I knew I wasn't staying.'

It's starting to really snow now. Big fluffy flakes are dancing under the twinkling lights. Not wet sideways snow that disappears as soon as it hits the ground like we get once a year at home. This snow is different. Everything is suddenly different now. John still loves me.

I take a deep breath and I'm about to explain about Jeff and what we have and how it's not so black and white at my end when John starts shifting from foot to foot and then he's gone.

He's down on one knee, both hands now clasped around mine. 'There's something that I want to ask you, something that I should have asked years ago.'

He's not. Oh, he is! He flips open a small square box, and for a second, I feel like I'm going to pass out.

'Aisling, will you marry me?'

CHAPTER 3

'**W**ould you get up, you clown?'

The snow is heavy now, and between the initial shock of seeing him and the fact he's down on one knee, I feel like I'm hallucinating. Could I have accidentally taken some indigestion medication earlier?

John looks up at me, stricken. 'Have I read the whole thing wrong? Do you not like the ring? The woman in Pandora in the airport said it was the most popular one. I was thinking we could pick out a real diamond one together tomorrow.'

I throw my head back and burst out laughing, feeling slightly delirious. John has never stopped loving me? He wants to marry me? Three years ago, I'd have said yes so fast the picture would have been up on Instagram before he'd had a chance to dust off his knee. But things are different now. I'm different. I don't know if it's because of the time that's passed, or whether my short stint in New York has given me a new perspective, but the idea of us suddenly getting married feels cracked.

He takes a step back. 'Ah, Aisling, don't laugh at me.'

'It's a lovely ring, but I can't take it, John.' I laugh again after a brief moment of composure.

He stands up, looking disappointed and unsure of himself. 'Alright so, will I just go?'

But I can't deny the feelings that have stirred in me since we've been talking again. Feelings I thought I'd put to bed the day I boarded that business-class flight. I couldn't admit it to myself at the time, but there were days recently I only picked up my phone in the hope of seeing his name in my inbox. The reason it didn't work out with James Matthews, and this intangible thing keeping me from committing to Jeff, is staring me right in the face. I might not be ready to marry him, but I'm not about to let him get away again either.

'Come on up before we both catch frostbite.'

****

Upstairs, I open the door to the apartment and this time I awkwardly invite John inside, tripping over a stray slipper on the way in. He catches hold of my arm before I snot myself, and even though the fabric of my parka is good and thick, the spot where his hand touches me feels like it's burning.

He throws down his holdall and I hang up my coat, both of us brushing the snowflakes out of our hair. The apartment feels like it's a hundred degrees, and I'm nearly afraid to look him in the eye because I don't know what I'll do. I'm giddy at the memory of him saying 'I've never stopped loving you.' It's like something out of a film.

'Do you want a towel?' I ask, gesturing in the general direction of his head. His shoulders are soaked, as is the left knee of his tracksuit bottoms. I'm trying to remember the last time the two of us were alone together, in private. It feels dangerous somehow, and for a second, I entertain the idea of asking Candice to come in and order us to leave room between us for Jesus just to break the tension.

John reaches up and touches his hair as if he hadn't noticed how wet he was until just this second. 'A towel would be mighty.'

'Back in a sec.'

In the bathroom, the sight of my reflection in the mirror is a cause for concern. The snow mixed with the heat inside has activated my frizz, and there's brown mascara smudged under my eyes. After dragging a brush through my hair and fixing my face, I grab a towel and force myself to walk-not-run back into the living room. When I open the door, John is standing in the middle of the room with his half-zip in one hand and his T-shirt in the other, looking around helplessly. The sight of his bare chest stops me dead in my tracks.

'I can't find the radiator.'

I'm struggling to breathe now. 'They don't have them here. It's all … vents.'

John was devoted to GAA long before I met him, and in the years we were together I don't think he ever missed a training session. But the body I'm looking at now isn't the body of the centre-forward-turned-coach I knew before. It's a whole new, very toned, borderline-chiselled John. I've always been a fan of his big hands and lovely forearms, but now I can't take my eyes off his abs and the V-shaped muscles that lead to the waistband of his boxers, just visible above his tracksuit bottoms. And then there's the unmistakable bulge below.

I clear my throat. 'You have a tan.' It comes out a squeak. 'I mean, not just your arms and your neck.'

He looks down at his pecs and impressive six-pack, his cheeks reddening. 'Er, yeah, I got into running. Topless. I didn't have much else to do. There was a gang of us who used to go from the gym I joined. The owner actually offered me a job but I'd already decided I was leaving.'

I can't tear my eyes away from him. 'You look great,' I whisper.

'You look great too, Ais.' There's a pause. 'You always did.'

The pounding of blood in my ears is near deafening as I walk across the room in what feels like slow motion, arm outstretched, holding the towel. Only, when I get close enough to hand it to him, my legs don't stop. They betray me and go forward another two steps until we're standing so close there's only a hair's breadth between us. I drag my eyes away from that V of defined muscles and look up at him. His bare chest is heaving harder than Michael Flatley's after that life-changing performance in Millstreet in 1994. My throat feels dry, and my palms are clammy, and I'm cursing myself for not brushing my teeth when I was in the bathroom.

As the towel falls to the floor an involuntary gasp slips out of me. Then his hands are in my hair and his mouth is on mine and we're kissing hungrily like we did on the night we met at my twenty-first after Mammy, Daddy and Auntie Sheila had finally left in Terry Crowley's taxi.

As my hands start to travel down his smooth, warm back I stop myself and pull away. It's excruciating, but I can't do it to Jeff.

He looks at me, puzzled, his hands cupping my face. 'Is everything okay? I didn't overstep the mark?' His voice is hoarse and his pupils are the size of dinner plates.

I nod. And then shake my head, a lump in my throat. 'It's just so good to see you.'

He brushes a stray strand of hair behind my ear and smiles down at me. 'I couldn't not come, Ais. I couldn't say that stuff to you over the phone.' Then he laughs. More of a chuckle, really. 'I can't actually believe I get to kiss you again.'

My eyes fall on the jumbo packet of Ruffles, abandoned on the coffee table, and the two wine glasses next to it.

I take a deep breath. 'I need to tell you something, John. About the guy who was here earlier. You better sit down.'

John sighs. 'Yeah, I was wondering why you shut the door in my face.' He adjusts himself as I lead him over to the couch. 'He's a big lad.'

He's an absolute unit, to be fair. 'He's a fireman,' I explain, sitting down at the far end of the couch. I don't trust myself to be close to him.

'Of course he is.' John's whole face is tight.

'So, we've been seeing each other for a while. Dating, like. I told him I wasn't feeling well earlier, so he left.'

John's face falls and he leans back into the couch cushions. 'You're going out with someone? Oh my God, you could have told me!'

'I know I should have. But the truth is, I was afraid that if you knew about Jeff, you'd stop texting and emailing me. I was worried I'd lose you for good.'

'Yeah, I might not have flown across the world if I thought you had a boyfriend.' He covers himself with a cushion. 'I feel so stupid.'

That doen't land right with me. 'Well, what did you expect? Did you think I came to New York to sit around pining for you? You were engaged, John. I had to get on with my life. Jeff has been so great for me. His taste in jewellery is questionable, but he's a good guy.'

He clasps his hands in his lap and looks down. 'I should have known you'd have lads fighting over you. I'm an idiot.'

'Well, it's not exactly like that.'

'Are you sleeping with him?'

It only takes a second of guilty silence for him to screw his eyes shut.

'Oh, and I suppose you and Megan were in separate beds?'

'You're not far off, Aisling. And at least you knew about Megan.' He has me there. 'Are you in love with him? Break it to me gently because I don't think I could take him if it came to that. Like, I'd try but I don't fancy my chances. He's not a little weed like that Aleksandr Petrovsky.'

I think for a minute about how meeting Jeff has brought so much into my life here in New York. The dates. The rides. The delights of his geography gaffes.

'I really like him, but no, we're not in love,' I admit eventually. 'He's been asking me to be his girlfriend – officially, like – but I've been avoiding it.'

'Oh. Right.'

'But I don't want anything else to happen between me and you.'

John still hasn't looked up. 'Understood. I shouldn't have landed in on you like I did. What was I thinking? I'm sorry. Forget you ever saw me. I'll go now.'

'Until I tell him.'

'Tell him what?' His eyes shoot up to mine.

I take a deep breath. 'Tell him that I'm really sorry but I can't see him any more.'

CHAPTER 4

'A re you –?' Majella's voice is muffled for a second and there's the sound of a struggle.

'Maj? Majella?'

'Sorry, I'm back. I'm just in the jacks.'

'Charming!'

'Calm down, it's just a widdle. Now, sorry, where was I? Oh yes – are you fucking joking me? Are you having me actually on?'

'I have beard rash on my chin, Maj. I feel berserk.'

'Did you have sex? Oh Jesus, I'd say it was wild horny. Talk about the mother of all make-up sex.'

'No, I couldn't. Not until I end it with Jeff. We just shifted for an hour and then I made him go to a little hotel up the street. I didn't trust us to be under the same roof.'

'You're a stronger woman than me. How did you resist? I have Pablo plagued at the moment. I think he's started hiding from me.'

'Maj, I'm blushing just thinking about it. He kept doing, you know, the leg thing?'

'Oh my God, where he pushes his leg in between …?'

'Yep, yep, that's the one.'

There's more fumbling. 'I'll ring you back, I have to find Pablo.'

I screech with laughter, despite the crazy anxiety coursing through my body. 'Maj! Maaa-aj!'

'I'm here, I'm here, I'm only messing. I do need to find him, though, because I am full, on, ovulating. Ya girl's an ovulation station.'

This revelation pushes me back down onto the couch where John was doing the leg thing not twelve hours previous.

'You're not? You're trying to get pregnant?'

I can hear the smile in her voice. 'I am. We are. Actually, I am. When people say "we're" pregnant it makes me violent.'

'Denise Kelly,' we say in unison, and my eyes roll so hard I think maybe I've pulled something.

'Can you believe she's talking about going for baby number three?' I can tell Maj has put the phone down again because she sounds far away. 'I can still remember my hangover from their wedding.'

'Oh Jesus, me too! Me and John nearly missed the break-fast and then had a row by the tiny croissants because he didn't want to get married.'

Majella returns to full volume, nearly choking on her laughter. 'And this is the man you were rolling around with last night on your couch in New York? I never thought I'd see the day, little miss married-by-twenty-nine.'

'He actually asked me to marry him last night. On the street. In the snow. I told him to cop on.'

Majella gasps. 'Stoppit. I'm not even pregnant yet and I'm about to go into labour.'

In the background, I hear Pablo coming into the room, singing operatically.

'Hiya, Pab,' I roar.

'I should never have brought him that *Les Mis* CD back from our Broadway trip. He's already after marking Bastille Day in the calendar for next year.'

'Between you, Tenerife, BGB and now France, that man really does have an infinite amount of love to give.'

Pablo's Tenerifian roots are never far from his mind, and he will often burst into tears even at the sight of the jamon section in the New Aldi. Ballygobbard is his home now, though, and he sort of has me and John to thank for that after we met him while on holidays and he followed us back.

More fumbling. 'Oh, it's so romantic, though.' Is that Majella crying? Now kissing noises.

'Okay, Majella. Maj? I'm going to go now.'

'Wait, Aisling! I wanted to ask you one more thing.'

I sit down on the couch again and glance at my watch. I know Jeff's break is at two and I've already had three texts from John telling me he's booked a hotel and wondering if I'm coming to meet him, along with nine selfies of him with 'a squirrel' in Central Park, although all I can see is grass. 'Go on.'

'Did you see Dr Trevor on CNN?'

'Of course I did – I watched the whole thing.'

'Your mam must be very proud?' Majella sounds hesitant.

Dr Trevor and Mammy are in a relationship. I've accepted this. It's been exceptionally strange being thousands of miles away while it's all been developing, though. Dr Trevor is something of a hero after he sort of became the face of the Ballygobbard lockdown during the terrible time of the Big Stink, and I'm actually happy for Mammy that she's found someone after losing Daddy so young. At least I think I am.

'She is. I was talking to her last night. Well, she was talking at me. They're all on cloud nine.'

There's a beat before Maj responds. 'Okay, so just to let you know, he has two daughters and he was in Filan's yesterday saying they were going to come to BGB now that the lockdown is over, and it was Sharon who heard him and she thought you should hear it from me –'

'Maj, Maj, it's grand. I know he has daughters. I get the feeling Mammy is worried about impressing them. She's only met them on Zoom so far, but I got ten minutes about their shiny hair on the phone the other day. They sound perfect.' The 'perfect' comes out a little harsher than I intended. Something about the way Mammy was talking about the daughters rubbed me up a bit funny.

'Maybe they'll have nice clothes you can borrow.'

'Maybe they will.'

'He's alright for an older man, isn't he, Dr Trevor? Marian landed on her feet there.'

'I suppose he's handsome enough, if you're into sparkly eyes and grey hair.'

'Don't let John hear you saying that.'

The mention of his name sends the nerves zinging around my body again.

Majella is still talking. 'Are you definitely not coming home for Christmas, by the way? It'll be mad to be in New York for it.'

'I know. But there's just so much work on. It's just another day. I'll live.'

'You will, of course.'

'And listen, Maj, don't say it to anyone, will you? About me and John?'

'Why not?'

'Because I don't know what's happening with us myself yet. And I definitely don't need it ending up in the parish newsletter.'

'Whatever you want, bird.'

In the background, Pablo is singing again. 'One Day More' it sounds like. I know their downstairs neighbour Carol Boland will already be well up and working in BallyGoBrunch, the café I opened, at this hour on a Sunday morning.

'Okay, Maj, I'll let you go. I've to meet Jeff and get this over with.'

'Will you be sad? Letting a New York fireman go? It's not to be taken lightly, I hope you know. There's girls, and lads, who'd kill for a go on the pole.'

'Do you know what? He's been lovely. So lovely. But the minute I saw John I just …'

'I know, I know, I get it. Right, go on. Pablo! Stop crying, it was two hundred years ago!'

****

I haven't even had time to get proper winter boots before the first snow hit New York, so I'm making do with my black Clarks and hoping to God I don't go on my ear in an icy puddle. Even though it's freezing out, I'm sweating a bit after racing to give my legs one more going-over with the razor and packing a handbag that will do me for a hotel but doesn't look like I plan on staying in a hotel. Why don't I want John to think I'm assuming I'm staying over? Why do I feel so nervous and excited for a man I've known for literal years? I bite the bullet and fire off an email to Mandy, my boss at Mandy Blumenthal Event Architects, telling her I won't be coming in to work tomorrow. Or Tuesday. For a second I consider pretending I have stomach flu, but I decide against it. Americans love saying they have stomach flu even though it's only a fancy way of saying you have scour. I don't want to endure two days of texts enquiring about my bowels. I decide to not even give her a reason in the end. I can fill her in when I'm back in the office.

On the subway ride downtown, I'm thirty per cent dreading having to break the news to Jeff and seventy per cent tingling in every cell with the anticipation of seeing John. Luckily a woman screaming bloody murder for several stops takes my mind off both. As I walk the final two blocks to Ladder Company 4, the anxiety starts to take over.

I turn the corner and the firehouse comes into view and I feel slightly sick. My phone goes and I pull it out, fully expecting another angle of John giving Trump Tower the thumbs down. It's from John alright, but this time it's just a picture of a hotel-room door. The number is 237. A text from him then: 'Let me know when you've done it and I'll tell you where to meet me. Good luck x.' A flash of fear courses through me then. What if Jeff gets mad? Or worse, what if he cries? I force myself to think back to me and John on the couch last night. I cannot wait to finish what we started. It will be worth it. It will all be worth it.

****

'Well, well, well. She lived to see another day.'

Jeff's head is poking out of the giant opening of Ladder Company 4, big enough to reverse a whole fire engine into. I did make a bet with him one evening that my Micra-reversing skills are so good that I could take on the fire engine, but I was all talk.

He comes out onto the street towards me, shivering a little in his work trousers and a long-sleeved T-shirt and just the one beaded necklace. 'Ya feeling better? You look good! You had me worried last night.'

'Hi! Yes, much better. Fine now actually.' He leans forward to kiss me but I manage to dodge him. I can barely meet his eye.

'You want coffee? I gotta pot on.'

'I can't really stay. I just need to talk to you for a minute if that's okay? In private.'

He stops dead and looks at me suspiciously as I shuffle from foot to foot trying to stay warm. November in New York is no joke.

'Well, I don't like the sound of that. Talk to me about what?'

'Will we go in? You'll freeze.'

'The boys are in there.'

Everyone is 'the boys', but there are actually three women on Jeff's crew. Two of them are called Cindy. My friend Sadhbh learned the hard way that joking about calling them 'Cinders' is not on. Jeff is good fun, but his lectures on fire safety are not.

'Well, go on then,' Jeff urges me. 'What do you want to talk about? Being my girlfriend?' He puts on a puppy-dog face.

'I really wish you hadn't said that.' I feel a bit of sick in my throat. I am the worst person in the world.

'Oh.' He looks as deflated as I've ever seen him.

'I'm just going to be honest with you, Jeff. The Holy Joe that came to the door last night? That was actually someone I know. My ex-boyfriend, John, from home.'

Jeff scratches his head. 'Your ex is a Mormon called Holy John?'

'No.' I speak very slowly. 'He's just John, and not a Mormon. I was improvising. I just got such a shock when I saw him. I had no idea why he'd come, and I didn't want to have to introduce you two.'

'The guy at the door? But he didn't even come into the apartment.' And then his eyes widen. 'That headache that came on real sudden? Did you have a headache at all?'

'No,' I admit sheepishly. 'I needed some time –'

'To screw your ex. Got it.' He folds his arms angrily.

'No! No, that's not what happened. I had to find out why he was there. We had this big long talk, and he told me he still has feelings for me.' Saying the words out loud makes it feel so real – and a little cruel to Jeff.

'And what about my feelings, huh? You don't care about those? I thought we had something, me and you. You're happy to trash it all for this guy who did – what? Did he hurt you? Then change his mind and come back crawling to you? What's he got for you that I can't give you?'

'He's got my history,' I say. 'He was my first love. I don't think we ever stopped loving each other. Jeff, I care about you a lot. But this is why I didn't want to get into a serious relationship.'

'And you really had no idea he was coming? He just arrived on your doorstep, blammo?'

'Well, not exactly. When everything started happening at home with the …'

'The Big Stink?'

'Yeah. We started talking a bit. We were both in the same boat, being so far away. I suppose it brought up some old feelings. I didn't think it would go beyond some emails, though. He was engaged to someone else. They were living in Dubai.'

'Oh, now you're just making up places.'

'Dubai is real, Jeff. It's a city in the United Arab Emirates.'

His face darkens a little. 'And then suddenly he's in the United States of America declaring his undying love to you? Sounds like some guy, this one.'

I bite my lip. 'It's all so complicated – I'm still kind of processing everything. I wanted to be upfront with you, though.'

'And let me guess, you're in love with Holy John?' he harrumphs.

'I think I am. I'm so sorry, Jeff. I wish it hadn't turned out this way.' I step forward and pick up his hand. 'I never thought it would end like this. I've had the best time with you. I didn't mean to hurt you. I'm sorry.' I let the silence hang for a few seconds.

'I was going to bring you home to meet my mom. I told the boys about you. Cindy wanted to double date.'

'I know. You deserve someone who's ready for all the brilliant stuff you have to give.' I glance up at his face and he looks so sad.

'You sure you're making the right decision here, Aisling? Once you choose him, there's no going back. I'm not gonna wait around.'

I think of John in that hotel room, maybe naked apart from a little pair of O'Neill's shorts. Yep, I've never been so sure of anything in my life. 'I think so.'

'Alright.' Jeff shrugs. 'I guess this is goodbye. Maybe I'll tell the boys I dumped you, eh? Try and save a little face.'

And with that, he's gone back into the firehouse. My first New York hook-up? Boyfriend? Situationship? Whatever they're calling it here on the mean streets of Manhattan. I wait until he's inside the building and then turn my face towards the bracing cold wind and fire a text off to John: 'It's done. Where will I meet you? x'

His reply is a picture of a hotel key card. On it is written 'The Plaza'. Oh my God, he didn't!

'Am I going to the actual Plaza Hotel? x'

'I'll meet you in the lobby. I've been waiting so long for this, Ais. x'

I am like a dog in heat, frantic to get to my Irish country boy in his big hotel. I make a start towards the subway and then stop and pull out my phone and open the Uber app. Arriving at the Plaza smelling like the 6 train is not the look I'm going for today.

****

Jorge is a talker, which suits me fine given that every street further uptown we go my nervous anticipation rises. I drag a travel brush through my hair and reapply my lip stain, adding a little bit to my cheeks too. Then I pull my Clinique Happy travel rollerball out and go hell for leather.

'The Plaza, eh?' Jorge looks in the rear-view mirror. 'Meeting someone special on this Sunday evening?'

'Do you know what, Jorge? I *am* meeting someone special.'

My phone goes again. It's John. 'I've sent champagne up to the room. Hurry up xxx.' This feels like maybe one of the most glamorous things I've ever done, and I recently sent out invitations for Barbra Streisand's dog's second birthday!

Jorge launches into a story about celebrities he's brought to the Plaza over the years. Mostly sportspeople, but I do make him go back and recount his Greta Gerwig story in detail. She said very little about Saoirse Ronan, which is disappointing. Jorge hasn't seen *Lady Bird*, but he promises he will watch it that very night. Our Greta chat takes us to within three blocks of Central Park, just as the snow starts up again in earnest. Christmas lights are twinkling on shopfronts, and there's a very drunk Santa fighting with a pretzel vendor on the street corner.

Just as the hotel comes into view, my phone starts ringing. Sadhbh. Shite! I forgot I said I'd meet her for a drink this evening. She's been based in New York for the past few months too, thanks to her job doing social media for her boyfriend Don Shields's band, The Peigs. Majella still can't believe she gets to be Don Shields adjacent. She stopped trying to play it cool years ago.

'Sadhbhy, hi.'

'Hi, Ais. Sorry, I know it's aggressive to cold call without a text first, but I'm walking and just want to make sure you have Friendsgiving in your diary. It's two weeks from Thursday. Tara has booked Shebeen and the whole Irish Mafia crew are going to be there. I know you're work–'

'Sadhbh? Sadhbh. I'll just stop you there.'

'Sorry, babe, go on.'

'Okay, this is going to sound bonkers, but I can't meet you for a drink later.'

'Not that bonkers, but why?'

'Because I'm in an Uber about to get out at the Plaza.'

'Okay, yes, bitch, we love it. Jeff is pulling out all the stops!'

'It's not Jeff.' She can surely tell by the pitch of my voice that it's not a work thing either.

'Who then?' she shrieks.

'I'm about to go in and meet John.'

Silence. Jorge breaks it by pulling up at the hotel and announcing my total.

'Thanks, Jorge. Hope you like *Lady Bird*.'

Sadhbh regains her voice. '*John* John? *Your* John? Is in New York?'

'Yes. He surprised me last night. Came all the way from Dubai to tell me he's in love with me.'

'You have *got* to be joking?'

'I'm not. I just ended things with Jeff, and now I feel like I might burst if I don't have my thighs around John's waist in the next two minutes.'

Another pause. I take in the magnificent hotel entrance.

'Okay, Aisling, this all concerns me, but it also might be one of the most romantic things I've ever heard.'

'Thank you. I'm standing outside the Plaza right now.'

'Oh my God. I stayed there once with Don and there was

a pillow menu! I cannot wait for the details!'

My feet do a little involuntary stamp of excitement. 'Well, I hope I won't be able to tell you ninety-five per cent of what goes on.'

Sadhbh squeals. 'I want a blow-by-blow account tomorrow. Well, not literally. Bye!'

I look up at the iconic building in front of me and take a deep breath.

CHAPTER 5

The front steps of the hotel are crowded and noisy with people sheltering from the snow and uniformed staff in peaked hats and white gloves trying to politely stop them trampling on the potted poinsettias. One man wearing a black wool overcoat with shiny gold buttons is fighting a losing battle trying to carve out a safe path through the slush to the front door with a monstrous shovel, while another is furiously blowing his whistle at a line of cabs with their lights off. It's bedlam.

'Sorry, coming through. Woman on a mission here.'

I squeeze past a knot of old ladies in fur coats and one of them tuts at me loudly. 'Do you mind? This is chinchilla.'

My hand is on the gold handle of the enormous glass door, but when I go to push it, it swings open so fast that I almost fall forward onto the logoed mat. I peer over the doorman's shoulder into the opulent foyer with its high ceilings and massive twinkling Christmas tree, the sound of laughter and clinking glass travelling through the air. It might be the most beautiful place I've ever seen, and I was in the VIP suite in Krystle once. It had a round pleather bed.

'Welcome to the Plaza,' the doorman says.

****

I make my way through the lobby anxiously scanning the faces around me, but there's no sign of John.

'Ais!'

My head snaps in the direction of his voice. He's jogging down the hall towards me in a faded grey T-shirt I recognise from a Christmas years ago when he got six different vouchers for Jack & Jones and won another one in Majella's school raffle. I helped him pick it out.

A bellboy walks past and I catch him also taking in the view appreciatively.

When John reaches me, he waves a hand in front of my face. 'Hellooo? Are you frozen solid or what?'

I snap out of it. 'The Plaza! What are you at?'

He laughs. 'I know, it's mad. Do you have any idea how hard it was to get a decent room in Manhattan during a snowstorm, though? And anyway, I wanted to take you somewhere special. So we're booked in for three nights.'

'Three nights?!'

He grins. 'I want this to be perfect.' Two puce spots high on his cheeks under the tan.

'I'm starting to get that impression, alright. Careful now, or I might get used to it.'

He steps forward. 'So how did he take it?'

Poor Jeff. Such a golden retriever of a man. He'll be snapped up by the weekend, though – I'm sure of it. 'He was a bit put out, but I think he understood where I was coming from.'

'So you're officially single?'

'I am.'

'That's funny, so am I.'

I feel weightless, like a helium balloon that could float off up into the rafters at any second.

'I'm going to kiss you now.'

My legs feel like they're going to buckle if he doesn't. 'Let's go upstairs and you can do more than that.'

I tilt my chin upwards and try to calculate how long it will take me to get him up to the room and finally get that track-suit off him. I've thought of little else since our PG romp on the couch last night.

His lips are millimetres from mine when a short bald man with a huge camera around his neck barrels in between us, jamming his gigantic lens into John's stomach. 'A bit of space, dude?'

Then, like lemmings, a group of around fifteen people of various ages and nationalities starts to gather around where we're standing under a giant crystal chandelier.

I step backwards, confused. 'What the …?'

A woman in a crisp black blazer with her hair in a French roll so tight it's giving her a facelift clears her throat. 'Good afternoon, ladies and gentlemen, my name is Valentina, and I will be your guide on today's tour of the historic Plaza Hotel here on the corner of 5th Avenue and Central Park South. You're all very welcome.'

'Oh, I'm sorry, I don't think we're meant to be here,' I say, taking John by the hand and skirting around a family wearing identical backpacks in the direction of the lifts. 'Come on,' I hiss.

Valentina's brown eyes flick over to where we're trying to sneak away. 'This is the last tour of the day, miss.

Complimentary for all our guests.' Her tone is gentle but firm.

'We'll catch it tomorrow,' John says, pulling me in to him and throwing an arm over my shoulders. 'We have somewhere to be.'

But Valentina is not taking no for an answer. 'Oh, but I'm afraid our tours only run on the weekend, sir. Gratuities are discretionary but very much appreciated.' Her eyes are stony and I can feel the rest of the group staring at me too.

I sigh, knowing full well how much the hospitality industry in this country relies on tips. 'Okay, then, you might as well lead the way, Valentina.'

****

An hour and twenty minutes later, and forty dollars lighter, we've finally managed to extricate ourselves from the group with promises to look up the Russell family if we ever find ourselves in Pigeon Forge, Tennessee.

After an excruciating twenty-second wait, the lift eventually arrives and is thankfully empty. John pulls me inside and jabs the close-doors button frantically. They inch together slowly, and finally, finally, after what feels like an eternity, we're alone again. He puts a hand on the small of my back and pulls me to him in one movement. My pulse starts to quicken at the hardness of him.

'This lift better be fast,' he murmurs.

'Excuse me, miss!' A white-gloved hand appears just as the doors are about to meet, and in steps a smiling uniformed woman. 'What room, please?'

John takes a step backwards, embarrassed, and I feel so frustrated I have to literally bite my fist.

My voice is shrill. 'It's okay, we can press the button ourselves.'

'I wouldn't hear of it, miss. It's all part of the Plaza experience. Now, what's your room number, please?'

'Two three seven,' John barks, and she jumps.

'Yes, sir.'

We travel the rest of the way in silence, my arse pressed firmly into his crotch.

****

'Your terrace room, madame,' John coos, pushing the door open.

My eyes quickly take in the luxurious carpet and antique furniture and the sweaty champagne bucket, and while I normally like to open every door and drawer before I make myself comfortable in a hotel room, my investigation can wait till after. Later.

John shuts the door with his foot and is already kicking off his runners while I run to the enormous bed, shedding my parka on the way, and throw myself on it.

'Quick, John, or I'll have to start without you.'

He smiles and pulls off his T-shirt, and the sight of him knocks the breath out of me yet again.

'Jesus Christ,' I croak. 'Get over here before I combust.'

He walks slowly and purposefully to the bed and climbs up so he's kneeling on the end of it. Then he pulls off my boots one at a time. His eyes never leave mine as I take in all six foot two inches of him. In the first of many new moves, he then takes the gusset of my eighty-denier tights in his teeth and starts to drag them down slowly. Painfully slowly. The anticipation has me in agony, but I don't want it to stop either.

When he eventually deposits the tights in a pool on the carpet, he glances up at my knickers and waggles his eyebrows. 'Now for these.'

I burst out laughing. I've never felt more weak or more powerful in my life. He's moving forward slowly when a sharp rap at the door stops him dead. My hands instinctively fly to my crotch.

'Turn-down service!'

I grab one of the many jumbo pillows on the bed, put it over my face and scream into it.

****

It's still dark when I wake up the next morning in a panic about work. It feels so bold to be here and not on my way to the office. John is sleeping silently beside me, and the bed is so vast and soft it takes me a minute to wade to the edge to locate my phone on the locker. I fire off a quick text to my colleague Aubrey to give her the heads-up that I won't be in today or tomorrow and to go ahead contacting the suppliers for Maggie Gyllenhaal's Thanksgiving Potluck. There's a state-wide shortage of free-range organic turkeys, but Aubrey said she'll raise and slaughter one herself in the next fortnight if she has to, rather than let Maggie down. That's the kind of dedication Mandy expects from her staff.

I sink back into the pillows and think about last night and John and the fact that we comfortably broke our previous record of three times. Well, I don't think the first time counts. My cheeks flame when I remember the use we made of the shower and the massive free-standing bath. It's a wonder one of us didn't drown. At one stage we were in the walk-in wardrobe! If that luggage rack could talk … I also spotted four robes. Maybe one is a day robe and one is for evening? Nothing would surprise me.

'Hey, what are you doing awake so early? C'mere.' He turns over in the bed and gathers me into his arms and I realise that I feel so happy, so content. I feel safe with him, and it's not just because I'm in the Plaza Hotel on a snowy Monday morning in November. It's because of John, and that scares me a bit.

'What are you thinking about?' He shakes me out of my little daydream.

'About you, you big gom.'

'Oi.' He tickles me in the ribs. 'Does it involve the luggage rack?'

'No. Well, maybe a bit.'

'There's a chaise longue in there with our names on it.'

CHAPTER 6

'**A**isling,' John calls from the bathroom while I'm perusing the pillow menu for the seventh time. Our pillows are actually lovely and I'm loath to order new ones, but it seems like an awful waste not to sample everything that's on offer. Maybe I'll do it this evening after I look up what buckwheat seeds are and why I should be resting my head on them.

'Yeah?' I call back.

'I think it's safe to say we missed the hotel breakfast?'

'It was worth it.'

He pops his head around the doorframe of the bathroom, eyes twinkling. 'Will you marry me?'

I shriek and fling one of the perfect pillows at him. He must have asked me six times last night. One time I nearly said yes, because he was on top of me and I've never felt closeness like it. Now, as he finishes up in the bathroom, I have a question for him. 'John?'

'Yep?'

'Why did you propose to me the other night?'

He turns off the tap and comes to lean on the doorframe, thinking for a second. 'Because that was always what you wanted.'

My heart sinks. I can't go back to this again.

'And now it's what I want too.'

We stare at each other, and then he frowns. 'No, wait, that sounds selfish, does it? Like, it's not just that because I want it now it should happen. I just mean that I was stupid before and now I'm, eh, less stupid?'

That gets a laugh out of me.

'Anyway, you didn't even say yes. What's with that?'

'Excuse me, I don't just say yes to any strange man who shows up on my doorstep proposing marriage.'

He feigns shock but quickly reverts to being serious. 'No, really, was it a terrible thing to do?'

'No, it was very sweet. And I can't believe you bought a ring in Dubai airport. That's extremely cute.'

His mouth turns down. 'Cute. Sweet. Just the words I was hoping for.'

I hate to hurt his feelings but the truth is marriage is not the priority it was for me a couple of years ago. And besides, not that long ago both of us were in relationships with other people.

'Look, I can't remember the last time I actually thought about getting married. Maybe that will change again, but it just seems a bit … what's the word? Like, kind of arbitrary to me right now. Obviously I love you.'

He smiles and then looks thoughtful for a second. 'I don't think marrying you would be arbitrary.'

'I know. But it's just not necessary right now. For me, anyway.'

'Okay, I respect that. Doesn't mean I won't stop asking, though.' He smiles cheekily. 'Are you getting up or what?

I'm starvers.' He's pulling on a navy wool jumper over a white T-shirt, and while the thought of him living in Dubai with another woman is not something I want to dwell on, between this and the Calvin Klein underpants he had on yesterday, the shopping over there did wonders for his wardrobe.

I slide out from under the luxurious duvet and feel for my nightdress, shy now that the mid-morning winter sun is coming in through the gap in the curtains.

'If this was a film, I'd have a big white shirt for you to put on.' John laughs at me. 'I'll wear a white shirt this evening and then you can wear it in the morning.' He's already over to me and pressing into me, not laughing any more.

'No, come on, we have to find some breakfast and do something.' I push him away gently.

'Right, grand, sorry. I just can't help myself. Pawing away at you.'

I feel an immense rush of power and confidence and kind of shimmy towards the bathroom, hoping my effort to drop my nightdress strap off my shoulder doesn't look like I'm having a stroke. 'Well, you can paw away at yourself there now while I have a shower.'

****

It's lunch we're looking at by the time we're out and about, dodging the slushy piles of dirty snow with our hands swinging by our sides, occasionally and painfully almost touching. Holding hands seems so intimate and couple-y, and I don't think either of us knows if it's the right thing to do.

'What are you hungry for?' I ask him after two blocks of peering at menus and hemming and hawing. 'Do you know what I'd love? Italian. Really good pasta.'

One of the dream meals that comes to mind when I'm really starving is Mammy's spaghetti Bolognese. I can still remember the first day she made it, after getting a taster from one of the Dolmio demo ladies in the supermarket. Life-changing stuff.

John looks at me, inspired. 'Jesus, yeah, that would be lovely.'

I pull out my phone. 'I actually starred a place near here. One of the girls told me the bread is amazing, and there are pictures of Martin Scorsese on the walls.'

'Sold!'

****

We're the first customers into Tony Baletti's for lunch. In fact, the door was locked when we arrived, but just as we were about to walk away a terrifying man – Tony? – with a pencil behind his ear and a phone in each hand ushered us in and silently pointed at a table for two in the middle of the small restaurant. And there *are* pictures of Martin Scorsese on the wall, along with Tom Hanks, Tina Fey and Will Smith. Our eyes are on stalks as we shuffle our coats off onto the backs of our chairs.

'Lookit, that's Jennifer Lopez,' John whispers, pointing to a picture of Jennifer Lawrence, and I don't bother to correct him because I'm sure there's a picture of JLo here too.

I grab his arm. 'Look, look, Liam Neeson. And Colin Farrell!'

I feel strangely patriotic seeing the lads up there with Tony and his staff. It's like when someone Irish appears on one of the late-night talk shows in America and they have to do the spiel about how demented Irish names are and we all roll our eyes at home even though we're actually delighted and smug that we know it's obviously pronounced 'Donal' and not 'Dum-nail'.

As we're gawping at the walls a waiter appears beside us and, in one fell swoop, whisks the coats off the backs of our chairs and lands menus, a wine list and a bread basket in front of us.

'I'll have the veal ragu,' John blurts after a quick scan, his eyes on the focaccia.

'Me too.'

'Oh and –' he scans the wine list '– the Montepulciano. The bottle.' He pronounces it perfectly and gives me a little smile and all of a sudden I have a lump in my throat. It's not even an emotion I can pinpoint. I just feel so content. Everything feels right – even with Tony now roaring into one of his phones and manning the door like he's expecting a Mob hit at any second. We tear into the bread as the first glasses of red wine are poured.

John lifts up his glass. 'To New York,' he says, and we clink. 'This is a trip I don't think I'll be forgetting in a hurry.'

'Yeah, about that,' I say, taking a delicious sip. 'You haven't told me how long you're staying for. Three nights in the Plaza and then what?'

'Well, we had other priorities.' He laughs, holding my hand across the table.

I feel the blush creeping up my neck. 'Of vital importance.'

'But my flight is on Wednesday evening.'

'That soon?' The feeling of disappointment takes me by surprise. We're only just getting to know each other again. The new us. We have so much to catch up on too.

'When I was booking it, I thought three nights would be enough to say everything I wanted to say, but I wish I could change it now. I had to tell Mam about me and Megan, though, so she said herself and Dad would pick me up at the airport. I think she thinks I'll be nursing a broken heart.' Then he adds quietly, 'I hate the thought of leaving you, Ais.'

'I know, me too. But maybe it's for the best. So much has happened in the past forty-eight hours.'

He looks disappointed but then jokes, 'And me after proposing to you? But yeah, okay. Maybe you're right.'

'I think the distance will be good for us.' I hope I sound more convinced than I feel. 'Let things settle and go from there. You're just out of a long-term relationship too, don't forget. I don't want to be your rebound.'

He looks mildly offended. 'You're far from that!'

'I'm sure your folks will be thrilled to have you back home anyway.'

He bites into the focaccia. 'Mam is already at me about getting a job. Jesus, this is good bread.'

John's an engineer and used to work in a big multinational company before becoming the toast of the parish as the county team selector and then moving to Dubai.

'No flies on Fran,' I laugh.

The waiter deftly places two plates of steaming pasta smothered in a rich meaty sauce in front of us.

'I have a plan that will keep her off my back, actually,' John says, picking up his fork and digging in. 'I've been thinking about opening my own gym in BGB. I think the village is ready.'

I mull it over for a second. 'That's a genius idea. Sharon looked into buying one of those Peloton bikes last year and nearly dropped dead at the price of it. If you do spinning classes I know she'd be all over it.'

'The gym I joined in Dubai did everything – spinning, weights, yoga, dance classes. It put the idea in my head.'

I pick up my glass. 'To good ideas.' I smile, but I can't stop thinking about him getting on that plane.

****

'I can't believe we were in there for nearly four hours! It felt like forty-five minutes.'

'I can't believe you made Tony take our picture for the wall. I wonder will he put it under the one of Sandra Bullock.'

I give John a dig as we carefully navigate the icy street, annoying New Yorkers just trying to get home before the snow gets any worse. 'Oh, you'd recognise Sandra Bullock, alright, wouldn't you?'

'You know Sandra and I have had a very special relation-ship since I first saw *Speed 2: Cruise Control* at The Truck's eighth birthday party.'

I slide my arm into his, grateful for the warmth and the sturdiness after the bottle of wine and three of Tony's limon-cellos. He said he'd email me his chef's famous tiramisu recipe so I can send it to Carol back in BallyGoBrunch, and he made me promise not to tell Mandy I'd been in for lunch too. Apparently she rented the restaurant out five years ago for Taylor Swift's intimate birthday dinner and then threw a shit-fit because he refused to take down the picture of himself with Jake Gyllenhaal.

'I bet Taylor didn't even care,' I reassured Tony. I was two glasses of Montepulciano in and felt like my dedication to listening to Taylor's *Red* album in my early twenties means I know her inside out.

'She didn't!' he shrieked. 'She thought it was funny!'

John is creasing himself doing his impression of Tony as we head for 'just one more' in the vicinity of Central Park when I hear a familiar voice behind me calling my name. Aubrey. It's Aubrey. I turn around to find her standing there in her ankle-length black puffer.

'I thought that was you!' Her cheeks are pink and her hair is frizzy from the snow. She's carrying multiple bags from Wag and Bone and looks from me to John, just dying for me to fill her in.

'John, this is Aubrey Weiss. We work together. Executive assistants.' John holds out his hand for a big firm shake. 'And Aubrey, this is my fr–, my … this is John.'

'Hello there, John. Aisling, I'm so glad to see you in good spirits. When you took off work so suddenly I was worried it was something to do with home, with that toxic stench thing.'

'Well, John actually is from home, so I suppose it is kind of connected. He's in town unexpectedly so I just wanted to, em, make myself available.'

John looks at his feet and I can tell he's trying not to laugh.

Aubrey, to be fair to her, glosses over my awkwardness. She holds out her bags. 'Well, I was just out getting some more supplies for a certain dog's birthday. Apparently, Clive Streisand can't be around any non-precious metals so …' She shrugs and I smile understandingly.

'What the celebs want, the celebs get,' I explain to John.

'Okay, well I'd best be on my way.' Aubrey rearranges the bags in her hands. 'John, it was so lovely to meet you, and Aisling, I'll see you on Wednesday? I've sourced Maggie's turkey so we can focus on Bella Hadid's menu. Her cousin is allergic to pecans.'

And with that, she's gone. John and I walk on again, our cosy Tony's glow pierced a little, but not completely gone.

'So that's Aubrey,' he says as we pass lines of horses and carriages just dying to take us into Central Park.

'That's her alright. Doing just one of the crazy things we have to do for work.'

'She seems really sound and really … efficient.'

'She is. She's been with Mandy for a few years now, but she's hoping to open her own wedding-planning business back in Long Island some day if she can ever tear herself away from the city. It's a tough job but the experience we get is second to none. I could do event planning in my sleep after this. I could do St Patrick's Day at the Áras.'

'It's mad – you're, like, really in it here. Working and knowing places to go and bumping into people on the street.'

'Hey, I'm walkin' heeya!' I do my best New Yorker accent because I can feel him getting soppy.

He stops and tugs on the sides of the hood of my parka.

'You'd think you'd get yourself a new winter coat.' And he bends down to kiss me, but before his lips meet mine he puts his mouth to my ear and in his best Tony impression he growls, 'Ais-a-ling, will you-a marry me?'

CHAPTER 7

'm up, showered and back in my Plaza robe, sitting on one of the ornamental armchairs well before ten the next morning. I was actually tossing and turning half the night after we decided to order breakfast in the room yesterday evening. We had hot ports in a little Irish pub by Central Park after bumping into Aubrey and then came back to the hotel too giddy, which led to the flaithiúlach breakfast order. John was asleep by nine and I wasn't long after him, wrecked from the wine and the carry-on of us. I woke with a jolt at three in the morning, unsure of where I was in the pitch dark of the room. John stirred in his sleep and reached out for me, so I made myself into the small spoon and folded into him. I was so afraid of missing the breakfast, though, that I was in and out of sleep and awake for good by half seven. I forgot to order any more pillows off the menu and now it's too late.

I'm back at work tomorrow and then John will be gone and this magic little interlude will be over. I have the same feeling in my belly as I used to get mid-morning on a Sunday when I was in school. There was still loads of the weekend to go, but with every minute that passed it was taking away the goodness. I give myself a shake and remind myself that it's only ten to ten in the morning and we still have the whole day together. I go over to the bed and jump up on it.

John moans and rolls onto his back, smiling. 'Have you the world set to rights? You've been up long enough.'

'Someone has to be ready to receive the breakfast.' I lie down beside him and he turns to face me. I blow on his eyelashes. 'Remember the hotel we stayed in that time in Tenerife? The two single beds?'

'And the hairy blankets?' John smiles and squeezes his eyes shut. I was allergic to those blankets. Flat out on the hydrocortisone.

There's a knock on the door then and I squeal and run for it. The uniformed bellboy from the day we first arrived has a whole trolley waiting for me, and after asking 'May I?' he wheels it beside the little dining table by the window. He starts opening out little hatches and drawers and I flutter around behind him trying to help until he gently tells me I can take a seat.

John eventually sits up in bed. 'Sorry, lad, coming now.'

The bellboy sneaks a peek at John nipping to the bathroom wrapped in a sheet before returning to the croissants and granola and pancakes and eggs. We really went for it. I marvel over the tiny trio of jams and the moulded butter and nearly pass out with delight when he produces a whole jug of fresh orange juice. Then he expertly flicks a crisp white napkin over my knees, and as he's gathering his bits to leave, John emerges in his robe and his bedhead slicked down with some water. He catches the bellboy just as he's leaving and slips twenty dollars into his hand. I'm extremely impressed as he sits down and tears into a pain au chocolat.

'That was incredibly smooth. Borderline erotic.'

He blushes. 'Ah, I did a bit of it in Dubai.'

There's a tiny part of me that dies when he mentions his other life in Dubai. But sure, I had a life without him too.

'And,' he adds, 'as soon as I booked the Plaza I looked up how to tip in fancy hotels.'

I burst out laughing. Of course he did. We hoof through the breakfast, looking out over our terrace onto the packed New York street below and making up stories for all the people busying along.

'She's late to meet her mother and is considering throwing herself under a bus.'

'The mother is going to have lots of compliments about her new haircut, all of them back-handed.'

'He's on his way to get his arse waxed.'

'He's kind of walking like he just had it waxed.'

John points to a woman wearing large sunglasses and a baseball hat down low over her face. 'She's after calling in sick and is absolutely haunted at the idea of bumping into her boss.'

I squint at the woman more closely. 'I think that's Lady Gaga.'

'Well, I hope she doesn't bump into her boss.'

The mention of work reminds me that I have to get back to reality in just a few short hours. 'So, I'm going to have to go home later. I have work tomorrow.'

John looks stricken. 'Ah but you'll stay here tonight though? Our last night together?'

'I can't. I don't have my stuff. I can't get in without my swipe card.'

'Go home and get it then? Please? I can't imagine staying here without you.' He holds out his arms and I go over and sit on his knee, digging my hands into his hair and scratching his scalp.

'Okay, I suppose I'll stay with you here in this kip for one more night.'

****

My Uber driver downtown is mercifully silent, and I lean back in the dark interior of the car to spend some time with my quiet brain. I can't believe I'm gearing up to say goodbye to John yet again. I distract myself by checking my emails. I set an out-of-office so there's nothing urgent but one from Mandy catches my eye. The subject heading is 'WEDNESDAY! LEO DI C!' and I'm too intrigued not to check an email that's potentially about Leonardo DiCaprio. Also I don't want to go into work tomorrow completely unprepared. I open it.

'Aisling, I respect your PTO, doll, but I also assume you're going to read this so don't come to the office tomorrow – come straight to meet me at Mad Susan's at eleven. Leo's looking for a new events team in the city so we're meeting with his people tomorrow.'

The fact that Mandy is bringing me to the Leo meeting is pretty big. I check the street address of Mad Susan's and it's only two blocks from the Plaza, which means I won't have to rush off in the morning.

My phone bips. Now a text from Mandy.

'Don't wear that sweater. M'

My jumper with the French bulldog on it is actually from Zara. I got it in the sale and thought it would be perfect for work because it's one per cent cashmere and people in New York are berserk for their little dogs. The last time I wore it into the office, though, Mandy said it made her nauseous and I tried not to feel too bad because she sent one of the Joshes home the previous week for wearing the wrong colour denim for a meeting about Nicky Hilton's baby-shower invitations.

The apartment is quiet as I open the door and throw my keys on the couch. Fatima is technically still renting the other room, but she's in Washington DC for the next three months at least, thanks to her new role on Congresswoman Dominique Devers's staff.

In my room I flick through work outfits for the Leo meeting. I look sadly at the Zara bulldog before choosing a plain blue shumper and a pair of black flared trousers that I'm absolutely thrilled are back in fashion. A-Wear would truly thrive with the resurgence of string tops and boot-cuts. I pull out some clean underwear too, going for a matching floral set I got in Marks and Spencer last year. The knickers are very flattering but itchy and the balcony bra makes my boobs look great, plus you can see my nipples through the lace. I start getting the fanny flutters at the thought of straddling John in this gear and have to sit on my bed with my legs crossed for five minutes looking at the news on my phone. But not before I lose the run of myself completely and send him a picture of the lace edging and the message 'Can't wait to get back.' He responds with a simple 'Jesus', and I do a little squeal before calming myself down with the *Irish Times* app. I'm halfway through an article about a two-bedroom house with half a roof in Harold's Cross for €955,000 when Paul's name flashes up on my FaceTime. Shite, I told my brother I'd ring him on Sunday but it got lost in all the John excitement. I answer.

'Aisling, tell Mammy it was Auntie Sheila who fell backwards into the coal bunker at Daddy's fiftieth.'

'It wasn't, it was Auntie Angela.' I remember it well because she was really quite wedged and there was talk of ringing the fire brigade at one point, once everyone had stopped laughing. 'Aunty Sheila broke the piano stool.'

'I told you it was Angela!' Mammy shrieks in the background.

I was half toying with the idea of telling Paul about John. I didn't want to say anything with Mammy there, though. Absolutely no need to light that fire.

'You'll never guess who I'm meeting tomorrow,' I babble. 'Well, probably. Maybe.'

'Marty Whelan,' Mammy shouts. Since Constance Swinford converted her to Lyric FM she hasn't looked back, although why Marty would be in New York is beyond me.

'No, Leonardo DiCaprio. Or his assistant, which is practically the same thing.'

'Oh Jesus, Mary and Joseph! I thought you and Majella were going to wear out that *Titanic* DVD rewinding it the way you did.'

Paul suddenly clears his throat pointedly. 'There's something I need to tell you,' he goes.

'Oh, go on?'

'I'm going back to Australia.'

'Oh! When?' Images of Mammy completely on her own at Christmas flash through my head, and the familiar old guilt about leaving home rears its head.

'January. A lad I knew over there got in touch about a really good job in his place, working on promoting Irish tourism, and they're looking for someone not just there on a year away, drinking and messing.'

'That's deadly, Paul, and you'd be brilliant at something like that.' Paul has grown up so much since he first went away to Australia and came back with a broken heart and a desperate case of depression. I'm thrilled that he's feeling well enough to go back.

'Oh yeah, they're all going off and leaving me. I'll be like Peig Sayers.' Mammy is messing but it still sends a pang of worry through me.

'Sure, you wouldn't even have time for us anyway,' Paul jeers her and she blushes. It's absolutely mad to see her in this new era of Dr Trevor. I'm kind of glad I'm removed from it. It might be just too weird.

My phone buzzes with a text from John wondering how long I'll be, so I say my goodbyes with a promise to ring at the end of the week with an update on Leo.

****

'Jesus, I forgot Donald Trump is in this!' John exclaims.

We're tangled around each other, naked and warm. My bra and knickers are on the floor somewhere and the whole hotel room is dark apart from *Home Alone 2: Lost in New York* blinking out from the telly. We keep exclaiming every time we see a Plaza landmark we recognise. They've changed the carpet in the lifts, but the phone Kevin uses is still in the lobby. I remind John about the time I got the haircut that made me look like Brenda Fricker, and he surprises me by telling me how stupid he felt the time he got me the same Pandora bracelet two Christmases in a row. It was the first time we had gotten back together, and neither of us had changed and it fizzled out. I didn't think he'd even realised he'd doubled up on the presents, and I cling to him even tighter as he whispers 'I'd never do that again' into my hair. By the end of the film, when Kevin is reunited with his family and legs it out of the Plaza to give Brenda and the pigeons a present, I sigh.

'What's wrong?' John asks, rolling me onto my back and looking down at me.

'I'm just sad that this is our last night.'

He's quiet for a minute. 'Me too. This is all my fault. If I hadn't gone to Dubai everything would be so much easier.'

'Nothing worth having comes easy.' I make myself even sadder by saying that. 'I saw it on Instagram this morning.'

'We'll figure it out.'

'We definitely will.'

'I can Skype you from Maguire's. I hear the karaoke machine has really taken off.'

'And we have Zoom now too. And there's always WhatsApp.' He nods, and then it's out of my mouth before I can stop myself. 'Unless you find yourself someone new in the meantime.' I try to say it jokingly but make a hames of it.

'Aisling, don't start that. You're the one wanting to take it slow. You know I love you. Only you.' He looks so sad now too. I just nod and squeeze him tighter.

In the morning he tries to convince me to book a flight home for Christmas, but I explain that I just can't.

'It's party season and I work in events,' I say with a shrug. 'You wouldn't believe how busy we are. Emily Ratajkowski is soft-launching her new boyfriend. Durex is sponsoring. It's a huge operation.'

'What about in the New Year?'

'Oh, I'll be all over the Aer Lingus sale.' I'm doing my best to stay in control, but the thought of us being apart again is overwhelming.

'And I'd be stupid to tell everyone at home we're back together, wouldn't I? I mean, are we back together?'

'You're not stupid, but I think it's a bit soon for all that, don't you?'

He smiles that lopsided smile. 'No.'

'I think we should take our time. Let's see how we feel once you get back home. Is that a good plan?'

'I have no idea, but it sounds better than nothing. Now, put on that bra again. It's only half nine.'

CHAPTER 8

I t's nearly seven o'clock by the time my Uber pulls up outside Shebeen and the place is hopping. Or maybe it just looks hopping because it's the only spot on the street open on Thanksgiving.

'I have to let you go, Gearóidín,' I beg, now ten minutes trying to get my father's first cousin off the phone. She put me up in her little place in Queens when I first got to New York. We still talk all the time because of our mutual love of the *Irish Times* crossword and Barry's tea. She was very disappointed when I told her I had to work and wouldn't make it out for dinner today, but what could I do. 'I'll come and see you soon, I promise. Bye, bye, byebye bye.'

The Irish Mafia are out in force for Stilettos and Skyscrapers blogger Tara's annual Friendsgiving get-together, and the air is thick with the scent of pumpkin spice. There are a few unfamiliar faces, but I immediately spot Stevie, who used to be in Sydney with Paul, chatting to his cousin Fiona Morrissey, formerly a political aide to disgraced congressman William J. McNamara. Joanne Collins is there too, on her phone as usual, which is what you need to do when you're as high up at Facebook as she is. Davy Doherty from Netflix is laughing at something Sandra Hayes is saying, and Gráinne Whelan is doing shots with a few of The Peigs at the bar. Rumour has it she's trying to get them to sign with Universal Music, but Sadhbh says she definitely won't be letting that happen now that she has a new role with Neptune, their record company back home.

Tara beckons me over and envelops me in a hug, and I feel a pang of pride at being welcomed into this high-powered group. She smells unreal. According to Majella, Jo Malone makes her a new signature scent for every season because she has nearly 800,000 followers on Instagram and occasionally shows one of her candles.

'The place looks great, Tara. Sorry I'm late.'

There's one huge table in the centre of the room, and it's heaving with food and decorative gourds and twinkling candles.

'No worries, girl. Food is coming out shortly. What's all this?'

I plonk down the stack of tinfoil boxes I'm struggling with and gratefully accept a seat from Stevie. 'Leftovers from work.'

Sandra's head shoots up. 'From Bella Hadid's Thanksgiving?' She's a producer for the *Today Show* on NBC and is forever trying to squeeze celebrity gossip out of me, even though she knows Mandy would have my guts for garters if her reputation for discretion was compromised.

'I couldn't possibly divulge that kind of information,' I say, pulling off my parka. The weather is gone bitter. 'Now don't be at me.'

'Just tell me what she had. I can get a segment out of it. Maybe two. Are potatoes in or out for supermodels?'

'You know how Mandy is.' No spuds for Bella.

'Nod if Gigi was there.'

'No!' She had all the trimmings.

'Blink if Zayn made an appearance!'

'Sandra!' No sign.

'Down, Sandra!' Stevie gently pushes her out of the way with a pop of his hip and drags his seat over next to me.

'Thank you,' I whisper gratefully, tipping the end of a bottle of white wine into the glass in front of me. I'm wrecked. Bella herself was grand, but her mother was a monumental dose and wouldn't let the caterers put squeezy cream on the pumpkin pie even though it was a special occasion. 'Where's Raphael?' Stevie is dating the painfully cool receptionist from my office who just about tolerates me.

'In Missouri. With his family.' He sighs, obviously still smarting because he had to work this morning and couldn't go home.

'Hang on, Raphael is from Missouri?'

'Oh yeah. Everyone assumes he's a New Yorker but he grew up on a farm. Don't tell him I told you that, though. So … Jeff was asking about you.'

'Ah, he wasn't, was he?' I don't think he's crossed my mind more than once.

'I was sorry to hear you guys were dunzo. You were so cute together! He was asking about my plans for today and who'd be here and blah blah blah. I had to explain that Irish people don't actually celebrate Thanksgiving the way we do.'

'I'd say that took a while.' Although he's truly one of the nicest men on the planet, Jeff really isn't the sharpest tool in the shed. He's never been outside New York and once asked me if we had ten-pin bowling in Ireland.

Stevie mimes wiping sweat from his brow. 'You betcha. I guess he was wondering why John wouldn't be here. How are things going there?'

I smile and start picking at a hangnail. Although we swore we'd take it slowly this time, things between us have certainly escalated these past few weeks since he went home. We originally decided to Skype every Sunday at 8 a.m. my time, 1 p.m. his time. But it just wasn't enough. He's under my skin in a way he never was before. I just can't get enough of him, and he's the same. So we're now WhatsApping all day long and FaceTiming at the drop of a hat. Like yesterday, he rang to show me That Bloody Cat asleep in one of Úna Hatton's planters. I was in a meeting with Mandy, Josh B and Aubrey at the time about how to lock down the contract for Nick Cannon's gender reveals. It was cute, though. I do miss That Bloody Cat.

'It's all good, thanks.' And then there's the sexting. It's not something I've ever really done before, apart from one time James Matthews asked me for a racy pic when he was away on a job and I was so mortified I did a close-up of my bent elbow that managed to pass for cleavage. John sent a shot of himself reclining in bed the other night that looked like something out of GQ. I wanted to reciprocate but I was already in my nightie and my knickers were just plain multi-pack ones from Penneys, so I did the elbow trick again to hold him off. Sadhbh said she'd give me some tips on taking nudes the next time I see her. She's well used to it, what with The Peigs being on the road so much and Don getting pelted with knickers on stage six nights a week. I scan the table and notice she's not here.

I turn to Tara, who's taking a selfie with the giant turkey that's just been placed in the centre of the table. 'Where's Sadhbh?'

'No sign of her or Don, and my photographer is leaving in twenty minutes.' She nods towards a bored-looking guy with a camera, wearing one of those little fisherman hats on the back of his head that don't look like they'd keep in a jot of heat.

I reach for my phone. There's a text from her: 'Sorry, I'm in an Uber.' That's Sadhbh for 'I'm getting out of the shower'. 'She'll be here soon, Tara.'

'Okay, we're gonna have to start without her, though.' Tara sighs. She knows full well that having Don Shields in a pic is a chance to get her blog mentioned in one of the tabloids and potentially go viral. It happened before when Davy scored them tickets for the premiere of some serial-killer documentary. Don was blinking and *The Sun* ran the shot with some made-up story about him suffering from exhaustion and going into rehab. Tara was delighted with the exposure, but his mam went mental.

At this stage everyone is seated at the table, and Davy in particular looks like he's going to go for the turkey if someone doesn't slice it up and serve it to him. I'm half thinking of tucking into Bella's leftover green-bean casserole myself.

Tara taps a glass with her knife and a hush falls over the room. 'Dearly beloved, we are gathered here today to mostly create content for my blog.' There's an immediate chorus of groans and boos and a chunk of bread roll goes flying past her. 'I'm joking! Just enjoy your free dinner and please ignore

Edson, who's going to snap away. Joanne, that pumpkin is decorative. And Davy, can you chew with your mouth closed for a change?' He mutters something in his thick Donegal accent that I don't catch. 'And between courses we're going to each say what we're thankful for.'

There's another groan as servers start passing around plates.

'I'll go first,' Tara says, ignoring the discontent and shovelling stuffing on to her plate. 'I'm thankful for you lot. I wouldn't have lasted a month in this mad city without you.'

There's an eruption of *aaah*s around the table. Tara's incessant need to create content can get a bit tiring, but she's sound out and generous with her freebies. Everyone understands that you have to be driven to survive in New York. I don't think I'd still be here myself if I hadn't met the Irish Mafia.

'Oh, just start without me, why don't you!' Suddenly, Sadhbh is in the doorway, stamping snow off her shoes. She recently bleached her eyebrows and has never looked cooler. I wave, and she gestures at me to scooch up and make space.

'No Don tonight?' Tara trills, looking anxious.

'Can't make it. Sends his apologies.'

'Hey, everything okay?' I whisper as she slips in beside me and the others get back to saying they're thankful for DoorDash and living in buildings with lifts.

'We had a fight in the hotel,' she whispers back, helping herself to nut roast.

'Ah, Sadhbhy, you two never fight. What happened?'

'He wants to have' – she lowers her voice another few decibels – 'a fucking baby.'

'A baby?!'

'A fucking baby. Since we're moving back to Dublin, he thinks the timing is right, even though I told him when we first got together that I didn't ever see myself having children. He knows about the ... you know ... and everything.'

Not long after I moved in with Sadhbh in Dublin, she got pregnant with her on-again-off-again boyfriend and had an abortion. She was the first woman I ever knew who'd gone through that, or so I thought, until Mammy explained she'd had to make the same decision years ago when I was a child.

'Is he set on the idea?'

She shrugs. 'Seems to be. He said he thought I'd eventually change my mind, that all women do.'

'That's a bit ...'

'Isn't it? So I just walked out. That's why I'm wearing my pyjamas.' She looks down at her outfit. It's a big T-shirt and she has on knee socks and loafers with it. It doesn't look any different than the gear she normally wears.

'Well, Don isn't the only one with baby fever. Majella and Pablo are going at it like the clappers at home by all accounts. She has an app that sets off an alarm for when she's ovulating. Apparently Pablo has developed a fear of it.'

'Aisling, I'm trying to eat my dinner here. I don't want to think of Pablo doing –'

'Now, you know Maj would be doing all the doing.'

'That's true. Ah no, I'm happy for them. It's lovely news. If they're both on the same page.'

She picks at her turkey, looking sad. Sadhbh and Don have always been rock solid – they even have each other's initials tattooed on their ring fingers! – so I'm not used to seeing her like this.

'Tell me about the new job at Neptune,' I say, trying to change the subject. 'Head of Marketing sounds very swish!'

She perks up. 'Doesn't it? And the office is on South William Street, so very handy. The movers are coming Saturday.'

'Why do you need movers? You came to New York with four suitcases.'

'It's mostly Don's guitars.'

I raise my eyebrows at her.

'Okay, it's mostly my clothes. I'm going to miss Aritzia so much!'

'Ah, I'm sure they deliver.'

Tara pokes her head in. 'Are you sure Don's not coming?'

Sadhbh shrugs. 'Sorry, Tara.' She turns back to me. 'What if I can't live without adaptogenic water and Trader Joe's cauliflower gnocchi and my edibles, though?'

'You'll survive. And you have a gorgeous house to go home to, remember?'

'I know, I know. I'm excited to get back and get settled. Ruby and Elaine are planning a girls' night, just like the old days.'

The wave of FOMO nearly knocks me off my seat. When me, Sadhbh and Elaine lived together, we used to order a takeaway and sit around drinking wine under blankets at least once a week. It was heaven, even when Elaine insisted we listen to some godawful techno mix.

'Oh Jesus, I'm so jealous, Sadhbh.'

'I'll tell the girls you said hello. Now, will you pass me whatever that is with the marshmallows on top and fill me in on what's going on with John?'

CHAPTER 9

Two weeks later, I'm standing in Macy's, suddenly aware it's definitely the wrong place to go for sexy underwear, especially on a Saturday afternoon two weeks before Christmas. The place is in bits and almost everything is seamless and flesh-coloured, which I'd normally be all over but not today. Sadhbh told me before she left for Dublin that if I want my nudes to be 'spicy' the best thing to do is start with lingerie layers and take it off bit by bit. She said it's basically like doing a striptease, only through pictures. Lads go wild for it. Then she got out her phone and tried to show me some examples from her own camera roll. I had to beg her to put it away. We're close but I don't need to see her in her pelt, thank you very much.

I give up and go home where I rifle through my underwear drawer before my eye falls on the floral M&S set that I wore in the Plaza that really got John going. God, am I really doing this? On the first day of my period when I'm bloated and have three new spots on my chin? Through the wall I can just about make out Candice wailing about the devil's ability to trick good God-fearing people into sinning. For a second, I wonder if he's pulled the wool over my eyes and then I remember, no, I'm definitely acting of my own free will here. I want to get John's blood pumping. That's why we've made this little WhatsApp date. It's been nearly a month since we've seen each other in the flesh and I'm missing that flesh something fierce, especially at night when I'm reading his texts about how much he misses me and wants me. Bloated and crampy or not, I want him too.

Per Sadhbh's advice, I've thrown my fears about fire safety out the window and a floaty scarf over my little reading lamp to give the room a soft glow and now, kneeling on the bed holding the phone above my head, I agree that the light is fairly flattering. I pull the bobbin out of my low ponytail and shake out my hair so it falls around my shoulders in what I hope is a sort of tousled, bedhead way. Not bad. I try to lean back on my heels but my hamstrings are screaming, so instead I sort of recline on my side and let one bra strap fall off my shoulder. Okay, better, although I get a stitch almost immediately. How do glamour models do it? And make it look so easy? I have a new respect for Jordan. I set the time on my phone and snap a couple of shots like that, hiding my discomfort and doing my best pout, and then unhook the bra entirely and throw it across the room. Next, I lie on my tummy and attempt Majella's favourite trick of squeezing the boobs together with my arms. She swears it brings her up two whole cup sizes, and she's not exaggerating. I take a few more shots in that position and another one over my shoulder and another one with my finger on my nipple. For a second, I even consider taking off the knickers and doing some full frontal, but I quickly get a grip and put back on my Winnie the Pooh pyjamas and fleece dressing gown and pour myself a glass of Pinot Greej.

His text arrives at 6 p.m. on the dot.

> *Well, Ais, how was your Saturday? Was just in Maguire's for a pint. Told Titch and Cyclops my gym idea and they both said they'd join. Sound! Sharon says hello. She and Cyclops did Fairytale of New York on the karaoke. Brought the house down X*

> *Hey, that's great news about the gym. And the karaoke. All quiet here. Did my washing and went to the shops for a few bits. Wrecked after last night. Mandy is in London so myself and Aubrey were holding down the fort. The Divorcees against Gum Disease Gala went off without a hitch TG X*

> *No better women. No big Saturday night plans to go out with the rest of the gang there later so? X*

> *Tara has tickets to some boxing match in Madison Square Garden but I'm happy enough staying in. Just chilling with a glass of wine now X*

> *Ah sounds so nice. Wish I was there x*

> *Wish you were too, John x*

> *I miss you so much, Ais. Seriously, this is torture. I can't stop thinking about you. About us in the Plaza. You were so hot x*

You were pretty hot yourself if I recall! X

Do you have any pics? I know you said you'd take some but no pressure. I'd love to see you x

I do actually. Here you go x

I throw a black-and-white filter on one of the first ones where I'm on my side and hit send. I don't know why I feel nervous – it's not like he hasn't seen me in the nip hundreds of times. There's a pause and then he's typing. Typing. Typing.

Ais, you look incredible. Your tits are unreal xxx

I examine the picture and feel a flush of pride. They do look good. When I think of the years I spent listening to WeightWatchers Maura shite on about points and boot-cut jeans being slimming and worrying about my body and what people thought of me I feel sad for that version of myself. But John always made me feel sexy, even in my BGB Gaels jersey and O'Neill's. *Especially* in my BGB Gaels jersey and O'Neill's.

Thanks. Do you have anything for me? X

After a second his picture appears. I recognise the arm-chair. He's lying back and his jeans are open. I can see his boxers. The look he's giving the camera can only be described as mischievous. He's such a ride.

Jesus, you're in the sitting room with your fly down! What if your parents walk in?

It's after 12 here, they're in bed ages. Have you got anything else for me, Ais? You're really turning me on here x

This time I take a drink and send him the over-the-shoulder one.

Ais, tell me you're wearing that underwear now, are you? You're driving me wild x

I glance down at my dressing gown. There's a little red tomato-sauce stain on my boob shelf from when I had a slice of pizza earlier.

Yeah, I am. It's a bit chilly x

I send on another one, the boob squeezing. I don't even put a filter on it.

Fucking hell. I wish you were here, Ais x

Then before I change my mind, I fire off the finger-on-nipple one for good measure because why the hell not? In for a penny and all that.

I wish I was too x

CHAPTER 10

'**A**isling! Get Charlotte on the phone! We might be just about able to fit in Leo's Going Green in '23 party on the twenty-third after all if we send out invitations tomorrow.'

It's taken weeks for Mandy to accept that Leonardo DiCaprio's assistant's assistant is as close as we're going to get to him and his philanthropy for the time being. Charlotte has been agitating for an event as close to Christmas as possible, but between the Real Housewives Holiday Hot Mess party we already have scheduled in for the 23rd and the Rockefeller Carol Singing in aid of New York Children's Hospital sponsored by Ben Dixon's tequila brand on Christmas Eve, we've been struggling to accommodate her and Leo. I leap up off my chair and follow Mandy into her office, thrilled that I made it to my desk three minutes before she arrived into work. I was up mad late voice-noting John, who was up mad early to have a meeting with the local enterprise board about his gym concept. It's crazy that no one else has come up with the idea yet. They've been selling protein powder behind the bar in Maguire's for months now, according to Majella, who spotted it between the clothes pegs and the yellow Snacks.

'So, it's really like you've never left?' I asked John at 3 a.m. my time, snuggling down into my bed and throwing a leg over a pillow, wishing it was his hairy thighs. I'm horribly homesick listening to him talking about BGB. When we finally said goodbye at half four, he said he had to do something to keep busy because he misses me so much. Then I cried for half an hour before falling into a fitful sleep and had an anxiety dream where Majella was up a tree trying to hold about fifteen babies all at once. Pablo was there too, juggling courgettes.

'What about the carol singing?' I ask Mandy, who's thrown her belongings on the chair I was about to sit on. I move the Birkin onto the floor and then quickly snap it up again and put it on her sideboard. I've seen enough screaming fits about the Birkin touching 'where your disgusting outdoor hooves have been schlepping in and out' to be caught disrespecting the bag. Luckily, I know Mandy well enough now to hardly be scared of her any more. She really trusts me and Aubrey, I can feel it. She left a Bellinis for Breast Cancer luncheon completely to us last week when she was in London, even though Oprah's best friend Gayle was going to be there and there was a chance I might 'do the word vomit about you shitting yourself'. I regret ever telling Mandy about the time I was home sick from school with a tummy bug and a temperature and I was watching morning telly and Oprah brought Gayle on and I hallucinated that she was an angel sent to save me. I managed to get through the whole luncheon, and it was only when Gayle was getting her coat and had had five bellinis that I discreetly thanked her. I also sneaked a picture of her, which is a big no-no in the celebrity event business, but Oprah's show was huge when I was in secondary school and WeightWatchers first came to BGB. We felt a kinship with her even though we're so white we're practically see-through. I had to send a picture of Gayle to the girls' WhatsApp. They were all in Denise's watching *The Muppet Christmas Carol,* and I got a video response of them screaming, which cut dramatically halfway through to Denise swearing as the sound of a toddler crying flooded down the stairs. I would have loved to be there touching Denise's grey velvet cushions and admiring her new bathroom. It's mad how I used to dream about my own grey velvet cushions and new bathroom and now I'm just happy for her that she has them but thrilled I'm not picking tiles and worrying about emptying the septic tank.

'It's been agreed that the tequila sponsoring the carol singing is in poor taste after all.' She can barely look at me while she's saying it. I was the one who suggested it might not be the greatest fit, but the placement would have been amazing and picked up for lots of TV news slots. We've only recently started working with Ben Dixon and the two other James Bonds on their tequila brand. Pierce Brosnan thinks he can get it into his next movie, and Daniel Craig seems happy to just go with the flow. I don't think it's going to be a hard sell at all, so I'm pleased the carol-singing gig has fallen through. Mandy has been making some rash decisions since she lost the McNamara contract after he was annihilated by Dominique Devers in the midterm election. She's well rid, and so are the carol singers.

'It might be a bit late in the day for Charlotte and Leo, no?' With Christmas Eve free that would mean a blissful four full days off work. We have the reality-star shitshow on the twenty-third and then nothing else until the twenty-eighth, when we have one of Hugh Grant's kids' christenings. It was supposed to be on the twenty-seventh but he forgot he had one of his other kids' birthdays. Maybe I can convince Mandy not to jump in with this Leo event. She looks thoughtful.

'I'm not sure they'll want to play second fiddle just because the Bonds got dropped.' We're not actually allowed use the James Bond name in conjunction with the tequila, so we've had lots of long strategy meetings about decoration and branding that just skirts the line of what's permitted. Aubrey has been battling with MGM over producing beermats with 'Never shaken, never stirred' on them. She had an hour-long debate with someone called Kai over what constitutes a recipe. No better woman.

'And I actually think waiting until the New Year would work well for the Leo event. Nobody usually makes a splash in January, whereas the Christmas events get lost on top of each other. There's an opportunity there.'

Mandy muses for another minute. 'And Charlotte did say that Leo is in the Caribbean for the New Year but can take the jet back to the city if needed.'

'How very green of him.'

'Don't start, Aisling.'

'Why don't I suggest an end-of-January gala to her? I bet Leo can get Harry and Meghan in January. I bet he can get Jack Nicholson.' Mandy has a soft spot for Jack Nicholson, who once tickled her ear with a cigar in the mid-nineties. She told Aubrey about it on a tipsy evening at a premium wedding planner convention in Vegas.

'Okay, but get her today, before lunch. I want her confirmed in writing before she goes to someone else.'

'And I can lock in the Christmas week schedule then?' I ask hopefully. I had all my presents wrapped and sent back home by the second week in November, but I still have some last-minute bits to do, including finding a Christmas crackers source. What else can change by next week?

'Lock it in.'

****

When I get home at a quite reasonable 7 p.m. that evening I send a message to Sadhbh on the off-chance she's still up. She's happily settling back into the gorgeous house she and Don renovated in Ranelagh and FaceTimes me straight away.

'Look at you, home before eight!'

'I know. I think Mandy is going easy on us before Christmas mania, which actually got a little bit less manic today.'

'Well?'

'The tequila choir thing is off.'

'Not surprised.' Sadhbh turns on the light in her bedroom and sits back on her gorgeous pale green linen pillows. 'So what does next week look like then?'

'Busy busy until the night of the twenty-third.'

'The Housewives thing?'

'The Hot Mess, yeah. I just reconfirmed the order of sugar glass today.'

Sadhbh laughs. 'I know it's meant to be safer than real glass, but if anyone can turn sugar glass into a viable weapon it will be a Real Housewife.'

'Don't tell me that, please – I'm the health and safety officer. And then I'm off until the twenty-eighth. I could have bloody gone home after all.'

This is the first time I've said it out loud, and I'm surprised by how angry I feel that the truth is that I could easily have done a few days in BGB. Well, not that easily, or cheaply, but it could have been done.

'Could you not still?'

'Ah, it's a bit late now. Imagine trying to get flights?'

'You never know.' She's quiet for a beat. 'Are you talking to him much?'

'Loads. I miss him so much. I ...'

'What? Go on?'

I start laughing. She's always at it, FaceTiming her rock-star boyfriend in skimpy bralets. It doesn't come as easy to me. 'We've been having phone sex. Like, loads of it.'

Sadhbh squeals and throws her phone in the air and then scrabbles for it. When her face reappears, she's laughing. 'I love this for you. I think. Just mind yourself, okay? Remember what happened the last time you got back together? It didn't work out and I don't know if you'd survive letting him go for a third time.'

'I know, I know. But this feels so different, Sadhbh. Being apart for so long really made me realise what I'm looking for. Not what I thought I was looking for. I have never fancied him this much. Or felt like he's a missing part of me or something.'

'Check the flights. You never know.'

When I open Skyscanner, there are a couple of seats available, but the price of one is equivalent to the GDP of a small country. I'd have to be certifiable to even consider it.

CHAPTER 11

y nerves are jangling when Tony Timoney heaves my suitcase out from the belly of the bus and passes me the handle with a flourish. I'm the last passenger on his final run of the day.

'Don't forget to tell your mother I said happy Christmas now, Aisling,' he roars before the doors hiss shut and he pulls off into the frosty night.

I already have WhatsApp open. 'Free now for a quick call? X'

John's response is so fast he must have had the phone in his hand too. 'Just in Maguire's with the lads. Should I wait until I'm in private? Hahaha xx'

'You wish! No, it's not that. Pop outside, it'll only take a second x.'

Without warning, his name flashes up on my screen. Shite. I was supposed to be the one ringing him. I panic trying to find a blank background that won't give away where I am and hit OK. He appears on the screen, making his way through the packed pub. I can see Mags from Zumba with Mags and Tessie Daly at the fire! And Eamon Filan nursing his pint!

'Well, did Mandy give you a five-minute break?' John smiles into the camera. Then a look of panic crosses his face. 'Shit, she can't hear me, can she?'

I can see the meat slicer and the shelves of tinned beans and the hanging wellies. He's almost at the front door now.

I hold the phone as close as possible so my face fills the screen entirely, trying my best not to laugh. 'No, I think you're safe there.'

The door swings open and suddenly he's standing on the footpath only feet away from me. Except he's not looking at me – he's mooning into his front camera. 'Go on, what was so important it couldn't wait till later? Miss me, do ya?'

I stifle a giggle. 'I do, yeah.'

When he hears my voice in stereo he looks so confused and vulnerable that I want to pick him up and put him in my pocket. My John. My heart.

'You can't be here,' he stammers looking from the phone in his hand back to me and back to the phone again.

'You're not the only one who can pull off a surprise, you know.' I smirk.

He's in front of me in a split second. He grabs me by the waist, spins me around and walks me backwards until I'm pressed up against Maguire's pebble-dashed wall. Inside, I can hear the faint strains of someone murdering 'All I Want for Christmas'. His kiss has an urgency that makes my stomach flip.

'My Christmas wish came true,' he croaks when we come up for air.

'Mine too,' I whisper.

He grabs the back of my thighs and hoists me up to his waist.

'Someone is going to catch us,' I squeal, wrapping my legs around him. I can feel his arousal and it's making me wish we were alone and not on Main Street, Ballygobbard, lit up by Mikey Maguire's bockety inflatable Santa.

'I don't give a shite. Do you give a shite?'

'No, I don't give a shite.' I laugh and lean in to kiss him again. A kerfuffle at the pub door stops us both dead.

'AISLING?'

It's Majella, frozen in shock, one arm in her coat and the other searching for its dangling sleeve.

'Surprise!' I roar, releasing the grip my thighs have on John and standing next to him shyly.

'You absolute bitch,' she screeches, running over and hugging me tightly. 'Why didn't you tell me? Pablo bawled through Mariah just now because he misses you so much. Well, you and Tenerife.'

Pablo's emotions run particularly high at Christmas, and especially when there's drink taken.

'It was very last-minute. And anyway, you're shite at keeping a secret. I wanted to get this lad back for landing on my doorstep in New York.' I nudge John and he beams down at me.

'Well, don't you look like the cat that got the cream.' Majella raises her eyebrows at him.

'Feeling fairly lucky alright, Maj,' he says.

Her eyes widen. 'Does your mam know you're back?'

'No, I'm going to head home now.'

'Jesus, she's going to lay an egg!'

'I know. She'll lay two if she finds out I came here first. I better leg it before I'm seen.'

'Ah, but Ais, you have to come in for a drink. Everyone's inside. It's Christmas Eve in Maguire's! Liam Kelly is trying to put together a *Paw Patrol* Lookout Tower behind the pool table.'

'Is Paul in there?'

She shakes her head. 'He just had one after mass. Your mam won't find out.'

I look from her pleading eyes to John's. He squeezes my hand. 'Just one? I'll bring you home after.'

****

There are so many people coming up saying hello and hugging me that I lose both Majella and John in the melee, and it takes me twenty minutes to get from the door to the bar, where Mikey is giving all his regulars their annual Christmas drink.

'And a West Coast Cooler for yourself, Aisling?' He slides the bottle over to me with a wink. It's like I never left.

'Thanks, Mikey.'

Carol Boland is at my side, filling me in on the record day they had at BallyGoBrunch. She looks exhausted but her eyes are shining. 'It was only because Skippy Brennan mentioned it on the radio, of course. A lot of people had reservations about sausagemeat stuffing, but the whole parish went crackers for it once he gave it his stamp of approval. Your mother even sent Paul out for some. He said she's having a crowd tomorrow. And she'll have one more now with you home, won't she?'

'A crowd?' Since Daddy died we've always gone to Auntie Sheila's. They cook the dinner between them. 'Did she say who?' It's probably Constance Swinford, Mammy's friend and partner in ShayMar eco farm, who's also part of the widow gang. She does sound like about fifteen people once she has a few brandies in her.

'I didn't have time to ask, pet.'

'Aisling, Majella said you were working the whole Christmas!' As the local hairdresser slash beauty salon owner, Sharon is always dressed to the nines, but she's outglammed herself tonight in a figure-hugging silver sequinned dress and thigh-high suede boots. She pulls me in for a hug and I squeeze her back happily.

'I managed to get a few days off. You look stunning, Sharon! Oh my God, show me the ring!' She and Cyclops got engaged shortly after I left. She dutifully proffers her left hand and I ooh and aah over the cut of the diamond and the band. 'It's so sparkly!'

'Fairy liquid, hun. Scrubs up like a dream. So, what are you drinking? West Coast Cooler still, is it? Another one there, please, Mikey, and a vodka and tonic for me and will you drop a pint up to himself?' She nods across the bar to where her boyfriend – fiancé – Eoin Ó Súilleabháin, aka Cyclops, is with Titch Maguire and Baby Chief Gittons. They've gathered a selection of parkas with furry hoods and are arguing over who gets to be Brian when they do East 17's 'Stay Another Day'. They'll have a tough job wrestling the microphone off Pablo, though. He's on the little make-shift stage in the corner belting out 'Feliz Navidad' while Majella shimmies over and back in front of him with a sprig of mistletoe in her teeth.

'Coming up, Sharon.'

'Ah, thank you, Sharon, but I can't. Mammy will kill me!'

'Stop, now. I have to buy you a drink. How long are you back for, hun? Will I book you in for a blow-dry on Stephenses Day? I'm only opening for friends and regulars, but I'll squeeze you in.'

Sinéad McGrath appears over her shoulder, followed by Dee Ruane. 'Jesus Christ, it's a Christmas miracle!' Dee pulls me in for a hug, and I'm surprised at how much I missed the whole gang. 'Mikey, another West Coast Cooler for Ais and a Bulmers Light when you're ready.'

'Right you are, Dee.'

'Dee, I can't, honestly. I have to go home.'

'I don't want to hear it, Ais – I haven't seen you in months.' Mikey puts a third bottle on the bar in front of me and Sinéad grabs my arm. 'Did the girls tell you what happened at mass?'

'No.'

'Mad Tom and Rocky were found in the crib.'

'Who's Rocky?' I feel so out of the loop, even though I've only been gone four months.

'His girlfriend,' Sinéad explains. 'She's the reason he switched out the real pig feed for the counterfeit stuff and nearly put the entire village in a mass grave.'

'Well, it was hardly Rocky's fault, hun,' Sharon interjects. She turns to me. 'He was trying to save money to buy her a new second-hand Subaru. Her hair is in one big dreadlock, Ais, but, you know, she can actually pull it off. I'm trying to get her to put Olaplex in it once a week.'

'No, I know she's not to blame or anything,' Sinéad continues. 'I'm just trying to fill Ais in. Apparently Billy Foran bet them thirty euro they couldn't go unnoticed in the crib, even though Father Fenlon dusts it himself every morning. They were in there for days! Nobody copped until Denise Kelly's little lad climbed the fence at communion time and got the fright of his life.'

Father Fenlon prides himself on the enormous life-sized crib that sits to the left of the altar in BGB's cavernous church. He used to even rope in some of the local farmers, Daddy included, to loan him livestock for his beloved Christmas Eve mass. It had to be nixed when one of Murt Kelly's donkeys ate through a cable and caused a blackout.

'No! Not Father Fenlon's crib!' Although I'm delighted to hear Mad Tom has fully recuperated from his porcine flatulence syndrome, I can only imagine the ructions this stunt caused. Poor Father Fenlon really thought moving midnight mass to 8 p.m. would put a stop to the rowdiness. 'I'd say they made a fine Mary and Joseph, the two of them.'

'That's the thing,' Sinéad says quietly. 'She was a Wise Man and he was in the manger.'

'Mad Tom was Baby Jesus?'

Dee cuts her off. 'Anyway, enough about BGB! Tell us all about New York. Maj said something about a ridey fireman. Jesus, Ais,' she lowers her voice, 'you're living out one of my biggest fantasies here. Have you been down the pole? I've been trying to get Titch into a yellow hard hat for years.'

'Mikey, will you get Aisling a West Coast Cooler there when you're ready?' Sinéad interjects with a grimace. 'Thanks!'

'No problem, Sinéad.'

'No, no, honestly, Sinéad, I've to go home!'

Over at the little stage, Majella is now pleading with Pablo to pass the microphone to Cyclops, and I remember what she said about them trying for a baby. I can really imagine her as a mammy. As much as she complains about some of the kids she teaches in St Anthony's in Santry acting the maggot, she has the patience of a saint and can operate on little to no sleep. I've seen her in action myself at Electric Picnic. I can hear her now, telling Pab that if he lets Cyclops and the lads have a go she'll let him open a present when they get home.

'Well, would you look what the cat dragged in!' Maeve Hennessey in a new green peacoat and an Orla Kiely bag on her arm snaps me out of it. 'I was in the chipper when I heard.' She's holding a steaming paper bag. The smell of vinegar and curry sauce makes my mouth water. It's been so long! 'Welcome home, Ais!'

Christ, if it's in the chipper already, I don't have long before the news reaches Mammy.

'West Coast Cooler is it, Ais? Drink for Aisling there, Mikey.'

'On the way, Maeve.' Mikey pops a fourth bottle on the bar.

'Maeve, I can't, honestly! I need to get out of here!'

She ignores me. 'I nearly screamed the house down when I saw you on Stilettos and Skyscrapers the first time. Please tell me Tara's a bitch in real life because I can't believe someone can be that perfect.'

'I'd say she Facetunes herself to bits, does she, Ais?' Sharon asks hopefully.

I shrug. 'Unfortunately, she's dead on. And gorgeous in real life. But I can tell you that her apartment has a cockroach problem. You won't see that on the blog.' Maeve looks delighted so I don't bother mentioning that that applies to half of Manhattan.

She turns to Dee. 'I told you! We all have our cross to bear.' Sinéad joins in, something about Colette Green that I don't catch, and I drift into a daze as the four of them start talking about bloggers and whose tanning mitt is the best and whether it's all the same white-label stuff coming from China or not. My eyes are wandering around the pub when they fall on John over by the fireplace and my heart jumps. He's looking back at me with a kind of half-smile on his face, and I return it, wondering how long he's been watching me chat to the girls. It feels so much like old times, but also so new and exciting. He makes a barely discernible nod towards the door, and as I gently extricate myself from my friends with promises I'll see them again on Stephenses night, Mikey rings the bell that signals last orders are up. It's time to go home.

CHAPTER 12

It's nearly half eleven when we get to the house, and even though I can feel the exhaustion setting in, I'm giddy with nerves and excitement and the two and a half bottles of West Coast Cooler I managed to throw back. The lights are still on and I can just about make out the twinkling Christmas tree in the gap between the sitting-room curtains. Paul is probably watching *Indiana Jones*. And I'd say Mammy's in the kitchen peeling acres of potatoes and getting her Brussels sprouts ready to bring with her tomorrow. She does a good sprout but she'd have them boiling all night if I let her. It was only a few years ago when me and Paul managed to convince her that vegetables are not really supposed to melt in the mouth.

I lead John in through the back door, but when we land into the kitchen there's no sign of her or Paul. There's not even a pot on the Aga. That Bloody Cat stands up when she sees me but just turns around on her chair and settles back in for another sleep. Our relationship has always been very one-sided, to be fair. She only ever had eyes for Daddy.

'Well, puss?'

Nothing.

'They must be inside, come on,' I whisper, abandoning my suitcase and tiptoeing into the hallway. I didn't want to mention anything about John and me talking again until I knew we were serious, but I think it's about time. It's only right that he should be with me when I break the news.

I take a deep breath, push down the handle and swing in the door. Maybe I should have given Paul the heads-up and got him to record my homecoming on his phone. It's the kind of thing that might end up in a heartwarming montage on tomorrow's *Six One*.

'Surprise!'

'Good lord!' It's a man's voice and it certainly isn't Paul's.

I'm as confused as Mammy is shocked. She shoots out of her seat on the couch when she sees me – us – in the doorway and gathers me into her. 'What the blazes? Aisling!'

It's Dr Trevor. He stands up and shuffles over to us, smoothing down his tie. What the hell is he doing in my house on Christmas Eve? It's a sacred day, like. A pang of sadness for Daddy hits me like a slap, but I try to shake it off for the moment that's in it.

Mammy holds me at arm's length and looks me up and down like she hasn't seen me in years. 'Look at you, you look great, love!' Then she turns to John, confused. 'It's nice to see you, John.'

Dr Trevor extends his hand. 'Aisling, very nice to finally meet you in person. Sorry about my reaction just now. I was afraid we had an intruder, God forbid.'

'Well, horse?' Paul stands up from the armchair and pumps John's hand. Then he pulls me in for a hug.

I shake Dr Trevor's hand gingerly, not sure what to say, and we all stand around in an awkward little group. I can feel a tide of irritation rising in me. I can't believe he's here tonight of all nights in his slippers, his feet literally under the coffee table. And why is there a big tub of Quality Street on it? We've always been a Roses house.

'Nice to meet you too' is all I can muster.

John leans in past me and shakes his hand. 'We haven't been formally introduced. John. How's it going? I think you know my mam, Fran? Arthritis in her left hip?'

Dr Trevor smooths his tie again. 'Ah, I take patient confidentiality very seriously, John.' Then he nods. 'But you can tell your mother I hope she's finding some relief with that new medication.'

'John was just walking you home, was he?' Mammy has her hands on her hips but she's smiling.

John puts his arm around my shoulders, and when I look up at him everything else just seems to melt away. I can't help but grin. 'Yeah, about us ...' His eyes are searching mine for confirmation. I stand up on my tiptoes and kiss him gently on the lips. Mammy's hand flies up to her throat in shock. 'I think we're back together.'

****

I'm all disoriented when I wake up the next morning. Where is the street noise? Why can't I hear Candice's omnipresent telly sermon through the wall? Then I remember I'm at home. It's Christmas morning! And I can smell the unmistakable aroma of Carol Boland's sausages drifting up the stairs.

After my surprise arrival last night, Dr Trevor offered to give John a lift home to Knocknamanagh. When Mammy was getting ready for bed I cornered Paul to get the lie of the land. He told me Dr Trevor hasn't moved in, but he stays over a couple of nights a week to keep Mammy company. They play bridge, apparently. Then Paul admitted he sticks in earplugs on those nights, just in case. We left it there.

I pad down to the kitchen where I find Mammy and Dr Trevor at the table tucking into a fry. I wasn't sure if he would, but no, he stayed the night. They stop talking when I push open the door, and I immediately feel self-conscious in front of him in my Forever Friends pyjamas and no bra.

Mammy hops up. 'There you are, love. I didn't want to wake you, what with the jet lag and everything. I have a plate for you under the grill. Sit down, good girl.'

There's a huge turkey out on the counter but not a single pot. Not even a hint of a sprout.

'Thanks, Mammy. Happy Christmas.' I nod at Dr Trevor. 'And you, Dr Trevor.'

'Please, just Trevor is fine.' I notice he doesn't eat the fat of his rashers. It's the best part.

Mammy puts the plate in front of me with a tea-towelled hand. Two sausages, two rashers, half a tomato and a runny egg. I've been dreaming about this.

'Are you behind on your veg, Mammy? I can give you a hand when I'm finished.'

She's about to say something, then hesitates, looking to Dr Trevor for reassurance. 'Not at all, Aisling.' She takes a breath. 'Síomha and Cara are bringing the vegetables for today.'

'I'm sorry, who?' I know well who she means.

'I'm only doing the turkey and the gravy.' She opens the fridge and takes out a roasting tin covered in tinfoil. 'And I have this, Carol's famous sausagemeat stuffing.'

'Who did you say is bringing the veg, Mammy?'

Dr Trevor dabs at his lips with a snowman napkin. 'They're my girls, Aisling. My daughters from my marriage to Valerie, now deceased.'

I look over to Mammy, who's now loading the turkey into the oven, studiously avoiding my eye. 'And they're coming here for Christmas dinner? Today?'

The trill of the doorbell sends her scurrying to the hall before she can answer me. 'That'll be them now!'

Dr Trevor stands up and heads after her. Why didn't I put on a dressing gown? The only way back up the stairs is through the front hall, but I can't go out there now. The front door opens and I can hear Mammy putting on her phone voice and a stilted chorus of hellos and how are yous and happy Christmas, darlings.

When Dr Trevor and Mammy come back in, they're followed by two petite girls I'm guessing to be in their early twenties. Mammy was right about the hair. Both have long, glossy, rich manes – one a shiny brown, one deep auburn – in what I recognise to be immaculate GHD curls. Sharon's would be the same on a night out. I've never mastered the GHD myself. I can't get the wrist action right.

'I think Paul is still in the shower, but this is my Aisling, home all the way from New York,' Mammy says proudly. She sounds like Úna Hatton, only less of a dose.

'Síomha, hi, how are you?' The brunette girl waves. Her make-up is flawless. She's wearing a navy Aran jumper with navy trousers and navy Mary Jane shoes, and there's a few delicate gold necklaces glinting on her chest.

I wave back.

'I'm Cara,' the red-haired one says, clearly taking in my pyjamas and the sausage dangling from my fork.

'Er, hiya, happy Christmas.'

She doesn't look like she'd ever let ketchup near her long cream knitted dress, which I suspect is cashmere. And, if I'm not mistaken, Mandy has the same brown crocodile-skin boots.

Síomha plops a Davenport's of Tralee paper bag on the floor, and Cara adds another two beside it.

Dr Trevor looks thrilled with this bounty. 'Ah, you got there in time.'

'Only just,' Cara says. 'The queue was out the door and down the street.'

'Did you get the winter root vegetables with honey and thyme?'

'It wouldn't be Christmas without them,' Síomha says with a tight smile.

'And you didn't forget the braised red cabbage?'

'As if we would,' Cara says. 'And before you ask about the heritage carrots and the redcurrant and port jelly, they're in there too.'

'We also got the festive stuffing. It sounds so good.'

I glance over at Mammy, who discreetly pushes the dish of Carol's sausagemeat stuffing to the back of the counter and throws a tea towel over it.

She turns around. 'You really went above and beyond, girls. I hope my turkey isn't too dry now. This all sounds lovely.'

'Yeah, lovely,' I add. To be fair, it does sound delicious, if a little bit fancier than what we're used to. Mammy is very suspicious of herbs.

'Well, Davenport's was Mum's favourite,' Cara says flatly.

CHAPTER 13

'No, they *are* nice,' I insist as Majella applies another layer of blusher to the apples of her cheeks. She's about five layers deep into what seems to be an endless application of layers of make-up. She's following the routine of Suzanne Simmons, the latest beauty influencer to take Ireland by storm. Colette Green is still number one, of course, but now that she's a mam to baby Bear she's moving further into her candles and cushions era. Suzanne Simmons has her own eyelashes range and has a picture on her Instagram grid of her with Rihanna. She's basically Kim Kardashian, if Kim Kardashian was from Cork City.

'I'm raging I missed them.' Majella is applying highlighter with a tiny brush in places I didn't know even existed on her face. 'I was hoping I'd meet them if I came early.'

She was actually forty minutes late arriving to the bedroom where we've gotten ready to go to the Vortex at least a hundred times, but seeing as it's Christmas I won't point it out.

'They didn't stay last night. Síomha was driving them up to Dublin to stay at her boyfriend's.'

'Ohhh, okay. I thought they'd be in a yurt.'

'I think Mammy would rather die than put them in a yurt.

They don't seem like yurt girls. One of them was wearing all cream.'

'On Christmas Day? That's brave. I'd be cascading gravy off my tits.' Majella's moved on to cream blusher. She told me to 'trust the process'. 'Okay, so they are nice, but why did you make a face when I asked?'

'It was just a bit awkward. Cara kept bringing up the dead mam, and Mammy was, well, I don't know what she was doing. Overcompensating maybe. It was her first time meeting them, since they couldn't come to BGB during the lockdown, and she was all nervous and talking posh the whole day. It was exhausting watching her. I felt really bad for her.'

'What a pair of bitches. It's not like your daddy isn't dead as well.' Majella crosses herself and looks towards heaven. 'Happy Christmas, Seamus. I hope all the *Indiana Jones*es are on telly up there for you.'

'No, they weren't being bitches, really. It was just a weird vibe. And like, their mam is dead seven years. Would they not want Dr Trevor to be happy? I was only thinking last night about how if Mammy hadn't met him she'd be facing into spending the New Year on her own. Paul is going to Australia next week and sure I'm flying back to New York the day after tomorrow.'

Majella turns from the mirror and looks at me sitting on the bed, watching her. I've already applied my black liquid eyeliner, made a balls of it, applied it again and done one eye perfectly while the other is passable. I'll straighten my hair when she's finished with her undercoat and gloss and top-coat and whatever else she's putting on her face.

'How do you feel about going back to New York?'

'I feel sick.' I'm surprised with how quickly I admit it. The thought of packing up and going back is giving me dread like I haven't felt since the night before Leaving Cert Biology, when Mammy found me crying in my room because it was 1 a.m. and I hadn't even started learning how to draw the male reproductive system. She suggested getting Daddy or even Paul out of bed to help, which brought on hysterics. It didn't come up, thank God. Now I'm back sitting in that very room and the thought of leaving again is panicking me.

'Ah no, Ais, do you not have a brilliant time over there? All your new friends and the shops and the celebrities?' Maj is furious I don't have more dirt on Leo.

'I do, I do. But I'm already homesick thinking about going back. It's like the worst bank holiday Monday feeling of all time.'

'Oh Christ, bird, that's bad.' Being a teacher, Majella knows the symptoms of The Fear all too well. She says it's the penance she has to pay for all the summer holidays.

'And it's John, too, obviously.' My cheeks flush.

'Would you think of doing long-distance?' I make a face and she nods. 'I know, bird. I don't know how people go weeks and months without seeing each other. Imagine me and Pablo being in different countries? He'd be walking on water to get to me.'

'How are we still here, after all these years, putting on make-up for the Vortex and talking about me and John?'

Majella pats glitter onto her cheekbones and under her eyebrows. She looks fantastic, in fairness to her. 'You can't help who you love, Ais.'

I say nothing, my emotions battling away in my head and my chest.

'Well? Can you?' She turns to look at me.

'No. And I do. I love him so much.' I burst into tears. The two glasses of Baileys I had with my turkey and ham sandwich are partly to blame. They were basically pints.

Majella springs into action. 'Your eyeliner! Stop crying immediately – I can't watch you doing it again. Think about Mad Tom on the rollerblades that time in the St Patrick's Day parade. Think about when Úna Hatton was caught rapid nominating herself as director of the BGB Musical Society. Think about Pablo's fear of squirrels!'

****

'I can't believe Jamesie Kelly is still the bouncer here!' I shout at Majella as we stride into the Vortex, legs out and heels already sticking to the same manky carpet that's been there since we were seventeen, and possibly decades before that. Jamesie is on two crutches now. All the better to clatter people with, I suppose. We've reserved our old booth for nostalgia's sake, even though the girl at reception tittered at me when I rang to make the booking earlier. I thought reserving tables might have caught on in the Vortex by now. Maybe even bottle service at the tables. Her snort and promise to 'stick a bit of paper on it' told me not much had changed, which is comforting in a way. We took the journey out in Terry Crowley's seven-seater taxi. He had fifteen of us in it, which might be some kind of record. I sat on John's knee and kissed him like we were teenagers and ignored the jeers and head rubs of all the people who've known us as a couple for about ten years, give or take the missing bits. We're short a few heads – pregnancies, kids and responsibilities tend to stand between you and your Down Home nightclub of choice on St Stephenses Day when you're in your thirties – but Maeve and Sinéad and Deirdre Ruane were sharing a bottle of prosecco down the back, and Cyclops and Sharon were joking about having their wedding at the Mountrath, the hotel the Vortex is stuck onto. They've already booked their reception at a gorgeous place just outside Cork. It has its own owl, which is the real mark of a top-notch hotel these days. The Mountrath isn't without its charm, of course, if you don't mind a menu that is exclusively funeral soup, chicken goujons and garlic mushrooms. 'Macarena' is blaring as we make for our booth – which has a 'KEPT' sign stuck on it with masking tape – and slide in along the cracked vinyl seats. We spill over into the adjoining booth and claim it for ourselves too with coats and bags. John tips my face up towards him and I smile innocently, fully prepared to let him go to the bar for me for as long as I can swing it.

'Coors Light? Wine? What does the lady desire?'

'Vodka and soda. And get yourself something nice too.' I nod at the wallet in his hand, and he grins and backs away before zooming back up to me to whisper in my ear.

'Remember the time we … in the toilets here?'

I kiss his neck and he backs away again, laughing.

'Vodka and soda? Very swish.' Majella has already sent Pablo up with an order to get two bottles of wine and two ice buckets. I'm interested to see what he comes back with. The

Vortex isn't known for its flourishes. It was one of the last nightclubs in Ireland to stop serving the 1 a.m. chicken curry, though. We'll take our accolades where we can get them.

'You can't even taste the vodka in it and soda is basically water. It's good for me,' I tell her, ready to defend myself against any accusation of New York notions. At least I'm not specifying my vodka like the Irish Mafia. I'm not sure if the Vortex has ice buckets, but it definitely doesn't have Tito's or Belvedere. Majella slumps a little in her seat as most of the gang spill onto the floor with the first few bars of 'I Gotta Feeling'.

'Are you not dancing?' Usually, the Black Eyed Peas would have her stamping on necks to get to the dance floor, but she looks genuinely glum.

'I actually wish I wasn't drinking, for once.'

'Ah, Maj, I'm sorry. Did you get your period?'

'No, it's not due till next week but I just know it's coming. Like, I'd feel something if it wasn't. Sore boobs or feeling tired or pukey or something. Anything. This is four months now with nothing taking.'

'Maj, that's nothing. You've hardly been trying for any length.' I grab her hand. 'You have to give it a bit more time before you start getting sad or worried. And anyway, you could be pregnant for all you know! It happens to people all the time and they have no symptoms. I saw a YouTube video about a girl who didn't know until she was crowning! She thought she was constipated and ate a load of prunes. The baby came out in the toilet.'

Majella grimaces. 'Jesus, imagine that, though. Going about your day, planning a weekend in Prague and next thing you're a mam.'

'Yeah, not ideal.'

'I did a test today, though. One of the early-early ones. NOT PREGNANT.' She moves her hand through the air like she's reading a giant pregnancy test.

'It's going to happen. And you'll be a brilliant mam. A little half-Spanish baby. Did you ever think you'd see the day?'

'Stop, Pablo is already onto level four on his Irish on Duolingo. The poor child will have languages coming out its arse!'

I nudge her and point over to another booth across the dancefloor, where Deirdre Ruane is arguing with a girl in her early twenties. 'Looks like Ais Ruane is wearing something belonging to Deirdre again.'

'Oh, I know. Dee said she was barely in the door for Christmas and Ais was rifling through her bags.'

'Can you believe we were ever that young? We thought we were so grown up, but they're just babies.'

We watch Dee Ruane's little sister and her friends for a minute, dancing and flirting and shouting. They have the same gaggle of lads in their good shirts and GAA half-zips. They have the same ease as a group of friends who've known each other in some way or another since childhood. They're dancing to the same songs we've been dancing to forever. They all squeal as 'Sex on Fire' comes on, and Ais dismisses Dee with a flick of her hair. Back on our side of the Vortex, Pablo is trying to dance seductively towards us while battling with the two bottles of wine in what look suspiciously like bathroom bins. John comes up behind him and relieves him of one of the 'ice buckets', and Pablo's hip thrusts get more energetic in Majella's direction.

Dying laughing, I lean over to her. 'If that man doesn't get you pregnant soon, there's no justice in the world.'

****

Much later, John lies squeezed in beside me in my childhood bed. 'I'm mortified that your mother assumed I was staying.'

'Well, I'm mortified she left pyjamas out for you. I don't know what's worse. My mother assuming you'll be naked and need covering up, or the idea of you in my dead father's pyjamas.'

He hitches a bare leg over mine and half covers my body with his. 'Well, isn't it lucky I have no intention of wearing them.'

'Terry Crowley was on fire with the Twenty Questions, wasn't he?'

We've joked for years that Terry must have been in the KGB in a former life. He'd quiz you until you had no breath left in your body and then still get more information out of you. John and I were the last ones into the taxi after getting carried away shifting by the cloakroom and had to sit up the front for the journey home. Any questions John and I had been dodging around for the last few days were laid bare right there while 'Wichita Lineman' gently played from the taxi's CD player and Majella roared at Terry to 'put on something that doesn't sound like death'. How long am I home for? Will I settle in America? Would I ever move home? Are we getting married? Is John moving to America? He also did a rapid-fire round about Mammy and Dr Trevor, but as with the other questions, I tried to fob him off with 'Ah, we'll wait and see' and 'You'd have to ask her that yourself now, Terry'. Now that I'm lying here with John, though, with the remains of the seven vodka and sodas running through my veins, I feel completely serene in bringing it up with him.

'I don't know if I want to go back to New York. To live, I mean.'

He shoots up in the bed. 'What?' He sees me smiling and flops back down. 'Don't be having me on, Aisling.'

'I'm not having you on,' I say calmly. 'I think I'm going to move home. It doesn't even feel like a big, massive decision. I want to do it, so I'm going to do it.' My bed has truly never felt so comfy. This must be what peace feels like.

John lies there for a second. 'What about your job? Will Mandy not kill you?'

'Ah, she'll get over it. Aubrey says she gets forty resumés in on a bad week. The good news is I won't have any problem getting another job with the CV I have now. Lisa Gleeson is a lovely girl but a dire wedding planner. I could take the Ard Rí to the next level. Do some proper five-star events. Or I could do event planning freelance. I need to think about it properly.'

'And your apartment? Will you have any hassle getting out of your lease?'

'I don't think so.' I narrow my eyes. 'Are you trying to talk me out of it or what?'

'Jesus, no!' He grabs my face and kisses me. 'This is just brilliant news. I was hoping you might come back eventually, but I didn't think it would be this soon. You're not doing it just for me, are you?'

That annoys me a little bit. 'Well, a big part of it is to be with you, yeah, of course it is. This is what we both want, isn't it? To be together again?'

His eyes go kind of glassy. 'I want it more than anything.'

He kisses me again for a long time, and when the sensation of the tip of his tongue dancing off mine becomes too much I climb on top of him and move until I feel like I'm going to burst. Afterwards, I lie on his chest and listen to his breathing getting slower and slower.

'Aisling?' he murmurs as my eyelids drop for longer each time.

'Hmmm?'

'I'm your boyfriend now, okay?'

'Okay.' His arms tighten around me.

'John?'

'Mmhmm?'

'Mandy *is* going to kill me.'

CHAPTER 14

'Aisling, this is Tameka. Tameka, this is Aisling, one of my executives. Excuse her accent, she's Irish. Don't get her started on potatoes.'

I've been trying to corner Mandy all morning to hand in my notice, but she's after the contract for a hot new start-up, FYI Testing, and to sweeten the deal she's invited them in to do free food-intolerance tests on the entire office. Since it's early January, people are keen to feel like they're improving themselves by cutting out stuff, but I'm sceptical about it myself. I obediently line up behind Mandy in the queue anyway. Anything for a quiet life.

'Hi, Tameka.' I smile, taking the iPad Mandy passes back to me.

'Your email address and signature on the bottom, Aisling,' she instructs. 'No need to get out your magnifying glass. It just gives Tameka here permission to run your blood through her state-of-the-art little machine. It's patent-pending and going to revolutionise the entire industry.'

'It's a blood test?' I was hoping they might let me taste a few things. I skipped breakfast to Skype Fatima about the apartment. Her name is on the lease, but since she's going to be spending most of her time in Washington she was happy to let it go when I told her I was leaving New York.

'Relax, it's just a little prick, Aisling. Much like my ex-husband. Ha!'

I smile politely and scrawl my details on the screen.

Then I pass the iPad over to Aubrey, who takes it with a sigh. 'I had to move my lunch with Jeremy for this.' She hates having to change plans at the last minute but we both know better than to defy Mandy's orders, especially when she's charming a potential client.

'You've been waiting for Jeremy to pop the question for three years. It won't hurt him to wait on you for twenty minutes,' Mandy says through gritted teeth. 'Your face screams gluten intolerance to me, Aisling, and if I'm wrong, I owe Josh B twenty bucks.'

A few people behind me in the line, Josh B calls up, 'Sodium causes facial bloating, not gluten!'

I ignore him. 'Can I have a quick word in your office after this, Mandy? It will only take a minute?'

She looks at her watch. 'I have a call with Leo's assistant's assistant at two. I can give you thirty seconds.' Then she disappears behind the white makeshift curtain to Tameka.

****

My throat is dry and my upper lip is sweating when I knock on her door five minutes later. She was right – it was just a little prick in the end. And Tameka gave me a mini Snickers for my troubles.

'Your thirty seconds has already started!' Mandy is at her desk leafing through the new issue of *Vanity Fair*. She flings the magazine across the room. 'They swore they'd include the Holiday Hot Mess in their social pages. Lying elitist bastards! Have I ever told you about the time me and Graydon Carter ended up getting wasted at Cipriani?'

Only every time she has three martinis. 'I think so.' I hesitate, slipping into the big leather chair opposite her.

'Fifteen seconds, Aisling. Spit it out already.'

'Okay, well, the thing is …'

'Twelve seconds.'

'I'm moving back home,' I blurt. 'This is me handing in my notice.'

I don't think I've ever seen Mandy stunned before. She shifts in her chair until she's sitting up straight. 'Aisling, is everything okay?' Her tone has completely changed. It's soft now, all the New York bravado completely evaporated. 'I thought you were happy here?'

'No, it's not that. I am happy. I love my job.' It's true, mad as it is, I do love this crazy business and get great satisfaction when an event goes well. Myself and Aubrey recently devised new, very detailed client feedback surveys and I sometimes read them in bed to get myself off to sleep.

'And you're fucking great at it. Do I not tell you that enough?'

Unlike most Americans, Mandy is not one for effusive praise, and I like that about her. But when I do something particularly well, she always compliments me on it. Yeah, she can be blunt and combative and a bit scary at times, but she's fair with it. She just has high standards. I can relate.

'It's not you, honestly, Mandy.'

'Well, what is it then?'

'It's John. You remember John?'

'Big guy from back home in Ballywhatever, never said a word?'

I nod. They met when Mandy was planning Emilia Coburn and Ben Dixon's wedding. He was terrified of her. 'Well, we're back together.'

'I thought he'd fucked off to the Middle East.'

'There was a change of plan. Anyway, I'm moving back to Ireland. And I just wanted to thank you for taking a chance on me. It's been some experience.' I'm not sure you're supposed to smile your head off when you're handing in your notice, but I can't help it.

'Do you have a job lined up?'

'No. I was thinking I could do some freelance event planning. You've taught me enough.'

Mandy suddenly looks thoughtful. She turns to her computer and taps a few keys. Then she swivels back to me. 'So your leaving is not anything to do with your role here. In fact, in an ideal world, you'd still work for me, is that what I'm hearing?'

I shrug. 'In an ideal world I'd do what I'm doing here, but at home.'

For a minute I'm afraid she's going to offer John a job to keep me here. For some reason, I can't imagine him squeezing Barbra Streisand's dog's anal glands or bitching about SoulCycle instructors with the Joshes on his lunch break.

She doesn't say anything, and leans back in her chair deep in thought. 'I'll head back to my desk, so? I have my letter of resignation drafted. And I'll do my two weeks' notice?'

I go to stand up but she indicates I should stay put with the flap of her hand. 'Just wait one sweet minute. This could be the best thing that's ever happened to me. You. Us, I mean. I might have to send your John a big fat Cuban.'

When I sit down, she leans back in her chair again, kicks off her heels and swings her feet up onto her desk. 'What I'm about to tell you, Aisling, is highly confidential. Can I trust you not to repeat a fucking syllable of it?'

'Of c–'

'Well, Aubrey knows. But apart from that, not a syllable?'

'You can trust me, Mandy.'

Her eyes light up. 'That's right. I can. Aisling, I'm expanding the company. I've always seen Mandy Blumenthal Event Architects as a global business. First here, then Europe, then Australia. Maybe. That's why I've been spending so much time in London recently. I was meeting investors and sussing out the market. There are a couple of pretty impressive event architects there I was getting ready to headhunt.'

'That's brilliant. You'll have an excuse to go in on that private jet with Bethenny Frankel now.'

'I've always thought London would be the perfect base for our European headquarters, for logistics alone, but I'm suddenly wondering if Dublin wouldn't be better. Less fucking Brexit shit to deal with anyway. Goddamn clowns.'

My patriotism immediately kicks in. 'Oh, you're dead right. Dublin is much better than London. All the big tech companies are already there, plus two Krispy Kremes. And don't get me started on the tax breaks – sure they'd nearly pay you to come.'

'And it's close to London anyway, right?'

'Only about a forty-five-minute flight away. Quicker than getting uptown in a cab. Haha!'

Mandy looks contemplative again. 'So, my original plan

was to relocate temporarily to London midsummer to kick things off myself. But now I'm thinking, why not shift the whole operation to Dublin and move things forward? What do you say?'

'I think you're on to something, Mandy. Now, it's five to two – I better let you go get ready for your call with Charlotte.'

She's now typing away furiously at her computer. 'So you're up for the challenge? Fan-fucking-tastic, Aisling. I'll get my lawyers to draw up the contract. Aubrey was already locked in to go to London to help with the set-up, but I'm sure she'll like Dublin just the same. If you're anything to go by, she already has the perfect wardrobe.'

'Draw up the contract for what?' I'm confused now. Did I miss something?

Mandy stops typing and looks me dead in the eye. 'Your new role at Mandy Blumenthal Event Architects. How does "Chief Operating Officer – Europe" sound? Twenty per cent on top of your salary.'

'Eh, ehm.' Sadhbh had warned me that she might ply me with more money or even the elusive top-tier health insurance, but I certainly wasn't expecting this.

'Your café and catering business was a start-up, right? It's on your resumé. You've got experience.'

'Yeah, but –'

'I'll get on to my realtor now and see what's available in Dublin. I promise you, Aisling, working for me will be far better than going out on your own. You'll have a salary – a good one – from day one and my name to entice all these new clients. We can talk about staff later. Right now, I'm thinking keep it skeleton. Aubrey will help you get a handle on the market and opportunities. She can do four months, six maybe. Do you know who does Kate Middleton's book club? Look into it, will you.'

On autopilot, I type 'Kate M book club' into my notes app while I try to digest what Mandy is saying. Could I actually start the European side of the company? I successfully got BallyGoBrunch off the ground, but I don't think that's the same. And most important, I had planned on moving to Ballygobbard to be with John. He's found a premises for his gym – one of the outhouses behind Maguire's – and is in the process of getting a grant from the enterprise board to renovate it. The location is perfect, and he's excited to get it off the ground, talking a mile a minute about skylights and equipment and retail opportunities whenever we're on the phone. I've told Mammy my plan to come home and now that Paul has gone back to Australia she's excited at the prospect.

'No, Mandy, hang on a second. This is all happening too fast. I need to talk it over with John. You can't just steamroll me into taking a job like the last time.'

She sits back in her seat. 'And look how well that turned out.'

'I'll think about it, okay? That's all I'm saying for now.'

The phone rings on her desk. 'Leo calling! Make yourself invisible, Aisling. We'll talk again tomorrow.'

****

My head is melted when I'm getting into bed after thinking about Mandy's proposition all evening. I've been so preoccupied with getting back to John but now the thought of actually taking this job is making my heart race. Would I be mad to turn it down? Dublin isn't far from BGB in the grand scheme of things.

I check my email quickly to see if Bella Hadid has finished her survey yet. No sign, but there is a message from FYI Testing with the subject line: 'Congratulations!' I bet they're officially telling me I have the constitution of an ox. I've always known it, but it will be nice to get the confirmation. I click in. The body of the email is short. It reads: 'Dear Aisling, please find the results of today's test attached. And congratulations on your pregnancy! I guess this explains why you were so excited about that Snickers. Best, Tameka.'

My hands are shaking so hard I can barely flick through the apps on my phone. Eventually I find my period tracker and hit the calendar icon. *Day 29. Period due.* The words are bright red, screaming at me.

My cycle has always been regular. Twenty-nine days long, no matter the month. You could set your watch by it. How did I not notice it was late? I grab my alarm clock. But it isn't late! It's only half eleven. It could still come tonight! I go back to the app and trace my finger backwards to the last fertile window. This time the letters are a soft pink. It spans a generous seven days, from 23 to 30 December. Christmas. John and me at home, on Stephenses night. Jesus Christ, how can this be happening?

I sink back into the pillow and try to listen to my body. When I was a teenager the period pain used to turn me green, and I'd have to be ferried home from school to Mammy by Sister Bernadette in her little Ford Fiesta. My symptoms have eased off somewhat over the past few years, but I still usually get cramps and an urge to watch *Beaches* and cry the day before it arrives. There has to be some mistake! Tameka and her blood machine are probably a scam. I hope she has a client survey I can fill in.

I hop out of bed and run to the bathroom. Sitting on the toilet, I inspect the gusset of my knickers. Nothing. Then I wipe and check the paper. Still nothing. Fuck. And suddenly I have a horrible realisation: I don't feel delighted. Whenever I thought of John and me having a baby, I presumed it would be a military operation. We'd be married for a start. Then we'd make the decision together, I'd come off the pill, and after three months max I'd be queuing for multipacks of babygros in the Next sale. And now here I am, possibly pregnant, and elated is not on the spectrum of emotions I'm feeling.

I check the time again. Quarter to twelve. That means it's quarter to five back home. I pick up my phone, take a deep breath and hit dial. It rings, rings and rings. Then goes to voicemail. 'Fucking turn on your bastarding ringer for once in your life,' I scream into my empty bedroom. Someone on the street outside shouts something back and I jab the dial button again, cursing the shoddy glazing on my window.

'Aisling, this is really weird, but you just popped into my head and I looked down at my phone and you were calling me! How insane is that?'

'You're already up? I thought I'd be waking you.'

'Babe, I'm a big deal now. I had to come in for a Zoom with the Tokyo office. If you could see my outf–'

'Sadhbh, are you alone? I need to talk.' My voice is shaky.

I can hear the volume of the background music going down several decibels. 'Of course. I'll just close the door. Not sure if I mentioned that I have one now?'

She did mention it. About two hundred times. She's thrilled to have put the tour-bus life and its lack of privacy behind her.

'Did you do it?

'Yeah, I handed in my notice but –'

'Woohoo!'

'No, that's not why I'm calling. Sadhbh … I think I'm pregnant.'

There's a weird muffling sound on the line. 'Sorry, Ais, for a second there I thought you said you were preggo. Imagine!'

'Sadhbh, I am.'

Silence.

'Hello?'

'Okay, have you actually done a test or is your period, like, five minutes late? I know how you get.'

'I haven't done a test myself …'

'Well then!'

'But I accidentally did. It was a blood test in work. And it says I'm pregnant.'

'And, I don't know how to ask this, it's … John's?'

'Yes, it's John's! What do you take me for?'

'I'm sorry! I know what the New York dating scene is like – I just wasn't sure if you guys were completely exclusive now that he's back living at home.'

For a second, I'm quite flattered that she thinks I might have John in BGB pining for me while I'm over here riding rings around myself.

'I don't know what to do, Sadhbh. When I was handing in my notice Mandy offered me a whole new job. It's a big opportunity.'

'I told you she'd do anything to keep you. I hope you stayed strong.'

'No, this is a job at home. In Dublin. She wants to open a

European headquarters. And she wants me to run the whole thing. It will be a lot of work but it could also be really amazing.'

'Oh my God, Ais, that's huge. You can stay with me! Don's going to be away again for a while.'

'Thank you so much, but I don't know if I'm even going to take it. And then I find out I'm possibly pregnant on the same day? I feel winded. The timing would be just so, so bad.'

'Oh, Ais, I wish I was there. You poor thing, dealing with this by yourself. You need to piss on a stick to be sure, though.'

'Will it even show up, though, if my period is literally due today?'

'Hang on a sec ... I'm googling it here. Okay, it might show up tomorrow if you get one of those early detection ones. And according to this thing I'm reading, if it doesn't, it could be a false negative. Keep testing. I think this article is for people who are, you know, trying.'

'I suppose I'll get a test on my way to work then.'

'And it says to use morning urine for best results. Whatever best results is.'

'Morning urine. Got it.'

'Are you going to tell John?'

I mull it over. Am I? Even if I am pregnant, I could make this all go away next week and accept Mandy's offer and everything would be so easy. He'd never be any the wiser.

'Things are so good between us now. I'm just afraid this will ...'

'Ruin it?'

'Exactly.'

'What's Majella's take?'

'I haven't told her. I literally just found out. You're the only one who knows.'

'You rang me first? Ais, I'm flattered.'

'You know I told you herself and Pablo were trying?'

'Oh yeah, right. You nearly ruined my Thanksgiving dinner.'

'Well, it's not exactly happening for them. She's getting pretty worried that it's taking so long.'

'Ais, no.' I can hear a wobble in her voice and I'm afraid it's going to set me off. 'Poor Maj, she must be stressed.'

'I know – it's early days, though. In terms of interventions, I mean. But I couldn't exactly ring her up and be like "Boo hoo, I think I'm pregnant", you know?'

'Totally.'

'How did you feel the time you had the … crisis pregnancy?'

'Oh, Aisling, that was completely different!'

'I know, but how did you feel?'

'Initially? Complete and utter shock. Devastation. I just knew I wasn't going to have that baby. Every single cell in my body was telling me not to go through with it. I would have swum the Irish Sea to that clinic if I had to. And wasn't it a good job I did? I love the life I have now. A baby would not fit into it. That's what I keep telling Don.'

'I think I'm in shock myself.'

'Of course you are. But just because you're in shock doesn't mean you don't want to have a baby with John.'

That hadn't dawned on me. 'Really? Do you think so?'

'Aisling, you're my friend, so I'm saying this with love: you're a control freak. My educated guess is the reason you're panicking is because you hadn't planned on getting pregnant.'

Well, she's right about that. 'We've only just become boyfriend and girlfriend officially! We haven't even talked about having kids down the line.'

'But when you were together for so long before, it must have come up. Even hypothetically?'

'I suppose it probably did. No, yeah, I know John wants kids someday. Back then he did anyway. He might have changed his mind for all I know.'

'And do you?'

I haven't actually thought about that recently. But I do, I've always known. Maybe not the football team I was planning when I was in my twenties, though. That seems mad now. 'Yeah. When the time is right.' I think of Maj and Pablo. 'If I'm lucky enough, that is.'

'So maybe, just *maybe*, you will want to have this baby once you get used to the idea. You're not even a day late. Very Aisling.'

'Sadhbh! I'm in my hour of need here.'

'What I mean is that if you're pregnant you're only four weeks gone. You've loads of time to decide.'

I place my palm on my lower belly. It feels warm and soft. Could there really be a part of John growing inside me? 'If it was you, would you tell Don?'

She harrumphs. 'Don would be delighted. He's still trying to wear me down.'

'He hardly wants you to have a baby right now? He's always on the go. And you've just started your new job.'

'No, but he wants me to say I'd be into it at some stage.'

'Oh God, I'm sorry to hear that. You'd tell him, though, would you?'

There's a pause. 'Yeah, I would. I tell him everything. How could I not?'

She's right, of course. If things are going to work between me and John, I have to be honest with him.

'And, Ais, if you do decide you want to have an abortion, I will do everything I can to support you. You know that, yeah? I'm here for you.'

'Thanks, Sadhbhy.'

'Call me again any time. No matter what you do, it'll all be okay.'

'I hope so.'

When my head touches the pillow I fall into the deepest sleep I've had in ages.

CHAPTER 16

I stop off at Duane Reade on the way to work the next morning and find a test that promises to tell you if you're pregnant six days before you even miss a period. Incredible technology, really. This must be the one Majella was talking about. I've been saving my morning urine per Sadhbh's orders, so by the time I get to the office I'm absolutely bursting and hopping from foot to foot. I slip into the unisex toilet in the lobby so I'll have less chance of bumping into Aubrey or one of the others from upstairs. There's a rumour that people save all their number twos for this one, so I've been avoiding it, but thankfully it's empty when I rush in and dive straight into a cubicle. No horrific smells either. With a shaky hand, I follow the instructions carefully and hold the little white spongy part of the stick under the stream of widdle, which is more like a waterfall, really. It's supposed to take three minutes to give you a reading, but I'm still weeing when the second line shows up. I double-check the pamphlet just to be sure that means what I think it means. Pregnant. One hundred per cent pregnant. When I text Sadhbh to tell her, she reminds me that I have loads of time to think things over and that she's here for the chats if I need her.

I tell Mandy I need Meeting Room 1 the whole day to research the Dublin events market in private, but instead I do up a pros and cons list called 'Have This Baby???' and stare at it for three hours. I feel so, so guilty for putting anything at all on the cons side, even though 'It might hate me', 'I might hate it' and 'Mandy will never forgive me for not telling her when taking the job' are all very valid.

I cry three times when making the pros list. Once when I write that it might have Daddy's eyes, once when I write that it might have John's little dimple and once when I just write 'tiny socks'.

****

After several sleepless nights and two instances of avoiding John's FaceTimes by saying I'm working late, the following week I decide I'd better go see a doctor and find an anonymous-looking walk-in clinic on Second Avenue that can squeeze me in on my lunch break. I wear my good knickers just in case, but I don't have to take them off in the end. The kind-faced doctor does another test and explains that I'm definitely pregnant, although a perfectly formed waving hand is not expected at this early stage. Going by my dates I'm around five weeks along, which initially gives me a land, but then she reminds me that they count it from the first day of your last period so it still makes sense for it to be a Christmas baby. I know the menstrual tracker app is just trying to steal and sell my data but it is fierce handy at the same time.

She's very gentle in asking me about birth control and says she's always interested when it's an unexpected pregnancy. I tell her I suspect it was St Stephenses Day because we didn't use a condom – I have to look at the floor while admitting that – and that I'd had a bit of a bad belly after my flight from New York so maybe my pill hadn't kicked in. I'm nearly falling over myself to tell her I usually double up, but she says she's seen people get pregnant no matter what they do. It's a wonder we're not all walking around pregnant all the time. Sister Assumpta had a point in school about abstinence being the only sure-fire way to avoid it. I'd like to see her resist John on St Stephenses night, though.

I spend the next week revising my pros and cons list and trying to imagine me and John with a baby. A family of three. Planning the FYI Testing rooftop launch party downtown keeps me from googling early pregnancy symptoms in work, but I still can't bring myself to talk to John on FaceTime until I've made my decision. He notices I've been dodging him and sends a string of panicked texts on Tuesday, worrying that he's done something to make me mad. I tell him I'm up to my eyes with Mandy's demands, which is actually half true. The FYI Testing people want a skywriter at short notice and it's up to me to find one. On Wednesday I finally call Sadhbh back. She answers the phone after two rings. Surely a record for her.

'Sadhbh, I need your help.'

'I told you, Ais, I'll do anything. Never be afraid to ask.'

I pause. 'Well, this baby is going to need an auntie with good taste in clothes.'

Her scream is so loud I have to hold the phone away from my ear. 'You're having the baby?'

I gulp. 'I'm having the baby.'

'Have you told him?'

'We're FaceTiming later.'

'I genuinely think he's going to be really excited, but are you prepared in case ...' She trails off but I know what she means. In case John decides he's not ready for this. In case I have to go it alone.

'I am. I'll cross that bridge if I come to it.'

'I'll start researching the internet's chicest and most tasteful onesies immediately.'

****

I tell Mandy I'm taking a personal day to mull over her offer and distract myself cleaning the apartment until it's time to call John. He has a meeting with the enterprise board until five Irish time, and I take at least fifteen breaks to pace the apartment while I wait for his text to say he's home. As the time on my phone clicks to two minutes past twelve, it finally pops up.

'Finished! x'

I take a deep breath, settle myself on the bed with my back against the wall and pile pillows on my lap so I can hold my phone comfortably at arm's length and face height. His smiling profile picture fills the screen before his actual one takes over.

'Hiya!' He's beaming. The meeting must have gone well. 'Long time no see!'

'Hiya. Yeah, sorry ... I've been up the walls.' I'm shy, like I've been so many times when faced with him over the years. I don't think it'll ever go away.

'I was so worried you were avoiding me. My mother accused me of having a gambling problem I had such a face on me. She thinks everyone has a gambling problem.'

'Sorry, sorry. Don't be worrying. How was the meeting?'

'So, the grant's pretty much in place. I've priced a lad to do the plastering and now know more about gym flooring than I ever thought was possible.'

'Brilliant! You have loads done already. Great about the grant. Plastering, brilliant. Floors. Floors are great.' I'm babbling. The nerves have overtaken me. I'd say my blood pressure right now would put me in the ICU.

John is looking at me like I have five heads. 'Have you been out on the sauce with your one from Sticks and Stones again?'

'Tara's blog is called Stilettos and Skyscrapers, and no, I haven't actually.' This gives me an in, and I go for it. 'The opposite, actually.'

He laughs. 'What's the opposite of boozing with Tara? Going to a funeral?'

Okay, no. I'm not going to dance around it. I'm just going to say it out loud and be mature about it.

'John?'

'Yeaaah?' He looks suddenly concerned.

'I –' God, my mouth is dry. I have to get the words out. 'I am p-pregnant.'

I smash my face down into the pillows, my entire body bubbling up through my throat with nerves and excitement and fear. There's two seconds of silence before he speaks again.

'Are you messing?' His voice is urgent.

'No, I'm due in September,' I mumble into the pillow.

'Show me your face. Seriously. Are you messing, Aisling?'

I bring my red face up to show him. Why am I so shy? There's something about this most shared and intimate thing that has me mortified and thrilled all at the same time. I take a deep breath. 'I am not messing. I am six weeks pregnant with our baby, and I'm sorry I'm doing this over the phone but I've known for a couple of weeks now and it was time I told you.'

'Oh my God.' His hand comes up to his mouth and then his forehead. He starts to smile like he can't fight it. But then he looks confused. 'But it's not like … I mean you're on the pill and we use condom–'

'We didn't on St Stephenses Night, and the pill is only –'

'Ninety-nine per cent effective.' He says it in kind of a trance. Then he starts to smile again, and I smile back at him. 'Are you really not messing?'

I shake my head.

'And are you happy?'

'I think so. I mean, it took a while to sink in. It's a bit unexpected. And scary.' Then I bite the bullet. 'How do you feel about it? I know you just found out. You might be in shock. I know I was for a while.'

'I'm delighted.' He says it so fast that I'm flooded with relief. He doesn't even need to think about it. 'Holy fuck, Aisling. Things have escalated.'

'I know.'

'Did you do all the tests and everything? The piss sticks?' We both burst out laughing.

'I've done twelve. I'll send you a picture of them all. I was going to wait to tell you when I get home but –'

'Ah no, I'm so glad I know. Jesus Christ. Oh my God. We're

going to have a baby. I'm going to be a dad. Ais, this would be a really good time to say you'll marry me.'

'Focus, John! There's another thing, too.'

'There's more? I think I might need a drink.' He's smiling, though, so I know he's only messing.

'Mandy's after offering me a new job. In Dublin but on a New York salary. She's expanding into Europe and she's offered me the chief operating officer role. I'd be overseeing the start-up and basically in charge of getting everything off the ground. I've decided to take it. What do you think?'

'Ais, that's brilliant! When you were talking about coming home I was trying to imagine you behind the counter in Filan's and I just couldn't.'

'Excuse me, I did a summer in Filan's when I was seventeen and my 99s were perfectly proportioned every time.'

His face falls. 'But the baby? Is Mandy going to lose her mind when she finds out you'll have to go on maternity leave?'

I shrug. 'If she does, she does. And I can work for another eight months. Aubrey will manage and it's just a job. This baby is bigger than all that … this is life. This is us, John.'

His face grows serious. 'And you know I'll support you with all this, don't you? We'll figure out all the logistics as a team.'

I nod. 'I do, but it's nice to hear you say it too.'

'And how are you feeling? Do you have morning sickness or anything? Is there anything you need? Should I come out and mind you?'

'No! No. I'm totally fine, apart from being a bit tired. I had a check-up last week. I'm grand. So is the baby. I'm a bit behind on my folic acid but I'm taking it now.'

'What's folic acid?'

'I'll fill you in when I get home. And John, I don't want you worrying about anything. We have so much time. I am the tiniest bit pregnant. Like, you don't start telling people for another month and a half.'

'Do you not? Okay, so I won't tell anyone so?'

'Oh no, don't. Not yet. My mother doesn't even know.'

'Is it not weird that we won't be living together? God, I'm still staying at my mother's. We'll need two bedrooms, won't we? At least. What about the apartments –?'

'It's okay, John, please let's not stress about that for now. I need to get home from New York first. Let me get over that hurdle and then we get into planning. And Sadhbh says I can stay with her in Ranelagh when I start the job, and you can stay as much as you like too. She has loads of room. We'll figure it out.'

'Jesus, Ais, I can't believe it. Two months ago I was a million miles away from this, and now I can't imagine being anywhere else. I cannot *wait* to see you.'

'Me neither. Not long now.'

****

Three days later I splash some cold water on my eyes in the bathroom in Dublin Airport before going out to wait for my two huge suitcases. The Irish Mafia threw me a going-away party last night and although I wasn't drinking, I have a social hangover. When I told Mandy I'd take the job she upgraded me to business class, and I slept for six hours on the plane. Didn't even watch one whole film and I missed the sandwiches they served for supper. If I wasn't pregnant, I'd think I was dying. I brush my hair, scrub at my teeth with the tiny Aer Lingus toothbrush and rub some lip balm on my dry lips. I know John is waiting for me in Arrivals, and the thought of seeing him fills me with such anticipation my knees are shaking. I still have to make it through the baggage-claim wait, so I put in my earphones and put on some ocean sounds, trying to drown out the crankiness of my fellow travellers until I can give John the biggest hug of my life. Another perk of business class is your bags come out first, so I'm not actually waiting that long. I take a suitcase handle in each hand and start to walk towards the Nothing to Declare customs line, feeling like I have the best thing ever to declare, actually.

His are the first eyes I meet when I walk through the door and I stop dead. The woman behind me tuts and loud whispers 'Sake!' at me. I don't give a shite, though, because John's big strong arms are around me in a split second.

'Welcome home,' he whispers into my hair. 'I love you.' I just tighten my arms around him. Then he drops down to his knees and speaks directly to my bellybutton: 'And I love you too.'

I burst out laughing, mortified, and he's at eye level again.

'I was going to get you flowers but they were crap and mad money in the petrol station, and I knew you'd be raging.'

And with that, I'm home to the love of my life.

CHAPTER 17

The next day John is like an excited child showing me around the building site that he swears is only six months away from being a top-notch gym.

'Have you decided on a name yet?'

'I'm going with B-Gym-B.'

'I think you made the right choice.' It was between that, BallyGoBulking and The J-Team, but I always said B-Gym-B was the cleanest looking and sounding. Plus, Sadhbh said BallyGoBulking sounded like a war crime and The J-Team sounded like a Korean pop band.

It's all raw plasterboard and concrete floors at the moment, but the building is huge with a vaulted ceiling and I can see why he went for it. So much potential. And there's parking for fifteen cars behind it. To think these outhouses were basically sitting idle only feet from BGB's Main Street until John came along with his vision. I'm so proud of him.

'Over here is the weights room and behind it there is Studio 1, which is totally accessible through the double doors at the side. There's going to be two more studios upstairs on mezzanine level. One will probably be just for Pilates if there's enough interest.'

'It looks mighty already, John.'

'Oh, watch your step there.' He flashes me a smile. 'Precious cargo and all that.'

I let him take my elbow as I navigate a river of cables coming from the boiler room. Underfloor heating for hot yoga, apparently. I can just imagine Carol Boland pumping sweat while doing her downward dog.

'And then down there to the left will be locker rooms, showers and toilets. What do you think about putting in a jacuzzi?'

'I'd join a gym just to sit in a jacuzzi.'

'Exactly!'

'I can't believe how fast things are coming together already. I have a couple of weeks before I start work so I can help you with the painting or the snag list or whatever.'

'That'd be brilliant, Ais. Come on, I'll bring you back to the office. It's the only room that's almost finished.'

John's idea of almost finished is obviously different to mine, because when we get to the door he has to hoof out a load of cardboard boxes to make room for us both. There are wires sticking out of the walls where lights should be and a giant roll of insulation propped in the corner.

'Cosy,' I say, taking a chair opposite him at his desk. I don't know whether it's the jet lag or the pregnancy but I'm exhausted already and it's not even lunchtime.

Something on his screen grabs his attention. 'Hang on a second, Ais, I just have to reply to this email. Bloody sparks ...'

As he taps away at the laptop I scan the desk. The usual half-drunk cups of tea on top of piles of invoices and receipts for gym equipment. Then my eyes fall on a book sticking out from under a packet of Bourbon creams. The cover is orange and the title on the spine reads *Dude! You're Gonna Be a Dad.*

'Sorry about that – all done,' he says, clicking the computer shut. 'Any interest in going to BallyGoBrunch for lunch? You're eating for two now, remember.'

I hold up the book. 'Doing some light reading, are we?'

He grins back at me. Then his face grows serious. 'I have a lot to learn, Ais. I'm glad you said you were already on the folic acid because it's so important for the baby's spine and brain development. Have you thought about taking some omega-3 too?'

I can't help but laugh. The man is as unflappable as they come. He's only known about the pregnancy for four days and now he's talking about foetal brain development.

He reaches under the desk and pulls out an Easons bag. 'I got a few more books too. Some are more just for you, but I'm going to read them when you're finished.' Then he starts firing them out onto the desk. There's *Bumpin': The Modern Guide to Pregnancy*; *Expecting Better*; *The Shit No One Tells You about Pregnancy*; and *The Womanly Art of Breastfeeding*. There's even *Drinkin' for Two: Delicious Mocktails for the Mom-to-Be.*

'Jesus, John, did you leave anything on the shelves at all?'

'I want us to be prepared. Turns out I had no idea what women go through. I finished *What to Expect When You're Expecting* yesterday morning when I was waiting on the plumber, and let's just say it was eye-opening. I couldn't eat my breakfast after finding out what an episiotomy is. Have you ever heard of perineal massage? Do not google it.'

I'm starting to feel a bit worried now. Maybe I should be doing more on my end. I'm too suspicious yet to download one of those apps that compares your baby to a fruit. It feels a bit early. I was up twice during the night to go to the toilet, though, which is very unlike me; I'm usually like a camel. And I don't feel sick in the mornings exactly, just a bit wobbly in my stomach. So there's definitely something happening.

'Have your feet gotten bigger? That's a thing, you know.'

I look down at my trusty Skechers. 'Still the same size, I think.'

'And how are your boobs? Sensitive, are they? You know they might go up as much as three cup sizes.'

'You weren't too worried about them last night anyway.' I smirk. He couldn't keep his hands off me after Mammy had tipped off to bed and pointedly said she'd be watching *Grey's Anatomy* on her tablet with her headphones on. I nearly threw myself out the window as she was saying it, but I was grateful in the end.

He grimaces. 'Yeah, sorry about that. I hadn't seen you in so long. It's fine to have sex, though, according to the book. I checked. In fact, it might even help bring on labour if you go overdue.'

'Can we not talk about labour, John? It's going to take me a while to get my head around that one. The baby is still basically a fish.'

'C'mere,' he says, beckoning me over to his side of the desk. I gingerly step across a toolbox and he scoops me up onto his lap. 'How are you doing, you know, emotionally? Your mood must be all over the place with all the extra hormones. I want you to talk to me about this stuff.'

'I'm grand, honestly. But I'm starting to worry about you. September is miles away. We have loads of time to prepare.'

'I just want to be a good dad,' he says into my hair.

I lean back and study his face. His serious brown eyes. The slight furrow in his brow. Those thick, long lashes that are absolutely wasted on a man. 'You're going to be an amazing dad, John.' I gesture at the books. 'You already know more about pregnancy than me, which I must admit is slightly annoying.'

He puts his hand on my lower belly, and for once I don't suck in or arch my back. 'Does it feel different in there?'

'No. I always thought it would, but no. Not yet anyway. I'm sure it will when I have a bump.'

'I can't wait for that part.'

'Me neither.' I sigh. 'I'm going to get one of those Baby on Board badges for when I'm on the Luas or the bus in town. Anyone who doesn't give me a seat will be getting daggers.'

'You're on week seven now. There's so much happening. Did you know that in two weeks it's going to be growing taste buds? Can you believe our little baby will have taste buds? How very advanced.'

'I can't really. I hope it doesn't start demanding weird foods.'

'Like olives?'

'I hate olives. That would be very spiteful of the baby.'

'Do you think it's a boy or a girl?'

I close my eyes and try to connect to this little bundle of

cells but I'm not really getting anything. 'I can't really tell. Maybe it's going to be gender-fluid. Or non-binary.'

'Hey, that's fine by me,' he says, rubbing my tummy. 'If anyone messes with them, they'll have Daddy to answer to.'

CHAPTER 18

'**M**ammy, I'm going over to Majella's!'

Her permed head pops out from the front hall. 'Before you go, will you tell me if I look alright, Aisling? I can't trust Geraldine.'

Geraldine's Boutique in Knocknamanagh is the number one local shopping destination for women of Mammy's ilk who are after a nice two-piece for a function or a good slip or maybe a feathery fascinator. Her sales technique is legendary. She once convinced Tessie Daly to buy a polka-dot dress and a matching hat for the Ploughing by telling her she was the stamp of Julia Roberts in *Pretty Woman*. Tessie is pushing seventy and was only going to jeer Úna Hatton in the brown-bread competition. She wore wellies with it.

Mammy is standing in front of the ancient oval mirror in the hall looking nervous. I nearly fall over when I see what she has on her.

'Are those' – I choke on the word – 'jeans?'

Her wardrobe has always consisted of a seemingly infinite number of pleated skirts in shades of navy and grey and the occasional pair of slacks, all of which she wears with a blouse and one of her many cardigans. Mammy stuff. But she has on a light-blue fine-knit jumper and a pair of navy boot-cuts with a crisp crease down the front of each leg.

She turns around shyly. 'Do I look ridiculous? You'll be honest with me, Aisling. I haven't worn jeans since I was a girl. They're a bit long on me. Geraldine said I'm all torso, whatever that means.'

I have to tell her the truth. 'They take years off you, Mammy. Honestly! And I love the jumper.'

'It's angora. Geraldine said I can put it in on a handwash cycle. I didn't even know my machine had one but she's right, it does.'

'The colour is fab on you.'

'I'm not a bit ... mutton dressed as lamb, am I?'

She sounds so vulnerable. I've never thought about how she might worry about her outfit same as I do when Sadhbh persuades me into one of her oversized jumpsuits that make me look like a beige Tellytubby. 'You look great, Mammy, and I'm not just saying that.'

'I just thought, feck it, I'll give them a go. YOMO, isn't that what you young people are saying now?'

Since I've been home I've noticed some subtle differences in her, especially when Dr Trevor is around. She seems brighter, more like the Mammy I knew before Daddy ever got sick. She's been going to Sharon in Strong Stuff to get her eyebrows tinted too, which has changed her face entirely, and has finally given in to Constance Swinford's years of pleading and taken up beginner's golf. And now this.

'Since when did Geraldine sell jeans?'

'They're new in. She said they're flying off the shelves. Trevor's ...' her voice falters a bit, 'Trevor's Valerie. She was very stylish by all accounts. And Síomha and Cara are too, of course.'

'Have you seen them since Christmas Day?'

'I haven't, but Trevor met them for lunch in Dublin last weekend. He said they were asking for you.'

I'm sure they were alright. She fluffs her curls in the mirror. 'Sharon was saying a bit of length in the hair might suit me. What do you think, Aisling?'

'Do not get extensions, Mammy. Majella let her put them in once and her heart was broke minding them. You have to blow-dry them and you need a special brush and everything.'

She chuckles. 'Oh, would you stop, I was just thinking of letting it grow a little bit. Maybe a few highlights or, what was it Sharon called them, lowlights, or there was something else beginning with "b" …'

My phone beeps in my pocket. A text from Majella. 'Will you bring biccies if you've any?'

I raise my hand. If I don't go now, I'll chicken out completely. 'Mammy, I'm on my way out.'

'Hang on there and I'll give you a lift. There's a bottle of Pinot whatchamacallit in the fridge left over from Christmas – you can bring it with you.'

'Eh, no thanks, I'm happy to drive.'

'Are you sure?' She looks suspicious. 'If Majella finds out you turned down a bottle of wine, she'll hit the roof.'

'I'm doing Dry January.'

'It's February.'

'February, I mean. Dry February. Nobody does Dry January any more. Too easy.'

'Right you are, love.' And thankfully she goes back to looking at her bum in the mirror.

****

When I get to the car park of Majella's building I dither outside BallyGoBrunch, watching Carol flitting around behind the counter. I'm absolutely dreading telling Maj about the baby, but at the same time I hate that John and Sadhbh both know and she doesn't. It feels devious. I know deep down she'll be happy for me, but I'm going in with no expectations, only one of my little packets of tissues I keep in the car. So handy.

My fingers have barely grazed the handle of the apartment door when she's in front of me.

'Did you bring the biscuits?'

Majella is wearing her new favourite thing – a 'snuddie', which is part hoodie, part fleece blanket. I can't say I don't want one myself, but she's fairly swamped in it.

I hand over the packet of Club Milks, which had been sitting in the biscuit barrel on Mammy's counter. Gone are her days of stashing them with the potatoes or behind the cistern.

Majella grabs them, delighted, and pulls me in for a hug. We've seen each other a few times in the fortnight I've been home, but this is the first time it's been just the two of us. 'Lifesaver! I was dying for something sweet and we've nothing in the house. Come in, bird. How are things? Are you looking forward to starting the new job?'

She ushers me into the kitchen-cum-living room and I take a seat under the massive black and white photograph of herself and Pablo on their wedding day. She had it blown up and put on a canvas. There are about seventeen similar pictures dotted around the room.

'Yeah, excited and nervous. I'm getting the keys next Friday with Aubrey. I'm going to stay with Sadhbh during the week. She has the space.'

'You lucky bitch! Will you take a picture of Don while he's sleeping for me?'

'Can't, I'm afraid – he's back in the States for a bit before the new album comes out here in April.'

'Oh. Well, at least you'll have Sadhbh.'

'Is Pab around?' She's in such good form I feel guilty at the thought of upsetting her but I know I need to get it over with.

'Doing a double shift in the Mountrath. The Rangers dinner dance is on tonight. Remember the carnage?'

I do. We used to go every year, the big gang of us, the lads in their good suits and us in dresses we'd beg, steal and borrow from each other and various older sisters. Between the medals and prizes we'd have funeral soup, supreme of chicken and a trio of desserts before tearing up the dance-floor. Then it was always back into Maguire's for a lock-in with Felipe playing a blinder behind the bar. My dedication to alternating every third drink with a glass of water helped keep me upright, but Maj was known for falling asleep in the ladies' more than once, no matter how often I told her it's a marathon not a sprint.

'Oh God, don't remind me.'

'Those were the days, eh, before we got old and boring.' She passes me a cup of tea and curls up on the couch beside me, battling with the snuddie to get her legs under herself.

'Maj, there's something I have to tell you.'

Her head snaps up from her Club. 'Oh?'

I take a deep breath. 'As in, I have … news.'

We both know what news means.

Her jaw drops open and she grabs my left hand. Nothing to see there. 'Did you finally say yes?'

I shake my head.

She looks at me blankly. Then she gasps. 'So you're …?'

'Pregnant. Yeah, I am. And, look, I know you and Pab are –'

She's bouncing up and down on the couch cushion now, sloshing tea everywhere.

She catapults herself across the room, down the hall and into the bathroom. When she returns she passes me a shoebox. I open it and inside is what looks like forty positive pregnancy tests.

I look up at her, incredulous. 'You're not!'

****

I'm still buzzing from the news when I get back home to Mammy's, three hours, two cups of tea and the entire sleeve of Club Milks later. Majella is seven weeks pregnant, just one behind me. Our due dates are only six days apart. When we were kids and we thought we'd be living next door to each other in mansions with our husbands Shane Filan (me) and Shayne Ward (her), we imagined we'd have babies at the same time too. And now it's actually happening, albeit without the popstar involvement. We're already planning a day in Dublin to test-drive buggies and maternity bras. She hasn't told a soul yet because it's taking all her strength to keep Pablo's emotions in check. Apparently he's see-sawing between singing the Canary Islands anthem to her stomach and wailing in the shower that he doesn't deserve the blessings of a new baby. It sounds exhausting, especially as she's had her head in a tiny toilet bowl in school half the day and can only stomach chocolate, and prawn cocktail crisps.

Mammy is at the Aga when I get home, back in her usual cardigan, skirt and slippers. She and Constance have had a family reunion staying in the yurts all week, and they had them run ragged letting kid goats and piglets escape the petting zoo.

'Are you hungry, pet?'

'Starving.'

She turns around with a plate in her hand. 'There you are so. I was too tired to put on a dinner, so I just made you this. Quick and easy.'

On the plate in front of me are three fried eggs, their orange yolks still wobbling. She looks pleased with herself. 'Don't wait for me now – eat up.'

The panic sets in quickly. Undercooked eggs are a big no-no when you're pregnant. You never know where listeria might be lurking, according to John. She bustles off to the fridge and I scan the room. That Bloody Cat might take one off my hands but there's no sign of her anywhere. Typical. And the bin is beside the fridge.

'And I was over in Knock Garden Centre – sorry,' she mimics Constance's posh accent, 'Lifestyle Destination – today, and you'll never guess what they have now.' Her voice is coming from inside the fridge. 'A fishmonger, if you don't mind!'

Knock Garden Centre thinks it's Avoca, honest to God.

'So, Aisling, I got you this. It wasn't cheap, let me tell you.'

She turns around and places a rectangular box of sushi in front of me with a smile. It's not chicken sushi like you might get in a petrol station, or vegetarian sushi or even a California roll, which is cooked crab. It's sashimi. Elaine and Ruby's favourite. Just literally slices of raw salmon and tuna. Another thing you can't eat when you're expecting.

'Didn't you say Sadhbh got you into it? There you go now.'

She's looking from the untouched eggs back up to me, and I swear to God there's a glint in her eye. 'And you'll have a glass of wine too, won't you? Go on, it's Saturday night.'

Soft eggs. Sushi. And now wine?

'Mammy, I …'

'What is it, love?'

'I'm sorry but I … I can't have any of this stuff.'

'And why is that, tell me?' She looks surprised. Sort of.

I have no other choice but to confess. I was going to wait a few weeks, and me and John were going to do it together, but my hand is being forced here. 'Because … I'm pregnant.'

She flicks a tea towel into the air. 'I knew it, pet!' Then she gathers me in for the biggest hug since Christmas Eve, when I landed in from New York and frightened the daylights out of her.

'Really?'

She pulls a chair up to the table. 'I've known it since you came in the door from the airport. I can see it in your face – your lips are puffy as anything, same as mine when I was having you. I got the big boobs with Paul.'

I've seen the pictures. She looked indecent at my cousin Doireann's christening. 'And you're not a bit disappointed?'

Her face falls. 'Disappointed? Why would I be disappointed?'

'Well, me and John aren't married. We're not even engaged.'

She looks at me sternly. 'Aisling, I don't care about that a jot. John is a good man, and together you're a good, strong couple. All I care about is that you're happy. Are you happy?' I nod, and she smiles back at me. 'I know you are. You're the happiest I've ever seen you. Congratulations, love. I can't wait to be a granny!'

CHAPTER 19

hanks to a raging bout of first-day nerves, I wake up an hour before my alarm the following Friday. I make the most of it, though, starfishing out in the massive bed, feeling extremely grateful to be at the receiving end of Sadhbh's taste for expensive bed linen. No Arnotts bargain basement for her. She's upstairs and she's paying full price. I wish John was beside me to tell me everything will be fine, but he was here the past two nights and I don't want us outstaying our welcome.

I put my hands over my belly and wonder what's going on in there. My bowels are feeling anxious, but that's probably more to do with today. It's mad to be going back into an office in Dublin. The last time was PensionsPlus, from which I was unceremoniously booted, along with all my co-workers, this time three years ago. I'm still friends with Des from Escalations on Facebook, and amid his mild-mannered posts about gardening and Sunday walks with his wife, Irene, his tagged posts give away that he's still an absolute divil for the Thursday nights on the razz. It looks like he recently broke his arm trying a flip on the dancefloor in Whelan's.

I went from PensionsPlus to setting up BallyGoBrunch and meeting James. Then on to my first experience working with

Mandy on the infamous BGB celebrity wedding that clashed with Majella's, when I realised I didn't love James and I did love John. Then over to New York for a fresh start and a salve for my feelings when John went to Dubai with Megan. And now here I am, back in Dublin, back with John and now expecting our baby, and about to set up Mandy's European office as her number one on this side of the Atlantic. Maybe I do feel sick after all.

My phone goes with a text from Aubrey. A green puke-face emoji and a thumbs-up. The green puke face does me in, and I race for the en suite just in time to get the acidic liquid into the toilet. I hope it's just nerves and not the beginning of a morning pregnancy routine. I stagger back to bed, glad now that I was awake early, and send Aubrey back a melty face and a strong arm. She arrived in Dublin two days ago and is staying in one of those sterile corporate short-let apartments. The new office is right beside where Crawdaddy and Tripod used to be but have now morphed into Starbucks and hummus-wrap emporiums. I went to Tripod once when I was in college because Majella was into a lad who was into, what was it again, either new wave or new rave. It was roasting, but once I got standing under an air conditioner I was actually grand and the music wasn't bad. Majella ended up shifting her mark and I shifted his friend who was 'out of his mind on pingers' and I worried about cross-contamination. I checked my pulse for twenty-four hours, though, and felt that I was out of the woods when I was well able for a chicken fillet roll the following evening.

I give myself another twenty minutes, then roll out of bed and back into the en suite for a hot shower that I hope will soothe any remaining nausea away. I laid out my clothes last night – a pair of soft black leggings and a black fleecy jumper. It'll just be me and Aubrey today, putting chairs together and getting phones set up. It'll be just us for a while, actually, as we build on the work Mandy's already done sussing out clients here and in the UK. I half dry my hair and put it in a low bun and go for my trusty brown mascara and the eyebrow pencil Sadhbh has bullied me into wearing. The first two days I thought I looked like one of the Super Mario brothers, but then John took a lovely selfie of us and my eyebrows actually looked dark and defined and not beetling and terrifying, so I've accepted the pencil into my routine.

I grab my laptop and tiptoe down the stairs. I haven't heard Sadhbh moving, so I'm not sure if she's up yet. She works from home three days a week so may be doing one of her classic 8.55 a.m. rises for a 9 a.m. start in front of the laptop. Don's still in LA with The Peigs, doing something called pick-ups for the new album, so she's been keeping weird hours talking to him for ages at a time. He's extremely stressed because it's their 'difficult second album', which means Sadhbh is also stressed, given she's his girlfriend but also works at the record label. As I swing into the kitchen to make my lunch, I get an awful fright because there she is standing right in front of me holding out a glass of green sludge.

'Morning!' she chirps, looking flawless as usual in a cropped grey T-shirt and matching leggings.

'Have you been there all night?'

'Very funny. I made you a smoothie. Hemp, kale, Greek yoghurt, agave –'

'Hemp? Sadhbh, I'm going into work, and there's this little thing I'm dealing with called pregnancy. I can't be going around getting stoned on your mad milkshakes.'

She sighs dramatically and sets the glass down on the counter, pulling the fridge open and taking out a bowl of chopped fruit, which she plonks on the breakfast bar with a spoon. 'Sit down and eat this and I'll put on some toast too. Hemp doesn't get you stoned, you lunatic. It's good for you. Drink the smoothie. You and the baba need it before a busy day.'

I can't control the familiar hot prick of tears at my eyes as I obey her. Jesus, I am a proper mess. My lower lip wobbles as I spoon in some strawberries. When Sadhbh turns back from the toaster, she's glassy-eyed too.

'You and the baba,' I parrot back to her as my face crumples.

'I know. I just heard myself. I can't believe you're having a baba.'

'You don't even like babies.'

'I don't want to *have* babies. It doesn't mean I don't *like* babies. And yours is going to be so cute. Imagine the freckles.' We stare at each other for a few seconds before she composes herself and throws a tea towel at me. 'Drink your smoothie.'

I take a sip to placate her, and while the initial taste isn't so bad, the aftermath of grass and muck is really something. I gulp it down in three goes because I believe her about it being good for me and the baba.

'Are you going Down Home after work?'

I nod through the last gulp of the greenery. Just like old

times, I'm hightailing it back to BGB on a Friday evening. I'm even back in the trusty old Micra. Paul kept it in good nick while I was in New York.

I can't wait to see John, even though we have an anxiety-inducing task to get through. 'We're telling John's parents about the baby. The baba.'

'Oh God. How do you think his mum is going to take it? She's a bit of a tough nut, isn't she?'

'Fran, yeah. Like, I think she's always liked me well enough, but she still goes to mass every week and I'm not sure she's a big fan of babies "out of wedlock", even in this day and age. And me and John are just back together.'

'Surely she'll be thrilled. And it's going to be the first grandchild, isn't it?'

'Yeah, John's older sister has lived in New Zealand for years and has no kids. We're telling them early because now Majella and Pablo and Mammy know there's no way to contain it properly. I'm only eight and a half weeks, though. It feels wrong to be saying it.'

'Ah, don't mind that bollocks. Tell whoever you want. I hate all the sneaking around women have to do to avoid upsetting anyone else. What about John's dad?'

'The world's most easy-going man? I'm not worried about Ray. He'll probably just shrug and say "Grand so".'

Sadhbh laughs. 'I never get tired of the BGB folk. How's Mad Tom? Is he still with the same girlfriend?'

'Jesus, Sadhbh, John is from Knocknamanagh, not Ballygobbard. Have I taught you nothing?'

'Sorry, sorry. Of course, the great Knock–BGB rivalry. You and John are like Romeo and Juliet.'

Now it's my turn to laugh. 'I did used to think that when I was younger, except with less glamour and more GAA dinner dances.'

'And fewer tragic misunderstandings,' Sadhbh muses.

'God, we've had enough of those. Anyway, I'm gone. Thank you for the breakfast. You're a star!'

'Say hi to Aubrey for me. Tell her I have a Peigs ticket for April with her name on it if she wants it.'

'Oh, lovely, I'll tell her. I still can't believe the boys are playing the Point. Majella is fuming she's going to be pregnant for it.'

Sadhbh's mouth drops open like she's in a cartoon. 'Excuse me, what?'

Fuck.

'Shite. I really wasn't supposed to say anything.'

I told Maj I'd call in tonight and empathise with her about not being able to drink, and now I'll have to confess I blabbed to Sadhbh. I don't think she'll care, though; she has enough on her plate already. Pablo has become obsessed with what their baby's star sign might be and what moon it might be born under, and she's already had enough of him holding crystals over her completely flat tummy to see if he can read anything from her aura. I might see if I can pick up a bottle of sparkling something that she can pretend is wine.

'Majella is pregnant? You two are pregnant at the same time?! This is like a Hallmark movie or a Mormon mommy-blogger unveiling on Instagram. When is she due?'

'September. She's like a week behind me.'

Sadhbh squeals. 'You couldn't make it up!'

CHAPTER 20

The Mandy Blumenthal Event Architects European Headquarters is actually a former international language school, and we've barely taken possession of the keys when the first lost student rings the buzzer.

'I did Spanish in high school,' Aubrey says with a shrug, as I try to explain in broken French that the premises he's looking for is now on George's Street and has a different name. I think a lot of these language schools are money-laundering operations, to be honest. After two more buzzes, I decide to put a little sign with a map downstairs on the front door and take the receiver off the hook. I can't be spending all day on Google Translate when we have a delivery of chairs and desks to assemble before we can actually start work.

Promising the Peigs ticket to Aubrey is a godsend because she's having a tough time settling into Dublin life. Unlike Irish people moving to the US, who grew up on a diet of American TV shows and films, she really hadn't a clue what to expect when she arrived here. She watched *The Banshees of Inisherin* on the plane over so was pleasantly surprised to see that Dublin is actually not all fields and donkeys. But she's already missing Jeremy like mad and is struggling with not being able to plug in her hairdryer in the bathroom. It's putting a dampener on the whole experience. Plus, she doesn't like being on the back foot when it comes to local knowledge.

'I promise the Luas isn't always like that,' I tell her softly after she recounts an unfortunate incident involving a group of tweens setting fire to a schoolbag while further down the carriage a fare evader was trying to wrestle the doors open. I would have thought after New York Aubrey would be up for anything, but the Red Line would test Jason Statham.

'I know, I know. I'm just missing home. And ranch dressing. I can't find it anywhere!'

'Right, I need a break from these IKEA instructions. Will we have an actual work meeting? Something to report back to Mandy on Tuesday? She's already scheduled a Zoom.'

I'm actually dreading having a face-to-face with Mandy. I feel so sneaky taking the job knowing full well that I'm going to be clocking off for at least six months while the company is still finding its feet. I've heard of women in New York sending emails between pushes and being back at their desks while their stitches are healing. I have every intention of taking all my maternity leave, though, whether she likes it or not. I know my rights. But I've decided I'm going to wait until I'm five months gone to tell her, because I probably won't be showing until then. I'm also considering wearing a wire in case she threatens to murder me and I do end up going missing. It could be crucial evidence.

Aubrey snaps right into work mode and opens her laptop. Luckily the Wi-Fi is working like a dream. That might have sent her over the edge.

She looks at me over the top of the computer. 'I have a lead on a waxing company – the Hairy Mollies – but it's small fry.'

'Small fry is good. It's something. We're starting at the bottom here. Anything else?'

'What do you know about hair?'

I self-consciously touch my damp bun. 'Not a huge amount.'

'Okay, well, when Mandy was in London she connected with a potential new client who's expanding into Ireland as a sort of tester before going to the UK. Paloma Porter Haircare.'

'I have her deep-conditioning masque!' I picked it up at one of Tara's charity beauty sales for a dollar. She has one every month to get rid of all the free stuff that's clogging up her spare room, with all proceeds going to a women's shelter on the Lower East Side. The masque normally costs $30 so I was keeping it for a special occasion, but I've opened the lid three times for a sniff. Divine.

Aubrey rolls her eyes. 'She's not a person – it's a corporation.'

'Oh, right.'

'So … any ideas? The budget is generous. Mandy wants to make it known that there's a new player on the events scene in town.'

I think for a minute. 'What about an awards show?'

Aubrey narrows her eyes. 'What, like, Paloma Porter sponsors the Irish Oscars or something? Do you even have an equivalent of the Oscars here?'

I'm about to launch into a defensive explanation of the IFTAs when I remember some of the guests got a bit pissed and rowdy one year and then they stopped televising it for a while. It plays into too many stereotypes.

'I mean we could create our own awards show from scratch. Something like' – it comes to me in a flash of inspiration – 'the Paloma Porter Style Awards. We can have categories for beauty industry professionals, celebrities, influencers. Anyone who's cool. Let people campaign and then the public can vote.'

I can nearly hear the cogs in Aubrey's head turning. 'How will people vote?'

'Josh B can make a website.'

'What's in it for the winner?'

'The glory.'

'And that's it?'

'A night out.'

'A night out?'

'You have to remember you're in Dublin now, Aubrey. There's not that much going on here, entertainment-wise. RTÉ might even show it. Well, maybe Virgin Media Two.'

'Okay, let's do up a pitch for Mandy,' Aubrey concedes. 'The sooner we get things moving and hire permanent staff, the sooner I can go home.'

****

'Welcome home!' John scoops me up in his arms on the doorstep of his parents' house in Knocknamanagh.

'Home? You know I'm BGB till I die, and don't get me started on the tiny jersey debate again,' I murmur into his shoulder.

'Okay, okay, you know what I meant.' He laughs and holds me at arm's length. 'I've already ordered two little hurls in the BGB and Knock colours. We can be bipartisan.'

'You big eejit!'

'Are you nervous?'

'A bit. Are they here?'

'They are. They know we have to tell them something. I think they're expecting an engagement. Oh, by the way, will you marry me?'

I roll my eyes and push past him. 'Come on, let's just do it.'

****

I'm shaking a bit when John delivers the news. His dad, Ray, strides over and gives him a big handshake, and after Fran has digested everything for thirty seconds, she comes to me first and wraps her arms around me. I wasn't expecting a hug.

'Well, isn't that lovely news? You're a great girl.' Over her shoulder, I raise my eyebrows at John and he smiles. This couldn't be going any better. I sensed Fran was disappointed that John and I seemed done for good when he went to Dubai with Megan, so maybe me getting knocked up is actually a big win for her. I'm just so glad there wasn't a lecture or a round of tutting.

'Will you have dinner, Aisling? You will, of course. You always had a good appetite. And you'll stay tonight? I'll do up the spare bed for ye.' She kind of mutters the end of the last sentence but I hear her well enough. Never in all my years of knowing John have we been allowed to share a double bed in the spare room. I was always in the single bed in his sister Rachel's old room and he was in his own. The fact that she's now giving us the nod to share is like getting a blessing from Rome. I don't know if I'll be able to look her in the eye in the morning.

I follow Fran into the kitchen while Ray and John go out to look at Ray's new car. As they go out the door, I hear Ray calling it a 'Granddadmobile' and it nearly sets me off.

'How far along are you, Aisling? Oh look, move those papers and sit down.' She points to the comfy armchair by the stove.

'Actually only nine weeks. So it's early days, although it has taste buds now. We just wanted to tell you and Ray because I already told Mammy.'

'The first grandchild on both sides. We'll have them spoilt between us.'

Fran busies herself draining potatoes and checking chops. I offer to help twice, but her second refusal is borderline terrifying, so instead I take up one of the papers I moved off the chair. The local weekly has a story on the front page about three Christmas wreaths that were stolen from front doors over the festive period. Hopefully the best minds are on the case. I'm just getting stuck into a review of the Knock Musical Society's run of *The Rocky Horror Picture Show* and the praise for Father Fenlon in the high heels when Fran asks me to tell the lads that dinner is ready and says she'll take a Romantica out for dessert since it's a special occasion. My heart feels so full.

****

'I'm surprised Fran didn't have long johns and a floor-length nightdress laid out for us,' John murmurs as we lie naked in the spare-room bed under a picture of Jesus Christ himself. We thought about removing the red bulb but it felt too blasphemous.

'I suppose she's thinking "what's the worst that can happen now?"' I whisper back, before sliding out of my side of the bed.

John grabs at my arm. 'Where do you think you're going?'

'I'm putting on my nightdress. What if Fran comes bursting in in the morning with a plate of rashers and sausages? I might be pregnant with her illegitimate grandchild, but I'm not having her seeing me in the nip on her good spare-room sheets.'

He sighs. 'Good point. At least they're going away tomorrow.'

I actually can't wait for that bit. Fran and Ray are off to a boules tournament until Monday, so John and I will have the place to ourselves. It's already been a pain going between Mammy's and Sadhbh's, so I'm looking forward to having a bit of privacy. We both are.

In the morning I wake up early and for a second I assess myself, checking to see if I feel sick. No nausea, thank God, but my belly hurts like I'm about to do a stinker in Fran's retro seaside-themed bathroom. I tiptoe across the hall and squeeze the door shut as quietly as I can. The sick feeling comes rushing back as I sit down on the toilet, and when I glance down into my pale-pink knickers a slash of bright-red blood in the gusset knocks the air out of my lungs.

I go to reach for my phone to google 'nine weeks pregnant blood', but I've left it in the bedroom. I stand up and close my eyes, afraid to look in the bowl before I flush, but I open them again to see more blood swirl away down the drain. I steady myself on the sink and just miss knocking over a ceramic lighthouse before crossing the hall back into the spare room to shake John's foot under the duvet.

'John, I think there's something wrong.'

CHAPTER 21

'**A**nd remind me of how far along your pregnancy is?'
It's John who answers Dr Trevor's gentle question
in the strangely familiar confines of Dr Maher's old
office. The de Valera picture on the wall is gone, but it still has
the same olive-green wallpaper and surprisingly comfortable
wicker chairs. Sadhbh would love them, although Dr Maher
definitely wasn't being trendy when he installed them about
twenty years ago.

'Aisling, do you want to lie down here while I examine
you? Nothing scary, I just want to feel your tummy.'

He walks over to the black leather bed in the corner and
pulls out a ream of blue tissue paper to cover it. It's still early
in the morning. After waking John up and racing back to the
bathroom to vomit, we waited another hour until it felt
decent enough to ring Dr Trevor. He told us to meet him at
his surgery. I wonder did he tell Mammy.

I slip my feet out of my runners and swing my legs up to
lie down on the rustling blue paper, grateful to have John
beside me. He stays in his chair, rubbing the back of his neck
and then his eyes. It all feels so surreal.

'Any pain when I push here?' Dr Trevor's hands are warmer
on my skin than I anticipated.

'No.'

'But you have been having cramps?'

'Yeah. Like period pain. A bit worse, maybe.' Tears leak out of the corners of my eyes because I know this is probably not a good sign.

'And how much blood would you estimate?'

'Not loads, maybe like the first day of my period. A couple of tablespoons.'

'And the colour? Red or more brown?'

'Red. Bright red.'

'Okay, Aisling, thank you. You can sit up now.'

Dr Trevor returns to his desk and starts tapping away at his computer. 'I'm referring you to the early pregnancy unit at the General. They'll do a scan so they can' – he pauses – 'so they can figure out what's going on.'

He taps away for another few seconds, and I just have to fill the silence. 'Do you think it's a, a thing? A miscarriage?'

He stops typing and looks from me to John and back to me. 'It's very hard to know without a blood test and a scan. I'm going to draw some blood now and then again on Monday morning so we can compare your hormone levels. You'll have the scan on Monday morning too, so we'll have a much clearer picture then.'

'Monday?' John's voice is surprisingly loud. 'She has to wait until then? It's only Saturday. That's inhumane!'

Dr Trevor nods gravely. 'I'm afraid so. They don't open at weekends any more and all emergencies go in via A&E. I don't want to put you through that unless absolutely necessary. It's better to wait if you can. Now, Aisling, I'll draw some blood if that's okay.'

I make a fist like Dr Trevor asks. Usually if I see or hear the blood whooshing into the little catcher yoke I feel a bit funny, but this time I watch it with fascination, thinking of all the secrets it's hiding. I look up at John and he's staring at me. I give him a little half-smile and he gives one back. It is absolutely berserk how brand new this situation is. I have a split second of positive clarity and think, 'Sure, everything will be grand, no matter what,' but then in the next breath I think about the tiny feet in the tiny socks and my eyes spill over.

Dr Trevor places a large warm hand over one of mine. 'Try not to worry too much.'

'What should she do between now and Monday?' John asks, still sounding incredulous about the wait.

'Because you're already experiencing some cramping and bleeding, I need you to be vigilant on observing more pain and bleeding and any signs of it intensifying.' Dr Trevor busies himself labelling the vials of blood. 'If anything becomes worrying or very painful do go straight to A&E.'

'Have you told Mammy? Like, did you tell her I was coming in?'

'No, no, of course not – God no. This is confidential. Completely.'

****

Back out in the car, we sit in silence for a minute before John reaches over and takes my hand. 'Are you alright?'

I shrug. 'I don't know.'

'What'll we do now? We can go back to my house? Fran and Ray should be gone by now. We'll have the place to ourselves. I'll mind you.'

I smile sadly and nod through my tears. 'That sounds nice.'

****

There's no need to be 'vigilant' for the pain because it comes with gusto from around lunchtime and continues in waves, along with what Google seems to think is 'standard' bleeding for a miscarriage at nine weeks. John takes away the stack of baby books and fills and refills hot-water bottles as I lie in the spare-room bed, one of the mattress-sized sanitary towels provided by Dr Trevor between my legs.

We watch episode after episode of the American version of *The Office* on John's laptop. I laugh along with it at times, and then feel guilty for laughing. I avoid a phone call from Majella and text her to say I can't talk and will ring her later, but I never do. I compose an email to Mandy and Aubrey saying I'm sick and think I'll need to take a few days off next week. I scrunch into a foetal position when the pain is bad, and John gets panicky and talks about A&E, but I know myself that there's no need for that. I just know that I have to exist with this pain and the blood clots I glance at in the toilet before scrunching my eyes closed.

We fall asleep before it gets dark on Saturday evening, and I wake up really early on Sunday morning. I can tell by the light behind the curtains. The giant pad between my legs reminds me that it wasn't all a horrible dream.

I turn over and John's face is illuminated by his phone. 'Stop googling it, there's nothing we can do to stop it happening,' I whisper to him, and he gathers me up in his arms as I cry for the millionth time. When I eventually stop he asks me if I want to watch something. 'Something cosy,' I say, and we go for the octopus documentary on Netflix. It feels safe. Majella said it was lovely, but she was convinced the lad in it was horny for the octopus, so at least we can look out for that. I find myself enthralled from the start. Yes, maybe the man is a little bit horny for the octopus, but she's his best friend. At the bit where it looks like she's gone missing I cry so much that John asks if we should turn it off and I say no. There's still a good bit left so there has to be some kind of positive news coming, I figure. The octopus makes a reappearance after a battle with a shark takes one of her legs, but she grows it back.

'I've never rooted for anything more in my life,' I say to John, but he just stoically nods.

As the film ends and the octopus dies after hatching her eggs, I cling to him, and as we watch the footage of the man swimming with his son and seeking out more octopus friends, I feel John's chest jerk up and down. He furiously wipes away tears as I look up at him.

'It's okay, it's okay, it's okay,' I say gently. I scooch up the bed and take him in my arms. He clings around my waist and lies his head on my belly and cries and cries. It's the first time I've ever seen him cry, which makes me cry.

When his sobs have petered out, I run my fingers through his hair. 'So, do you think he was horny for the octopus?'

It's a relief to laugh.

****

Later, John gets up to heat up some soup and make toast, and Dr Trevor rings. I tell him about the pain and the bleeding, and his voice sounds serious as he tells me that it is likely I am miscarrying. Like I didn't already know. Sunday night brings more of the same, and I worry about ruining Fran's sheets. John tells me, 'They're only sheets,' and skips the whole season of *The Office* where Pam is pregnant. We stay in bed when we hear the back door announcing Fran and Ray's arrival home.

'I don't want to go downstairs,' I tell him. 'I don't want to see anyone.'

'Stay here. I'll bring up some crisps. I won't say anything until we know.'

'I wish we had our own place. Just the two of us.'

'Me too.'

****

On Monday morning, Dr Trevor takes more blood and gives me a referral letter for the hospital, where he says they'll do an ultrasound. I wish he'd been more specific about the type of ultrasound because this one involves a wand going right up my vagina. They confirm that there's no heartbeat and tell me my body is doing everything it should and advise that I continue the miscarriage without intervention. 'Conservative management' they call it. Neither of us cries during the whole hospital visit, but when Dr Trevor rings when we're on the way back to Knocknamanagh and says the blood test results seem to confirm what the hospital has said, John pulls in to the side of the road and we cry together until the Micra windows have steamed up.

'What'll we do now?' John asks as he starts the car. I'm at a loss, but I feel like I need to tell Mammy. Dr Trevor knows. It's not fair that he has to hide it from her.

I tell John he can drop me off if he wants and he looks upset. 'I don't really want to leave you.'

'Okay, good, I didn't really want you to go.'

I love him so much in that moment.

CHAPTER 22

Mammy cries a little bit but tries to control it so she doesn't 'upset me'. I think of her all those years ago when she went to England to get her abortion, a procedure that was surgical and invasive. I'm glad that it looks like I won't have to go through anything like that, as long as the miscarriage continues the way it 'should'. I tell her that I have to go back for another scan in two weeks, as long as I have no fevers or complications, and she cries again.

'I'm so sorry this is happening to you, pet.' She looks at John. 'And you too, John. I know ye were excited.'

We drive back to John's house to tell his parents, but I can't bring myself to go in. When he comes out, I can tell he's been crying again, and my heart continues to break. The little hurls had arrived. We watch *My Octopus Teacher* again that night, this time in my bed in Mammy's. It feels cathartic. Mammy gallantly leaves the hot-water-bottle making and tea and paracetamol trays to John, even though I know it's killing her not doing it herself. There's no sign of Dr Trevor, but when I hear him arriving later that night, I feel comforted to know there's a doctor in the house.

****

On Tuesday John cancels the plasterer for the gym and stays in bed with me. The cramps have lessened along with the bleeding, although I'm still wearing the mattress in my knickers in case of clots. When he suggests the cinema, I comb the listings for something safe to watch. There's a new *Mission Impossible*, which seems unlikely to have a pregnancy storyline. I fret over what to tell Mandy, and John insists on ringing her as soon as it's a reasonable time in New York. He goes outside to do it and it's over very fast.

'What did you say?'

'I told her the truth, of course. She was dead sound,' he says, immediately easing my catastrophising that she was going to fire me. 'She wants you to take two weeks off and will let Aubrey know, as long as it's okay with you?'

I get an email from Mandy twenty minutes later.

> *My darling Irish doll,*
>
> *You gotta look after yourself now. I'll square things with Aubrey. She can handle the hairdressers and the wax thing. Take as long as you need. You wanna go to a spa? I'm paying.*
>
> *Love ya,*
>
> *M*

The wax thing. Aubrey must have landed the Hairy Mollies' new clinic in Dún Laoghaire. Fair play to her.

****

On Wednesday I leave John for the first time to go to Majella's. I have to tell her before she sends me any more daft nursery-decoration ideas. She and Pablo live in a one-bedroom apartment, and I don't know who she could get in BGB to paint the cast of the *Lion King* on her walls anyway. Ciara Connelly was good at art in school, but she made a balls of Sharon's salon windows at Christmas. Rudolph looked like Marty Morrissey.

I take a deep breath as I stand outside the door of her apartment. I know Pablo is at work in Maguire's. He's picking up shifts wherever he can now that Maj has set her sights on a baby travel system that costs over a thousand euro.

She opens the door as soon as I knock. 'Come in, come in. I wish I could say I have wine in the fridge, but I have some fizzy apple juice that my mother bought in Marks and Spencer instead.'

I say nothing and sit on the couch, feeling sick with nerves and crampy from my ongoing miscarriage.

She clocks my face. 'What's wrong, bird?'

'I don't want you worrying over this, but I've had a miscarriage.' I just needed to get it out.

Her face crumples immediately. 'Oh, Ais. What? Are you sure? Oh my God, I'm so sorry.' She's down on the couch beside me, arm awkwardly around my shoulders. We've never been the biggest huggers. Not sober, anyway. After a second, she scuttles away from me though. 'Sorry, there's nits in my class and I can't use the usual poisonous stuff because of ...' She trails off and I know it's because she's pregnant.

'It's okay. You can say it. You're pregnant. And look, I don't want you fretting and worrying that something is going to happen to you. You'll be fine.'

She looks down at her hands, crying. 'Okay. But are you okay? When did this happen? How are you feeling?'

We drink the fizzy apple juice, even though I suppose I could have something stronger if I wanted. I wouldn't have the stomach for it, though. I try not to tell her too many specifics because I really don't want her constantly thinking it's happening to her.

'And I don't know if you should tell Pablo yet,' I say, 'He'll go berserk worrying.'

'I don't know – he's gone very zen with his crystals. He's made two best friends on Etsy already. I'm worried they're taking advantage of him. I might have to cut him off. If you don't want me to tell him, though, I won't.'

'No, it's okay, you can tell him. I've actually just realised how much miscarriages are kept a secret. Like, you're not even supposed to tell anyone you're pregnant until you're three months and out of the danger zone or whatever. Oh God, not that you're in the danger zone or anything.'

'Ais, it's okay. I'm a big girl. Let's worry about you for now. And the bloody nits.'

'Can you use anything at all?'

'Ah, some organic shite that they're probably lapping up like it's kombucha and having a nit party in my cow's lick.'

I go to the bathroom to change my pad, and she gets us water when we can't hack any more of the fake wine.

'Did you tell Mandy?'

'John rang her yesterday. She's been very sound about it, especially since I've only done one day of work.'

'Eh, of course she has. Who wouldn't be?'

'There's no paid leave for miscarriages – did you know that? Mandy's given me two weeks, but she doesn't have to.'

'Why am I not surprised? And you're so right about the secrecy thing. It's like people don't want to acknowledge that these terrible things happen.'

'Oh, sure, Sadhbh is already campaigning for period leave in her new job. They're all foosball tables and Domino's on a Friday so she thinks they might go for it.'

Majella looks thoughtful. 'I'm fairly sure I mistaught multiplication in school one year because of a bad period. It'd be for the good of the country if they gave us a bit of time off. And here, how is John?'

'Ah, Maj, it's the first time I've ever seen him crying.'

Her eyes instantly fill with tears again. 'Are you serious? That's so sad. The poor fucker.'

'I know. And he was crying with his parents, and I think he was crying in the bathroom earlier. He was all snotty.'

Maj pulls her sleeve across her face. 'And now I'm all snotty.'

'This is worse than the time Shayne Ward got engaged.'

'Ah, Ais, nothing is worse than that.'

We're crying laughing when Pablo comes in from Maguire's, complaining that his socks are full of Guinness after spilling a pint all over himself. He looks from Maj's face to mine. 'You're crying? Why are you crying, my love?'

'Ah, nothing, I'll tell you later.'

'Maybe the babies make you cry,' he calls behind him as he goes to change his socks. If only he knew how right he is.

****

Every morning this week has felt like waking up on St Stephenses Day. The excitement is gone. The magic is over. John has stayed with me every night. He was due to start a personal training teaching course this week, but they've let him push it back a bit. As we lie in bed on Friday night he says glumly, 'This time last week we were in a different place.'

'Don't remind me.'

He bends down and kisses the side of my head. He's sitting up in bed and I have my head in his lap, curled up against him. 'I'm sorry.'

'S'okay.'

'Here, do you think your mother is okay with me being here all week? Maybe I should go back home.'

The very thought of it brings me to tears.

'Ah, Ais, I'm not trying to upset you.'

'I know. I just don't want you to go. You're the only one who gets it. My mother doesn't care that you're here. She's beside herself making wholesome dinners.'

'Okay. Just, if you get sick of me let me know. Or you can come and stay in Fran and Ray's if you want.'

'Okay, maybe we'll stay with them next week or something.'

'It's a pain in the hole, isn't it, all this living out of bags and going between houses?'

'It is. I don't know where I left my deodorant.'

We're quiet then, watching an old episode of *University Challenge*. We figure nothing is safer, content-wise, than quiz shows.

'*Jane Eyre*!' I shout.

'*Terminator 2*,' says John.

'*The Tempest*,' says one of the nerds on the telly. He's right, of course.

'John?' I say, not lifting my head from his lap.

'Yeah?'

'I don't think I'll ever get sick of you.'

He bends down to kiss me again. 'And you won't even marry me. Such a tease.'

I laugh. He hasn't asked me to marry him in a week. I'm relieved to hear him bring it up again. Last night I started to panic that he was only with me because of the baby. But maybe we'll be alright.

'Classical music now,' says Jeremy Paxman from the TV.

John groans. 'I'll get the tea and biscuits.'

'Don't forget my –'

'Hot-water bottle. Already on it.'

I actually get the first classical music question right. Finally, learning Beethoven's Ninth Symphony on the recorder in Transition Year has paid off. As John returns to the bedroom I'm ready to gloat, but he has a serious look on his face.

'What's wrong? Is it the cat? I swear there's something dead inside it. The farts are noxious.'

He puts the tea tray down on my desk and sits on the edge of the bed. 'Aisling, will you marry me, though? I'm dead serious.'

I stare back at him for a long time – probably only twenty seconds, though. Thousands of images race through my head. Me in a wedding dress, him rolling down a grassy hill for some reason, me watching him and Megan dance at the wedding, me alone in New York, us with two blonde Instagram kids, us crying in the Micra.

'Not now, John. It's too much.'

It's his turn to stare back at me. For a split second, I wonder if he's going to get mad. But then he sighs. 'Are you sure? Because I really mean it.'

'I know. I know you do.'

CHAPTER 23

ubrey looks relieved to see me when I arrive back in to the office. I probably could have come back after a week, but I took the two Mandy offered. There's a huge bouquet of flowers waiting for me on my desk.

'How are you feeling? Can I get you anything? Mandy sent those.'

I pick up the card. It reads: 'Whatever you need, just ask Aubrey x.'

'I'm actually happy to be back into a routine. The distraction will do me good.'

'Amazing. I've been having to pretend we have a receptionist and then doing a different voice when I put clients through to me. My Irish accent isn't great. I'm not sure they're buying it.'

'The phone's been ringing? That's a good sign! Maybe it's time to hire someone new.'

'I've already mentioned it to Mandy and got the green light. We're good.'

Physically, I'm feeling almost normal again, but emotionally I'm all over the shop. It was a real struggle getting out of bed this morning. A big part of me wanted to just stay there and wallow and never have to deal with anyone or anything again. Everything just feels so unfair. Sadhbh says I'm going through the seven stages of grief and that if I don't acknowledge each one then I won't heal. Sit with the feelings, she said, even though it's hard. She thinks I'm at stage five now, depression. I feel bad that she's paying €120 a week to talk to a therapist and I'm getting the benefits for free. I must bring her up some eggs from home next week as a thank you.

'What else did I miss?'

'The students have stopped buzzing the door. I think the language school updated their website.'

'Finally!'

'And I had a Zoom with Mandy on Friday and updated her on some Paloma Porter Style Awards ideas. She loved them and will be bringing them to the PP team tomorrow. If they approve, we can get the ball rolling. And the Hairy Mollies contract is in the bag too. They're wondering if you want to go in for a Hollywood?'

Sharon gave me one of those once. The positions she had me in on the table – let's just say I left my dignity at the door.

'I think I'm alright for the moment.' The truth is there's no point – me and John haven't had sex since the miscarriage. I've never felt closer to him, but at the same time I can't let him touch me like that. Not yet anyway. 'So how are you finding Dublin? Are you all settled in now?'

Her face falls. 'Did you know there's no Barry's Bootcamp here? Or even a SoulCycle?'

'I thought your building had a gym?'

'I wouldn't call two treadmills and a rowing machine a gym. I tried three Pilates studios in Ballsbridge and couldn't find a class with a single free spot. One of them didn't even open on Sunday.'

'Did you manage to get some exercise in the end?'

'Yeah, I joined a walking tour last weekend.'

'Oh, lovely.'

'It went to eight pubs.'

'Yeah, a lot of them do that. Did you do anything else?'

A cataclysmic change comes over her. 'I found that store you were always talking about – Penneys!'

'Which one did you go to? There are loads.'

'I think it's Mary Street?'

'Ooh, that's my favourite. It's a monster. Three storeys and a Scrumdiddly's. If there's ever a zombie apocalypse, that's where you'll find me.'

Her voice goes up a few octaves. 'It's everything you said it was and more! I even got my eyebrows done.'

Aubrey was well used to me complaining about how much I missed Penneys when we were in New York. It's hard to believe that there's no American equivalent. As much as I love Target, it doesn't come close. 'I knew you'd like it. Did you buy loads?'

'Too much. This sweater was only sixteen euro. Look, see this collar and these cuffs? They're just sewn into it. They're part of the sweater! It's so genius. I don't know why Michael Kors isn't doing them.'

'It's a shumper. I swear by them. You'll never look back, I promise you.'

'I also got the cutest Minnie Mouse pyjamas. And some new pantyhose and fluffy socks and lingerie for when Jeremy comes to visit.'

'Is he really coming over?'

'He's thinking about it. We're just trying to sort out dates.'

'What did you think of the homeware section?'

'It has a homeware section?! I was there for three hours and didn't see it.'

'It's downstairs.'

Her perfectly groomed eyebrows shoot up. 'I can't wait to go back.'

****

At lunchtime I take myself out to Stephen's Green for a walk, even though it's freezing. I just need to clear my head. There was a flurry of emails from New York just before I left, when Mandy must have woken up. She wants a suggested guest list for the Style Awards and some location ideas, but thankfully they can wait until this evening. The time difference is already coming in handy.

I'm wandering past the duck pond, which is actually overrun with slightly terrifying, burly seagulls, when I spot the first pregnant woman. She's waddling towards me, her long mustard coat stretched over a sizeable bump, talking animatedly on the phone. I catch a few words, something about haemorrhoids and not being able to sit down, as she passes me, and I wonder does she know how lucky she is.

The next one is carrying a blue bag from JoJo Maman Bébé. There's a man walking beside her with his arm thrown protectively over her shoulders. Her cheeks are flushed and she's gesticulating with one hand while the other rests on her full belly. They turn off towards a side gate before they reach me, and I can hear him laughing at whatever she was saying. My eyes sting with tears. That should have been me and John in a couple of months, going out buying tiny clothes and bath toys and getting really excited.

When I see the third one, holding on to a small child who's hurling bread at the seagulls, I decide to call it quits and go back to the office. I'm not made of steel. My phone rings as I'm just crossing onto Harcourt Street. It's Mammy.

'How are you getting on, love?'

'I'm alright. It's actually good to be back in work. Keeping me busy.'

'Now don't forget to take it easy, Aisling. You're not doing too much, are you?'

I know she means well but I can't take the fussing. You'd think I was working down a mine and not sitting behind a desk filling out spreadsheets. 'I am taking it easy, Mammy. I'm just out for some fresh air now. Dr Trevor said walking is fine. It's good for me, actually.'

'Well, he's right about that. Speaking of Trevor, he had an idea that I wanted to run past you.'

'Oh?' I don't know why, but I immediately feel on edge, even though Dr Trevor has been nothing but kind to me.

'He's had an idea for us all to go away together. On the Easter bank holiday.'

I pause for a second too long. That's only a month away. 'Us all?'

'Well, myself and yourself. And John, of course.'

Me and John and Mammy and Dr Trevor on holidays together. I just can't imagine it. But, oh, she's still talking.

'And Síomha and Cara and their two boyfriends. All eight of us.'

My heart sinks. The girls were so rude and cold to Mammy at Christmas. I wouldn't give them the time of day if I was her. She must be really into Dr Trevor to want to spend a whole weekend with them.

'Did you get the link to their podcast I sent you? Trevor says it does very well for them.'

I have no idea what the eight of us will find to talk about, but Dr Trevor has been so lovely, I haven't the energy to try and get out of it. 'No, I haven't listened yet. That sounds like a nice idea, Mammy. How do you feel about it?'

There's a tiny pause. 'I think it would be nice for the girls to get to know us. And it's Trevor's treat. It's a hotel in the west that he's very fond of. It has a spa. I've never been to a spa in my life. I'll have to go back to Geraldine for a new swimsuit. Do you even wear a swimsuit? Everyone's not running around naked, are they?' She sounds anxious.

'Ah, Mammy, don't be fretting. I'll be there to help you. And yes, you wear a swimsuit. We're not in Germany.'

I've only ever been to a spa twice, once for Róisín Flood's hen and another time when Majella got four numbers in the Lotto and brought me, Maeve, Denise and Dee to Monart for a weekend. That was the end of her winnings.

'Are you sure now, Aisling? I know it'll still be very soon after everything.'

'A hundred per cent. It'll be nice to have something to look forward to. I'll have to check the dates with John, but I'm pretty sure he's free.'

'Well, you can let me know in a day or two.'

I pull open the door of the building and step into the lift. 'I have to go now, Mammy. I'm back in the office.'

'Alright, love. Mind yourself now.'

I wish I felt as gung-ho about spending the weekend with Síomha and Cara as I've just let on. Truly, I'd rather have elective bunion surgery, but I can suck it up for her sake. The bunions aren't covered on my health insurance anyway.

CHAPTER 24

'**S**upport her head, Aisling! She's only eleven weeks old.'

Sadhbh has invited Ruby and Elaine over for a Friday night takeaway and wine. It feels a lot like old times, except there's an uninvited fifth presence in the room now.

'I don't think she likes me,' I yelp, holding down the Sphynx kitten who's desperately trying to escape my lap and coming dangerously close to ripping a chunk out of my forearm. Every part of her is angular and sharp, apart from two little patches of velvety hair on either side of her rump. She hasn't stopped hissing since they arrived.

Ruby turns to Elaine. 'She might be cold. Did you bring her pink blankie? That always calms her down.'

Elaine looks alarmed. 'Balls. Should I go back for it? I think I have her little fleece here somewhere.'

'Guys, you know it's only a cat, don't you?' Sadhbh can't hide her impatience. 'There's one outside happily living off chia seeds in my bin.'

Ruby and Elaine arrived twenty minutes ago and have spent the whole time laying out the cat bed, litter tray and all the toys and bits they claim are absolutely essential to little Marsha's comfort and happiness. The kitten leaps out of my arms and heads towards the kitchen. I'm a bit relieved, to be honest. She's not very cuddly. I know That Bloody Cat can be a pain in the hole, but at least she'd occasionally sit on your lap without drawing blood.

'Marsha is a she, Sadhbh, not an "it".' Elaine hasn't changed a bit – she's having none of Sadhbh's attitude. They've known each other since college and behave like sisters sometimes, stealing each other's tops and bickering over nothing. I would have said they were very similar, but Elaine's gone full cat mammy now, and Sadhbh is just not an animal person. Or a mammy person.

'Sorry.' Sadhbh is contrite as she tops up our wine.

'Oh, not too much for me, Sadhbhy,' Elaine says. 'She'll be up at six in the morning whinging to be let out.'

I catch Sadhbh rolling her eyes and try to defuse the situation. 'What made you want to get a hairless cat anyway?' The question has been bubbling up inside me since they walked in with her in a carrier on Ruby's back. She's one of the weirdest-looking animals I've ever seen, and I remember when Mad Tom had a pet stoat he used to keep in his coat pocket.

'What do you mean?' Elaine says tersely.

Feck. I try to backtrack. 'It's just that they're so unusual. I've never seen one in real life before, only on *Friends*.'

Ruby's face darkens. 'That episode has done untold damage to the Sphynx cat-owning community.'

Elaine pipes up. 'They are unusual, though. We had to go all the way to France to adopt her.'

Everyone turns to look at Marsha, who's sitting in the kitchen doorway glaring back at us.

'Yeah, she seems like she was worth the trip,' Sadhbh mutters.

This evening was supposed to be a relaxing catch-up, but it's been pretty tense so far, not helped by the fact that Sadhbh is milling into the Pinot Greej and our takeaway is running extremely late. I always thought the Japanese were meant to be punctual.

'Anyway, enough about Marsha,' Ruby says, settling back into the cushions on Sadhbh and Don's lovely couch. 'I feel like she's all we've talked about for the last two weeks. I actually wanted a puppy. Ha!'

Elaine leans forward in her armchair. 'How many times do I have to tell you? Lesbians owning a cat is not a cliché!'

'Can someone please tell my wife she's in denial?'

Sadhbh clears her throat dramatically. 'I think Don is going to break up with me.'

The words hang in the air. All three of us turn to the fireplace, where she's standing. Even Marsha has stopped licking her naked paws.

'What the hell, Sadhbh? Where did that come from?' Elaine is up off her chair in a flash, her hand on the small of Sadhbh's back, guiding her to the couch between me and Ruby. 'Sit down, sit down.'

I don't know what to say. She's been a bit withdrawn lately, but I had no idea a break-up was on the cards. Don is still in LA, but they talk every day. How could things between them be so bad she thinks he wants to end it?

'It's not his fault,' Sadhbh sniffs. 'I told him to do it.'

'Hang on a second, I'm confused,' Ruby says, reaching for the wine bottle. 'You told him to break up with you? Why the hell would you do that? You two are made for each other. I read that on Her.ie last week. There was a poll.'

Sadhbh takes a gulp of wine. I gently release the glass from her hand and put it on the coffee table. 'Easy on the lady petrol there, Sadhbhy.' If her sushi doesn't come soon, she's going to be on her ear.

'It's very simple.' She shrugs. 'He wants to have a baby and I don't. I just don't. I thought I was very clear about that from day one.' Then she turns to me. 'I'm sorry, Ais, I don't want to upset you.'

Then Elaine looks at me. 'Why would that upset you? You're not telling her to just have his baby to keep him happy, are you?'

'Jesus Christ, Aisling, are you for real?' Ruby is incredulous. 'Get a grip!'

Now it's Sadhbh's turn to backtrack. 'God, no, Ais would never. It's actually been so lovely having her here.' She squeezes my hand. 'I've been feeling so lonely. She has enough on her own plate.' Then she whispers, 'It's okay to tell them, isn't it?'

I nod, feeling a lump form in my throat. 'Of course.' We've seen each other through plenty of ups and downs over the years, not least the time I got us all into Berghain and then got off my face on Nurofen.

Sadhbh clears her throat. 'Aisling had a miscarriage a few weeks ago.'

Elaine gasps and immediately tries to hug me.

'I'm fine, I'm fine. Honestly. It happens to so many people all the time.'

Elaine looks horrified. 'You two are dealing with all this,

and you let us talk about our new cat for the past forty minutes?'

'Really and truly, we're mortified,' Ruby adds, shooting Elaine a you-and-your-bloody-cat look.

'I'm grand now, I swear,' I reassure them, not willing to go into the whole sad story. 'Let's focus on Sadhbh.'

'It's fine, I should have said something sooner.' Sadhbh sniffs. 'I just wanted to let you know where things are with me and Don. We tried seeing a counsellor on Zoom to figure it out, but there was a time delay, and between that and her asking us to hold space during the session for her cat that had recently died –'

'Oh God.' Ruby reaches for Marsha.

'– Don lost the head and said he wasn't doing the counselling again.'

'That doesn't sound like Don.'

'I know, but he's so stressed about the new album, I think it all just got to him. I love him and he loves me, but if he really wants a baby, I've told him it will have to be with someone else and to go ahead and pull the plug on us. It's not like he doesn't have girls in his DMs twenty-four hours a day.' She smiles. 'And I'm not just talking about Maj.'

'Jesus, Sadhbh, you poor thing. That's a lot to deal with.' Elaine turns to me now. 'And you too, a miscarriage. I'm so sorry, Aisling.'

I pick at the cuff of my hoodie. 'Thanks. But it's okay. It wasn't like it was planned or anything.'

'That doesn't make it any less hard, Ais.' Ruby's voice is so sweet it catches me off guard. Very out of character for her.

'Thanks. No, I know. I'm okay – I'm a bit worried about

John, though. He took it hard.' That's when I start to cry. More betrayal from my body.

'John? As in … John?' Elaine is reaching for the wine again and I don't blame her. It's a lot to take in. 'What's it got to do with him?'

I take a deep breath. 'He's Down Home. We're back together. The baby was his.'

'I'm sorry,' Ruby shouts, sitting up straighter. 'I'm really struggling to keep up here. You and John are a couple again?'

'They're BGB's own Jennifer Lopez and Ben Affleck.' Sadhbh laughs. 'He won't stop asking her to marry him.'

'And you're not saying yes?' Elaine is incredulous. 'That's not the Aisling I know.'

I flick my hair. 'What can I say? I've changed.' Then I reach for Sadhbh's hand. 'You and Don will sort things out, I know you will. I think you're right to be honest with him. Your body, your choice.'

The buzz of Sadhbh's doorbell app sends the cat flying under the coffee table, but no one pays her any notice. 'Finally,' Sadhbh says, heading out into the hallway, slightly wobbly in her Ugg slippers. Then she pops her head back into the room. 'And did you hear Majella is pregnant?'

'She's almost twelve weeks,' I add.

'I think we're going to need to open another bottle.' Elaine sighs, sinking back into the couch.

CHAPTER 25

I breathe a sigh of relief when I finally spot the sign for Castlefarrow House ahead on the left.

'Thank God, I thought we'd never get here,' John says, flicking on the indicator. We're fairly clocking up the mileage on the Micra between me going between Dublin and BGB a few times a week, and then John using it to bop around whenever I'm home. He's waiting until the gym is up and running before he buys his own set of wheels from Eamon Filan. That shouldn't be too long now, with the grand opening set for July. It's not nearly ready but he's confident three months is plenty of time to get everything finished and up to code. There was some initial animosity out of Mags from Zumba with Mags, but he convinced her to forsake her classes in the town hall for one of his new state-of-the-art studio spaces, and she had to admit her customers will be delighted to have access to showers and potable water, rather than a horrifically squeaky floor and condensation dripping down the walls. It won't be long till he's running a fitness empire, I tell him. There's already a waiting list for his HIIT classes.

Me, Sadhbh and Elaine or Ruby have had a couple of nights out and they really helped me start to feel like myself again. One of them was in a vegetarian restaurant – and you'd hardly miss the chicken at all, although it was very mushroom-heavy. We had another night in with Marsha the cat, and she took a fancy to Sadhbh and wrapped herself around her neck like a scarf. I've never seen a person so uncomfortable.

I flick off the stereo as John swings the car into a long, winding avenue. After the Rangers match, we listened to three episodes of *Blood and Bordeaux*, Síomha and Cara's podcast, on the four-hour journey from BGB. I'm not pushed on the concept – they drink wine and discuss famous murders – but the one about conspiracy theories was good. I sent it on to Majella for her commute. She still thinks Princess Diana's car crash was an inside job. She sent me back a thumbs-up picture, and with her cardigan open I swear I could already make out a little bump. She officially told the girls the news once she hit the twelve weeks, but it wasn't like everyone hadn't guessed the first time she turned down a drink in Maguire's. I've obviously already gone ahead and made a Majella's Baby Shower WhatsApp group, even though it's a bit early yet. I tried to suggest a Boho Baby or Vintage or even a Twinkle Twinkle Little Star theme but she's adamant she wants it to be *Magic Mike*. I'm hoping the planning will keep my mind off what was supposed to be my own due date.

Up ahead, Castlefarrow House comes into view. It's very *Downton Abbey*, but with a modern-looking glass extension to one side. John throws his arm over the back of my seat to reverse into a particularly tight parking space, and I feel that familiar tingling. We still haven't had sex, but I think I might be ready. Ever since our time in the Plaza, hotels really get me going. I can't even watch *Four in a Bed* any more.

'Like a glove,' I sigh, and he kisses me on the forehead while pulling up the handbrake.

'Is that Trevor's car over there?' He nods at a black Volvo to our right.

'I think so. Mammy said they were leaving early to beat the traffic.' I don't know what traffic she thought would be on the N7 at eight o'clock on a Saturday morning, but I said nothing. She's been up the walls worrying about this trip. All I want is for her to relax and have a good time, and for Síomha and Cara to be nice to her.

The foyer of the hotel is warm and inviting, with a polished marble fireplace on the right-hand side and a wide mahogany reception desk straight ahead. There's a round table in the centre with a massive flower arrangement and what looks to be a big bowl of something red and a stack of little glasses beside it. Very swish.

'It's complimentary for guests – I already asked.' Mammy is suddenly beside me in a cloud of perfume that I don't recognise.

'Hiya, Mammy, you look lovely.' She's wearing the new jeans with a pink blouse and her hair is freshly blow-dried. Then I cop what's on her feet. 'Are they my good boots?'

'You don't mind, do you, Aisling? You left them under the stairs, and sure you're not wearing them. I didn't have time to get the jeans taken up.'

I suddenly feel a bit scruffy in my dress, fleece-lined tights and loafers. I didn't even think to put heels on for our arrival, even though she told me several times it's a four-and-a-half-star hotel.

John gives a shy nod. 'You're looking well, Marian.' As if he doesn't see her at least four times a week.

'Help yourself to some fruit punch there, John – it's included,' she says, patting her hair. 'Trevor is just inside in the bar watching the end of the rugby. We're all checked in. Do you want to join us for a cup of tea?'

I catch John's eye. 'Er, no thanks, Mammy.' He gives me the faintest smile. 'We're a bit wrecked from the drive.'

'I'm the same myself, truth be told, but he won't miss the match,' she says, looking at her watch. 'It's just after four o'clock now, so we were thinking we could meet for dinner at seven?' She passes me a little paper key-card wallet. 'You're in room 212.'

'Great, thanks. Are the others here yet?' I'm only asking because I'm hoping to avoid them for as long as I can. I can't really be arsed making small talk for two days and two nights, and I'm pretty sure Síomha and Cara feel the same.

'Still on the way – Trevor was just talking to Cara. They stopped off to do some shopping.'

'Well, we'll see you back here at seven, so.'

'Now don't forget to take some of that punch with you.'

****

It's ten past seven when John and I are getting out of the lift. We ordered a bottle of prosecco to the room and one thing led to another and we ended up making good use of the four-poster bed. It was very romantic.

'I missed this,' he said afterwards, when I lay on his chest. 'So did I,' I told him, and I meant it. Our room has its own fireplace, and the bay window looks out over manicured gardens and beyond to the sea. If the thumping coming from next door was anything to go by, we're not the only ones who were enjoying some afternoon delight.

I spot Síomha and Cara as soon as we walk into the restaurant. They're sitting at a big table across from two dark-haired lads who look uncannily alike. I mean, it's almost spooky. No sign of Mammy or Dr Trevor, and there I was worried about getting in trouble for being late.

'Do you have a reservation this evening?' The dicky-bowed maître d' is nearly under my feet.

'We're with them.' I gesture over to where the others are sitting.

His face lights up. 'Ah, you're guests of the Byrne family. Such a pleasure to have you here at Castlefarrow.' He rustles up a stack of leather-bound menus. 'Please follow me, and do let me know if there's anything else you need this evening.'

Everyone at the table stops talking when the maître d' arrives with me and John in tow. 'And here you are,' he announces, depositing the stack of menus. 'I'll bring more bread.'

Cara stands up first and we awkwardly hug. She's wearing a gorgeous green velvet blazer. Mammy was right – they're a very stylish family. 'Aisling, hi. Nice to see you.'

'Hiya. Love the jacket.'

'Thanks, I just bought it in Kildare Village on the way. It was forty per cent off.'

Maybe we're not that different after all.

'This is Denis,' she continues, pointing to the lad opposite her. 'And that's his brother, Matt.'

'Hiya, lads.' I give the boyfriends a little wave. Síomha leans towards me and we sort of press cheeks while I want the ground to open up and swallow me. John steps up like a hero and is friendly as anything, kissing them on both cheeks. Double-cheek kisses are something he's seemingly embraced in his thirties, along with jalapeños on a pizza and an occasional espresso. My worldly man.

He breaks the ice with the boyfriends right away. 'So you two are brothers, did I hear that right?'

'We're actually twins,' Denis says.

John's eyes narrow and they dart between him and Matt for a second.

'Go on, you can say it,' Matt sighs.

'You're identical!'

I cannot believe Mammy didn't tell me that the sisters are going out with a set of twins. She knows I've had a fascination since I first started reading *Sweet Valley High*.

'So which one if you is evil, then?' John asks, pushing a bread roll onto my plate and spearing a curl of butter with his knife. 'Go on, one of you has to be.'

Síomha and Cara exchange a look, and for a horrible second I'm terrified they're going to storm out before we've even had a chance to order. But they both just burst out laughing.

'It's definitely Denis,' Cara says with conviction. 'He forgot our anniversary last year. Three years and not so much as a text.'

'Hang on a second,' Síomha says, holding up her hand. 'Matt is clearly the evil one.'

'Go on.' Denis is delighted that the heat has shifted. 'I might have some evidence to support this theory too. Aside from the fact he has my number saved in his phone under Organ Donor.'

Síomha folds her arms and looks at me. 'I let him take my Beetle to Carlingford for a stag and he wrote it off.'

'That was an honest accident, I swear!'

She turns to John. 'He forgot to put the handbrake on and it rolled off the pier and into the Irish Sea.'

'Yikes!'

'It wasn't my fault.'

'Tell them why you were too distracted to remember the handbrake.'

'I was trying to drive over a seagull,' Matt admits solemnly.

Síomha shakes her head. 'I told you, the actions of an evil twin.'

The two sisters and their twin boyfriends continue bickering over who's good and who's evil, and I feel myself start to relax. They actually seem kinda normal and sound. Maybe I was worrying about nothing. John squeezes my thigh under the table.

'You alright?' he whispers in my ear.

'Thanks for being at your most charming,' I whisper back. 'You're the dream buffer.'

'Any time. You can make it up to me upstairs later.'

Suddenly a hush falls over the table and I hear one of the girls groan, I don't know which, and mutter, 'I almost forgot why we were dragged here.'

When I look up, Mammy and Dr Trevor are making their way towards our table with a carrier bag full of Easter eggs, followed closely by the maître d'.

'Girls, you made it,' Dr Trevor bellows. 'Sorry to have kept you waiting.' Then he turns to me. 'Lovely to see you again, Aisling. Isn't the view just spectacular? I believe we're neighbours up on the second floor. '

CHAPTER 26

'John, I'm actually afraid they might be planning on murdering her. Think about it. They probably pick up loads of tips researching the podcast.'

'Okay, you have officially lost the plot. You're gone, Aisling. You're in another dimension.'

'I'm serious. I'm going to have to watch them like a hawk. Now, go on. Just a little fracture please.'

He ignores the poker I've just pulled out of the coal scuttle and am trying to pass to him. 'I'm not going to break your leg, so put that down and go!'

Dr Trevor has booked me, Mammy, Síomha and Cara into the spa for a private rasul treatment, whatever that is when it's at home, and I'm running out of ways to get out of it. Surely they wouldn't make me go with a broken bone.

Dinner last night ended up tense, despite John and the other two lads getting on like a house on fire. Once Mammy sat down, the sisters barely said a word to anyone other than each other, even though she tried to make conversation about the menu and the food and even their podcast. They were like a stone wall. I ended up overcompensating and talking a mile a minute about house prices and the war in Ukraine. At one stage I was reading Matthew Broderick's

Wikipedia page out loud for the table. John had to intervene. I was never so happy to see the bill coming. Poor Mammy was a bit shook-looking when we were saying goodnight, and Dr Trevor didn't look too thrilled either. I know he wants us all to be friends, but it has to be a two-way street.

'Go on, you're going to be late,' John says, pushing me towards the bedroom door. It's alright for him – he's going clay pigeon shooting with Dr Trevor, Denis and Matt. They get to bomb around the estate in golf buggies. I've already heard talk of bets and hip flasks of whiskey.

'Will you make sure and count those rifles when you're putting them back? And ask if they're kept under lock and key. I wouldn't want one of them falling into the wrong hands.'

'Go!' he roars and sends me out the door with a slap on the arse.

****

When the lift opens in the basement, I'm immediately self-conscious. I know the robe and slippers are meant to make you feel relaxed, but I'm always afraid I'm doing something wrong, like I'm too naked or not naked enough underneath. I'm still a few minutes early so I pop into the bathroom for a quick nervous piddle. I'm sitting in the cubicle with my new Speedo togs around my ankles when the door opens and a couple of people shuffle in.

'Aisling is alright, to be fair. I had no idea Ferris Bueller had a house in Donegal. We should go up and stalk SJP sometime.'

I know the voice. It's Síomha. What am I about to hear against my wishes? She's already said my name, so if I cough or make a noise now she'll only be embarrassed. My arse is rooted to the toilet seat.

'And John is such a sweetheart. I think Matt has a bit of a man crush.' That's Cara. I still think it's suspicious that they grew up in rural Kerry and don't have a hint of an accent. A definite red flag for notions.

The door of the cubicle next to me slams shut, and I hear a robe landing on the tiled floor with a thud. Then a tiny fart. 'Sorry!' It's Síomha laughing. And weeing. 'I just cannot be arsed with *her*,' she moans. 'How are they still together? I thought it would last three months max. Did you see the state of her boots yesterday? Dire.'

'Oh, they were hideous.'

My neck starts to redden. They must be talking about Mammy. And Carol Vorderman has those boots! The bolt of fury hits me so hard I stand up – and sit back down when I realise I can't really go anywhere unless I want to get into a confrontation. And I never want to get into a confrontation.

'Did you hear her wittering on about the food last night? You'd think she'd never heard of celeriac before,' Cara says, mashing the lid of one of the dispensers at the sink, probably the hand and body lotion. Voya. They have it attached to the wall, understandably.

'At least she's a bit nicer than the last one. The florist? I can't think of her name. Was it Madeleine? No, she was the one with the peanut allergy.'

'The florist was Bernie. She had a big thing for carnations. Rotten.'

The last one? That's a bit worrying. It sounds like Mammy isn't the first old lady Dr Trevor has romanced since his wife died. Is he some kind of love rat, like Darren Day or a premiership footballer?

'I think he's definitely more serious about Marian,' Cara continues. 'He's never brought any of the other ones to Castlefarrow, for starters ...'

'Do you not think that's weird, bringing her here?' Síomha says, now ripping out toilet roll sheet by sheet. Give me a full roll over this system any day, although I suppose it does save paper. The melting ice caps are never far from my mind.

'I think he's trying to show off,' Cara says.

'Stop, please. I do not want to think about Dad like that.' There's a pause. 'You're right, though. Why else would he make us come?'

'He obviously wants us to be a big happy-clappy family. Yeah, good luck with that, Dad.'

'I don't know how he can bear living in Ballygobbard. God, that village is a shithole.'

'Agreed. It's a kip. I have no idea how he sticks it either. Apart from the café, I suppose. Those sausage rolls are like crack.'

I take the briefest of seconds to silently acknowledge the praise for Carol's sausage rolls but I cannot believe what I'm hearing. BGB? A shithole? It got Highly Commended in the Good Windows section of last year's Tidy Towns competition! The €500 prize money was funnelled straight back into new bunting and a decorative flower bed. Shithole, my eye!

I accidentally let out an enraged squeak and cram my fist into my mouth.

'Cara?'

'Yeah?'

'Did you say something?' Síomha asks.

'Nope.' A pause. 'Balls, it's nearly five past. We better get this over with. Hurry up in there.'

There are the muffled sounds of a robe being re-tied from next door, then the flush of a toilet. 'He was only supposed to work there for a year and then retire back in Kerry where at least he has neighbours and family. But that's all gone out the window now because of *her*.'

The cubicle door opens and someone turns on a tap.

'Look, it mightn't last,' Cara says, a hopeful note in her voice. 'Something could happen. He was grand before she ever came along. I'm sure he'd be grand again eventually if she was gone.'

'Oh, absolutely. We just have to make him realise it,' Síomha replies glumly.

****

The four of us – me, Mammy, Síomha and Cara – are sitting in our togs in a tiny tiled room that's rapidly filling up with hot air. Katerina, the no-nonsense therapist, is telling us exactly what a rasul is while Mammy unsuccessfully tries to keep her glasses from steaming up.

'It's an ancient Arabian practice,' Katerina explains. 'This steam that you are feeling now coming from the ceiling will open up your pores. This is very good for your circulation. And your cellulite.' She slaps her own arse so hard that Mammy jumps.

'How long does this go on for?' Cara asks. She sounds bored already and we haven't even started yet. 'It's just I have a peel later.'

'The chamber is private but that is up to you,' Katerina says. 'It is booked for an hour.' Then she points to one of the two big gold bowls at her feet. 'Here we have salt from the Dead Sea. You can use it to exfoliate any dead skin on your bodies.' She sort of mimes rubbing her limbs. 'Once you've done that, you apply this.' She points to a bowl full of something that looks suspiciously like what Mammy's alpacas produce organically several times a day. 'It's mud. Very mineral rich. And very good for the delicate skin on your' – Katerina grabs her own bust – 'bosom! Take off your swimsuits and help each other, not forgetting those hard-to-reach places on your backs. You are family, yes?'

Síomha mutters something that I don't catch, and Cara elbows her. I shoot them a poisonous look.

Katerina continues, 'Afterwards you can shower outside and spend some time in the relaxation room. Don't forget to drink plenty of water to flush out those nasty toxins. Enjoy!'

With that she turns and leaves the chamber deathly silent except for the plinky-plonky spa music. The panic is etched on Mammy's face, even though her eyes are completely obscured by the steamed-up glasses.

'Sure, I'll go first,' I say, peeling my arse off the wet tiles and deliberately bumping into Síomha on my way to get the salt. 'Excuse me.'

She follows me, then Cara and then Mammy, self-consciously pulling at the neck of her new floral swimsuit. We all sit there in the steam rubbing salt into ourselves, and to be fair to Katerina, my skin does immediately start to feel smooth, although it agitates a patch of carpet burn on my knee. A little souvenir from me and John's carry-on upstairs yesterday afternoon.

Mammy clears her throat and breaks the silence. 'Trevor says you've been coming here since you were small – is that right, girls? And did they have all this here back then?'

Cara sighs, like answering her is exhausting. 'We used to stay for a fortnight every summer,' she says, scrubbing salt into her elbows.

'Castlefarrow is Dad's favourite place in the world,' she continues, bending down to rub the salt into her heels and between her toes. 'I'm pretty sure this is the first time he's been back since Mum died. Shoot,' she sits up and slaps her forehead theatrically, 'that reminds me, Sheev. We forgot to invite Uncle Donagh to Dad's birthday dinner. He'll go nuts.'

'I'll text him later,' Síomha says. 'We have loads of time. It's not till next month.'

'Are you planning a party for Trevor?' Mammy asks. 'That's a lovely thing to do. I'm sure he'll be thrilled. I can bake something if you like? He's a fan of my Black Forest gateau.'

Síomha gives her a side-eye. 'We're having it catered. And it's just going to be something intimate. Only his close friends and family from Down Home.'

'All of Dad's favourite people, basically,' Cara adds airily.

I feel Mammy stiffen beside me, and I can tell in my heart of hearts that there will be no invitation for her forthcoming. I can't believe the rudeness of these girls. It feels so pointed. What the hell did Mammy ever do to them other than make their widowed father happy in his old age? It's not easy to whip up a Black Forest gateau. I know that first-hand.

'It must have been hard to lose your mother at such a young age,' Mammy says charitably, clearly trying to move the chat away from the party. 'Your father showed me some pictures of her. You're all very alike. She was a beautiful woman. Very striking.'

'Of course it wasn't easy watching our mother die of cancer,' Síomha mutters.

Then Cara adds, 'And you know, Marian, it might seem like Dad is ready to move on, but he's definitely still not over it. He's certainly not ready to get into something serious, no matter what he might be telling you. We just don't want you to feel led on when he eventually moves back Down Home, which he always does.'

Mammy just stares at them, mouth slightly open, speechless.

Síomha continues in an equally patronising tone. 'That's where his life really is and, you know, the sooner he comes to his senses and realises that, the happier we'll all be, and we can stop this happy-families charade.'

I'd like to think the tide of anger had only been rising inside me since dinner last night, but truth be told, my emotions have been all over the place since the miscarriage. If that hadn't happened maybe I'd have kept my cool. But after overhearing them in the toilet and now this, it's too much. The absolute weapons. I stand up, walk calmly over to Katerina's second golden bowl, pick up two handfuls of mineral-rich mud from the Dead Sea and hurl them straight at Cara's and Síomha's faces.

CHAPTER 27

'**A**is, stop! I can't! What came over you, you mad bitch?'
The following weekend Majella is nearly under
the table in BallyGoBrunch when I'm telling her
about my rasul experience. Thankfully the first sausage bap
rush of the day has just died down, so the place is quiet, save
for Úna Hatton in the corner nursing a cappuccino with her
gratitude journal. I can hear the meat grinder going in the
kitchen, gearing up for lunchtime.

'I think I just saw red. And you know what, it felt really
good. Cara screamed like she'd been shot and Síomha started
crying. You'd think people who grew up in the country would
be okay with a bit of muck. Then Cara went for me, and
Mammy had to physically separate us.'

Majella grabs both my arm and the side of the table. 'Stop.
It. I wonder have they CCTV.'

'By that stage the floor was slippery as anything, so Cara
ended up on her arse. I skidded off to the showers then and
decided to skip the relaxation room, which nearly killed me.'

'Because of the free juice.'

'Exactly. And then me and John had bar food that night,
hiding from them, and we had breakfast in the room the
next morning and left Castlefarrow shortly after.'

'Go on, was the breakfast in bed any use?'

'Not a patch on the Plaza, anyway. My rashers were a bit cold, but it was worth it not to bump into those two wagons at the omelette station.'

'And was your mother just with them then for the rest of the time?'

'Well, the worst part was that I was the only one she gave out to in the spa, and she hasn't even so much as texted me since.'

'Oh my God, she's hardly taking their side?'

'I don't know. I've been mad busy because we're finally hiring staff so I've stayed in Dublin all week. I'll be going home after this to face the music.'

'Are you going to tell her what you heard in the jacks, about the other women?'

'I don't know. Maybe? I feel like she should know what she's getting into.'

'They sound well dodgy, those sisters. Did you listen to yesterday's episode of the podcast?'

'Majella, you traitor!'

'It's not my fault – my app just autoplayed it and I was driving. I can't get any more points or I'll be back listening to Tony Timoney singing showtunes every morning.'

'What were they talking about?'

She lowers her voice. 'A girl who murdered her stepmother. Cut the brakes of her jeep. The police had to call in her dentist to identify her remains.'

'Jesus, Majella. Do you think I should be worried?'

She flicks her wrist dismissively. 'It happened in Florida. I swear to God, they must be putting something in the water over there. They're another breed.'

'It's probably the humidity. It's not normal to live under those conditions.'

It feels so good and normal to be having tea and scones with Maj that I almost forget she's pregnant until she sits back in her seat and I notice the bump. You can't miss it now, and I hate myself for feeling a stab of jealousy. 'So enough about me, how are things going with you?'

'Oh, grand, grand,' she blusters. 'Not a bother. Up to my eyes with confession prep. Kids these days have no imagination when it comes to sins. I'm trying to tell them if they want a decent penance, they'll have to do better than' – she mimics a little voice – '"I said a bad word". Rob a few Skittles, you dry shite.'

'No, I mean, like, with the …' I gesture at her belly. 'The baby and everything.'

She folds her arms over her bump. 'Oh, all grand, thanks.' Then she swings around to look back at the counter. 'Do you fancy another scone? My one was a bit stingy. It's not like Carol to be tight with the cranberries.' She pulls a laminated menu out of the little holder between us on the table and studies it. 'Maybe I'll have a sausage roll, actually. Harissa and sage sounds good.'

'Majella?'

She doesn't look up. 'Yeah?'

I take a deep breath. 'I want to hear about the pregnancy. About the baby.'

She puts down the menu and finally meets my eye. 'Ah, it's all going grand. Nothing much to say there.'

'C'mon, Maj. I want to know.'

'But I don't want to upset you, Ais.' She says it so softly I only barely hear her.

'I know, and I really appreciate that. But I wouldn't ask if I wasn't able for it.' I plaster on what I hope is an excited smile. 'How far are you along now?'

Her eyes bore into mine. 'Are you sure you really want to know?'

Of course, I already do – our due dates were only a week apart. I still have them both circled on my desk calendar in work. 'I'm sure, I swear!'

She grins. 'Okay. Sixteen weeks, six days.' She rubs her bump happily. 'The size of a small turnip, although it's measuring a bit bigger. A medium turnip, maybe. Mammy says she's not surprised – I was nearly ten pounds myself and Shane was over eleven. She needed sixteen stitches and goes pale anytime anyone mentions it. I'm in for my big scan next month.'

'That's exciting. Are you going to find out the sex?'

'I don't know. I want to because I want to have a gender reveal, obviously, but Pablo says no. He's actually dead against it. Remember his Abuela Sofia from my hen?'

How could I forget. Trying to wrangle dozens of women in Tenerife, including several of Pablo's relatives who don't speak English, put years on me. I wouldn't mess with Abuela Sofia if my life depended on it. A formidable woman, and mad as a brush too.

'I got her into her "Abuela Up for It" T-shirt, didn't I?'

'Yeah, well she's very superstitious. And religious. She doesn't want us to find out the sex or even buy a buggy or anything before the baby gets here. And she's been in Pab's ear about it and now he's on the same page. But I want to get organised, like! The New Aldi is having their baby event next week. I have the catalogue and the bargains are stunning.'

'If you want to buy a few bits on the sly you can keep them in Mammy's. She won't mind.'

Her face lights up. 'Really?'

'Yeah, sure Paul's room is empty.'

'That'd be great, Ais. Just a little bath and some nappies.'

'So have you come up with any names yet?'

'Urgh.' She tops up our tea. 'Another bone of contention.'

'Go on.'

'I want something a bit different. Unusual. Like, I love Kinsley for a girl, after my mother.'

'Your mother's name is Liz.'

'Yeah, but, like, kin means family. My mother is my family? It's more of a nod than a carbon copy. I just like how it sounds. Anyway, Pablo's not a fan. He's insisting we call it something Canarian, or at the very least Spanish. He likes Ainhoa because it means Virgin Mary.'

'When was the last time he even went to mass?'

She thinks for a second. 'Christmas Eve, same as the rest of us.' She sighs. 'So anyway, that's where we are. We've downloaded an app called Kinder, which is like Tinder but for baby names. If we both swipe right on the same name it's a match. But we've been on it for weeks now and nothing. He doesn't even like Jaxon for a boy, which I love. I'm trying to see if I can get a "y" into it somewhere to make it more unique.'

Me and John never got as far as fighting about baby names, so I suppose that's something. 'I'm sure you'll find one you can agree on. There has to be something that ticks both your boxes.'

'Well, I'm not calling my baby Caconaymo if it's a boy, that's for sure. I don't even know if I'm saying it right.'

'What does that one mean?'

'"Son of Tenerife". I mean, would you be well? How's work going anyway?'

I fill her in on the new office, the latest client we snagged – influencer Suzanne Simmons – and all of Aubrey's recent Penneys purchases. 'I can't wait until we have an extra pair of hands. We've already had' – I flip over my phone to check my notifications – 'around thirty applicants for the job, so that's looking good. The next few weeks are going to be busy.'

Maj suddenly looks shifty. 'Listen, I don't want to be gossiping, but it's not true about Don and Sadhbh being on the rocks, is it?'

'Where did you hear that?'

'I'm a member of several Peigs message boards, Ais. The rumours I'm hearing are nuts. There's a TikTok going viral saying they haven't been photographed together in three months, but I refuse to believe it.'

I shake my head emphatically. I was getting a loan of Sadhbh's Dyson AirWrap on Tuesday night – she paid €500 for a hairdryer even though she still has that Mia Farrow crop, which is what I was going for the time I ended up with the Brenda Fricker – when I overheard her on the phone. Don's nearly finished in LA and is finally coming home. I could tell from her reaction that she's thrilled. I hope they manage to sort things out. 'He's been in America – how could they be photographed together? They're going through a rough patch but working on it. You know how mad they are about each other.'

'Don't remind me.' Majella sighs looking out the window wistfully.

'I'm actually going to get my own place, I think. I don't want to be under their feet when he's there.'

'Good luck with that one, bird. It's near impossible to get anywhere decent inside the M50 at the moment. One of the SNAs in work has been sleeping in the PE hall on the sly for a month now.'

'I was actually thinking of looking in BGB.'

'Seriously? Oh my God, that would be deadly, Ais.'

'I've been thinking about it for a while now. It's been so hard bouncing between houses. I'm sick of packing up my washbag every day. Me and John need to get our own place.'

Majella leans back in her seat. 'Why don't you give Dee Ruane a ring? See what she has on the books.'

'Way ahead of you. Say nothing to John, but I'm actually meeting her in Maguire's later. That's if Mammy doesn't kill me stone dead in the meantime.'

****

Mammy is hanging out sheets when I swing into the yard. It's still cold for April, but the sun is high and the sky is cloudless. I heard on the radio we're expected to get record temperatures again this summer. I'm still washing out my Müller Light pots before recycling them, but it does sometimes feel like I'm fighting a losing battle.

'Hiya,' I say, taking a white fitted sheet out of the basket at her feet and pegging it on to the line. 'Good drying it looks like?'

'I was wondering when you'd show up.' She's still in a huff, anyway.

'I texted you last night that I wouldn't be down until this afternoon.'

'Well, I didn't see it,' she says haughtily, even though I know right well she did because it has two blue ticks.

I decide to let her away with it. 'Sorry about that.'

'And is that all you're sorry for?'

I fold my arms indignantly. 'Mammy, I wasn't about to let them talk to you like that and not do anything! They crossed the line. I could see that you were upset.'

Mammy sighs. 'I don't think they really knew what they were saying. Cara in particular is carrying a lot of anger since her mother's death – Trevor explained it to me. She says things without thinking sometimes. She'd gotten herself very het up, and Síomha was going along with her. I shouldn't have mentioned Valerie at all.'

I can't believe what I'm hearing. 'Eh, my dad also died, and I've managed not to be a complete wagon to Dr Trevor. I can't believe you're letting them off the hook so easily and having a go at me!'

Mammy tuts like she's going for Olympic Gold in tutting. 'Well, I was mortified of the show you were making of me. Castlefarrow is a four and a half-star hotel. Trevor gets a Christmas card every year from the manager!'

'Can you not see I was only defending you?'

'I'm a grown woman – I can defend myself. You went too far. Some of those minerals got in Cara's eye. Síomha thought she might have a scratched cornea. What in God's name possessed you?'

'I had to do something! They were the same at dinner, being so obnoxious. I don't know which is worse. They're awful, the pair of them.'

'Excuse me, you had a puss on you at the dinner table yourself the previous night, if I recall correctly.'

Did I? 'No, I didn't.'

'You did so, when Síomha asked you to pass the tender-stem broccoli. You barely looked up at her.' She picks up a pillowcase and flaps it viciously to turn it right side out. 'Whether you girls like it or not, Trevor and I have become very fond of each other these past few months. It's not a big ask to expect you to be civil to one another.'

'And what about being civil to you?'

'I have sympathy for them, Aisling. They were very close to their mother. I never expected them to welcome me with open arms. It's going to take time. You need to understand that too.'

'But I was nice to their father from the minute I met him, wasn't I?'

'You're that bit older, Aisling. Can you not be the bigger person here? Please. For me. Just promise me that you'll try a bit harder, will you?'

I sigh. 'Fine! If it means that much to you.'

'Thank you. It does. And Trevor feels the same. And just so you know, he had a word with them too. He actually suggested you three should get together yourselves some time without us oldies cramping your style. He thinks we might be the problem.' She starts to look shifty. 'He was telling me they're big fans of young Don's band. What are they called again?'

I narrow my eyes. This is all sounding suspicious. 'The Peigs. What did you do, Mammy?'

'Nothing! I heard Ryan Tubridy on the radio talking about the new album.'

'It's gone straight in at number one. Isn't that brilliant? They were so stressed about it.'

'Oh, Cara and Síomha probably have it already bought.'

'What are you getting at, Mammy?'

'Well, I might have mentioned you could get them tickets to that concert you're going to next week.'

'Mammy! It's completely sold out. Sadhbh is already putting me and John and Majella and half of BGB on the guest list. I can't ask her for any more tickets! It's a health and safety issue.'

'Ah, Sadhbh wouldn't mind. I'll give you some lettuce and kale to bring up to her tomorrow. She'll be delighted with that.'

'So you expect me to just text Síomha and Cara out of the blue after what happened last weekend and ask them to come to the gig with me and a whole rake of people they don't know?'

'That would be perfect, thank you.' She beams. 'Otherwise, maybe another weekend away to sit down together and sort this out might be on the cards. And I don't think any of us wants to do that, do we?' She picks up the empty basket and jams it on her hip. 'Now, come on – I have some lovely chicken Kievs for dinner.'

CHAPTER 28

Aubrey and I have been interviewing for the junior executive position for nearly four hours, and there hasn't been one standout candidate among them. The number of no-shows? Three. And the number of duds? I've lost count. One girl kept her iPhone in her hand and started scrolling Instagram when I was telling her what the role involves. We urgently need to find someone, though, because the two of us have slipped into a dangerous stand-off over answering the phone. I'm officially Chief Operating Officer – Europe, so I'm hardly going to be the one to do it. And she claims that being 'acting receptionist' is nowhere in her job description, so she's flat out refusing too. If we keep letting calls go to voicemail we're going to start missing clients. Or worse, Mandy is going to notice and rip us to shreds when she visits at the end of the summer.

'I'm so hungry, can we please break for lunch?' Aubrey pleads after seeing out a twenty-four-year-old with a master's from Trinity who asked if his mother could sit in on the interview because he was nervous. 'I need my fix.'

She's been hooked on chicken fillet rolls since I persuaded her to skip Starbucks and try a local delicacy from the Centra across the road instead. I caught her sobbing after the first bite.

'Let's just get this one over with first,' I say, scanning the next CV on top of my pile. 'No real experience but has three summers in her uncle's B&B under her belt, doing a bit of everything. She signed off her cover letter with "keep slaying", so, you know, we'll see.'

The door goes and Aubrey buzzes her in.

I settle back and take a sip of water. Dee Ruane texted earlier to say she has news for me and she'll fill me in later at the Peigs gig. Síomha and Cara finally replied to my message and sort of reluctantly said they'd come, so I'm already a bit stressed about merging the groups. They'd better be on their best behaviour.

The office door swings open and a tall brunette with the most incredible head of waist-length curls strides in. She's wearing patchwork denim flares and a cropped purple cardigan with big pink buttons and has a tote bag with 'Dump Him' printed on it.

'Hey … Aisling?' She walks over to where me and Aubrey are squashed behind my desk, and I reach out to shake her hand. Good grip. Firm. No sweat. It wouldn't be me.

'Lovely to meet you, Hannah. This is Aubrey. Have a seat there. So, tell us, why would you like to work at Mandy Blumenthal Event Architects?'

Hannah tucks a strand of hair behind her ear and sits down. 'Um, because Mandy Blumenthal is an icon. I'm obsessed with her.'

I glance at Aubrey, who shrugs. None of the other interviewees could even pronounce Mandy's name properly, let alone knew who she was. Two of them kept saying Bloomingdale.

'So what have you heard?' I ask, flipping open my notebook.

'Only that she's in a league of her own when it comes to luxe events,' Hannah gushes. 'Her aesthetic always slaps. I mean, did you see the table settings for Bella Hadid's Thanksgiving dinner? I die.'

I picked out the china pattern myself. 'How do you know about that? It was a private event. All the guests had to surrender their phones.'

'Oh, I can always find pics when I want to. One of the chefs has a private Instagram, but I created a Finsta using a profiler from her second cousin's yearbook and, boom, I'm in. I'm the CEO of stalking when I need to be. So ...' Hannah's eyes flick around the room. 'Mandy isn't going to be here today?'

'Unfortunately not. But the successful candidate will of course get to meet her.'

'Oh my God, seriously?' Hannah looks ecstatic. 'I can get her to autograph my dissertation.' Her demeanour quickly changes. 'I mean, if I'm lucky enough.'

Aubrey's eyes narrow. 'You want Mandy to autograph what now?'

'My dissertation. The topic was the "Challenges of Fundraising Events Involving A- to C-List Clients". I used William J. McNamara's Fall Ball as my case study.'

I'm trying to conceal my surprise when the phone in front of us starts to ring. Aubrey immediately looks down and starts fiddling with her new fake jade bracelet. Penneys, four euro. I smile tightly at Hannah, who glances from me to the phone to Aubrey to the phone and back to me again. She looks a little confused. The phone continues to ring. And ring. And ring. And ring.

'Mandy Blumenthal Events, Hannah speaking. How can I help you?'

Aubrey's head snaps up and she looks straight over at me, her eyes wide.

'No, we're not a language school. I swear to you. Look, I've got to go. *Oui. Merci.*'

'Hannah,' I say as soon as she hangs up, 'can you start Monday?'

****

There must be hundreds of people milling around outside the 3Arena, but I spot the gang from BGB immediately because Majella is wearing the most Peigs merch I've ever seen in one place, and all of it is clearly unlicensed. Sadhbh is going to murder her.

'Here they are, Aubrey, come on. You remember John, don't you? And this is Sharon and Maeve, and that's Dee and Denise and Pablo there with the banner. What does it say, Pab?'

He passes it to Majella, who holds it above her head glee-fully. Three big words. It's. Yours. Don. And a massive arrow pointing straight down to her and her bump. He'll get a laugh out of that, for sure.

The girls say their hellos and do their hugs while John gathers me into his arms with a 'hey you' and kisses my hair. 'Nice to see you again, Aubrey. What do you think, is Dublin better than New York or what?'

'It is, yeah,' Aubrey scoffs, accepting a premixed tin of gin and tonic from Sharon. Then her face lights up.

'Oh my God, Aubs!' I laugh. 'You're assimilating.'

I check my phone. According to a text from Elaine, herself and Ruby are already upstairs in the VIP bar waiting for Sadhbh. I scan the crowd for Síomha and Cara. They said they'd be here at half seven and it's quarter to eight now. The night is not off to a great start.

'Lads, can we go inside?' Majella pleads, pulling her Peigs trucker hat down over her eyes and wrapping her Peigs scarf around her neck. 'I'm cold and sober and I want to make sure I have a good view of Don.'

'Just let me knock this one back, Maj!' Maeve shouts.

'I don't know how she has any left,' Majella hisses in my ear. 'She made me stop the minibus three times on the way up to widdle in the ditch.'

Dee Ruane squeezes in between us while John moves away to relieve Sharon of her last tin. 'Quick word, Ais?'

'Absolutely,' I say, making sure John is out of earshot. 'Tell me everything!'

'So you know Murt Kelly's mother's cottage that I was telling you about? The one just outside the village?'

'Yeah.' It's a tiny place, with two small windows on either side of a half-door. The back garden is massive, though.

'I've checked it out and it's actually in really good nick, considering it's been vacant for a few years. It could do with a bit of modernisation, but it's definitely liveable. Are you interested? The Kellys are thinking of renting it for a while before they decide if they're going to sell it or not. I have the keys. You can look at it at the weekend if you like? It won't be ready for a couple of months, but it'll be cheap.'

I glance over at John, who's rubbing Majella's upper arms vigorously to warm her up while Pablo re-rolls the banner. I've been seeing him less and feeling more in the way in Sadhbh's now that Don is home and they're having tense conversations about coffee and laundry and anything but the 'having kids' issue.

'I'll take it.'

Dee looks surprised. 'Without viewing it? Are you sure?'

'Certain. Don't let anyone else look at it and don't say anything to anyone either, will you?'

'My lips are sealed,' she says, miming doing the zip and throwing it away and nearly losing her gin in the process.

'That's it, I'm going in,' Majella roars, throwing her arms in the air. 'I'm not missing Don walking out on stage.'

Everyone starts getting their stuff together, but there's still no bloody sign of Síomha or Cara.

'Okay, you guys go on to the guest-list kiosk and get your wristbands. They're all under my name. You can go up and find Sadhbh, and I'll wait out here for the last few stragglers.'

John grabs my hand. 'I'll wait with you.'

'Are you sure you don't want to sample the VIP amenities? Ruby says there's three different kinds of chicken wings.'

'No way am I leaving you – I haven't seen you in two days,' he replies, pulling me in for a kiss.

'Good, because I have a surprise for you,' I say, tapping my nose.

As the others head off to get their sparkly gold wristbands, me and John find a bench to sit on. It's after eight now, so the plaza in front of the 3Arena is empty save for a few touts and a man selling T-shirts from inside his trench coat. The band is going to be on stage any minute.

'So what's the surprise?' John goes, taking my hand.

I stand up and face him square on, my pitch already in my head. 'I've decided I'm moving back to BGB and I'm moving into Murt Kelly's mother's cottage, and I think you should move in there with me.'

'Okay, whoa!' And then he laughs.

'I'm deadly serious. I miss you too much when we're not together. I think it's finally time for us to move in together.'

He jumps up and takes out his phone.

'What are you doing?' I laugh.

'Getting a taxi to BGB. Come on.'

'Now, it needs a bit of work, so we'll have to wait a while. It'll be summer before it's ready.'

'The summer?' He looks disappointed. Then he sits back down and pulls me with him and scrapes his stubble on my cheek. 'You big tease.'

'So you think it's a good idea?'

'I think it's the best idea you've had in years.'

A roar from inside the venue announces that The Peigs must be taking to the stage. I swear I can hear Majella screaming.

John stands up. 'C'mon, time to call it, Ais. You can't say you didn't try. I'm not missing "Pierce Brosnan" waiting for them. You know that's my favourite song.'

I let him pull me up and look back over my shoulder. 'Where the hell are they? They knew I was pulling strings to get them in tonight.'

'Come on, we can leave their tickets at the box office. Just text them and let them know.'

****

We make it into the front pit just as The Peigs finish their first song. I've never heard screaming like it. The gang are over to the left, and several young ones are trying to sneakily get a pic of Sadhbh. She's wearing a harness that I know she got in a sex shop on Camden Street, but over the frilly pink blouse it actually looks great. I'm wearing a new dress from Zara that I didn't think would suit me because, historically, shirt dresses and my boobs are not great bedfellows, but I do feel pretty great in it and won't mind if I get in the background of any pictures of Sadhbh and Don.

'Where are the evil stepsisters?' Majella roars as Don sings the opening lines of 'Homesick for Henry Street', one of the songs off their new album. She nearly brains a fan with her huge sign.

'No sign. Left the tickets for them.'

Majella looks shook. 'They've already missed two songs! Animals!'

The Peigs fly through their set, and it's incredible how many people in the 3Arena already know all the words to the new album. Pablo has to keep restraining Majella from trying to get on his shoulders. 'You are four and a half months with our baby, mi amor. Please keep your feet on the ground.'

I repeatedly check my phone for an update from Cara and Síomha, but it's not until the whole place is roaring along to 'Will You Meet Me Friend?' that I finally get a text from Cara.

'So sorry for the late notice, something has just come up. We won't make it after all.'

I show the screen to John and he rolls his eyes. 'Don't mind them. You just enjoy yourself.'

I shove my phone back in my bag, seething.

When Don is handed his acoustic guitar to play 'Bábóg Blues', I glance across at Sadhbh and then grab her hand when I see tears in her eyes. Don says this one's about missing her, but she's convinced it's about him missing his phantom baby. It's a beautiful song, and we're all in floods by the time he strums the last chords and blows her a kiss. I swear I hear a girl behind us hissing at her. It seems like way too soon when they go off for their pretend ending and then come back to finish with 'She's the Business' and 'Pierce Brosnan'. I squeeze John's hand so tight as we scream, 'God bless you, Pierce Brosnan, please God you'll return some day to Navaaaaan.'

****

We're able to slip backstage and out a side door to a minibus Don has arranged for us to bring us to the Clarence for the afterparty. There are lots of fans waiting outside the hotel, basically showing Don their knickers as he tries to go in. He's super polite and stops to sign things and take selfies, while Sadhbh barely notices and drags us inside after her so we can get some good seats. Truly she is the perfect level of cucumber-cool to deal with his rabid following – and Majella. Don seems relaxed when he finally joins us and pulls Sadhbh onto his knee. The whole band look wrecked, and I'm not surprised. They're touring the album for a month in the UK, then taking a few well-deserved months off before going back to the US for more gigs. Honestly, I don't know how they do it, but I am excited about them playing a tequila event in Vicar Street in October that me and Aubrey are already hard at work organising. Ben Dixon will be flying in from the new Bond movie set, and Daniel Craig's assistant's secretary has acknowledged the invite. If we can get Brosnan there it will be the hat trick. Majella has already asked if she can bring a four-week-old baby.

'I still can't believe those two little face-aches didn't come!' No amount of mocktails will get Maj over the Cara and Síomha snub.

'I know. I left them on read. That's the last time I do anything nice for them.'

She finishes her virgin raspberry fizz and gestures at Pablo to get her another one. He's flitting around her like a nervous moth. 'Have you and John any holidays booked? I need to get away before I'm not allowed to fly.'

'No. All his money is in the gym, and I'm just going to be hammering away at work all summer. Plus – this is exciting – Dee has the perfect place. Murt Kelly's cottage. I told her I'd take it.'

'No way! Is it not in bits, though? Mammy said there was a very cranky badger living in there last time Murt checked.' Murt Kelly is Majella's godfather and a bit of a cranky badger himself.

'They're doing it up. Dee reckons about three months until it's ready for finishing touches.'

'This *is* exciting!' She shoos away a clinger who tries to slip into the seat momentarily vacated by Don and Sadhbh. 'It's mad that you and John have never even lived together.'

'I know. I have a good feeling about it, though.'

'Will you stay with Sadhbh until then?'

'Ah, I'll be nomading around a bit between there and BGB. But Sadhbh and Don are going away for a month, so at least I won't be in the way too much.'

'The Maldives. Must be nice. I wonder will they get engaged.'

'As long as they stay together, I don't care what they do.'

CHAPTER 29

'Do you think Farrow and Ball are bitter about the paint-mixing machines?' I ask idly as I watch the hardware man strap a tin into his mega mix so we can copy Dead Salmon for our bathroom for a fraction of the cost. It's the perfect amount of pink, very muted, so I suppose Dead Salmon is a fair name for it. John finally picked it out, along with Omelette Surprise for the sitting room and Scent of Brown Paper for our bedroom. He also suggested a pale blue called On Porpoise for the kitchen, and I honestly couldn't tell if he was making up the name or not.

After months of renovations, we slept our first night in Kellys' cottage last night, our king-size bed the only piece of furniture in the whole place and the window left slightly open to the warm July night air and the sound of sheep squawking in the next field. We thought a sheet would be enough to keep us warm, but I woke up freezing in the middle of the night and John could only find bath towels, so he draped them on top of the sheet, and I just about climbed inside his skin. Denise Kelly says she sometimes feels like her toddler wants to climb back up inside her and I kind of get it.

The walls are freshly plastered, waiting for our Farrow and Ball knock-offs to be applied. We're not even paying for the paint – the Kellys might be selling the house down the line – but I couldn't in good conscience go back to them with a receipt for extortionate paint. The couch is coming next week, and I found an almost new fridge for a hundred quid on DoneDeal. Majella is flat out getting baby bits on DoneDeal and storing most of them at Mammy's. Pablo's superstitions are still not ready for a vibrating bouncer or a bottle steriliser.

John takes the paint tin from the man and swings it into the trolley with the others. 'What's next? Bathroom bits? His and hers towels?' He nudges me with his hip and I go pink immediately and feel a familiar spit of something in my throat. It's not shame exactly, or embarrassment. It's whatever the closest emotion to 'He's got me' is. I am more excited about us moving in together than I ever thought I could be. Even his joke proposals are starting to get me misty-eyed, and we've only been back together for six months. I suppose when you've known someone for ten years you've already ironed out the kinks. I nearly said yes when he interrupted me carefully applying my Dead Sea mud face mask in the bathroom in Sadhbh and Don's the other evening. Between the greyish mask and the leave-in Paloma Porter conditioner in my hair, I looked like Beetlejuice, but John still got down on one knee with a flourish and told me I was ravishing.

The Dead Sea mud mask is now packed up in a box along with all my stuff from my bedroom in Sadhbh's. Giving her and Don space couldn't have come at a better time. Since getting back from the Maldives, they've definitely been at each other more than I've ever seen before, and Sadhbh told me they're still not seeing eye to eye over the baby thing.

She says she's sad to see me go from the house but can tell I'm excited about the move.

'Do you think I'm a big sap being this happy about moving in with my boyfriend?' I asked her as I reefed the sheets off her guest bed.

'Eh, no! And don't you deserve happiness?' She was sitting with her back against the wall because I refused to let her help after allowing me – and John half the time – to stay in her house.

'I know, but me and John have been so on and off over the years. I know that can be a dose.'

'Ah, who cares what anyone thinks? And haven't you been through enough at this stage to deserve a happy ending?'

'God, I hope so.'

After the miscarriage I was worried I'd never look forward to anything ever again. I had been ruminating and worrying that I'd always have the disappointed and heartbroken feeling, but the prospect of moving into a new place with John gave me hope.

'We might have time to look at backsplash tiles in the morning if you're meeting Hannah late?' John's voice breaks into my daydream in the middle of the screws-and-nails aisle.

I groan. 'Don't remind me.'

Hannah is taking the lead on the event walk-through for the Paloma Porter Style Awards, so I'm meeting her at the hotel at eleven. The Silversprings is just off the M50, so it makes more sense to go from BGB rather than going to Dublin and doubling back on myself. Mandy was disgusted that we didn't get a more central venue, but when Aubrey backed me up that it actually made sense to use a hotel more accessible from all around the country, Mandy reluctantly agreed that it could go ahead. She even said the ballroom wasn't as sad as she was expecting from the pictures.

'Are you still afraid of Hannah?'

'I'm not afraid of her! I just think she could rein in the confidence a tiny bit. And stop sending emails like they're texts. Seven emails, one after the other, she sent on Friday. Like a stream of consciousness.'

John's eyes widen and he points at me in recognition. 'Seán Óg is the same. He called me a "boomer" the other day, and when I asked him what he meant I had to tell him I was born in 1989, not 1959. He was still pure horrified.'

Seán Óg is Titch Maguire's nephew and John's first hire for the gym. He's only twenty-two but has terrifyingly defined muscles and is developing his own range of protein powders for his TikTok following. Meanwhile, I've become self-conscious of what I wear around Hannah. Last week she was able to somehow sniff out that my new posh sleek black runners were actually made by Ecco and insisted on taking multiple photos and a video to make a TikTok about seeing 'Ecs' as they're supposed to be worn. Apparently, Eccos are the latest footwear Gen Z are appropriating as 'cool', but I suspect Hannah was not taking photos of my feet because she thinks I'm cool. I wasn't wearing the runners ironically. I just couldn't believe the arch support on a shoe that looks like something Amy Huberman might wear with a little pair of jeans and an effortless blouse.

'Is Hannah any use with the awards, at least?' John is straining up to look at hooks on a high shelf. I can't relax unless I know my tea-towel hooks are in place.

'She is, in fairness. She has great ideas for social media too. She's currently going viral on her TikTok with a nostalgia series about the ugly houses of the Celtic Tiger. So many chrome breakfast-bar stools. Of course, she's nearly too young to even remember the Celtic Tiger.'

John grimaces. 'That's not depressing at all.'

I give him a shove. 'Give over. You're having the time of your life in B&Q, old man.'

'Still, though, maybe I'll get Sharon to give me a mullet so I can stay down with the kids.' He does a little twirl and gets in the way of a proper old man and immediately goes puce.

'Speaking of Sharon, I need to ring her. What time is it? Ah feck, I'll do it tomorrow.'

Sharon's salon is nominated for four hairdressing awards, and it wasn't even anything to do with me. She got hundreds of nominations in through the website and I couldn't be prouder. I want to give her first choice of her table on Wednesday night.

****

John and I get chips on the way back to BGB, and I wash two of our new plates and glasses while he unloads the rest of our DIY bits. We were very keen to move in as soon as possible so said we'd do a lot of the finishing touches ourselves. We have a power shower and the bed, and the gas cooker is already installed so we're flying. Having the cooker and the original Aga feels extremely decadent and is worth sacrificing a full-size dishwasher for. The one we're getting is as dinky, but it's just for the two of us anyway. The only hitch so far has been

John's indecisiveness about things like paint colours and flooring options. His past few months' experience kitting out the gym has given him an inflated sense of interior-decorating knowledge. Honestly, you think you know someone until they're staring at Dead Salmon and Barely a Rose for two hours. It's a good thing I love him because otherwise not a jury in the land would convict me if I did a homicide over the 'Which grey tiles?' debacle.

We try to eat the chips sitting on the ground in the sitting room with a candle, but after two minutes I admit to him that what I thought seemed romantic is actually cold and uncomfortable, so we sit side by side on the bed instead.

'Are you finishing that battered sausage?' He pokes it with a chip.

'Yes, I am, actually. The end is the best part. I told you to get two.'

'Alright, alright. I was only asking.' He swipes two of my chips instead.

'What time are you in at in the morning?'

'I've an induction session with Mad Tom at eight. He insisted on taking off his top when he was booking in, and I actually think he has the potential to be a beast.'

'That's all we need, a superstrength Mad Tom.'

'How did your mother get on yesterday?'

Mammy was seeing Cara and Síomha for Matt and Denis's birthday lunch. I'm surprised they didn't invite John now that they're practically besties on Instagram. I had to get really cross with him after they all followed each other so they could talk about hurling and *It's Always Sunny in Philadelphia*. Sometimes I envy how low-maintenance men can be about things. Me and the sisters are basically mortal enemies, and John, Denis and Matt are simply oblivious. They're probably planning a minibreak to Berlin.

I'm still extremely put out that Cara and Síomha didn't show up for the Peigs gig back in April, but I'm trying to be mindful about Mammy's accusation that I wasn't being overly friendly to them either. She ended up going to Dr Trevor's birthday party in the end, when he just flat out invited her himself. She was nearly breaking out in hives with the nerves, and I had to hold back from texting the evil stepsisters to rip into them about stressing her out. In the end, she had a good time, and the girls were distracted with other people. The twins' birthday lunch will be just the six of them, though. I don't know why they're so obsessed with these constant celebratory meals. I'm surprised they don't all have ulcers from the stress and gout from the truffle fries. It seems to be a real thing for their family, though, whereas when I was growing up we went out for dinner about once a year, and it was to a Chinese restaurant called Joe Wong's, which was above the place Daddy got his tyres. Joe always gave us extra prawn crackers.

When I called in to Mammy last night, she had her arms around Dr Trevor in the kitchen and they sprang apart when I came in the back door. I didn't know where to look, so I pretended I was looking for something, anything, in the Important Drawer and didn't ask her about the lunch.

'She really loves him. It's the only explanation for putting up with those two.'

'Do you not think you'll have to make friends with them?'

I glare at him, furious and feeling attacked. 'They're the

ones who don't want to make friends with me. They mortified me not showing up to The Peigs. Those tickets were like gold dust! And I told you what I heard them saying about Mammy and BGB. They think they're it. And you should be on my side.'

John holds up his hands. 'Okay, I'm sorry, I really wasn't taking sides. I just think it might make it easier on your mother?'

'Well, I tried to with the Peigs tickets and they didn't show. And I'm not going to just sit back and let them make Mammy feel like shite for the next however many years or months. I'm not letting them away with being little bitches.'

'Is there another mud fight on the way then? Maybe some manure? Throw them in the slurry pit?'

'I mean, it is a legitimate way to murder someone. And I feel like I'd have a decent defence in court too. That's if they don't murder us first.'

'Are you finished?' John nods at my abandoned plate and the uneaten nub of battered sausage.

'Yes. I suppose so.'

He smiles and pops it into his mouth before lifting both plates and heading for the kitchen. When he comes back, I'm lying across the bed, bracing myself to go into my WhatsApps. Fifty-seven new messages in Majella's Babe Shower. She changed the 'baby' to 'babe' herself after I made her an admin in the group. She insisted on both being in the group and being an admin because, despite all my protestations, she says she doesn't think it's fair for me to do all the work on my own, and I know without her saying it that she's worried about me and all the baby stuff. I really am doing grand, though. Mostly grand. It pops into my mind a few times a day, but I try not to dwell. I don't bring it up with anyone, really, apart from John. It makes people uncomfortable, I think. Even John and I have stopped mentioning it much because it tends to make me sad.

I sigh and go into the WhatsApp group just as John returns to the bed and lies across me, belly down, winding me a bit but providing a delicious sensory calm. This must be what Sadhbh is on about with her weighted blanket. She's been on at me to get one, but I can't fathom either having to carry it out of a shop or paying to have it delivered.

'What's up?' He shifts himself slightly so he's not completely squashing me.

'The baby-shower WhatsApp. Fifty-seven. Oh no, wait, sixty new messages. Majella's aunt Shirley hasn't seen a single *Magic Mike* film so the girls are trying to fill her in. Her other aunt Carmel seems to be a big fan.'

John is silent for a minute, making space for the roaring sheep. 'Are you okay with all that stuff? The baby shower?'

My bottom lip wobbles a little bit. 'Ah, yeah.' My voice comes out weird. 'It's for Majella. I don't mind doing it.'

He rolls off me completely and scoots around so we're lying face up side by side. He takes my free hand in his and laces our fingers together. I rest the phone on my chest. 'You'd tell me if you were struggling with it, wouldn't you?' He squeezes my hand and I squeeze back.

'Yes.' We're quiet again and then a thought pops into my mind. 'John?'

'Yeah?'

'And you'll tell me if you're struggling with it?'

He's quiet for one, two, three seconds. 'Okay, yes, I will.'

CHAPTER 30

It's 2 a.m. by the time me, Aubrey and Hannah get to sit down for a debrief after the Paloma Porter Style Awards. I'm exhausted but thrilled. The evening was a huge success, with salons from the thirty-two counties well represented and the sponsor trending on Twitter all evening. One of the executives even flew in from LA to present the biggest award of the night – Stylist of the Future – and she was blown away with what we'd put together in such a short space of time, while also coming in well under budget. She told me she was very impressed with the valet at the Silversprings too, which was worrying because I'm a hundred per cent sure they don't have a valet here. I hope she gets her car back.

The style was off the charts and, according to Hannah, the social pics are doing numbers on all the usual online outlets' Facebook pages. It nearly kills Hannah to have to go on Facebook. She says she's betraying her Gen Z comrades and jokes about being radicalised into getting a curly blow-dry even though she already has curls for days. Speaking of blow-dries, a manager from a chain of blow-dry bars gave me her business card before she left – they're looking to launch a new crimper next year and they want us involved. I also had a very promising chat with a dry shampoo entrepreneur from

Leitrim who wants to enter the US market. She's using ingredients from the bog, which the Americans will go stone mad for. Mandy Blumenthal Event Architects Europe is officially on the scene!

Sharon took home gold for the county in the Best Perm (Short Back and Sides) category, which caused a bit of a stir among the local contingent. Catherine Cantillon from Dyed and Gone to Heaven in Knock ended up storming out of the ballroom and accidentally spilling a glass of red wine all over Colette Green's silver sequin dress from her new premium Colette G collection. According to Hannah, they're now feuding in Colette's Instagram comments, and Carmel's salon is up nearly five thousand followers with people tuning in for a gawk.

'The starters and mains were out on time, but the desserts were three minutes behind schedule,' Aubrey says, stuffing her headset into her new Penneys tote bag. 'I'll feed it back to the hotel manager tomorrow.'

God, I love her attention to detail. 'Thanks, Aubs. How do we think the 360-degree photobooth went down?'

'I had to literally drag one eyebrow influencer off the platform after her third go,' Hannah says. 'She'd brought a change of clothes.'

'There was a queue all night – it was brilliant.' Aubrey nods. 'And the tan-cam was a massive success – shoutout to you, Hannah.'

Hannah had created a stage and camera set-up especially for guests to show off close-ups of their fake tans. They could then share the pics online with all the relevant hashtags. This is above and beyond what the client expected, even if there were a few people who could have laid off the ultra-dark to avoid being problematic.

'Okay, I'm going to head now, guys.' Hannah stands up to leave. 'I've done nine hours' overtime tonight plus another hour's travel back to Dublin, which brings it up to ten, so I guess I'll see you at' – she consults the calculator on her Apple Watch – 'noon on Friday?'

The thing I've learned about twenty-one-year-olds in the two months since Hannah has been with us is that they're very big on boundaries.

Aubrey stifles a laugh. 'We have to send out the press release in the morning. And then we have a call with Mandy. You can't just not come in. Staying out late is part of the job.'

Hannah shrugs. 'I'm contracted to work from 9 a.m. until 5 p.m. If I'm not being paid an hourly overtime rate after that, well, I'm gonna take the time in lieu.'

Aubrey is getting cross now. 'Do you not care that it makes you look bad?'

'I work to live, not live to work. You should try it, Aubrey.'

'You'll never climb the corporate ladder with that attitude. Tell her, Aisling.'

'I'm thinking about pivoting into crypto next year anyway. The money is way better and I want to travel.'

Even though she's constantly calling me cheugy, I admire Hannah. I was always excellent at keeping track of my over-time at PensionsPlus, but even still I'm sure I did plenty that went unaccounted for. It probably added up to thousands of euros over the years. And for what? To be made redundant without a by-your-leave? 'Safe travels, Hannah, and thanks for all your help tonight. Text me when you get home.'

She blows us both a kiss. 'I'll bake you something yummy. See you Friday!'

****

The next afternoon I'm waiting for Mandy, two of the Joshes and Alexia to hop on our Zoom from New York when Josh C sends me a text. 'She met someone!!!'

'Who met someone?' I fire back.

'Mandy! She was at Ina Garten's Annual Oyster Shuck in Southampton yesterday and hooked up with some real-estate mogul. They left together and she's been offline since. The office is *funnn*.'

I can only imagine the giddiness. Mandy is never offline due to training herself to sleep no more than four hours a night. On the extremely rare occasion she took a personal day when I was there, there was always a vague air of hysteria in the building, like the last hour at work before you clock off for a holiday. For a minute, I feel a pang of homesickness for New York. As much as I love being home and settling in with John in our little cottage, I think I left a part of me there in the Big Apple. I also think I found another part of me. I hope it all cancels out.

I have to ask. 'Are you sure she's not dead?'

'She'll never die. Who'd do her funeral?'

It's a good point, so I tell Aubrey to head out for lunch and take the opportunity to check the Majella's Babe Shower WhatsApp. She's due on 23 September. We've finally nailed down a date of 24 August to suit all twenty-eight – and counting – shower attendees. Mandy's due to visit the second week in August to check out how the Irish operation is going, so it's going to be a hectic month.

As much as it would be lovely to invite the Tenerife cohort, Maj decided it was best for her blood pressure if Pablo's mam, Juana, his sisters, Maria and Paola, Abuela Sofia and all the assorted aunts and cousins waited until after the birth to descend on BGB. That hasn't stopped her inviting more guests closer to home. Three more teachers from her school have been added to the WhatsApp in the last week, and we've had to go through explaining the *Magic Mike* theme once again, and once again I've been reminded that my mother is also in this group. Majella is adamant she wants to dance to 'Pony' with a virgin margarita in her hand, even though the baby shower is three weeks away and she's already struggling to put on her own socks. Her ankles are the size of basketballs and Pablo is having to shave her legs for her, according to the voice note she left me at 6 a.m. She also nearly started crying over something called pregnancy nose, which I had to google and then FaceTime her the second I was in the office to check her face.

'Maj, your nose looks the same as always.' It definitely looks bigger. How is this a thing?

'You're just saying that. You have a perfect nose.'

My nose is one thing I've never much fretted over, so I accept the compliment silently but warmly. 'Maj, I googled pregnancy nose and some of them are absolute honkers. Like, the person is unrecognisable. You are still very much Maj.'

'Pablo wasn't able to lie to me when I asked him about it. I could see him going cross-eyed zooming in on my schnozz. I'm hideous.'

Hannah pushes her wheelie chair over to my desk to show me pregnancy-nose TikToks, each pregnant person more disfigured than the last.

'Maj, I think you should have a lie down, and I'm going to send you some TikToks to make you feel better. You're just hormonal, I'm sure. And overwhelmed. With an absolutely tiny nose.'

'Thanks, Ais. What would I do without you?'

'Promise me you're going to be excited for your baby shower? No more nose talk? And leave poor Pablo alone. He worships you.'

'He does, I know. He'll be ringing me from work shortly to sing to the baby.'

'Oh, that's fierce cute.' My voice catches unexpectedly.

'Ah, Ais, I'm sorr–'

'Don't be. Please, don't be. It's just very cute. I'll be updating the group with times and stuff later. Bye bye.'

****

Now, with some quiet time in the office, I start typing.

'Ladies, I've confirmed the time with the Mountrath for 24 August, so we'll be kicking off at 4 p.m. sharp.' Pregnant woman emoji. Present emoji. Champagne bottle emoji. Pony emoji.

Maj was hoping the Ard Rí, the fancier of the two BGB-adjacent hotels, would be able to accommodate her, but unfortunately it's booked solid until the New Year. According to Lisa Gleeson, there are people getting married on Mondays and Tuesdays now. I couldn't in good conscience do it myself; annual leave doesn't grow on trees. But each to their own.

Liz Moran is typing. As Majella's mam, if something doesn't work for her, I'll have to go back to the drawing board and find a new date. Maybe even a new venue.

'I have a hair appointment at 2. Will I be ready on time @Sharon???'

Sharon starts typing, but before she sends her reply Majella is straight in. 'Mammy, feck your hair! Aisling's organising a stripper!'

I've actually yet to find a male entertainer who has the authentic *Magic Mike* gear and can live up to the role, so I'm going to get Hannah on it tomorrow.

'You'll be grand, Liz, I'll have Cliodhna with me on the day and she's fast with the GHD when she needs to be.' Smiley emoji. Thank you, Sharon.

'4 p.m. seems late for a baby shower, but not your baby shower @Maj.' Cry-laughing emoji, berserk emoji. 'Works for me,' Maeve Hennessey adds.

'Me too.' That's Dee Ruane.

'And me, as long as I'm gone by 6,' Denise Kelly says. 'Liam has a work do.'

'We'll just be getting started at 6, bird.' Smiling devil face.

Majella might just be the only pregnant woman in history who wants her baby shower to still be raging by midnight.

CHAPTER 31

'**W**hat are you two whispering about?' Majella and Sharon are supposed to be folding napkins for the sausage roll station at B-Gym-B's grand opening.

'Nothing.' Majella says it too quickly and I look to Sharon.

'I was just asking Majella if I'll do those little balloons inside bigger balloons for the shower. Just so I'm doing something, like,' Sharon trails off.

'For the hundredth time, I'm grand to do the baby shower. Plus, it's in three weeks. I have all that organised. I have the decorations ordered. I have the tiny sandwiches ordered. I'll be asking everyone for baby pictures this week. I'll be photoshopping the little heads onto male-stripper bodies.' I actually have Hannah on the case for a lot of the decorations. I figure this can be a test case for the market going forward, and it would be good to familiarise ourselves with suppliers. Hannah is horrified by the very idea of baby showers and treated both Aubrey and I to a ten-minute rant about how getting married and having babies isn't an achievement and the continued celebration of patriarchal and heteronormative structures is what's wrong with the world. Aubrey was barely listening because her fiancé Jeremy is visiting in a couple of weeks, and she was spending her lunchtime planning the perfect Wild Atlantic Way road trip. She was almost fooled by the Ireland's Ancient East marketing campaign, but I convinced her that the west coast would probably give her more bang for her buck. I couldn't in good conscience have Jeremy in Kildare on his holidays.

I've taken the edge off Hannah's protests somewhat by having her investigate what's new and up-and-coming on the stripper/raunchy entertainment scene in Ireland. Maybe Majella's 'Babe Shower' idea could catch on with more grown-up fun for all involved. Hannah hasn't had any luck either in sourcing a stripper who will live up to Majella's *Magic Mike* standards, so I'm thinking of throwing a little curveball and sourcing the perfect palaeontologist costume for the entertainer instead. Before Shayne Ward, any of Westlife, Pablo or Don, Majella's first love was Dr Grant from *Jurassic Park*. I'd actually be surprised if Pablo hasn't already dressed up as him behind closed doors. My first film crush was Aladdin, but I don't think it would be culturally appropriate to get John into the trousers and little waistcoat, although he is wearing a little waistcoat this evening for the opening. I have a fierce weakness for men in waistcoats just on the cusp of being too small for them. Majella interrupts me as I'm gazing at him across the room, where he's cleaning footprints off his brand-new mats.

'I just don't want anything to upset you or overwork you.'

'Maj, you have to stop worrying about that. Can this be the last time we talk about it? I promise you, I'm so happy to do it and I'm dreaming up some surprises. And, sure, you're all over the WhatsApp.'

It's a blessing in one way having Majella in the group to police it, but at the same time the numbers have swelled even more, and we're now at thirty-nine. Úna Hatton cornered Majella in Filan's and said Niamh from Across the Road will be home visiting from New York that weekend, so Niamh has been added to the group, and Majella has already cut her off at the pass when she started inquiring about ethical balloons. Majella asked her if many ethical balloons fly past the window of the plane when she's crossing the Atlantic Ocean in her Airbus. More teachers from Majella's school are now coming, as well as Constance Swinford. Úna Hatton herself will be invited next.

'Well, isn't this the perfect little place?' Speak of the devil: Úna Hatton calls in the door of B-Gym-B and deposits her coat across the handlebars of an air bike. She makes a beeline for John and presses a bottle of bubbly into his hands, which is sound of her, I suppose. I almost make an escape into the shower room just before she catches me, but she's impossible to dodge.

'Is your mother not here yet, Aisling? I was hoping to catch her before I have to fly off again. One of my poems has come first in the Knocknamanagh Literary Club's writing competition and I'm receiving my prize at a ceremony this evening. Don is outside right now in the Prius.' With that, her husband appears at the door, holding an envelope.

Úna shrieks. 'The card! I forgot the card. It's actually one of my own watercolours. I found a website that turns them into cards for you, so I'm sending out all my own work for all occasions. Niamh thinks she could get them into some stores in NYC.'

Niamh is an out-and-out dose, but I do forget sometimes that she has to humour Úna like the rest of us.

'Mammy has a big group checking into the yurts, Úna, so she and Constance will be down later.'

Úna shakes her head. 'Your mother works too hard for a woman of her age. I'm five years younger and have been able to devote myself to my arts and passions.'

I know for a fact that Mammy and Úna Hatton are exactly the same age because for Úna's sixtieth Niamh sent an ethical balloon arrangement and it was left outside the front door for a whole day. Rumour has it Úna abused her position as the choir leader at her Protestant church and made them sing 'Happy Birthday' to her three years in a row, claiming to be turning fifty-nine.

'I think the eco farm is one of Mammy's passions, in fairness,' I say, somewhat bristly, as Úna's husband intervenes to remind her they're in a rush.

'She won first runner-up in her poetry competition. Lovely composition about her flower beds.'

Úna grabs him by the arm and drags him to the door, calling over her shoulder, 'It's basically joint first. Congrats on your little gym, John. You're a great boy. My Niamh –'

The door closes behind her before we hear what her Niamh might have to say or do to John, who looks stressed as he waves Úna off.

I go over and hug him around the waist. 'Are you alright?'

'Yeah, just wondering will people show up. Will enough people sign up. Úna kept calling it a "brave little venture". I've all my savings put into it now.'

I hug him tighter. 'Loads of people are going to show up. Sadhbh and Don are on the way and Elaine is with them.

Majella has most of the baby-shower WhatsApp bullied into it. Sumira Singh is making three different kinds of high-protein samosas. And so many people have signed up already. I've had Dee Ruane on to me complaining that she can't get into a spinning class.'

'I've only five bikes, in fairness.'

'Yeah, and you'll get more. You'll be brilliant.' I go up on my tippytoes to meet his lips. 'I'm very proud of you.' His eyes go kind of glassy and I get a fright.

He blinks it away, though, and smiles at me before nodding at the door. 'Here's your mother. And Constance. And Mad Tom.'

****

Thirty minutes later, and there are so many people in the gym we've had to open the front and back doors to let the air flow through. Air-conditioning wasn't a top priority in the budget, but to be fair, B-Gym-B isn't supposed to hold the entire population of a small town. Constance Swinford is holding court by the sausage rolls, her regal grey curls bobbing up and down as she lectures Majella's mother and father on the particulars of breeding Afghan hounds. Given that the only dog the Morans have ever had is Willy the Jack Russell, I don't know what they'd be doing with hound-breeding knowledge, but Constance is, as ever, hard to ignore. She's the only person I've ever known to wear a wax jacket in the height of summer.

Despite her early declaration of civil war, Mags from Zumba with Mags is now a complete convert to the gym.

She's in a corner with John discussing the music system and demonstrating some borderline lewd hip thrusts. Mad Tom's cut-off T-shirt has caused quite the stir. He's cut off not only the arms but also turned it into a crop top. He's already one of the gym's most devoted members and is obviously proud of his progress so far – if you squint you can make out at least one ab. His girlfriend, Rocky, showed up on a motorbike with a sidecar, and while I haven't yet witnessed it myself, I believe Mad Tom is quite the willing passenger. They seem besotted with each other. She keeps touching his ab with one hand and eating sausage rolls with the other.

Sadhbh, Don and Elaine are outside while Elaine puffs away on her vape. I haven't had time to talk to Sadhbh yet, but she and Don seem to be getting on okay. When I spoke to her on the phone the other night she said he's eased off on the baby issue, so hopefully they'll be able to move forward. Speaking of babies, Denise and Liam have brought their two with them to the opening, and the smaller one has been trying to climb up on anything within her reach. At one stage, John had to pry her tiny fingers off the weights rack and I felt my heart break a little bit.

Mammy and Dr Trevor are talking to Tessie Daly, and by the way Tessie's arms are going I can tell it's flower-box related. The Tidy Towns committee are at an impasse about replacing the half-barrels that have been holding daffodils and busy Lizzies for the past fifteen years. They're due an upgrade but Tessie can be very resistant to change. She refused to take euros in the charity shop until 2005. Majella and Pablo are in a world of their own, him with his hand on her bump and is he …? Yes, he's singing to her. He stops every few seconds and lets her smell his glass of white wine. Seán Óg is in John's office, welcoming in anyone who wants to sign up for the free trial or take the plunge and go for the full year, and there's a steady stream going into him. I'm just about to see if he needs anything when there's a touch at my elbow. It's Dr Trevor.

'Aisling, could I grab you for a minute?'

We sit on the spare breeze blocks stacked outside the back door beside the bins and wooden pallets that once held Seán Óg's protein powders, now displayed proudly beside the water fountain inside. Dr Trevor is smiling but looks nervous. He fiddles with the bottom of his wine glass.

I break the mild tension. 'So how are things? Who's dying?'

He looks a little shocked. 'Well, I can't be telling –'

'Oh God, I know! I was only messing. And hopefully nobody's dying.'

'Nobody right this minute, anyway.'

We laugh awkwardly. Ever since my miscarriage, Dr Trevor has been so lovely and kind to me, but I haven't really been on my own with him. Maybe he just wants to check in. I have an awful feeling this might be about Cara and Síomha, though. It's like a huge elephant in the room anytime I see him and Mammy together.

'So how have you been, Aisling? You've been feeling okay, I hope?'

Just checking in. Phew. 'Yeah, I'm doing grand, actually. Time heals and all that.'

'Good, good. It would be very normal to have all kinds of reactions and feelings – just know that.'

'Oh, I do, yeah. I have the odd wobble but I'm mostly grand. My granny used to have a tea towel that said "What's for you won't pass you" on it, so I've been keeping that in my head a good bit.'

'And John? How is he doing?'

'Yeah, okay, I think. We both got a land and I think he was really shook, but we've been made even stronger, I think.' I feel my cheeks go pink. 'Is that really sappy?'

'Not at all, not at all.' He has a voice that wouldn't be out of place on one of those mid-morning radio shows introducing Glen Campbell or Paul Brady songs. No real accent, but somehow posh and rural at the same time. Kind of Constance-lite. 'I might get a bit "sappy" on you, actually, if you don't mind?' He drains the end of his wine and I wonder does he know people are lying to him in his GP's surgery when he asks them how many units they drink a week. Sure, you'd drink your weekly allowance just doing your make-up before you go out.

He opens his mouth to speak but is interrupted by John stepping out the back door. 'Oh, sorry, I didn't know ye were out here.'

He goes to go back in but Dr Trevor stops him. 'No, no, John, please join us. I'm sure you need a breather.'

John nods and sits down gratefully on some blocks, sipping from a glass of white wine.

'I could actually do with talking to both of you.' A tiny shiver runs down my spine as Dr Trevor speaks. 'Has Marian said anything to you, Aisling, about Cara and Síomha?'

I freeze. I don't want to throw Mammy under the bus, but I don't want to miss an opportunity to point out how nasty they've been. 'Em, she *has* been a bit worried about it, I think. Like, it's been a bit awkward? She said you talked about what happened at Castlefarrow?'

He nods, and I'm so glad he's acknowledging it. 'We did, and I agree it's not ideal. I spoke to the girls about their behaviour. I know Marian's worried, and I've been doing my best to smooth things over. But I might need your help.'

I swear to God, if he asks me to take them to another Peigs gig.

John interjects. 'Aisling's tried her best with them, in fairness. The girls haven't made it easy.'

'I know they haven't, and maybe that's partly my fault. I've introduced them to a few new friends of mine over the years, I can't deny that. And they've stood by me for the most part when things haven't worked out. The thing is, peculiarly, that I think they realise that I'm really serious about your mother. And they're afraid that means big changes.'

He's looking at me for a reaction, so I just nod. When Daddy died and I had to finally grow up fully, I realised that parents have lives and loves and losses of their own. That they had lives before their children and want lives after them too. It suddenly dawns on me that Cara and Síomha are probably struggling to come to that same realisation, and I feel a pang of empathy.

'I wonder would you give the girls another chance? Maybe get together with them? See if you can be friends? For your mother?'

I feel my jaw tighten. This feels a little bit like emotional blackmail, but at the same time if Dr Trevor isn't going anywhere, then what choice do I have?

'John, you and the boys are already good pals, I understand? Maybe we could build on that?'

John shoots me a look quickly and clears his throat. 'Eh, yeah, I mean, whatever Aisling wants, but I get on great with the lads. Happy to help if I can.'

Dr Trevor smiles gratefully. 'I appreciate it, John. And you too, Aisling.'

He stands up and raises his glass. 'Time for a top-up. And maybe a gym membership.'

'Hah, tell Seán Óg to give you the family rate.' John chuckles awkwardly, before turning back to me and slapping his hand over his mouth. 'Sorry,' he muffles. 'I don't know why I said that.'

I bring him in for a hug in between my legs and he rests his chin on my head as I look down at my feet. I need to get my toenails done. Cara and Síomha wouldn't be caught dead with chipped toenails. Then, a spark of inspiration. 'I can't believe I'm saying this, but I could invite Cara and Síomha to the baby shower. Maj wouldn't mind. She'd invite the whole country if she could.'

John steps back. 'That would be sound of you.'

'And you could bring Matt and Denis on Pablo's, what are you calling it?'

'Dadchelor party. He got the idea from the DadsToBe hashtag on Instagram.'

John and a few of the lads are bringing Pablo out on the same day as Majella's do. They were thinking go-karting or paintball and then some drinks, but Pablo has requested a shopping trip for 'dad clothes' followed by karaoke in Maguire's. Nobody has been able to deduce what he means by 'dad clothes' but the boys are bringing him to Dublin nonetheless.

'Yeah, no problem at all – we could meet them in town.'

'Pablo won't mind, will he?'

'He'll probably start crying at having more friends. He's already in bits because he gets a new best friend when the baby is born.'

The silence hangs between us after John says that and I swallow a lump in my throat. He holds out his hand and I follow him back inside.

****

The gym's music system is playing a Bell X1 album for a third time when I fill Sadhbh in about Dr Trevor's chat. Don abandoned the idea of driving back to Dublin hours ago. Mammy said she has a yurt for them. Don and John are idly lifting weights with one hand and cans with the other. Me and Sadhbh are sitting against a pile of mats, and Elaine is on an exercise bike scrolling through pictures of the cat. I can't believe Ruby stayed at home to keep it company. A cat, like! Mad Tom and Rocky are slow dancing near the front door. She offered us some magic mushrooms earlier, and while Sadhbh chewed down a handful I said no thanks. I have a fear of going off my nut and sawing off my foot or something. Sadhbh just laughed like a maniac for twenty minutes and then returned to normal. Knowing my luck, I'd be found on O'Connell Bridge in the nip.

'It's very generous to ask them to the shower. Will Maj behave?'

'I asked her earlier, and she said it was totally fine to invite them, and she promises she won't roast them or try to poison them, even though it will be difficult for her. She's just happy to get two more presents.'

'I wonder is Dr Trevor gearing up to propose or something?' Sadhbh muses, giving me a fright.

'No, hardly! That would be so weird. They're only together a wet weekend.'

'I know, but older people are better at knowing what they want. God, he'd be your stepdad. I have a stepdad but I don't know him at all.'

Sadhbh is not close with her mother – or any of her family, really. She calls me and Elaine and Ruby and Don her 'chosen family', which I think is lovely, but I wonder is it lonely for her sometimes. She says it's fewer people to worry about or feel obliged to, which is a good thing, I suppose.

'Then they'd be your evil stepsisters. I spent an hour on their Instagrams in the car down. Obsessed. How do they get their hair so shiny? And the podcast! It does really well!'

'I know. Majella confessed that she was addicted to it. She's agreed to a self-imposed ban going forward as an act of solidarity.'

'She's so cute with the bump.'

'I know.' I don't mean to leave a silence there but I do.

And then Sadhbh has to ask. 'Are you sure you don't m–?'

'I'm sure. I'm so happy to be doing it for her.'

'I know you are.'

'And, like, I'm thrilled for Maj. So it's not hard seeing her or whatever. I do think about the fact that we'd be kind of going through it together at the same rate, though. Like, doing milestones together. So that's hard sometimes. But I really don't think too much any more about what the baby might have been like or anything, which I'm glad about. That makes it way easier. Did you ever do that?'

'Like, very briefly. But I was so sure about the abortion that I didn't dwell on it either. It must be torturous to find yourself doing that.'

I look over to where Don and John are deep in conversation, the weights forgotten. 'How are things with you and Don? Any more baby chat?'

'Some. But I think I've finally gotten through to him that a mini Don and Sadhbh combo is not going to happen. I get more solid about not having kids with each day that passes. I just don't have any yearning for it at all. Like, I don't even understand the yearning. Is that weird?'

'No? I don't know? I've always had a bit of yearning, although I never really thought about it properly until I was pregnant. I was always just thinking, "Oh, it's just what you do, you have children." Now I've had to actually think about raising one.'

'And?'

'Yeah, I think I'd like it.' My eyes tear up and Sadhbh grabs at my hand.

'And you'll be brilliant at it.'

****

Later in bed, I'm just drifting off when John says softly, 'Aisling?'

His voice sounds strangely choked and I turn towards him quickly. 'What's wrong? Are you crying?' I touch his face just under his eye and it's wet. I grab him and hold him as tight as I can. 'What's wrong?'

'I said I'd tell you if I was struggling. I'm struggling.'

I gather him even tighter. 'I'm sorry. I'm so sorry you're struggling. I'm so sorry.'

He laughs a bit, in spite of himself. 'I feel stupid. I'm the one who should be comforting you.'

'Don't be silly – there's two of us in it. What can I do to help?'

'Maybe I should talk to someone. A counsellor, like, or something. I was talking to Don about it.'

Is there anything Don Shields isn't good at? Music. Being sound. Being a ride. Looking after his mental health.

'I think that's a great idea.'

'Yeah, Don was saying he's been working through the idea of not having kids, which is kind of a loss in itself, in a way.'

'Is the person Don is seeing good? Although it would probably be weird to go to the same therapist.'

'Oh, Don isn't going to anyone, I don't think.'

'I thought it was Don's idea?'

'No, it was mine. He said he might do it too, though.'

I take his head in my hands and kiss him all over his face where his tears were. Don who?

'It can't hurt anyway, can it?' John says as we settle back down.

'As long as you don't start leaving crystals around the place like Pablo.'

'Talk about a madman.'

I think I'm laughing as I fall asleep.

CHAPTER 32

'Hi gals, can we all welcome Cara and Síomha to the group? They'll be joining us on the twenty-fourth.' Two girls dancing emoji. Firework emoji. Baby emoji.

I had sent them polite texts saying Maj and I would be delighted if they'd join us for the shower, seeing as Matt and Denis are invited to Pablo's do. Dr Trevor had obviously been on to them because they immediately and civilly consented to being added to the WhatsApp group.

Maj is straight in with the over-the-top welcomes. 'Delighted you're joining us, gals. It's *Magic Mike*-themed but you can wear what you want and please don't be getting any presents, but if you can't resist, we love a voucher.'

'Majella Moran!'

'Ah, Mammy you're the one who told me to ask for vouchers.'

'Welcome, Cara and Síomha. If you want to chat presents you can message me privately.' Thank God for Dee Ruane taking on the responsibility of the present. She's going to get money from anyone who wants to go in on a big Dunnes voucher and is going to buy Majella a pair of shoes that she's been coveting from River Island but won't fit over her pregnancy cankles. She can look forward to wearing them once she's had the baby and is exploring her new life as a loolah mam on the lash.

'Has anyone finished the *Crawdads* yet? I'm finding it slow going.'

'I flew through it, Amanda. I'm onto the new Marian Keyes now. Have ye any book recommendations, Cara or Síomha?'

The group has slightly spiralled out of control. It's evolved into part book club, part TV reviews, part make-up recommendations and part Don Shields fanfic. I swear half of them forget that his literal girlfriend is a member. Denise sent in a pic of Don on stage the other day and said she could imagine what his sweat smells like. She deleted it ten minutes later, but we'd all seen it and she's been lurking ever since – mortified, no doubt.

Cara and Síomha don't immediately respond to the request for book recommendations, and I tell myself to chill out about it. I'm worried about them thinking the group is a pain, but I'm also worried about them being pains in the group. I'm sure they'll just mute it if it's too much, especially if Aubrey goes on another one of her 'things that are amazing about Ireland' monologues. We get it, Aubrey, you went to Kilkenny for a weekend and touched a castle. It was nice of Majella to invite her, though. Which reminds me, I must add Hannah to the group. She's now integral to the running of half the shower. Oh, wait now! Cara is typing!

'I actually just read an amazing biography of the Yorkshire Ripper, if anyone is into true crime?'

Several people are typing.

'Love it.'

'Beat into it.'

'I listen to murder podcasts before I go to sleep and then have nightmares.'

'Cara and I actually present a podcast, *Blood and Bordeaux*, in case anyone's listened?' Síomha is straight in with the self-promotion.

'Oh my God, that's ye? I love that podcast. I love the "Irish Eyepoppers" bit. Who knew there were so many mysterious happenings in Roscommon?' Alright, Denise, you turncoat.

'That's about all that's happening in Roscommon.' Cry-laughing emoji. Cry-laughing emoji. Cry-laughing emoji.

'And that Lidl Malbec ye had the other week was savage.'

'It's a very popular podcast, I hear.' Ah God, that's Mammy. She told me she has the whole chat muted because she just couldn't keep up the day Majella and Elaine were discussing Mormon baby names, but I suppose she's all over it now that Cara and Síomha have been inducted.

'The whole true crime fascination is a little troubling for me. Like, making entertainment out of horrific deaths? No thanks.'

You can always trust Ruby to put everyone in their place. There's a lull after she posts and I start imagining Cara and Síomha side-texting each other about what a bitch she is. Luckily, Maj gets things back on track with a straw poll on fake tanning before the birth. She says she just feels like a more complete person with a layer of medium bronze on her legs. There's bit of debate – 'Go for it girl' from Dee Ruane and 'I'll do a sprayer for you' from Sharon, while Elaine warns Maj that she doesn't have to emulate celebrities with their 'perfect' post-birth selfies.

'Fuck the selfies, I just don't want the child's first thought to be that they're inheriting my blue milk-bottle legs.'

'With any luck, the baby will favour Pablo.' Sun emoji. Sun emoji. Sun emoji.

'Oh well, that's just lovely, Mammy.'

'The Morans have lovely skin!'

'Leave her alone, Liz!' I knew Majella's aunties wouldn't stand for that.

'My sister met a Spanish man on a passage to India and they had the most divine babies. Rupert and Estrella.'

This is Constance's first contribution to the group and why am I not surprised there's a mention of a passage to India? The other sister is probably married into Monegasque royalty.

'Rupert is a cute name!'

'Majella, you're not having a Ballygobbard baby and calling it Rupert. And imagine poor Pablo trying to bring a Rupert back to Tenerife? No offence, Constance, they're lovely names.' I had to interject before Maj gets any ideas.

'Maj, do you really not know what you're having? I'm dying to get you some clothes.' Denise would want to get on with having that third baby or else she's going to steal Majella's when it's born.

'No. Pablo wore me down about not having a gender reveal because he saw a viral video about a whole town going up in flames after a gender reveal smoke cannon backfired.'

'That was in America. They're dopes. No offence, Aubrey.' Speak-no-evil monkey emoji.

'You can buy some really lovely gender-neutral stuff. I've already bought too much.' Sadhbh, of course.

'Tiny baby linen sacks and dungarees, just like Auntie Sadhbhy.' Heart-eyes emoji. I can nearly hear Majella squealing.

'I have almost a full outfit crocheted.' Maj and Rocky hit it off at the B-Gym-B opening, bonding over a shared love of macramé, which Majella has been doing in the evenings to stop herself thinking about wine. So far in the WhatsApp group, Rocky's revealed a diverse range of interests, including both astronomy and astrology, psychedelics and the music of Boney M.

'Aisling, Liam says they have an itinerary for Pablo's day out. So cute.'

John was working on it just last night. They're having their lunch in Eddie Rocket's because Pablo loves the chips so much. 'I know. They've even allocated time for each shop.'

'Keep them out of that surfy place in Stephen's Green. Pablo thinks he can pull off board shorts but his legs are too stumpy.'

'I'll let John know, Maj.'

'His legs? *Que?*'

Oh God, I thought all the Tenerifian relatives were gone from the group. Good luck with this one, Maj.

CHAPTER 33

With my new pine table and six matching chairs finally in situ, Mammy is on her way in for a cup of tea. I've lured her over with the chance to nose around the cottage, but I really want an update on the Trevor/Cara/Síomha situation. I think I've gone above and beyond with the baby shower invite, and I want to talk to her about what I heard in the toilets in Castlefarrow. It's still niggling away at me. She's been keen to come in for a look since the place has come together, but I've been up the walls between planning the launch for the Hairy Mollies new at-home wax kit, commuting up and down and trying to keep Majella's Babe Shower on topic. One of her cousins posted something yesterday about an amazing opportunity for stay-at-home mams. She said they could be earning €40K a year in their spare time while being their own boss. I had to stop Denise Kelly from investing her life savings in what is clearly an essential oils pyramid scheme.

Majella has mentioned several times now that she doesn't want the usual baby shower games and has explicitly banned the one where guests have to eat melted chocolate out of nappies. She's excited about the Guess the Baby Photoshopped onto the Stripper Body game I've devised, and thrilled with the DJ arriving at seven because she's hoping it goes all night.

I'm not sure a sesh is what Americans intended when they exported the concept of baby showers, but I suppose they've been around long enough now that we're putting our own Irish spin on them, a bit like what we've done with Chinese food.

The noise of the front door handle rattling interrupts my rearranging of tea towels on the Aga.

'Hellooo?' I swing around to see Mammy's face pressed against one of the windows. 'Anyone home?'

'Why didn't you just ring the bell?' I ask when I open the door. 'It's right there.'

'Ring the bell? At my daughter's house? Well, la-di-da!'

Between New York and the time I spent living with Sadhbh in Dublin, I'd forgotten that BGB operates a strict open-door policy. You simply have to be ready for callers at all times, whether you like it or not. The Truck nearly caught me in the nip the other night when he was dropping in a soundbar for the gym. I had to hide behind my new Orla Kiely oven glove. It's a stressful way to live, so John and I have decided to keep the door locked. Since we've no front hall, it's the only way to get a bit of privacy.

Mammy bustles in, shaking her coat on to the back of one of my new kitchen chairs. 'Oh, they're gorgeous, Aisling. Not a mark on them.'

'Thanks, I'm delighted with them, I must say.'

The table and chairs were a display model in Knock Garden Centre – a bargain at forty per cent off. And I got them to throw in free delivery too. Although I would have made John pick them up if I'd known Mad Tom was the driver. He took the wing mirror off my Micra backing the van into the driveway. All his training is starting to pay off if the way he was able to carry two chairs in each hand is anything to go by. He's getting great wear out of his crop top too.

'Guess who did a line with Murt Kelly back in the seventies?'

'Ehhh, Tessie Daly?'

'Jesus, no, she'd never land a man like Murt. Auntie Christine.'

'No way!' Daddy's sister lives in Scotland now and sends Christmas cards with ten-pound notes in them every year.

'Eileen Kelly raised a family of seven here. Murt was the eldest.'

'In two bedrooms?'

'It was what people did at the time,' she says, depositing a white cardboard box from BallyGoBrunch on the kitchen table. 'Madness, really, what women put themselves through. I got us some of Carol's coffee choux buns. Is the kettle on? Show me everything, now, go on.'

I take her around the cottage, pointing out the new floor in the bedroom which John sanded and stained himself, the pedal bin with sections for normal rubbish, recycling and food waste, and all the Carolyn Donnelly Eclectic bits I've been picking up in Dunnes on my lunch breaks. Carolyn never puts a foot wrong, as far as I'm concerned.

'You have the place looking gorgeous,' Mammy says when she eventually takes a seat at the table and I pass her a cup of tea. 'I'll have to get you a few cuttings from Úna Hatton's hydrangeas. You can put a planter on either side of the front door. It'll look very dressy. How's John?'

'Flat to the mat in the gym,' I say, helping myself to a choux bun. 'Literally. He's doing strength training this morning with the Rangers under-seventeens. He has the Knock Rovers then in the afternoon. They have to be kept apart – you know yourself. And Sumira Singh is going to do an over-sixties yoga class on a Tuesday evening. You should go. Keep you limber.'

'I have bridge club on Tuesdays, love. Trevor is after joining us.'

God, it's like they're joined at the hip. 'Oh lovely.'

'Constance is a bit put out that she's had to pair up with Padraig Whelan. She says he smells like creosote. He's a mighty bridge player all the same.'

I clear my throat. 'And how is … Dr Trevor?'

Mammy's face lights up. 'Oh, he's very well, and asking for you, of course. I'll tell him you say hello.'

'Yeah, do.' There's an awkward silence as I try and figure out how to phrase this without her losing the head. 'About him, actually, Mammy. I heard something I think you should know.'

'About Trevor?' She puts her cup on the table, a look of concern crossing her face. 'What is it? Nothing bad, I hope.'

'No! No. Well, actually, I don't know.'

'Go on, spit it out, Aisling. You obviously have something you want to get off your chest.' There's an edge to her voice now that I recognise from when I used to leave behind bits of lamb from her stew because you can only chew meat for so long without getting a tension headache.

'He's had' – I decide to just blurt the words out – 'loads of other girlfriends since his wife died. I just wanted you to know because I can see things are getting serious between the pair of you. I'm worried he might be a serial romancer or something.'

She picks up her cup and takes a sip, one eyebrow raised. 'A serial romancer?'

'You know what I mean. A bit of a ladies' man.'

'And who told you this?'

'His own daughters. Well, not in so many words. I overheard them talking in the hotel. They were being little rips.'

Mammy puts her cup down with a sigh. 'I thought you girls were getting along a bit better now?'

'Well, I invited them to the shower. And I didn't have to. I'm just telling you what I heard.'

'Aisling, Trevor and I are in our sixties. Still. Just about. We've both been married before. You don't get to our age and think keeping secrets is a good way to go on in a relationship. You don't keep secrets from John, do you?'

'God no.' I mean, I used to when we were going out the first time around. I never told him my hopes or dreams for our future together. I thought he'd just figure it out himself eventually. That was my biggest mistake, and what drove a wedge between us. It all seems so silly now, how angry I used to get every time we went on a Pigsback discounted mini-break and he didn't end up down on one knee. Since we've been back together, I'm an open book, even more so since the miscarriage. I showed him a chin hair yesterday.

'Well, Trevor and I have no secrets either. He's been very honest about the companions he's had since Valerie died, thank you very much.'

'Are you not afraid he might, I don't know, do the dirt on you?'

'Do the dirt? What are you on about, Aisling?' She's getting exasperated.

'Like, cheat on you. Go out with someone else while you're golfing with Constance.'

She rolls her eyes. 'No, I'm not one bit afraid of that. I know all about the other women. Bernie, they were stepping out for just a few months before she left him for a Welsh train driver. Very callous by all accounts. And Madeleine from Kilkenny, the chemistry just wasn't there. They're still in touch. And there was also Doreen, and Mary before her. Síomha and Cara don't know about them, but he told me because communication is important. He's a handsome man, Aisling. Of course he has women interested in him.'

My eyes are rolling before I can stop them. Sometimes when I'm around Mammy I revert back to being a teenager. Not that I was particularly angsty, and I certainly wasn't a troublemaker, bar the one time me and Majella drank a naggin of Bacardi in the calving shed and were found under a pile of straw with That Bloody Cat the next morning, but I just become a little wagon. I usually hate myself for it afterwards, and when I see Mammy's eyes filling with tears I want to throw myself headfirst through the front door. 'Ah, Mammy, I'm sorry. It's just all a bit wild, you know? So much is changing.'

'I know, pet. I've been throwing a lot at you, and you've been a great girl. I just feel very –' She cries harder here and I pull my chair closer. 'I feel very lucky to have met him. I know you'll be skitting at me saying that.'

'I'm not skitting, Mammy. I promise.' I can't deny it is way out of my comfort zone to be talking with her like this, but I have to remember I'm an adult.

'Well, if Paul was here he'd be skitting.'

'He would, that's fair.'

She takes a deep breath and picks up her cup. 'I actually have something I want to talk to you both about, but I'll tell you now because it will probably affect you more. I'll get Paul on the Zoom later.'

My stomach drops. They're getting married. They're already married. She's pregnant. No, almost certainly not. She's sixty-six.

She puts the cup down. 'Aisling, I want to sell the farm.'

It's as if time momentarily slows down. The sound of the sheep bleating outside becomes a roar, and I know that if I try to stand up my knees will buckle under me. My heart is pounding. Mammy wants to sell the farm? Our home? Where is she going to go? Where will *I* go?

She reaches out and puts a hand on my forearm. I notice she's still wearing her rings from Daddy. 'Love, I know this will have come as a shock to you, so I'm not expecting you to say anything or do anything for the moment. I just needed to let you know.'

'But why? Why would you even be thinking about selling it?' It comes out a wail and I'm immediately embarrassed. If I regress any more, I'll be sucking my thumb next.

'I just think it's time, pet,' she says quietly. 'It's a lot of work, and someone younger could make a much better fist of it. Paul has no interest and neither do you.'

'But you love running the eco farm. Were you not only saying recently that it gave you a new lease of life?'

She nods. 'And it did. Throwing myself into setting it up helped me get over your father's death. I believe it was his last gift to me, I really do. I want to enjoy my old age, not work myself into the grave. Trevor and I want to travel and make the most of our time together. The thoughts of facing into another winter is too much. I'm ready to retire, Aisling.'

'And what about Constance? She's your partner – does she not get a say in all this?'

'She's in the same boat as myself. She wants to play golf and go to the races of a weekend.'

'But where will you live?'

'That's the other thing. Trevor and myself, we were thinking I could downsize in or around Ballygobbard. An apartment or maybe one of those new townhouses in Knocknamanagh where Constance lives.' There was fierce skitting when the sign went up for the 'townhouses', especially from BGB-ers thrilled to point out that Knock is getting above its station. 'And Trevor wants to look at buying something in the west. Maybe a little bungalow with a garden. We'd both love to be by the sea.'

'So you'd …?'

'Move between both, ideally. We'd be able to see you and have a base to see Cara and Síomha, and then you could come and visit us on the Wild Atlantic Way anytime you wanted.'

Wow. They really have it all figured out. I struggle to take it all in, fighting conflicting emotions of sadness and anger and guilt before blurting out, 'Don't sell it, Mammy. Me and John can help you. We can't let it go. What would Daddy say?'

She gives me a sharp look. 'Aisling, I can't have you holding that over me. I won't. Daddy would be happy that I was happy. Would you have me hoovering out yurts into my seventies? I know he wouldn't. And he'd hate anyone to be sticking with the farm out of obligation. And anyway, when would you help me?'

She's got me there. I'm fairly busy myself, and so is John. 'On the weekends.'

'That's a nice idea, Aisling, but I'm going to retire. I've made up my mind.'

'We can hire someone to run it! There has to be another way. You can't just sell the farm. Granny would hate it.'

'Granny is long gone, Aisling. I think it will be okay.'

'Paul might want it – you never know.'

'Paul is happy out down in Oz. He has his own life, and I won't be interrupting it and putting it on him to run the family farm. That's what happened your father and I won't be repeating history. Times have changed.'

'What do you mean that's what happened Daddy? He was never in Australia. The furthest he ever went was Wales on your honeymoon.'

'I mean he was obligated to take it over. He was the eldest and none of his siblings had a blind bit of interest. I've spoken to them all and they're happy for me to do what I want.'

This is news to me. In my head, Daddy was born in a pair of wellies and a tweed flat cap talking about moving sheep. 'How do you mean forced? Couldn't he have said no?'

'His older brother died, pet. Your uncle Malachy, God rest him. Long before your father and I even met. But his death changed the course of your father's life in more ways than one.' I knew Uncle Malachy had died, of course. He drowned off the coast of Wexford in a fishing accident along with one of his friends. He was only twenty-two. There's a plaque down there to commemorate it. 'He had aspirations to train as a carpenter but the obligation put paid to that.'

'But he loved being a farmer. He did it his whole life.'

'That was your father through and through. What point was there complaining about it? So he threw himself into it, but you can be sure it wasn't his first choice. It's not an easy life.'

My eyes dart over the surface of the pine table, taking all this information in. I can't imagine anyone but us on that farm, feeding baby lambs and always, always watching out the back kitchen window for the weather to turn. Could I put myself at that window for the next forty years? 'Okay then, how about I take it over?'

Mammy looks at me sceptically. 'You'll take it over? Take over the animals and the eco farm and run the whole place?'

'Yeah? Why not? I'm the eldest. Isn't that how it goes?'

'And what about John?'

'He'll run it with me. He can do courses. We both can. I get loads of farmers popping up on my Instagram. It's gone very modern.'

'It would be a huge undertaking, Aisling. You have your own job, your own career to think about. I'm happy to let the farm go.'

'Well, I'm not.'

CHAPTER 34

'I know you said it was bijou, darling, but are you really taking meetings with clients in that minuscule room?'

I knew Mandy would think the European offices were on the small side, and that's why I told her countless times the place is 'bijou', because that's what Sadhbh called it when she came to visit.

'There are only three of us and we have most client meetings out,' I remind Mandy, 'and the meeting room is big enough for Hannah to do her TikTok dances on her lunch break.'

Hannah regularly goes semi-viral with her dancing videos, which she uses to show off her 'thrifted' work outfits while also passive-aggressively getting at Aubrey for her truly unstoppable fast-fashion Penneys habit. I think she has the whole of her sterile corporate flat decked out in the Sunflower Fields homeware range, even though she's almost due to go back to the US.

'Ah, speaking of lunch?' Mandy's boyfriend – or partner, surely: she's probably too old for a boyfriend – Seán has been patiently sitting in our tiny lobby while Aubrey, Hannah and I have been filling Mandy in on how the client books are looking and what the scope is for expanding. I know Mandy has her eye on the Windsors, ultimately, and while she's disappointed Ireland doesn't have its own royal family we can chase up, I've convinced her that landing Amy and Brian's eldest's birthday party is basically the same as hosting for Prince George. Hannah also has a meeting with three of the big Instagram comics tomorrow with a view to setting up a showcase for them. I'm still reeling from an interaction yesterday where I asked Aubrey where she was at the turn of the millennium and Hannah mentioned that she was born in the year 2002.

I've been feeling like a bit of a fraud carrying on with my event architect work when I'm still contemplating leaving to run the farm. Mammy's told Paul that she wants to sell and he's happy to go with the flow, so it's making it all seem very real. I cried to John the night Mammy broke the news, and he said he'd of course support me if it's what I want to do, but made it clear that I'd be taking the lead. I cried more when I thought about our babies, if we have any more babies, not growing up around the yard like I did. John has started seeing a woman over Zoom for therapy and tried to get me to do some breathing exercises with him, and we eventually fell asleep listening to some rainforest sounds with the sheep as backing singers.

'I could eat a donkey.' Poor Seán.

'I've booked us into Le Cochon Vert for lunch, supposed to be lovely.' I asked Sadhbh for recommendations. Nothing too fancy, because we don't want Mandy to think we're squandering, but fancy enough that they'll have different-shaped wine glasses and at least a few raw meats on the menu.

'And we'll have a pint afterwards? Grogan's is still in the same spot?' Seán's Irish accent just about comes through the evidence of his thirty years in New York. His head is unmistakably Irish, which is just the right amount of puce and potato, even though his teeth are most definitely New York born and bred. I'm not sure I would have picked an Irishman with veneers and a Gucci belt for Mandy, but she seems besotted. And this is a woman who famously stood Bill Murray up because she had a working pedicure booked. Now she's bringing her boyfriend on business trips and assuring him that we can definitely go for pints in Grogan's after lunch. I wince when she butchers the word 'pints'. There are some words Americans just have no business saying, in much the same way Irish people cannot wrap their gobs around 'garbage' or 'chipotle'.

Mandy is horrified when I suggest that we stroll to the restaurant on George's Street. Aubrey had already laid the groundwork for the walk by reminding Mandy that Dublin is much more higgledy-piggledy than New York's grid system and how it's often much quicker to just walk. I'm also ready to head off her assertion that 'we'll just Uber' with the devastating news that we don't really Uber here, and actually if we hail a taxi we might get stuck with a talker – or even worse, a conspiracy theorist. Mandy is not a big fan of unsolicited talking. We're actually three-quarters of the way to the restaurant before she's over the Uber revelation.

****

'Welcome to Le Cochon Vert, I'm William, and our specials today are a beef tataki and a venison with cavolo nero, and please let me know if you need the vegetarian or vegan menu options.'

Hannah sighs with relief and immediately asks for direction on the vegan dishes. I knew by the way William's kerchief was tied around his neck and by the bustling lunch crowd already sitting down that Sadhbh had steered me in the right direction. Just the right level of notions and a waiter who seems to know what he's doing.

'Oh hey, Aisling, there's chicken on here for you.' Mandy guffaws and elbows me. It really tickles her that I always order the chicken. It's just usually such a safe option. I don't know what beef tataki is, but I've seen a plate of very pink meat brought out to the table beside us so I'm not taking any chances. And I really do like chicken. Very versatile.

Across from her sits Seán, who's gleefully reading the restaurant's stockists list at the bottom of the menu to Aubrey like a who's-who of childhood Irish holiday locations. 'Clawn-a-kilty black pudding. I went there every summer. Every damn summer.'

Aubrey, who's across from me, is genuinely interested. Jeremy is due to arrive in two days, and she's settled on Cork and Kerry for their minibreak. Hannah tried to get them to do it in a converted HiAce but I begged Aubrey to book hotels, if only for the breakfasts. I couldn't bear their first Wild Atlantic Way experience to be sleeping on a bed that somehow converts into a shower and a dining table. They need helpful concierges and bain-maries of sausages and rashers to get the real American-on-holidays-in-Ireland experience. Over lunch, we discover that Mandy has no intention of going on a trip down memory lane with Seán on the highroads and byroads. They're staying in the Merrion for the few days and then over to Powerscourt for the weekend and then back to New York. I think he mentioned a helicopter at one point. He's absolutely loaded by the looks of things. The perfect man for Mandy, it would seem.

'You are mad about him!' I whisper and nudge her as he excuses himself to the bathroom after they all order coffees and I cannot resist the praline profiteroles. I wouldn't usually be elbowing her or whispering to her about her private life, but I'm emboldened by three glasses of Pinot Greej, and she's been hoofing into the Malbec.

She turns around a little in her chair to face me. 'Aisling, I had forgotten what it was like to have fun with a man. This fool has me laughing all day and night.'

She really does laugh a lot at his extremely cheesy jokes. But sure, look, there's a boot for every foot.

'I'm thrilled for you Mandy. You –' I'm about to tell her she looks ten years younger, but she would probably fire me on the spot or have me served up alongside the beef tataki. 'You look so happy.'

'I suppose I am, Aisling. And how about you? How's my favourite mute man?'

I break into a huge smile. 'He's good. I don't know if I told you, but he's opened his own gym Down Home in Ballygobbard.'

'An entrepreneur!'

'Yes, I'm very proud.' I would love to see the look on Mandy's face if she saw John's gym compared to the multi-floor mecca to wellness she goes to in the West Village, and even more if she caught sight of Mad Tom doing his squats in his wrestling singlet.

'And you're living down there, down in Ballywhatsit? I thought you were setting up in the city?' She laughs at herself at this because she can't believe Dublin has the audacity to call itself a city. Aubrey was actually its staunchest defender over lunch and gave a very passionate speech about the Luas, its characters and its 'quirky' logistical layout. Hannah nearly choked on her wine when she called the Red Line 'spirited'.

'Actually, now that I'm older it's not that bad of a place to settle.' I swallow a lump in my throat thinking about the farm and wishing I could ask for Mandy's advice.

She nods in barely concealed disbelief at the idea of BGB being a decent place to live. Seán returns, exclaiming that he's just met his second cousin in the toilets. Mandy is gobsmacked, but Hannah and I are less surprised. It's determined that the cousin and his wife should join us in Grogan's, and I say a prayer to the pub gods that we're able to get a table. The sun is out and it's just the kind of day that would have it packed.

'Hannah, Hannah,' I hiss across the table at her. 'Will you run on ahead and scout for tables outside Grogan's?' She dons a determined look and slinks out of the restaurant as I finish my glass of wine and promise myself to have two waters if and when we get seats outside the pub. I'm hosting and I can't be on my ear trying to show Mandy and Seán around.

****

After another show of incredulity about having to walk, Mandy does graciously apologise when we arrive at Grogan's and she realises that it was literally a two-minute stroll. To my delight, Hannah is guarding two tables pushed together in the glorious sunshine the same way a dog might guard a slice of ham. She's even managed to corral an assortment of chairs and stools and, after some convincing, Mandy does eventually sit on one. Two people stop to say hello – Des from Escalations, who's definitely had hair plugs, and Sandra, a weapon of a girl I went to Irish college with. Between that, the creamy pint in front of her and the August sun, Mandy accepts that it's actually a pretty special place to drink and be merry. As Seán and the cousin launch into another FaceTime to a disbelieving relative, she leans over to me. 'Okay, I can see why you'd want to come back here.'

I glow with pride at this coming from the queen of New York. 'Thank you, Mandy. I knew once you'd sampled some Guinness while a guy plays "Bohemian Rhapsody" on an accordion you'd get it.' He was alternating 'Bohemian Rhapsody' with 'Runaway' by the Corrs, and both were definite crowd-pleasers.

'How's your mom? I'm sure you've worried about her being alone since your father passed.'

I don't remember ever telling Mandy that. Did it come out of my pores like I was channelling Saoirse Ronan in *Brooklyn*? Maybe Aubrey told her.

'I have a mom too, you know?'

I genuinely can't imagine Mandy ever being a baby, ever having her nose wiped, ever being parented. 'Mammy is good, actually. She has a new, eh – boy– eh – partner.'

'And they live in the same town as you and John?'

'They do, yeah.' I let out a sigh. 'Mammy's actually wanting to sell her house and the farm and all that. Where I grew up. She wants to retire fully, you know?'

Mandy puffs out her cheeks. 'Yikes, that's gotta be hard? The childhood place? That's a big decision.'

I feel a swell of love for Mandy that she recognises how huge the prospect of selling is. It means she really was listening that one time she joined us for post-work happy-hour drinks because she had an hour to kill before a Thai boxing class. After two huge glasses of Pinot Greej I was showing her pictures of the three-legged lamb me and Daddy once nursed back to health in front of the kitchen radiator. It *is* a huge decision, and it's one that I feel hangs on me now, because unless I take on the farm, it has to go.

'You couldn't live there?' Mandy continues before I can answer.

'Well, it's a farm and it has yurts and a shop and all, so it would be a full-time job.'

'Oh, I see. And you already have a full-time job.' She raises her glass to me, but her tone is odd.

'Yes, I do.' I know it's come out sounding odd as I clink my glass with hers.

She stares at me for a moment and then talks, low and serious. 'Are you looking for a new job or are you happy with the one you have? Because, if you can't tell, I think you're doing a great job here with the new office, and I'm excited about the trajectory and where you can take it.'

I go to reassure her, not because I'm one hundred per cent sure of what I want but because I don't want to be in trouble with her.

She holds up her hand a fraction and then keeps talking. 'But if what I'm picking up here about shacking up in Ballygobatshit with your dream lover and running the family farm being a possibility, then you need to tell me because I am going to need to move Aubrey into your position asap and break it to her that she lives in Dublin now. Understood?'

I just nod at her, trying not to cry. Crying with work people at a pub is still technically crying at work, and I saw an Instagram reel about how you're not supposed to cry at work because it's bad for peer respect and career progression. Or maybe it was that you *are* supposed to cry at work. Either way, I don't want to cry in front of Mandy, so I just nod.

'Okay then. Phenomenal. Hey, fella, know any other songs?'

Turns out, for fifty of Mandy's dollars he knows any song you want.

CHAPTER 35

The farm shop is closed on Sundays, and check-out time is twelve o'clock, so I know Mammy and Constance will be playing golf in the afternoon. They're becoming very dedicated to getting their nine holes in every weekend. Word in the village is that Constance is gunning for the Lady Captain role since Tessie Daly was forced to step down over a landscaping contract scandal. Mammy is hoping she gets it, if only to annoy Úna Hatton, who's been talking about going for it for years now.

I leave John dozing on the couch in front of the match and head over to the farm to see if I can genuinely imagine myself running the place. In the heat of the moment when Mammy was telling me about everything Daddy sacrificed to take it on, I was sure I wanted to follow in his footsteps. But after my chat with Mandy I could feel my resolve starting to wane. I couldn't bear the possibility of handing my job over to Aubrey after all the work I've put into it. Could I?

That Bloody Cat appears as I get out of the car, rubbing herself against my shins, looking for something. 'And where would you go if she sold it, puss?' I scratch her under her chin. 'You don't like change at all, do you? No, me either.'

She stalks off as soon as she realises I have no food on me. Brat.

The sun is still high in the sky and the piglets and goat kids barely notice as I make my way around the petting zoo, past the wooden playground and over to the vegetable garden, where it looks like everything is just about ready to come up. There's lettuce, carrots, turnips and, of course, an abundance of spuds. I don't know how many varieties this year. The rhubarb is thriving. And then there's the fruit: bushes buckling under the weight of strawberries and raspberries and the very start of the blackberries and gooseberries. Constance is forever braying on about her source for superior manure, and I have to hand it to her, it's going to be a fine harvest.

I head across the yard, past the polytunnels and green-houses full of tomato plants. The yurt resort is quiet now, but I know they were busy on Friday and Saturday with a crowd of women down for a thirtieth. They drank Maguire's out of prosecco last night, according to Mikey. He's thinking of installing one of those taps on the bar, but I told him to hold off until September. If Majella got wind of it while she's still pregnant it might push her over the edge.

I continue on past the toilet and shower block and right up the hill to the wide gate that opens into the Far Field. I clamber up onto the top bar and settle my arse down. From here I can see the house and yurts and all the outhouses in front of me. Behind me is the rest of the land, nearly sixty acres of good grazing. The best in the county, or so I was always told.

I loved living on a farm when I was small. Feeding pet lambs with Mammy. Playing in the bales when Daddy was bringing in the hay. Me and Paul sitting beside him in the tractor, bouncing along the winding Knock Road, all ears when he was telling us who lived in which house. I wasn't so fond of it in my teenage years, when I longed for the glamour of a house in an estate with next-door neighbours and a patch of grass to hang around on. I was always pleading for lifts, and I resented having to help after being in school all day, standing in gaps in the freezing cold when Daddy was moving cows and having to serve dinners to a houseful of men when it was silage-cutting season. But Mammy always just got on with it, and Daddy never said a word, only talked to me about land and how important it was to own land and mind land.

I close my eyes and try to imagine myself in charge of it all. The house, the yurts, the shop, the fields. So much to do. What do I know about keeping sheep and cattle and now the alpacas? I could do those courses I was telling Mammy about, I suppose. Majella's always talking about the fine things on Farming TikTok. There's probably loads on YouTube too. John was able to find a video showing how to take the deck off a treadmill after Mad Tom dropped his monocle into the mechanism last week.

The first time Sadhbh, Elaine and Ruby came down from Dublin, I tried to see the farm through their eyes. I'd never really noticed how tall the trees behind the calving shed were before they pointed them out, or how nice it is to be able to look far into the distance out to the horizon. I hadn't realised you can't really do that in a city. Too many buildings. Too many walls. They talked about how the air smelled fresh and sweet and how safe and calm it felt to be so far away from other people. I didn't mention that, even though the Morans' bungalow is two fields over, I was often able to hear Liz and

Majella fighting over the right way to load the dishwasher or why the vodka in their drinks cabinet was tasting very watery these days.

Across the road from the house, I can see Don Hatton wandering around their front garden with a yellow hose. That's the other thing. Even if I decided that I could manage the farm and working seven days a week and never being able to take a holiday as long as I live, could I really cope living so close to the Hattons again? Not if the rumours that they're putting in a pergola and outdoor kitchen are true. Úna would have me absolutely mithered going on and on about it.

I'm trying to do up a mental list of pros and cons in my head when my phone beeps. A text from Denise Kelly. 'Does she have any lanolin, does anyone know? It's great for the nipples.'

With the Majella's Babe Shower official WhatsApp group reaching near hysterical levels with only a week to go before the big event, Dee Ruane has set up Majella's Babe Shower (Minus Maj) to finalise the presents. She has literally hundreds of euro from the now almost forty-strong guest list so wants to add some more actual gifts to the vouchers and the River Island shoes. Maeve Hennessey suggested the Orla Kiely nappy bag, but Liz said she'd already picked one up in the Christmas sales in Knock Garden Centre. Majella wasn't even pregnant then, which makes it very cute but would absolutely crucify poor Pablo if he knew. His superstitions and his crystals are nearly cancelling each other out at this stage. John has made him sign up for Sumira Singh's yoga to help him find some peace.

'No lanolin bought yet, Denise, great suggestion.' Dee is all over it.

'Did you put the go-kart on the list?' Poor Rocky isn't reading the room on the go-kart idea. It's just really not a newborn essential.

I have to admit, the farm is fairly glorious now in the summer with everything looking so green and birds cheeping in the hedgerows. But Mammy's right, it's a different story the rest of the year. Winter is particularly grim. I remember sitting at the kitchen table eating my Ready Brek before school and Daddy coming in the back door, stamping the frost off his wellies, after being up before the sun feeding the livestock. Can I really see myself at that for years to come? Maybe. I do love a frosty morning. John mightn't be so rose-tinted about freezing early mornings on a farm, though. He's already talking about expanding the gym business, which sounds mad at such an early stage, but the demand seems to be there. The old bookies beside Dick's in Knocknamanagh is up for rent, and with the waiting list for membership growing every day he's really considering going all in. Skippy Brennan had him on Solas FM talking about his new men-only pole-dancing classes last week and someone texted in to say he's like a young Ben Dunne, albeit without all the scandals. He was delighted, mostly.

The sun is warm on my face and I close my eyes, grateful for the bottle of factor 50 I've taken to keeping in the glove box of the car. I wish it was an easy decision, but no matter how long and hard I think about it, I just don't know what to do. I wish Daddy was here. More than ever. As I head back towards the house my phone dings with an email alert. It's from Mandy. Classic Sunday behaviour.

Aisling,

Simone will be drafting up the permanent contracts for Ireland this week. Just so you know.

M

CHAPTER 36

Mandy's email is on my mind as I drive to work on Monday morning. She said so much in so few words. How does she know I've been agonising away? I swear she can read minds or auras or whatever. Nothing would surprise me with the amount of lasers and steams and needles and wraps she subjects her body to.

It's quiet in the office without Aubrey. According to her Instagram, she and Jeremy are having a wonderful time on the Wild Atlantic Way, even if the weather has been extremely mixed. I really hope it's nice on Saturday for Majella's baby shower. It's a real sign of how much I love Majella that I've agreed to take her to Dundrum on Thursday evening to find her a suitably sexy outfit. None of the stuff she's ordered online is working, and although her frame is as small and wiry as ever, her bump is absolutely enormous now and so is her bust, which is new and exciting for Maj. She's been a slave to the chicken fillets and clever use of bronzer all her life, so she's dying to make the most of the new curves. I had to stop her when she started talking about how much Pablo is enjoying them. The accompanying actions were too much. I'm about to crack into a new spreadsheet for Suzanne Simmons's eyelash glue launch when Hannah gasps from her desk opposite me.

'What? Don't tell me the Hairy Mollies have vetoed another balloon arch?'

'Aubrey's engaged!'

I gasp too and grab my phone, opening Instagram. There at the very top of my feed is Aubrey, clutching onto a beaming Jeremy at the Cliffs of Moher and displaying the tell-tale Hanging Hand beside her cheek. I personally love those freshly engaged photoshoots where the hand and the ring are manipulated to be the centre of every picture. It's Sadhbh who christened it the Hanging Hand and ever since then it's all I see, but I still love the joy of the moment.

'OMG, OMG, so thrilled for you!' I comment underneath, adding at least seven heart emojis. It was only a few years ago that I was looking at Hanging Hands on Instagram and wishing I was one of them, waiting and hoping for John to propose. It's like looking back on two babies now. Only telling each other half of what we were feeling and thinking. 'We'll have to get a cake for when she's back on Thursday.'

Hannah rolls her eyes but spares me a monologue about the patriarchy. She even smiles a bit. I think she's happy for Aubrey too.

****

'Is the ring nice up close?'

Majella is struggling to get the seat belt around the bump and sweating a little after our trawl around Dundrum. Unfortunately, most of the things she tried were either indecently booby or not quite booby enough. We eventually found a black tuxedo dress in the Mama section of H&M that she decided will do the job once her mam takes it up a couple of inches. I must admit, looking at the maternity clothes stung a little bit. I'd be right there with her, the size of a house, if things had turned out differently. She also bought two pairs of leggings that go right up to her bra and a silky nightdress.

'It's gorgeous. Oval diamond on a gold band.'

'Lovely. Very classic. I haven't been able to wear mine for months. If it wasn't for the big boobs, I'd be absolutely fuming.' She finally clicks the seat belt and leans back with a sigh. 'How many times has John proposed to you this week?'

I smile and bite my lip. 'Just the once.' Last night as we lay side by side in bed, our bodies covered in a sheen of sweat, our chests heaving in unison. The surge of oxytocin nearly made me say yes.

'Why don't you bloody say yes? What's stopping you?'

'We're only after moving in together. We're only back together, like, nine months. I'll know when the time is right. As long as nothing goes wrong. Nothing else.'

'You don't need to be worrying any more. You're safe with John. And if not, I'll simply murder him and his body will never be found. All the *Blood and Bordeaux* will come in handy.'

We've just hit the N7 when I circle back to the conversation about John, but really as an excuse to bring up the farm. I'd told Majella straight away about Mammy's revelation, hoping she would have an answer for me somehow. All she could offer was surprise and consolation, though. Maybe if I try again.

'Maj, can you imagine John living on the farm?'

'Eh, I can, I suppose. What does he say?'

'He says he'd be grand with it but can't see himself as a full-time farmer.'

'And you're still thinking of becoming a full-time farmer yourself?'

'Well, yeah. Can you imagine any other family living there? What if they changed the whole place? Or levelled it to the ground? Or put in the conservatory Mammy always wanted?'

'Well, what were ye planning to do with it when your mother passed away?'

She's got me there. It's a question I've been asking myself for the past four days. Truth is, we hadn't had that conversation yet, me and Mammy and Paul. I just assumed we'd sort something out and keep it in the family, no matter what.

'I don't know. I just didn't see selling up in the equation.'

****

After dropping Majella back into Pablo's literally open arms – he was in the car park outside their apartment waiting for her, I don't know how long he'd been there – I tip into Mammy's to give her some shortbread I'd picked up in Marks and Sparks. She developed a fondness for it when I had to make shortbread biscuits for my Junior Cert home economics mock practical. I only got a B2 in the end because I forgot to sprinkle a tablespoon of sugar over them before they went in the oven, not that I'm still thinking about it or anything.

When I swing the Micra around, she's standing at the back door, a cardigan slung over her shoulders. 'Aisling! The very woman,' she calls as I get out of the car with the biscuits.

I can tell from her expression that something is wrong. 'What's going on?'

'It's nothing, really.' She's looking past me out into the yard. 'I just can't find Tiger, the little rip.'

I can't remember the last time someone called That Bloody Cat by her first name. It usually means she's in trouble. 'When was the last time you saw her?'

She rattles the packet of Dreamies in her hand. 'Here, puss! Here, puss! *Pspspspsps!*'

We both freeze and wait to see her tail bobbing out from behind the strawberry beds where she likes to sleep in the shade. Nothing.

'When was the last time you saw her, Mammy?'

'Tuesday morning.'

'You haven't seen her since Tuesday?' Now I'm worried. That Bloody Cat has always been very independent and is a regular gift-giver – rats, rabbits, mice, even a hare bigger than herself once. But I can count on one hand the number of times she's missed a meal. 'That's really not like her. Yesterday was Wednesday. Ham and cabbage. She loves a bit of ham fat.'

'I know,' Mammy admits. 'She hasn't really been herself recently.' She raises her voice like the cat might be listening. 'Have you, puss?'

The pair of us turn around to scan the yard but again, nothing.

'What do you mean?'

'Ah, just a bit mopey. I'm sure she's fine, wherever she is.'

A feeling I recognise as dread has started to creep over me. 'Have you looked in the house?'

'Of course I have.'

'In the washing machine?'

'Aisling! Stop that!'

'Sorry, I had to ask.'

It used to be That Bloody Cat's favourite place to nap until Mammy went to put on a wash one Christmas Eve and she nearly met her maker.

'I'm sure she'll turn up when she's hungry,' Mammy says huffily. But she doesn't sound so sure.

My phone rings. It's Sadhbh on FaceTime. I hurry into the sitting room and answer. 'Did you see Aubrey's Hanging Hand for today? I think she might do a full week of daily po–'

Sadhbh is crying.

'What's wrong?'

'Me and Don have broken up.'

My heart drops. 'Ah no, Sadhbhy. What happened?'

'We had another row, a big one.'

'About the baby stuff?'

'Yeah. He's just so worried he'll regret it. And I can't live with that.'

'Oh, Sadhbh, I'm so sorry. Maybe he just needs time to think, on his own.'

'Yeah, maybe.' She bursts into tears again.

I'm truly at a loss for what to say. 'He'll realise he can't live without you. I'm sure of it.'

'We've agreed to just go no-contact. He checked into a hotel. It's only been an hour and I feel like he's died.'

I remember reading a quote on Facebook once that said a break-up was nearly worse than a death, because with a break-up someone chooses to leave. With death they usually have no say. 'You poor dote. Do you want me to come up?'

'No, no, it's grand. You have to get ready for the baby shower. I'll see you on Saturday, sure.'

'Don't come if you don't feel up to it. Majella will understand.' But will Majella be able to accept that Don Shields is no longer in her life?

'Okay, bye'

I've never heard Sadhbh sound so down. 'Bye, my love. You'll be okay.'

****

Back in the kitchen, I can hear Mammy out the back shaking the Dreamies, calling the cat. We've had That Bloody Cat since Daddy came home from the mart one Saturday afternoon with a scrawny little kitten in a shoebox. She was destined for the Rices' cat pond, or so the story goes, until he intervened and said she'd come in handy keeping mice and rats away from the animal feed. It didn't take long until she'd laid claim to her own chair in the kitchen and was on Daddy's lap in front of the fire every evening, not that he'd admit she was becoming a house cat, of course. That must have been fifteen years ago now. I definitely remember her weaving around my legs when I was practising my shortbread.

I go outside to Mammy. 'I'll have a look in the polytunnels. You stick the kettle on. If she's not there, I'll get on to the Morans.'

'I met Liz this morning when I was doing the Lotto. She hasn't seen her.'

'Have you asked Úna Hatton?'

'Ah, Aisling. It hasn't come to that yet.'

'Mammy, she's your closest neighbour! And you know she always has an eye on the house and garden. How else did she know to text you when your knickers blew off the clothesline?'

Mammy rattles the bag of Dreamies again. 'Let's give her one more night. I'm sure she'll turn up.'

God, I really hope she does. The last time she was gone this long was years and years ago – she'd been hit by a car and it was Daddy who eventually found her at around 5 a.m. one freezing morning. He carried her all the home and spent a fortune at the vet's to fix her broken leg.

'Oh, and I'll be over to collect the baby shower decorations on Saturday so I can give you a lift if you like?'

'Will you not be having a drink, pet?'

'I will later on in the evening, but I have loads of decorations to bring and I want to be the hostess with the mostess for a couple of hours at least. I can leave the car there and come back for it on Sunday.'

'Should we, eh, will we offer Cara and Síomha a lift as well?'

'Can they not drive themselves?'

'I said they can stay here or in one of the yurts if they want to have a few drinks at it. Some of Majella's cousins are booked in, and Matt and Denis will be out with Pablo and John and the lads.'

I take a calming breath in the name of the peace process. 'Yes, okay, that's grand then. I'll text them.'

CHAPTER 37

I reach for my phone the second I wake up the next morning. A text from Liz Moran: 'I've looked everywhere, love. Shane even checked under the bonnet of the Subaru. She's not in the washing machine again, is she?' There's also forty-six new notifications in the Majella's Babe Shower group but I don't have the bandwidth to go in and explain that the cake I ordered a month ago is a regular three-tier round one with a fondant baby on top and not the life-size replica of Channing Tatum's torso that Maj found on bloody Pinterest and shared at 2 a.m. last night. Sometimes that website does more harm than good.

John is already at the gym – he has a Pump 'n' Grind class at 7 a.m. on Fridays – so I decide to do something I've been putting off. I booked today off work months ago, thinking I'd need time to finalise things for the shower. Now I have a missing cat, a heartbroken friend and a major life decision to make, on top of making sure Maj has the night of her life. The bedroom window is open and I can already tell it's going to be another balmy day. I throw on a sundress, brush my teeth and am about to hop into the Micra when I stop and check under it, just in case. No cat.

'Well, Daddy, how're things?' I say when I get to his grave, trowel and gloves in hand. I'm the only one in the whole place and grateful for the privacy. Daddy was never a brilliant one for doling out advice, but he was always a good listener. Often by the time I was finished explaining whatever drama was happening in school I'd have figured out what to do by myself. It's how I got over my crush on our substitute maths teacher, Mr Wickham, in second year. Between the wedding ring and the fancy lunches I realised he was probably married. That did the trick.

I kneel down on the little foam pad I keep in the boot of the car and start methodically raking through his gravel looking for weeds. A small part of me was worried Mammy's weekly visits would peter out after she took up with Dr Trevor, but there's barely a dandelion sprout to be found, which is a relief, although if she moves west she'll hardly be weeding every week. I'd have to make sure and step up. I couldn't bear the thought of him being left alone with only his neighbours – Sinéad McGrath's great-great-grandmother on one side and Pat Foran on the other – for company. Nobody could ever understand a word Pat Foran said he was such a chronic mumbler, and Angela McGrath had an incredible disdain for all men that Sinéad said stemmed from the fact she was mother to eleven useless boys. Sinéad tried to get her a plot in the feminist corner of the graveyard between Maureen Kelly – killed by a donkey – and Pansy Doran, who was Mo Mowlam's second cousin, but Father Fenlon wouldn't budge on his strict policy of new plots going in chronological order. Sinéad was bulling and told him to stick his little pink envelope for donations up his hole. Her mother made her apologise afterwards, but she swears Father Fenlon hasn't made eye contact with her since.

'I'm sorry it's been so long since I came to visit, but work has been busy and then me and John have been renovating Murt Kelly's mother's cottage – you know the one just outside the village with the orchard? I think you'd really like it.'

I decide not to mention the fact that his sister did a line with Murt. Mammy's told me since that Daddy wasn't happy about it because Murt had a big mouth for telling stories about his way with the ladies.

'I'm not sure if she's said it to you herself yet, so I'm sorry if this is a bit of a shock, Daddy, but Mammy wants to sell the farm. You probably know Dr Trevor? They want to move in together, maybe over in the west, if you can believe it. He has two girls. They're weapons.'

I sit back and wait to see if he sends me some kind of a message that he's as put out as I am. I can hear the distant hum of a tractor and some chirping from the little tree that hangs over the grave, but otherwise nothing.

'I have such mixed feelings about it. She says she's too old and tired to keep the farm going and that she wants to retire.' I can nearly hear his voice in my head – 'Again' – and of course he's right. Mammy has already retired once, from her first job as a nurse. But when you live on a farm, you never actually stop working.

'And I know she deserves that. She deserves to be able to relax and prune her roses and – oh my God, did you hear she's taken up golf? It's hard to say no to Constance, to be fair, but she's really enjoying it. I'm so torn about what to do, Daddy. I'll take it over, I think. Do you think I'd be able for it? You taught me well enough.'

I shift my position on the foam mat and cross my legs,

spinning the trowel in my hand.

'Mandy, my boss, wants me to make a big commitment to expanding the business in Dublin, and I really want to do that too, but I suppose I'm scared because the farm and Ballygobbard is such a big part of me and who I am. I'm afraid of losing my home, but then John would have to make it his home too. And we have our own little home in the cottage as it is. I wish I knew what to do.'

I take a breath. 'I've also been planning Majella's baby shower, which I'm sure you've already heard about.' I glance across the graveyard to the older side. Majella's granny is buried over there, but there's absolutely no chance that the news wouldn't have travelled by now. 'I'm delighted for her, of course, but I suppose I'm a bit sad as well, because I was supposed to be having a baby too, but things didn't work out and I had a miscarriage and, well, I think I'm still dealing with it but, you know me, always trying to keep busy.' As the words are tumbling out of me, so are the tears. He would have been the best granddad. The thought of passing him a little bundle to hold gives me such an ache in my chest that for a minute I'm afraid that I'm going to be sick, but I keep going.

'I'm a bit worried about John, to be honest. He was really looking forward to it so it hit him hard. He's doing therapy now, which he says is helping, but I'm scared that deep down he might blame me because we don't know why I lost the baby. Even that saying, "I lost the baby", makes it sound like it's my fault, and part of me thinks that maybe it is. Maybe I did something wrong. Maybe I'll never be a mammy. Majella and Pablo are so excited, and I'm excited for them, but with the timing and everything I don't know if I'm going to be able to get through this baby shower, despite all my talk. And if I do have babies then Mammy wouldn't even be around to help me, and if I don't end up on the farm I wouldn't be able to teach them how to hold the bottles for the lambs the way you did with me. But sure, I might not have any babies anyway.'

I sniff. 'So yeah, that's all my news.' And then I remember. 'Oh, and That Bloody Cat is gone missing to top it all off.'

'Hello, Aisling. And Seamus, God rest your soul.' Her brusque voice gives me such a fright I nearly impale myself on the trowel. She always had an ability to pop up when you least expect it, like the time I was in the County General checking on John's old flatmate Piotr, the one I kissed when I was in bits with grief. I was never so mortified.

'Fran,' I stammer, standing up and patting my cheeks dry with a gardening glove, wondering for the millionth time in my life what John's mother must be thinking of me. 'I didn't hear the car.'

'I'm on the electric bike. Úna Hatton had the cheek to give me a lecture about carbon emissions one day in BallyGoBrunch and, well, she made a valid point about shorter journeys, so we're trying to use the car less, especially in the fine weather.' The Granddadmobile. Ray would have been a brilliant granddad too, and every child needs one terrifying grandmother to keep them on the straight and narrow. It was Granny Reilly for me.

She hesitates for a second. 'I didn't mean to eavesdrop, but I was cutting back my mother's hostas when you were talking. You were upset.'

I nod mutely, swallowing continuously to get rid of the lump in my throat. 'I was just filling Daddy in on everything that's going on. I like to keep him in the loop.'

'Yes, well.' She picks at the hem of her cardigan. 'We haven't really had a chance to have a chat, have we? Do you have a minute now?' She points over towards the low limestone bench near the graveyard's pedestrian gate. 'There's some shade over there.'

'Oh, right, yes. Sure. No problem.' I always felt that Fran slightly disapproved of me, especially when me and John first got together. But I think it's just that the Holy Joe in her feels the need to scare people a bit, even when those people are picking out her Mother's Day cards and reminding her son his car tax is due. John always said she was very fond of me, so I've made my peace with that just being the way she is.

We wander through the graves towards the bench, Fran automatically tutting at withered flower arrangements and lopsided headstones along the way. John is so easy-going – it's hard to believe they're related.

We sit down in unison, and for a second neither of us says a word. Then Fran clears her throat and puts a small hand gently on my forearm. 'I wanted to tell you this before, Aisling, but there was never a good time. I had two miscarriages myself. After Rachel and John.'

I shake my head. I had no idea. I don't think John even knows.

'Ray and I always wanted a third. Me more than him, I suppose. I used to do nights in the General back then. It was a juggle, but I felt our family wasn't complete. Sometimes I still feel like that.'

I've spent many hours with Fran over the years. On the sidelines at matches. Sunday dinners. Anniversary masses. Christmas masses. A lot of masses. In all that time I don't think the two of us have ever had a conversation deeper than whether the ref's call was right or who's applying for planning permission in BGB. When we told her and John's dad about the pregnancy it was the most we'd ever bonded, but even then it was brief. This is new territory, but I'm glad she's telling me. I feel closer to her instantly. Like we're equals. Two women grieving.

'I'm sorry to hear that, Fran. Really.'

'The first one was early. I hadn't even told Ray yet, but I knew myself. I could feel the changes in my body without even doing a test. A woman knows, especially after two pregnancies. I was going to have it confirmed by the doctor and then give Ray a pair of John's baby shoes wrapped up, little navy patent ones, to break the news. But at six weeks I started to bleed, and then there was nothing to tell.'

'That must have been hard.'

She sniffs. 'It was. I told Ray then, of course, but he didn't have the same attachment that I did. By the time he knew, it was gone. Just an idea. It stayed with me, though, and I worked out that the thirtieth of June 1990 would probably have been my due date. The whole country was gone stone mad for Italia '90. Ireland played Italy that day. I still light a candle every year.'

For a minute, I'm envious of her faith. 'That's lovely. It's nice to have that.'

'The second one was worse. I was eleven weeks gone and even showing a bit. Well, you see, I have a very small frame. I was at work when it started, which was both a blessing and a curse. It would have been born on the fourth of August 1991. I light a candle that day, too.'

'I'm so sorry, Fran.'

'I already had two little ones at home, so I tried to focus on that and count my blessings.'

'I really like your idea. Of doing something to remember.'

Fran smiles. 'The sense of loss never leaves you, but it does get easier to bear, Aisling.'

'That's what John's therapist told him too.'

'He mentioned he was talking to someone, alright, and I'm happy to hear it. They need to talk more, men. A bit like you and me.' Then she laughs, and I think it's the first time I've ever heard her make that noise. 'Anyway, I wanted to tell you, Aisling, because I've always thought very highly of you. I don't think John knew how lucky he was when he found you, but I'm glad he came to his senses. You're a good match. I have faith that you'll always look after each other.'

I look across to Daddy's grave and wonder if he's trying to tell me something. I walk Fran out to the gate of the graveyard and wave her off before hopping in the Micra and heading for the farm. Mammy texts to say there's still no sign of the cat today, so I'm going to walk all the hedgerows calling for her and then head home to personalise the last twenty baby-shower party bags and curse myself for ever deciding to personalise them in the first place. Then a very large glass of Pinot Greej and at least three episodes of *Succession*. It makes me feel extremely cutthroat when I watch it. Maybe it'll spur me into making a decision.

CHAPTER 38

I crawl into John's arms the second I wake up, still so early
according to the light and the birdsong. Mostly asleep, he
turns on his back and allows my head to rest on his chest,
his arm tight around my shoulders.

'John?'

'Hmm?'

'Will we plant some flowers?'

'Whatever you want. Shhh. It's very early.'

'For the baby, I mean. Something that comes back every
year. Like a thing to remember it by. Is that silly?'

He stretches his neck, waking himself up. 'That's not silly
at all. It's actually a lovely idea. Where will we do it?'

'We could just do it here at the cottage? Out the kitchen
window?'

'What if we mo– actually, never mind. That's perfect.'

'Let's do it next weekend.' I close my eyes then, but ten
seconds later open them again. 'John?'

He sighs. 'Yes, my sweet angel of the dawn.'

'You should talk to your mother.'

'About what?' The gentle mocking tone is gone from his voice.

'Nothing bad. Nothing to worry about. Just talk to her. Ask
her about her babies.'

He twists his head to look down at me, curious. 'Okay, so.'

We settle into a few minutes of silence again. He's next to speak.

'Aisling?'

'Yeah?'

'Are you feeling okay about today?'

Am I feeling okay about today? I know I'm feeling anxious that it all goes well. I'm feeling wary of Cara and Síomha. I'm feeling excited about spending a day with my friends. I'm feeling sad for Sadhbh and Don. But I don't know how I'm feeling about the fact that this could have been a joint baby shower and this cottage could have been full of flat-pack baby furniture and a big bouncy ball. I couldn't have done anything differently, so I can't even wish I could go back in time and change things. I'm aching for what could have been but excited for what is.

I reach around John's head and scratch behind his ear, like a dog. He immediately turns and presses himself to me.

'I'm feeling okay about today. I don't know how I'll feel later, but right now I feel okay.'

He kisses my face and down my neck. 'Good. Me too.'

'How are you getting to the bus later?'

'Titch is picking me and Pablo up, and he'll leave his car in the village.'

'Tony Timoney won't know what hit him.'

Three hours and a hearty breakfast later John is heading out the door for the lads' day out with Pablo.

'Did you hear from Don if he's coming?'

'He was never able to come – he had something with one of his old schoolfriends this weekend so he's out. Has Sadhbh decided if she's going to the baby shower?'

'She just texted me there to say she is.'

'It'll be a good distraction for her, maybe?'

'She's my diversion for when the stripper arrives.'

John puts his bus cans into a backpack, shaking his head and laughing. 'Should I be worried about this stripper?'

'You should be worried *for* the stripper when Maj claps eyes on him.'

Titch Maguire pulls up outside and gives a little bip. I stand at the door and wave them off, Pablo already in the front seat wearing a 'Papa to Be' baseball cap.

'Have fun. Don't lose Pablo. Majella's going to really need him in about a month's time.'

****

I want to get to Mammy's before Cara and Síomha so I can collect some of the decorations I have stashed there and not have them watching me loading them into the Micra and sweating. Or even worse, having them help. I try calling the cat as I walk from the car to the house, even though Mammy has already texted me to say there's been no sign. In the kitchen, my eyes sweep around all the usual places – on the armchair, on top of the presses, on the windowsill – but she's not there. Maybe she's gone off somewhere to die, like an elephant. Maybe she somehow got wind of Mammy wanting to sell the farm and she's taken off before she can be removed by force.

Up in my bedroom, I take down the balloon stands and bunting I ordered online from the top of the wardrobe. I feel under the bed for the box full of packets of balloons, pumps, tinsel curtains, penis straws, soother necklaces and fake dollar bills. Truly the most deranged set of party decorations ever collected together. Mammy gives me a hand bringing the stuff downstairs and I take it out to the car, stacking it in the boot. I race back upstairs to change into my dress for the shower but end up sitting on my bed in my underwear for a few minutes to cool down. It is a hot day to be drinking in a ballroom with a pregnant lady and a stripper.

I try to imagine this as me and John's home. Us running the farm and the gym and the house. Maybe we'd get a dog. Maybe we'd have children here. Or maybe it will be someone else's house entirely. And they'll never know that me and Majella did a seance in the sitting room and nearly burnt the place down when Majella's granny made herself known by knocking over the Forever Friends candle we were using to summon her. They'll never know that Paul broke his leg falling down the stairs and I got in trouble for laughing instead of getting help straight away. In my defence, I thought he was messing, and he had recently been kneeling on my neck telling me to stop hitting myself. Not a jury in the land would convict me. They'll never know how many nights I cried in this room over boys or fights or quadratic equations.

Through the open window, I hear Mammy out the back calling the cat again, so I throw on my dress and run down to her, grabbing the Dreamies as I go out the back door. Just as I do, Cara's Volkswagen Beetle swings in the gate and crunches up the driveway. Great, it looks like we're out here as a welcoming party for the two queens of Sheba. Síomha gives a half-hearted wave as Mammy directs Cara to park on the far side of the Micra. I shake the Dreamies absentmindedly and then stop abruptly as I hear an unmistakable and plaintive cry coming from what seems like the far side of the small shed.

'Mammy, listen.' I shake the Dreamies again, and around the corner of the shed pops That Bloody Cat, roaring like she hasn't been fed in a week. Well, maybe she hasn't, in fairness. She stops and stretches as if to goad us into waiting even longer for her. Mammy is overcome and shouts joyfully at Cara and Síomha, who are still in the car, 'The cat's come home to welcome you girls!' Cara gestures a circling motion at Mammy, obviously not getting that this raggedy animal has been missing for days, and probably not caring either. Puss starts to trot towards us just as Cara shifts her gears and her reversing light comes on. I barely have time to let the 'No!' leave my lips before the car moves back and, *THLUNK*, rolls over its victim with a tiny bump. Cara looks from me to Mammy, taking in our stricken faces. The car jolts forward and cuts out as she lifts her feet off the pedals in a panic. I squeeze my eyes shut and then open them a tiny sliver to confirm that if the cat wasn't lost to us before, she certainly is now. We all sit and stand in silence for ten seconds, Mammy with one hand over her eyes and the other pointing to Tiger's mangled body. The reality of what's just happened hits Síomha, and she steps out of the car and looks towards the back wheels as I roar out another 'No!'

'Omigod, omigod, omigod.' That's Cara hyperventilating in the driver's seat. Síomha stands stock still with her hands over her mouth. Cara slowly pulls the handle on her door and exits the car, moving towards the rear. Mammy, eyes open now, shouts at her, 'No, Cara, no, don't look at it. There's no need.'

Cara bursts into tears. 'I'm so sorry. Omigod, I'm so, so sorry. It was an accident. Oh my God, I can't believe I did that.' She leans on the car for support. 'I think I'm going to get sick.'

Mammy moves towards her then. 'Come on inside with me – you got an awful fright. Come in where it's cool and get some water.'

Cara allows herself to be led inside while Síomha just stands in the same position, eyes darting around like a trapped bird. For some reason, I feel like I'm going to laugh. The shock, maybe. I turn on my heel and follow Mammy and Cara inside, grab the cordless and go into the hall to punch in Willy Foley's number, which is handily Sellotaped to the back of the phone along with the nearest Garda station and the Chinese. Willy answers on the second ring.

'Hiya, Willy, are you around on the farm by any chance?' Oh great, could you come down to the house? There's been an incident with the poor cat. Yes, she came home but, eh, there's just been an accident. Look for the Beetle.'

Síomha is inside when I go back into the kitchen, silently sitting on a chair. Cara is still gasping, and Mammy is patting her shoulder in circles, making shushing noises.

Cara looks at me in desperation. 'It was an accident, Aisling. I really didn't mean it.'

'Of course it was an accident, pet.' Mammy continues her patting. 'That old cat had already used up twenty lives anyway.'

'We didn't see it at all.' Síomha finds her voice. 'We didn't know anything until we hit it.'

Cara breaks down in tears again. 'How are we going to explain this to Dad?'

'We'll all tell him it was an accident and it couldn't be helped.' Mammy catches my eye. 'Aisling, get the brandy from the front room.'

When I come back with the bottle, Mammy has two little glasses out and then goes back and gets a third one for herself. She pours three decent measures before raising her eyebrows at me.

I shake my head. 'I have to drive us to the Mountrath.' As I sink into the chair opposite Síomha, I hear Willy on the four-wheeler pulling up outside the house. I think he'll be able to figure it out for himself.

Mammy takes a swig of her brandy before encouraging the girls. 'It's good for your nerves. Come on, for the cat.' They both take swigs, screwing up their eyes in disgust.

'Hang on.' I run back into the sitting room and grab two tiny cans of ginger ale from the drinks cabinet. I thrust them at the girls across the table. 'It'll be much nicer with this. My dad said brandy and ginger ale could cure anything.'

Cara tries to smile and Síomha mutters her thanks.

My phone dings and I grab it off the counter. It's Sinéad and Dee in the baby-shower group that doesn't include Majella, wondering where I am with the decorations. They said they'd help. Aubrey will be arriving shortly too, with Hannah in tow. Might as well make a workday out of it.

'Do you need to get going, Aisling?' Mammy asks, and Síomha groans.

'We can't go now. We can't kill your cat and then go to your friend's baby shower with all your other friends. Someone will deck us. And I wouldn't blame them.'

Mammy knocks back the rest of her brandy. 'Of course you can come. Girls, this is a farm and animals come and go. Ye were very good to be making an effort to come for Majella, and for me. It means a lot.' She puts a hand over Cara's. 'Isn't that right, Aisling?'

'Oh yeah, yeah, of course you have to come. And like Mammy said, the cat was on her last legs anyway.' If I'm honest with myself, despite the shock, I'm relieved. At least we know what happened to her, and we know she died quickly and hopefully painlessly. I had awful visions of her never coming home, or coming home and then getting slowly sicker and having to be put down. At least it's over now.

Cara grabs Mammy's hand now. 'You're being so nice to us.'

'Sure, aren't you great girls? Now, will we get ourselves together and hit the road?'

I really could have done with that brandy.

CHAPTER 39

'What's the story with those two? They look like they've seen a ghost.' Dee pauses from blowing up a gold balloon to nod over at Cara and Síomha, who are hanging tinsel curtains around the perimeter of the room, giving it a slight Studio 54 vibe. Majella will be thrilled. The ballroom has been halved in size with a big accordion divider, and if the majority of the fiftyish-strong guest list arrive, we'll be packed. 'Are they raging to be here?'

I feel sorry for the girls after the trauma with That Bloody Cat. They were like two children with Mammy looking after them, and they asked her questions about Tiger all the way in the car. Mammy was thrilled to tell stories about the cat's escapades, and I was thrilled to see them being nice to her.

'No, they're grand. They just got a fright earlier. On the road. They're grand.' No need to be spreading the story about them reversing over the cat in a room full of strangers. I check the time on my phone. 'Only ten minutes until people start arriving. Pump like your lives depend on it!'

I have Majella scheduled to arrive half an hour after everyone else so she can walk in to a hero's welcome, and as the time ticks closer to her grand entrance the room fills up nicely. Sadhbh, Elaine and Ruby arrive together and cause a mini riot when they reveal the buggy they're pushing isn't a present for Majella – it's a cat chariot for Marsha. At one stage, I catch Mammy's eye and burst out laughing. Rocky arrives in a jumpsuit she crocheted herself, and the barman drops two pints staring at her. Tessie Daly and some of the older ladies set up camp at one of the tables and order five bottles of wine straight off the bat. I see them hoarding some of the fake dollars too. They must be gagging for the stripper.

Niamh from Across the Road arrives with Úna Hatton in tow and cradling a tiny bump of her own. Rumour has it her boyfriend is a distant Trump cousin, which is probably why we haven't heard her mother boasting about it. I find myself staring at her and feeling a little bitter that she's managed to get even that over on me. Then Rocky shows me some earrings she's made out of baby booties and I catch a hold of myself and congratulate Niamh, who's terrorising a waitress about every single ingredient inside the tiny sandwiches. Majella's aunties and cousins and our neighbours are all getting stuck in to the finger food while Aubrey sucks her prosecco through a willy straw, looking thoroughly confused, and Hannah talks the ins and outs of brow lamination with Sharon. One of Majella's cousin's has brought her baby, which would be against the 'no children' rule, but she's breastfeeding so she gets a pass. I've already seen most of the guests getting a go of the baby. She seems like a very agreeable little thing, which is lucky because she looks a little bit like Danny DeVito. Right on the dot of half three, I get a text from Liz Moran telling me they're outside.

'Queen Maj is on her way in! Everyone on your feet!' Dee is on the tunes until the DJ arrives at seven, and I gesture at her to press play on 'Baby Love' on the laptop that's hooked up to the sound system. We scream and cheer as Maj makes her entrance in the tuxedo dress, which is now so short that if she was crowning we'd be able to see the baby's hair colour. We're so loud that she stops suddenly, a look of panic flashes across her face. But after a split second she screeches again, 'Jesus, I thought I was going into labour there.' Sinéad McGrath is flat out taking videos like a paparazzo to send back to Pablo's relatives in Tenerife, and I can tell by Majella's face that she is living for the attention. She makes her way over to me and engulfs me in a hug. 'It's perfect, bird. The chocolate willies and all. Perfect.'

Everyone sits and eats and gets their drinks orders in for the first half an hour or so. I'm delighted to be able to chat to Maj and the girls before we get into the games and the main event: Dr Grant himself. Hannah has made sure he has the right colour blue shirt and everything. She's even made a 'Jurassic Cock' visitor's badge for him.

'How are Cruella and Drizella?' Majella asks, nodding at Cara and Síomha, who are smiling politely as Úna Hatton recites one of her poems.

'Oh, Maj, something awful happened earlier. They reversed over That Bloody Cat and killed it.'

Majella stops chewing mid vagina cupcake. 'I'm sorry, what?'

'They were in bits over it. I actually felt sorry for them. Mammy was so nice to them. And they've actually been nicer since it happened. That's what it feels like anyway.'

'Maybe they needed to feed their bloodlust – they did a podcast episode about a guy who needed to do that, actually.'

'I thought you were quitting *Blood and Bordeaux*?'

'It's too addictive, Aisling, I can't. I'm sorry. I know they're your mortal enemies.'

'I don't know if they are any more. I saw a more human side to them today. And I'm probably a bit too grown to be fighting with my mother's boyfriend's children. As long as Mammy's happy, I should be happy for her.'

Majella nods, finishing off her cupcake with its startlingly realistic buttercream pubic hair. Carol Boland didn't even blink when I asked her to make two dozen. They're going down a storm. Sumira Singh and Constance Swinford are tucking into one each across the room right this second.

'Speaking of being grown up, Ais, have you thought any more about the farm?'

'Ah, I have and I haven't. I feel sort of at stalemate. My pros and cons lists are dead equal, and I cannot decide which to go with.'

'For what it's worth, I think you'd be wasted selling cabbage and shovelling sheep shite. You're so good at event architecting, or whatever you call it. Farming's such a hard life. I think you're mad, I do. Remember your dad didn't take a day off in thirty years? He missed our fourth-year musical because a bullock got out.' Maj was the Artful Dodger. She kept the accent for months.

'I know. Farming is a vocation, but I just feel like we can't sell it. What if Daddy is turning in his grave?'

'Bird, I'm not being a bitch here, but that isn't true and you know it. Seamus was a sound head. He'd want her to be happy. Marian has years left in her.'

Deep down, I know she's right. 'The thoughts of somebody else running it, though. Paul says he doesn't really care, but it's easy for him. I don't think he has any intention of coming back home. Not for a long time anyway.'

'So let her sell it, bird. Let her live her life. Unless … are you worried about her? And Doctor Love?'

'I've asked you to stop calling him that. Please, Maj.'

'Sorry.'

'But, yeah, I think that's part of it. I just don't know if it's a good idea to put all her eggs into his basket, if you know what I mean. Then she'll be tied to him.'

'After selling the farm, she'll be independent. She can have her own basket. And, look, your mother's no lovesick teenager. She'll probably have a prenup like Kim Kardashian.'

'It's our home, though, Majella. I've lived there all my life. I just always thought it would be there.'

'It's just a house and some sheds …'

'And sixty acres. And all my childhood memories. And … and … and … Daddy.' As soon as I say it the lump forms in my throat. I've already said goodbye to him once – this would be like doing it all over again.

'That's why we have graves, Ais,' Majella says gently. 'You can visit him there. And your memories are already in your head. You don't need to be in the house to remember your dad.'

'I suppose I'm just struggling with the idea that I won't have a home any more.'

'But, like, what's home? Really, when you think about it? My family home burnt down and, look, here I am, not a bother.'

She's right, it did. Three years ago, an inferno caused by a build-up of lint in the tumble dryer. Liz Moran's greatest shame. 'That's different. Your dad was able to rebuild it. It's still there.'

'It's not the same, though – it's all open-plan now. And anyway, it's not really my home any more. It's Liz and Shem and Shane's.' She places a hand on her bump. 'My home is the apartment with Pablo. And with this little fecker soon. Is your home not wherever John is? Wherever you are?'

I think about our plan to plant the tree. 'It is, I suppose.'

We've made it so nice and so cosy. My heart sings every time I open the front door and walk in after the drive down in the evening. More often than not, John is at the Aga whipping up dinner and dancing around to Bon Jovi with a tea towel over his shoulder. It's all I've ever really wanted. 'But we don't own it or anything.'

'What does that have to do with anything? Plenty of people in this country don't own their home and never will. Pablo says Irish people get too bogged down in owning land. On the continent people rent all their lives – it doesn't stop them having a home. His abuelo on his father's side was a nomad. Mardonium, meaning warrior. I gave it a hard pass before it was even out of his mouth.'

'Imagine having a Mardonium starting in Junior Infants. You made the right choice.'

'I know. Mardonium Moran.' She flashes me a look, probably to see if I object. 'The child is taking my surname, obviously.'

'Oh, obviously.' I couldn't care less what the child is called as long as it's healthy and happy and not called Mardonium. 'Thanks for the advice, Maj. You're very wise, you know?'

****

We split into teams for 'Guess the Babby with the Booty', and Sumira Singh turns out to be surprisingly good at figuring out whose baby picture has been photoshopped onto the body of an exotic dancer. Constance Swinford was a very handsome infant – we all say it. Majella allows a poll on whether it's a boy or a girl, even though she swears Pablo's spidey superstitious senses will be tingling. It results in a dead heat, and we make the barman cast the deciding vote. He goes for boy, but the poor divil has started to look very shook. It's not even five o'clock and the dancefloor is already in use. He definitely didn't come in for his shift working a baby shower and expect to see this much twerking before dinner time.

'Drink, Ais?' Sadhbh is heading for the bar after a therapeutic cry in the toilets with me, Elaine and Ruby. She keeps swinging wildly between acceptance and denial about her break-up with Don. To be honest, none of us can believe it, but we have to be good friends and tell her she's a ride and a catch and will find someone even better than Don when she's good and ready.

'Do you think there's anyone better than Don?' Elaine whispers as we leave the bathroom.

'God, no, although losing his shit over the baby thing has lost him a few points.' Ruby, matter of fact as always.

I refuse the offer of a sandwich, just waiting to get the stripper out of the way before I relax completely. I check with Hannah that he's on his way and then start gathering up bundles of dollar bills for the poor craythur. I hope he knows what he's in for.

I pass Cara and Síomha sitting at a fairly empty table – Mammy, Tessie Daly and Úna Hatton are over at the cake, fighting about the best way to cut it – and smile at them. They're looking a bit less shook, thank God. Then I double back to them. Might as well be friendly and have a chat. 'Hiya, girls, mind if I sit down?'

Cara indicates the empty chair beside her and starts talking immediately. 'Aisling, we just wanted to say again how sorry we are. The poor cat –'

'Honestly, girls, it's fine. Don't beat yourselves up. It could have been me or Mammy that did it. It was just bad luck. Mostly for the cat. C'mere, are you enjoying yourselves?'

'It's really lovely,' Síomha says. 'Good fun, and surprisingly non-PG?'

'That's actually a great way to sum up Majella.'

'Your friend Niamh is lovely. The one who lives in New York. She has such a glamorous life over there. I can't believe she knows Bono's daughters.'

'Oh, she told you all about that, did she?' I know for a fact that Niamh from Across the Road met the Bono girls precisely once at a fancy magazine awards event and they couldn't pick her out of a line-up. Tara was there too, shoehorning them into pictures for her blog, and the closest Niamh got to being friends with them was holding one of their drinks. Still, though, let her have her glory in the ballroom of the Mountrath. She's in a delicate condition, after all.

'Is there really a stripper coming?' Cara looks incredulous. 'I thought the people in the WhatsApp group were joking.'

'Oh, he's definitely coming. Hopefully in about twenty minutes. Here, have some dollars.'

They exchange a look as I stuff the fake bills into their hands. 'We actually wanted to talk to you about something.' Cara leans forward. 'It's about our dad.'

CHAPTER 40

'**W**e just can't believe he's thinking of getting rid of it. It's our family home. And he says your mum is selling her farm. Do you not think it's all a bit much too soon?'

I find myself in a place I couldn't have even imagined one or two or three months ago: relating to and empathising with Cara and Síomha. 'I totally get where you're coming from. I've been really struggling with the idea, too. So much so that I'm considering taking over the farm myself.'

'Dad says it's just bricks and mortar and we carry our memories with us, but, like, that's where Mum was when she died. It's like he doesn't care.'

'I don't think it's that he doesn't care, Síomha.' Cara shakes her head. 'Like, obviously he'd be sad to sell it, but he just doesn't think we have much of a say.'

At least Mammy has entertained the idea of me taking over the farm, although my earlier conversation with Maj rings in my ears. The money she'd make from the sale would give her financial independence. I've just been selfishly and ignorantly assuming she'd just walk away and give everything to me. 'Maybe your dad wants the money from the house to retire on?'

'He's a GP. He has plenty of money. We actually –' Cara breaks off there.

'What?' I push her.

'We thought maybe your mum was after his money for a long time.' She has the good grace to look a bit ashamed.

I feel myself bristling. 'My mother is not after his money or anything else. I think she's shown that she's mad about him just by putting up with you two, to be quite honest.'

'Well, it's not like you were the most welcoming yourself!' Síomha fires back. 'You looked like you wanted to die at Christmas, and you literally assaulted us at Castlefarrow.'

I will acknowledge that it doesn't sound great when they lay it out like that. 'Okay, I'm really sorry. It really wasn't like me. I was just …' I sigh. 'I had had a rough few months and I was worried about Mamm– eh, my mam. But also, I invited you to The Peigs and you didn't even show up. It wasn't easy to get those tickets.'

'We are genuinely sorry about that, and to this day I'm raging we didn't go,' Cara admits. 'But it just seemed so overwhelming. You with all your friends – you're besties with Sadhbh, for God's sake. She's as inner circle as it gets.' I spare them the details of Sadhbh's heartache. 'We were afraid you'd be laughing at us or resent us for being there. We know our dad asked your mum to sort the tickets.'

'Yeah, and she was really hurt that you wasted them.'

'We know. We got it in the ear from Dad.'

'My mother is a nice person, you know? She's not an evil-hag stepmother.'

'I know, and she was so, so nice to us today after the … the thing with the cat.' Cara looks ready to cry again.

'Well, since we're being honest, for a minute I thought you might try and murder her. Or us. To get us out of the picture. Your podcast is full of great ideas.'

Síomha bursts out laughing. 'We were hoping she might just end things with Dad, but she didn't, in fairness to her. We probably took it a bit far.' Síomha looks at Cara and they both nod.

I smile. 'We all took it a bit far. But at least no one died. Well, except the cat.'

There's a squeal from across the room and we look over to see Geraldine from Geraldine's Boutique recoiling from the cat chariot. She's not the first person who's peered in expecting a baby, only to be greeted by Marsha.

'Did you know they want to move to Connemara?' Cara has a note of incredulity in her voice.

'Yeah, Mammy mentioned something about the west, alright.'

'Although Dad sent me a link to a place on Achill. Did you get that, Síomha?'

I didn't know Achill was now in the mix. Mammy hasn't shared any of this with me. I suppose how can she when I'm still humming and hawing over the farm.

'Oh, Achill's cool. I was there with Matt last summer.'

'Still, though, are we really willing to sacrifice the Kerry house?' Cara slumps in her chair, and I realise how unreasonable she sounds. How unreasonable we all sound. And at least I have Mammy saying she wants to keep a base in BGB. The girls won't have anything similar in Kerry.

'Are you genuinely thinking about running the farm, Aisling? Do you not have your deadly job in Dublin? And you're living with John. Would he come with you?'

I think about leaving the little cottage again so soon, after all the work we've put into it. I think about the dodgy boiler in our old farmhouse and the draught that gets under the carpets. I think about how long I've been storing my memories in that house and those sheds and those fields and imagine packing them up and bringing them with me.

'Do you know what? Maybe I will just let it go. Now that I think about it, it feels a bit selfish to insist on keeping it.'

Cara and Síomha look unsure.

'My friend Majella, who's very wise and insisted on this baby shower, said something to me earlier about home being what you make it. If Mammy and Dr Trevor's home' – the girls snigger at me calling him Dr Trevor – 'if it's in Achill or Connemara, then that'll kind of be our home too, if they let any of us ungrateful wagons visit.'

'Sounds like you've made your decision.' Cara shrugs.

'Any clearer on the Kerry house?' I look from one face to the other.

'Maybe,' Síomha says, 'but we might give him a hard time for a bit longer.'

'I'd well believe it.'

Hannah appears at my side. 'Aisling, he's outside. Get her in the chair.'

I hurry over to Sadhbh and tell her to initiate the diversion as I prepare the floor for the stripper's arrival. She dutifully asks Majella to show her photos of her meeting various Westlife members, a pastime that will buy us precious minutes of set-up time. I race out of the ballroom and down to a large storage cupboard where I've stashed the chair gussied up to look like a throne. As I drag it back into the ballroom, Aubrey is passing out giant baby bibs with 'I've got a boner' printed on them, plus a cute dinosaur to make them a little less crude. Dee is in place to man the music, and all that's left to do is send Hannah the text that we're ready to roll. I fire it off, give Dee the nod and as the iconic *Jurassic Park* music fills the room, I escort a confused Majella to her throne, startling her from a monologue to Sadhbh about Shane Filan's eye creases.

'What the hell, bird?'

With that the ballroom door swings open and in struts Dr Alan Grant. Well, a small but very well-built version of him, anyway, wearing the blue shirt, chinos, red kerchief and an Indiana Jones hat. He even has dust on his trousers and boots. Hannah's attention to detail is up there with Aubrey's.

'Oh my God,' squeals Majella, as Dr Grant strides towards her and bellows, 'I'm here to jump some bones.'

Majella grabs my hand. 'Aisling, I really do think I might be going into labour.'

'What? Really?'

Dr Grant crosses the dance floor towards Majella, loses focus for a second when he sees just how pregnant she is, but then he's back in the game and he's undoing the upper buttons of his shirt.

'No, actually, I'm alright,' she hisses, shooing me away.

The palaeontologist stripper is better than any *Magic Mike* impersonator we could have gotten, and even plays along when the sweeping *Jurassic Park* music segues into 'Pony', humping and grinding like nobody's business. His pièce de résistance comes when he whips a little brush out of his tiny pants and flicks it up and down Majella's body. I'm glad Pablo isn't here to see it. The room is going wild as he finishes his set, running around the room and rolling his hips at anyone who'll stand still for two seconds. I've never seen Constance Swinford so puce. Before he leaves, I press two fifty-euro notes into his hand as a tip. He's earned it. And I've earned a drink. Majella toddles off to the bathroom to cool down after her hectic time in the throne, and I tip over to Sadhbh and Ruby to see if they want a top-up.

Sadhbh is staring at her phone in disbelief. 'It's Don. He's outside.'

'Oh. What? Is he okay?'

'He wants me to come out. I suppose I'll go?' Her cheeks are flushed and she's practically giddy. So much for no contact. It hasn't even been forty-eight hours.

Before she can even make it to the door, a frantic Don is entering the ballroom, eyes swivelling around looking for her. He spots her and pounces, taking both her forearms in his hands. 'I thought you weren't going to come out.'

'In fairness, she didn't get a chance,' Ruby pipes up, and is silenced with a glare from Elaine.

'Sadhbhy,' Don pants, 'I barely got through one day without you. I'm in absolute bits. Please can we stop this stupid thing we're doing and just go back to being us. I'm in hell.'

The whole room is agog. Denise Kelly has even produced popcorn from somewhere.

'What about the baby issue, Don? If I haven't changed my mind and you haven't changed yours –'

'I have changed my mind. I have changed it, Sadhbhy.'

'How? Since Thursday?'

'I can't live without you. You're more important to me than any stupid baby that doesn't even exist.'

'Interesting language for a literal baby shower,' Ruby mutters, before being shushed by several people.

'Plus,' Don continues, 'I was staying with Marc and his wife last night, and they have a two-year-old and a newborn, and it was so awful. The older one was terrorising us.' Some of the mothers in the group nod sagely. 'I'm pretty sure I can live without that, but I can't live without you.'

Sadhbh collapses into his arms and a cheer goes around the room. Even the barman is looking misty-eyed. The cousin with little Danny DeVito elbows her way through, thrusting the child at Don. 'I know you said you're not into babies, but I absolutely have to get a photo for Facebook.'

Don accepts the infant, somewhat blindsided, and then turns on his delicious smile for the camera. The cousin forces her phone on her mother. 'Get one with me in it.'

As the posing continues, Majella pushes her way through, much more composed after a little time out. She stops dead in her tracks as she takes in the scene of her one true love – after Pablo – standing in the middle of her shower, cradling a tiny baby. She gasps and grabs her bump.

CHAPTER 41

ajella stares down between her feet where a slow trickle of clear liquid is starting to pool. She looks like a deer caught in headlights, her eyes darting from it to Don and the baby and then back to me.

'Shite, Maj, that's … I think your waters are after breaking,' I hiss, grabbing her by the hand and dragging her back towards the toilets before someone slips on it and knocks themselves out. Luckily, Don's dramatic declaration and photoshoot has completely distracted everyone else. Even characteristically cool Niamh from Across the Road is looking flushed and fanning herself with a photograph of a lithe dancer with the head of baby Pablo in a bonnet.

We scuttle towards the bathrooms, and at the last minute, I steer Majella away from the ladies' and into the disabled toilet for a bit of privacy. When I lock the door, I wheel around, expecting her to be in a state of panic, but instead she's calmly topping up her nose contour with a tiny compact she's just pulled out of her bra. The liquid is still running down her leg.

'What are you doing, Maj? You're going into labour. For real this time!'

She catches my eye in the mirror. 'Bird, relax! I'm only thirty-six weeks. I have to get to forty. Loadsa time yet.' Then she starts carefully combing her eyebrows. 'I need to get a selfie with Don before he whisks Sadhbh away for a ride in the car park.'

The liquid is now gathering in her shoes and trickling down onto the floor. I walk over and take her gently by the shoulders and turn her around so we're facing each other. She's shaking slightly.

'Majella,' I say, as evenly as I possibly can, 'I don't think you understand. Forget Don Shields! Either you are very slowly pissing yourself here or you're going into labour.'

'No,' she says defiantly. 'I'm at my *Magic Mike*-slash-*Jurassic Park* baby shower, Aisling. We've been planning this for months. Well, you have anyway. I'm absolutely fine. I haven't even done my birthing class yet. I don't even have a bag packed.'

I glance down at the puddle between us. 'Well, I don't think the baby cares about that.'

I only got to read the first couple of chapters of *What to Expect*, but I'm pretty sure that once the waters break, there should be no hanging around. I need to get Majella to the hospital fast, and I need to get Pablo back home from Dublin to hold up her legs and listen to her telling him what a prick he is for knocking her up in the first place.

Majella is putting the compact back into her bra when she suddenly stops dead and sort of winces.

'What was that?'

'I don't know.'

'Was it a contraction?'

'Hard to say. It's passed now.' She fluffs her hair. 'I think we should go back out. I haven't opened any presents yet.'

For a second, I consider slapping her across the face, but instead I carefully guide her by the shoulders backwards to the toilet. Then I flip down the lid and sit her onto it firmly. She's starting to look a bit dazed.

'Majella, I think you're in denial. You're in labour! I have to go out and get my phone. I'll be back in a sec.'

I don't think she's taking in a word I'm saying, though, because she's starting to babble.

I kneel down in front of her so we're eye to eye. 'Are you okay there?' Then I plaster on a smile. 'This is exciting, Maj. It's happening!'

She meets my eye then, looking stricken and clutching her bump. 'I can't really be in labour, Aisling,' she whispers. 'That means the baby will be premature. It's only a cucumber yet. It's supposed to be a watermelon.'

'Don't worry about that. Everything is where it's supposed to be at this stage, isn't it? The baby just fattens up the last few weeks anyway. Remember Tara Cowman?'

'Midfield for the Gaels?'

I nod. 'Her little lad was born at thirty-two weeks, and he was grand. Only four pounds and she called him Boris, but grand. The baby is fine, but we really should make our way to the hospital. I'm going out to get my phone, okay? Don't let anyone else in. We're very close to the girls wanting to piss in pairs.'

A look of panic crosses her face. 'Don't tell anyone, will you not, Ais?'

'Why?'

'My mother's three sheets to the wind, and so are my aunties. They never get together any more except for funerals. Let them enjoy the evening. I don't want everyone going all weird and sitting around thinking about me and waiting for news.'

'Absolutely. Whatever you want, Maj.'

Her face screws up.

'What? What's wrong?'

'I didn't even get to see the DJ. I always wanted a baby shower with a DJ.'

I leg it out of the toilet and back into the ballroom, where Dee and Maeve are shimmying around the dancefloor to 'Mamma Mia' with Constance Swinford, Liz Moran, Mammy and Hannah. A few of the cousins and at least two aunts are at the bar handing out baby Guinnesses. It's all turning out exactly how Maj planned – it's just a shame she's missing it now.

Aubrey catches my eye as I nip around her to grab my phone off the table. She is deep in conversation with Sharon about wedding venues that don't frown upon a dove release. I've seen a dove drop dead in upstate New York after flying straight into the trailer of an articulated lorry, but I say nothing. Hopefully Tom Hanks's son and his fiancée managed to enjoy their engagement pictures in the end despite the bloody carnage.

'All good?' Aubrey mouths at me, and I give her the thumbs-up. Hopefully Hannah didn't notice or I'll never hear the end of it. She accuses my thumb emojis of being cringe.

When I slip back in to the toilet, Majella is still sitting there looking disorientated. 'Are you okay?'

'Yeah. I think so.'

'Any more pains when I was gone?'

'A small one. Are they having loads of craic without me? Is Doctor Grant gone? Is there cake left?'

I hit dial on John's name. 'I'll get Aubrey to save you some.'

It's ringing.

'Ais? How's the baby shower?'

I can hear a racket in the background. It doesn't sound like Arnotts or anywhere you might buy chinos or an anorak. 'John! Thank God.'

Majella winces again, screwing her eyes shut and holding her bump. 'Is … Pab … enjoying … himself?' she gasps.

'Majella's gone into labour! Do you have Pablo?'

'Good one, Ais.'

'John, I'm deadly serious. You need to get Pablo home – fast. Everyone's pissed, so I'm going to have to bring her into the General myself. How long till you can get there, do you think?'

'Oh shit, um …' He sounds cagey now. 'Matt and Denis wanted to catch the New Zealand match …' The din in the background is picking up. Then there's an unmistakable roar. 'And, oh, Ireland just scored, I think!'

'John, you have to get Pablo to the General!'

Another roar. 'Yep, the TMO's confirmed it.'

Is he really going to give me the ins and outs of the game at a time like this? 'You're not in Maguire's!' They wouldn't be showing rugby. Felipe would sooner wear a poppy.

'We're still in town, Ais.'

'I thought you were getting the five o'clock bus?'

'Oh, fuuuck.' Majella gasps, rocking slightly on the toilet seat. 'Did … he … buy … a … polo … shirt?'

I haven't been timing the contractions properly, but I'm guessing they're around five minutes apart now.

'We were going to get the next one at quarter past eight.'

'That's two hours away!' I lower my voice. 'Her contractions are getting closer. You have to get him home, John!'

I shove my phone in my pocket and sink back down on my knees in front of Majella, trying not to think about why the floor directly in front of the toilet might be so sticky. 'Stay calm, Pablo's on his way. How are you doing?'

'Ais, I think I change my mind.' Her chest is heaving and I can see the whites of her eyes.

'Change your mind about what?'

'About the baby.'

I'm tempted to tell her it's a bit late for that, but instead I reach out and take her by both hands. 'Majella, there's no need to be scared of childbirth.' I sound calmer than I feel. 'You'll be fine. Anything Denise Kelly can do, twice, you can do better. You're always saying it. And once we get to the hospital, they'll give you the gas and air so you can get mad out of it. You're excited about the lovely drugs, aren't you?'

She shakes her head. 'It's not the birth I'm worried about, Ais. It's … everything else after it.'

'What do you mean?'

'I don't think I'm ready to be a mam,' she wails.

'Of course you are! You've been dying to be a mam since we watched *Mermaids* and wanted to get dresses like Cher and Winona Ryder. Shoop shoop?'

'Yeah, but I don't know if I thought it through properly. I'm not Cher. Like, what if I forget I have a baby and accidentally leave it in a car on a sunny day?'

'You won't, Maj.'

'It happens all the time!'

'Not in BGB. You couldn't leave your purse in the car here

without getting a text from the Community Alert crowd giving out to you.'

'What if I don't know how to stop it crying?'

'You will know. Mams just do.'

'Well, what if Pablo loves the baby more than me? I'm scared I'll be playing second fiddle for the rest of my life.'

'You'll be happy for the baby! And we all know Pablo has plenty of love to go around. You're not going to be second fiddle to anyone.' Then I add, 'I'm sure everyone feels this way when they're getting ready to give birth.'

'But what if I'm not responsible enough? You know the way I'm a bit of a, well, a hames –'

'Excuse me,' I interject, 'you used to be a hames. Not any more. When was the last time you lost a phone?'

She thinks for a second. Then her face lights up. 'Not since my work Christmas party!'

'There you go! That's more than nine months ago. You've a new personal best.'

'And I didn't lose it – it was actually robbed after I left it behind me in the toilet cubicle in McGowan's.'

I bite my tongue. 'See? I told you. You're all grown up. You're going to be a brilliant mam.'

Her face suddenly crumples.

'Oh God, another contraction?'

'No,' she sobs, 'I'm just afraid, Ais. I'm afraid everything is going to change and things will never go back to the way they were.'

'Ah, Maj, don't be worrying. Change is good. You tell me that every time you dye your hair. Things will be better than they ever were. You're ready for this, I promise you.'

She's still sobbing. 'I thought I'd feel grown up by now, but I don't. I still feel like I'm twenty-two. Am I a weirdo?'

I contemplate it for a minute. 'You're not a weirdo, you're normal. I feel like that myself. I even have the same boyfriend as I did when I was twenty-two! Although we're in a much better place now than we were back then.'

'If you love John so much then why don't you put him out of his misery and say you'll marry him?' She practically screams it. 'You're driving us all mad, bird!'

'Majella, would you keep your voice down?!'

'I can say what I want – I'm the one in labour,' she sniffs.

'I told you, we'll get engaged when the time is right. Now can we start making a move?'

She squeezes my fingers so hard a little whimper falls out of me. 'What kind of a mam hoovers up coppers, Ais? And I hate cleaning, and I leave my clothes in the washing machine for ages until they start to smell and then I have to turn it on again before I can hang them out.'

I stroke her hair. 'You'll be grand, Maj, you'll be grand.'

'You don't do that stuff, though, do you?' she gulps.

'I never did, to be fair. And, look, don't forget you're not doing this by yourself. You have Pablo. You're a good team, the pair of you. You'll be brilliant parents together.'

She gives me a watery smile and sniffs. 'And you and John will be too.' She squeezes my fingers again, more gently this time. 'Some day.' Then her face contorts and she starts to pant. 'Oh … bollix.'

'I think we better get you into the Micra.'

CHAPTER 42

I really have to force myself to avert my eyes when I'm dragging Majella through the kitchen of the Mountrath. I don't think I've ever seen so many food-safety violations in one place, and we were only in it for thirty seconds max. There was a pigeon on one of the counters.

I slide the passenger seat back as far as it will go and throw down one of John's fleeces for her to sit on. 'Okay, you just lie back there and get yourself comfortable. We'll be at the General in twenty minutes.'

Then I pass Majella my phone, which we've been using to time her contractions. They're three and a half minutes apart now, and judging by what she said to the kitchen porter who told us to have a nice day, they're getting stronger.

Majella lowers herself slowly into the car and eventually gets the seat belt around her on the fourth attempt. 'Take the Knock Road, bird – it's three minutes faster. Pablo's been doing drills.'

'Would the main road not be better? The Knock one is so narrow –'

She grits her teeth and starts to pant. 'Oh ... fuck ... another ... one. *Shiiit*.'

I've let the ball drop on *Call the Midwife*, so I can't really remember what you're supposed to say when someone's in labour. 'Breathe, Majella!' I chance. 'Don't forget to breathe!'

After a minute of huffing and puffing her face relaxes and she melts back into the seat. 'That was the worst yet. Pablo better be on his way. I won't get through this without him. I'm meant to have his stupid crystals in the delivery room.'

'He won't be long now.'

'Do you have anything I could take? I'd dry gargle a couple of Solps at this stage, Ais.'

'I might have a paracetamol in the glove box there – have a look.'

'For fuck's sake, what is wrong with you! I need real drugs!'

'How long between those last contractions?'

She checks the phone. 'Three minutes and fifteen seconds. Let's move it, come on!'

'Knock Road it is so,' I concede, and start the Micra.

We're only gone about two kilometres and one contraction so strong that Majella asked the Pope for forgiveness when I fly around a bend and nearly go straight into the back of a trailer piled high with round hay bales. It's crawling along and we won't have any chance of overtaking it till the Rathborris crossroads, which is about ten kilometres away. This never would have happened if we'd taken the main road.

'Shite, anyway,' Majella groans. 'Who is it?'

I pull slightly to the right to try and see who's driving the tractor, but I don't recognise the hat. 'I don't know. It's a ninety-eight reg.'

'Ford?'

'John Deere.'

Majella closes her eyes. 'Ninety-eight John Deere. Let me think. It's not Kellys. Is it Maguires?'

I take another look. The driver's shoulders look very defined, and I can make out his impressive biceps from here. 'I think it's Seán Óg!'

'Beep him, Ais. Go on! Beep him to high heaven!'

'He has on those big noise-cancelling headphones.'

'His life's in danger if he doesn't get out of our way. I'll strangle him myself.'

I lean on the horn but we crawl along behind the tractor for what feels like an hour but is actually an agonising eighteen minutes, which I measure in Majella's contractions that are now coming every three minutes. At one point I debate stopping the car and getting out to catch up with the tractor on foot, but I can't leave Majella when she's in this state. After another contraction and a full twenty-one minutes behind Seán Óg it dawns on me. 'John will have his number! Ring him there and stick it on speaker.'

The sound of the dial tone fills the car as we inch along. It rings and rings.

'Oh, here's another one already,' Majella shouts. '*Fuuuck!*'

'Ais! How's Majella?' Just hearing John's voice makes my shoulders relax a bit.

'I'm … not … fucking … well … arrrgh,' Majella roars, her voice about five octaves deeper than normal. She's red in the face now.

'Holy shit,' John shouts back. 'Maj, from the sounds of it I think you might be going through transition already. Did your mam ever say if your own birth was fast?'

'I … was … born … on … the … kitchen … floor …' she gasps.

'What's transition?' I ask, hoping it means that the baby might be having second thoughts about coming out any time soon.

'It's basically the part of labour just before the shit hits the fan,' John explains.

'The midwife told me they scoop that away so fast nobody sees it,' Majella shrieks, panting now.

'No, I mean, the baby isn't far from being born,' John says, his voice sounding serious. 'You better put the foot down, Ais. And Majella?'

'Yeah?'

'I want you to think of the contractions as waves. Ride the wave. Breathe in through your nose and out through your mouth. In through your nose and out through your mouth – that's it.'

Majella does as she's told, and I can see her face start to soften. 'It's easing off,' she gasps. 'I'm riding the wave. I'm just riding the wave. Ahhhh.'

'John, we're stuck behind a tractor on the Knock Road. I think it's Seán Óg Maguire. Can you ring him?'

'He'll never answer. I'll have to send him a video on Snap.'

'Since when do you have Snapchat?'

'I'll have to download it. I hope I have space on my phone now. Hang on, I might have to delete something …'

Majella interjects. 'Where is Pablo, John?' she wails. 'I need him.'

'Don't worry, he's here beside me. We're just coming off the N7 now.'

'Pablo, can you hear me?' Majella cries. 'Pab, the baby's coming! It's really coming!'

'He's asleep, Maj. He passed out when I told him you were in labour. When he came to, Matt and Denis gave him a brandy for the shock, and he's been asleep ever since.'

'Jesus Christ! How did I ever fall for a man who can't hold his drink! Oh shit, here comes another … wave! Aarrghh!'

'Keep breathing, Maj,' John shouts. 'Imagine your muscles are like jelly. Relax your jaw. Let the wave just wash over you. Your body knows what to do. You know what to do. Deep breaths, good woman. You can do this.' Then his voice changes. 'Horse, it's me. Aisling is behind you in the Micra. It's an emergency. Pull in as soon as you can, will you? Good lad.'

'Aaarrrghhh,' Majella groans. 'Oh Jesus, I'm starting to feel pressure down below. Is that good or bad, John?'

'Well, it depends how you look at it.'

I can feel the sweat pooling in my bra now. This is usually the part of *Call the Midwife* when people are boiling water and tearing up sheets. Beside me, Majella's eyes are screwed shut and her chest is heaving.

'Ais, I'm really scared,' she gasps. 'I can't have a baby on the Knock Road. I'm not calling it Knocknamanagh.'

'Anna, if it's a girl,' John shouts.

'We're going to get you to the hospital in time, Majella,' I say, my eyes trained on the trailer in front of me. Come on, Seán Óg! Check your phone! I've seen you do it behind the wheel a hundred times before! But there's nothing. We just continue to crawl along at a snail's pace. Then suddenly the left indicator on the trailer starts to blink.

'He's opened the Snap!' cries John.

'He's turning in! He's turning in to a gateway, Maj!'

'Fuuuck … here's … another … *waaave*!'

'John, I'll let you go. See you at the General.'

'I love you, Ais.'

'I love you too.'

'And Maj,' he calls, 'remember your body is made to do this. And don't forget to breathe. We'll be with you in ten.'

CHAPTER 43

'Look, there's the hospital up ahead, Maj! We're here! We made it!'

'Ais, I feel like I want to push,' Majella shrieks, 'Give … me … the … drugs!'

'Remember what John said,' I shout, indicating in to the hospital gateway. 'He's read about fifty baby books. He could nearly give birth himself at this stage. Relax into it. Let your body do its thing. Come on, breathe through the pain! Almost there.'

Out of nowhere, a white limousine speeding in through the gate cuts me off and I have to jam on the brakes. My left arm instinctively flies out to stop Majella lurching forward and the engine cuts out.

'Christ,' she roars. 'What the fuck was that? Oh shit, here … comes … another … one. *Arrghh!*'

She's given up timing the contractions now because they're coming so fast. In fact, they're nearly on top of each other. Bastarding doublers, she's calling them.

I start the car and lurch forward into the hospital car park, then I speed up again following the signs for the Emergency Department, which is around the back.

'When we get there, I'll run in and get them to come out with a stretcher. You're in no fit state to walk. I'll only be a second.'

'You can't leave me,' Majella screams. 'If another contraction comes my body is going to start pushing – I can feel it!'

I flick on Solas FM. 'Just focus on the music. Look, Skippy is playing the Saw Doctors. It's like he knew.'

I'm planning on throwing the Micra into the ambulance bay, but when I turn the corner that bloody white limo is taking up the whole space, the driver's door hanging open.

'For God's sake,' I shout, banging my hands on the steering wheel. Then I lean on the horn. The limo doesn't move, but the back door shoots open and out staggers Pablo, looking dazed and confused. The Truck unfolds himself from behind him and takes his arm while Liam Kelly takes the other.

Majella spots them immediately. 'Pablo!' she screams. And then, 'Oh my God, I think it's coming out!' She turns to me, looking as terrified as I've ever seen her, and I was there the first time she went on the Cú Chulainn in Tayto Park. 'Ais ... I ... can't ... help ... it ... I'm ... pushing!' The screech that comes out of her can only be described as bloodcurdling. In the ambulance bay, Pablo starts to wobble and grabs The Truck to try and steady himself.

I can read his lips – 'Mi amor!' – then he faints, slithering down The Truck's body in slow motion before falling gently into a crumpled pile on the tarmac.

The glass doors at the entrance to the Emergency Department slide open, and John and a man I assume is the limo driver appear, looking winded. John looks frantic. 'We couldn't get anyone's attention. It's bedlam.'

Majella lets out a scream and the limo driver is the next one to go wobbly, leaning against the front of his car. 'I really feel like it wants to come out,' Maj shouts in a panic, looking from me to John. 'I need someone to tell me what to do.'

In what seems like two strides John has stepped over Pablo and has the passenger door open and Majella's seat belt off her before I know what's going on. 'Majella, look at me!' he says admirably calmly, holding her face in his hands while she writhes around grunting. He's on his hunkers in front of her, his knees resting on the door jamb. She's moaning and groaning and making sounds I've only ever heard before in the calving shed. 'The Truck is gone in to get a doctor.' He looks up at me and I stand up and make eye contact with The Truck, who turns on his heel and heads for the sliding doors, followed by the entire Dadchelor Party. John is back in the zone with Majella. 'You're going to be alright. I just have to check under the bonnet to see what's going on – is that okay?'

Majella nods mutely while looking at me for, I think, permission to allow John to do what he said he was going to do.

'Yeah, of course I don't mind,' I roar. 'Go on, John! Get up there!'

He has her knickers off and his head under her dress before the words are out of my mouth.

'It's coming!' Majella screams. 'The … baby …. is … really … coming! *Arrrghhh!*'

'You're not wrong, Maj!' John's voice is muffled and slightly panicked. 'I think the head is coming out. It has black hair. Loads of it!'

I lean over and take her hand. 'Oh my God, Majella, you've always said you didn't want a bald baby!'

'I know,' she pants. 'They … look … so … creepy. Oh … shit!'

There's a flurry of clattering and footsteps coming towards us, and a gloved hand takes John by the shoulder. I breathe a sigh of relief to see a doctor and about twenty other medical staff surrounding the car. John shuffles back on his hunkers and the doctor takes his place.

'You're doing great,' the doctor says. 'Majella, isn't it? I think the shoulders are going to come out on this contraction. Keep breathing now. Bear down. Pant! Pant! Pant!'

I jump out of the car and race around to Pablo. He'll never forgive himself if he misses this. 'Majella needs you, Pab,' I scream into his ear, shaking him into consciousness. 'Come on now. Do it for Tenerife.'

His eyes open immediately. 'Where is she?' he whispers. 'Take me to my love!'

'She's right here, hup now, you're about to see your baby being born.'

With that, he clambers up, and I half drag him the three feet to where the doctor is coaching Majella with her breathing and a nurse is starting an IV from the backseat

'Maj, he's up!' I shout, propping him onto his knees behind the doctor so he can see what's happening. He rallies for a second, and then if anything he starts to look even paler.

'Keep panting, Maj, that's it, and now just go with your body,' John coaxes from my left, and I grab his arm and squeeze.

I can't believe how calm he is and how much he knows. 'Did you learn all this from those books, John?'

'I watched a few videos as well. Loads of videos.'

The doctor holds her hands above her head, and a nurse places a towel into them. 'That's it, Majella. Good woman, you're doing it! Go on, now *puuusssh* like your life depends on it. Right down into your bottom!'

Majella screws her eyes shut and lets out a roar loud enough to lift the roof off the car just as 'I Useta Love Her' segues into Westlife.

She's a five foot ten in catsuit and Bambi eyes

I close my eyes, saying a prayer to anyone who's listening that everything will be okay. And then I hear a sound ... it's the faintest little cry, like the mewling noise a kitten makes.

Everybody who's staring wouldn't believe that this girl was mine

'Congrats, Mummy, baby is out,' the doctor announces. When I open my eyes, Maj is clutching the smallest little creature I've ever seen – pink and purplish and covered in white stuff and flailing away like it would definitely rather be back inside.

'Pablo, it's our song!' Majella wails, looking shell-shocked. 'The baby came out to our song!'

The tiny thing is passed to another doctor, who wraps it tightly in the towel and takes a funny-looking scissors from a nurse. 'Would somebody like to cut the cord before we can get these two inside?'

'Pablo?' Majella smiles at him hopefully, and for a second it looks like he's about to stand up, but then he slumps back down on top of me. Gone again.

'I think his blood sugar is a bit low,' I explain. I can't take my eyes off the little bundle in the doctor's arms. The pink face, peeping out from inside the blanket. The little nose. The perfect eyelashes. A copy and paste of Majella's lips. How was it inside her body five minutes ago? And now it's out here, another person in the world?

'Ais, would you do it?' Majella's voice snaps me back to reality.

'Me?'

'Well, John did most of the labour.' She laughs. 'Ow. How the fuck am I still having contractions?'

'You need to pass the placenta still,' the doctor says. 'But it'll be a breeze compared to what you've just done. So, who's doing the honours?'

I hold out my hand. 'Pass me the scissors, so.' And then I stop. 'Hang on, do we know what it is yet?'

'I forgot to ask,' Majella gasps.

The doctor takes a peek inside the blanket. 'Congratulations.' She smiles. 'It's a girl!'

****

A couple of hours later Majella and Pablo and their new baby daughter are settled in a private room, a gift from the hospital manager for being so understanding about having to deliver her baby in the car park. It turns out there had been an accident at a local hotel where fifteen women attending a baby shower had tried to make a human pyramid. A&E was dealing with multiple concussions, two sprained ankles and one dislocated hip. They were overrun. Majella said nothing.

'Pablo, will you please stop crying,' she pleads from her hospital bed. 'Come on now, you'll set me off again. We have to get our shit together – we're parents now.'

He's sitting in an armchair holding the baby, staring at her perfect little heart-shaped face. She's five pounds one and is swimming in the spare onesie and hand-knitted pink hat the hospital was able to rustle up. Only a handful of people even know she's been born.

Pablo nods solemnly. 'She is my world, this little girl. I would die for her. And I would kill in her honour!'

I search Majella's face, but there's absolutely no sign of the jealousy she was so worried about. I've never seen her look so happy. Exhausted and pale, but so, so happy.

There's a knock on the door and John pops his head around. The man of the moment. I can't stop thinking about what might have happened if he hadn't been there. Our hero. 'Okay if I come in?'

'I don't know why you're knocking, lad – you've seen my cervix.' Majella roars laughing at her own joke and he blushes ever so slightly.

He's carrying two bouquets of flowers and her overnight bag. 'I got you those few bits from home,' he says, passing one bouquet to Maj and giving the other to me. 'The limo driver said he's never had a day like it. I was up the front with him. Some car.'

'How did you end up in a limo anyway?'

'There was a hen party in the pub we were watching the match in. When they heard why we were desperately trying to get a taxi they made us take it. Sound girls.'

Then he produces the biggest packet of nappies I've ever

seen. 'And I thought you might need some of these so I stopped in Filan's on the way back. Since she came so early you probably need to buy loads of stuff, do you?'

John sits down beside me on the foot of the bed while Majella shifts in her pillows, looking at Pablo out of the corner of her eye.

'Well, actually, I have pretty much everything already bought,' she says quietly. Pablo shoots her a confused look. 'I know you didn't want me to, Pab, but the deals were too good to pass up just because of some stupid superstition, so I've been keeping everything in Aisling's mam's house. I even got you one of those carriers so you can wear her like a backpack.'

Pablo's jaw drops, and for a second I think we're going to see some mad, angry side of him, but he just moans. 'Oh no, mi amor! I have been doing the same! Buying all the tiny things!'

'What?' Majella shrieks so loud the baby's forehead furrows. Then she whispers, 'I mean, what?'

'I have them all. The carrier. The steriliser. The breast pumps. They are in Eamon Filan's garage. This is why we should not keep secrets from each other!'

Majella rolls her eyes. 'You big dope! Now we have two of everything.' Then she yawns and I remember she's just pushed a baby out of her body with not a drug to be seen. She must be wrecked.

I stand up. 'We better make a move and let you get some rest. It's been a big day. C'mon, John.'

'I can't believe I missed my own baby shower. I'm actually raging, bird.'

'Well, you do have the best excuse, in fairness,' I say, going over to Pablo for one last look at the baby before we leave. Then I whisper, 'You be a good girl for your mammy tonight.' There's not a peep out of her. She doesn't take after her mother anyway, that's for sure.

John puts his arm around my shoulders and gives me a squeeze. 'Look after your girls now, Pablo.'

'Ah, please stop, John,' Majella says, but her eyes are glassy and she's blinking a mile a minute.

'Let me know if you need anything, Maj,' I say. 'And congrats again. You're a legend.'

'Before you go, there's something we want to tell you,' she says. 'Isn't there, Pab?'

'Oh?'

'We've decided on a name. Finally!'

Pablo beams. 'Yes, just an hour ago, when Majella was getting the stitches, our decision was made.'

Majella winces. 'Please, don't remind me.'

'Don't keep us in suspense,' John says.

Majella bites her lip. 'Since she came so early, it was obvious really. We both suggested it at the same time. The first name we've agreed on.'

'Well?' I look from Majella to Pablo. 'Tell us.'

Majella takes a deep breath. 'We're calling her Aisling.'

And that's what sets me off.

CHAPTER 44

I t's getting dark when we're eventually leaving the General after several rounds of tears and hugs over gorgeous baby Aisling. Majella was keen for her middle name to be Joan, a tribute to the man who helped bring her into the world, but John insisted he couldn't have a little girl with such an old-woman name on his conscience and that she didn't even look like an Aisling Joan anyway. Maj was relieved and then decided she wanted to implicate Don Shields in some way, since he was the one who sent her into labour, but Pablo wasn't keen on Donielle or Donatella, and Maj rejected Donna on the grounds that it's too basic. They were bickering away over Donica when myself and John eventually sneaked out of their room unnoticed.

'Well, that was a day I won't be forgetting in a hurry.' John laughs, raking a hand through his hair, as we make our way down the front ramp. 'I saw a few things that I can't unsee. It's nice to be leaving the General happy for a change, though. I think the last time I was here, apart from us the other month –' I squeeze his hand '– was when my father was kicked in the hand by that bullock. His knuckle never really healed right.'

I stare at the ground. 'I remember. The night Daddy died.'

He squeezes my hand twice as hard. How could I forget? We were broken up. John was seeing Ciara, the camogie-playing vixen we'd met on holiday in Tenerife. I was so distraught I'd forgotten to pay my parking. I got clamped for the first and only time in my life. Very unlike me. But while I was in the hospital, John paid the fine and had the clamp taken off. He left a note on my windscreen too: 'Now you can pretend it never happened.' But he wasn't just talking about the clamp. He was talking about us and him and the break-up. All of it. When I went to Dublin to pay him back, I ended up kissing his housemate Piotr in a moment of grief-induced madness. It was all such a mess. And then John didn't show up for Daddy's funeral, and I thought that was the final nail in the coffin for us. It was only later I discovered he'd been at home all along, paying the ultimate tribute to Daddy by minding the house when we were out saying our final goodbyes. He may not have been the perfect boyfriend, and I know there were times when we were younger that he definitely took me for granted, but we've both grown up a lot, even since then. I can't believe I used to worry about us so much. Now I just feel so certain that he's the one for me and he always has been.

'John?' I stop dead in my tracks and put down the flowers. But he's looking over to his right, squinting at something, not really paying attention.

'I think this is the spot right here, Ais. Although I thought there was a tree in front of it. No, this is it! This is where you got clamped. There should be a plaque or something.'

'John!' I say it louder this time, and he swings around so we're facing each other. The sky behind him is streaked with bright orange and pink but further up the stars are already out.

'Yeah?' His hair is all messy and he looks like he's been through the wringer. He's such a ride. I fancy him so much, but more important, I don't ever want to be away from him again, not even for a minute. We belong together.

'Will you marry me?' I just blurt it out. There's no other way to say it. And then I hold my breath.

He looks back at me with a dubious smile. 'You're not really doing this, are you?'

I actually am. I start to sink down, stop to check for any glass or dog muck, and then go fully down on one knee, wobbling over a bit and then righting myself properly so I can ask the question he's been teasing and begging me with for months. 'Will you marry me?'

His face is straight now. 'You're serious.'

'I'm deadly serious. I've never been so sure of anything in my life.'

'Please stand up so I can look at you properly.' He helps me back to my feet and kisses me so softly on the lips.

'I said I'd know when the time was right, and the time is right. Don't you feel like it is?'

He scoffs and squeezes me. 'I've felt like the time is right all year. I was just hoping that at some stage you'd be ready to say yes.'

I push back from him. 'I'm not just doing this because I have a contact high from Majella and Pablo.' I'm reassuring myself as much as him. 'I just want to lean all the way into it. And they're not the worst role models anyway. We'll be lucky to have what they have.'

'A baby?'

'Yeah, a baby. Why not? And to be married. And a picture of us on our wedding day on the wall in the cottage. When I'm with you, I'm home, John.'

'Home is wherever I'm with you,' he sings into my ear, and then we both jump as a car beeps at us. Two eejits swaying in a hospital car park. 'I promise I'll always mind you, Ais.'

'And I'll mind you.' I lace my fingers between his. 'I promise to always put on the fresh duvet cover. I know how much that stresses you out.'

He bats his lashes. 'My dream woman.'

'I've nixed the idea of us taking over the farm. I came to my senses earlier.'

'If that's what you want. I was worried it would be a lot, but I would have stood by your decision.'

'I haven't even told Mammy with all the drama.'

'Do you think maybe she already knew?'

I muse over that for a second. 'Well, she knew more than me then.'

I shiver, even though it's a warm night and I still have a feather boa around my neck. John envelops me once again and then starts fumbling in his pocket. He steps back and slowly starts sinking down on to one knee. 'What are you doing?' I squeal. 'No, I wanted to ask you. Get up, you clown!'

'I do need to ask you, Ais, I absolutely do. So I'm going to do it again.' He holds out the same square box he had with him in New York.

'Have you been carrying that around all this time?'

He smiles. 'You mean you didn't know?'

'It's been years since I checked your pockets for engagement rings. Turns out that was a huge waste of time.'

'I must admit it got me in the balls a few times when I sat down quickly, but you're worth it. I needed to be ready for when you came to your senses.'

I throw back my head and laugh. I can't help it. He never stops surprising me.

'So, Ais, I'm going to ask you an important question again. I think I know what the answer is going to be this time, but I'm asking because you deserve to be asked, and there's only one answer I've been waiting to hear.'

I smile. 'Go on, so.' I'm afraid if I say anything more, I'll start to cry and ruin the moment.

'Aisling, will you marry me?'

'Of course I will. And John, will you marry me?'

'I can't wait to.'

EPILOGUE

Three months later ...

'Okay, now another one with Don and Aisling.'

'I'm guessing you mean baby Aisling?'

'Well, I have enough pictures of you and Don,' Majella hisses at me, thrusting her daughter into Don Shields's arms. Luckily, she looks nothing like Danny DeVito. She's the cutest baby on earth, the perfect mix of Majella and Pablo, who've taken to parenting like ducks to water, bar one unfortunate incident when Pab got the baby's ears pierced while Majella was in Strong Stuff having her roots done. Sharon said Maj needed two glasses of prosecco and three Lindors to get over the shock.

Pablo flits around taking pictures and providing back-up soothers as the DJ segues into Counting Crows. My eyes search for John and find him at the bar, already bouncing up and down on the balls of his feet. I smile as he mouths the opening lyrics to 'Mr Jones'. In his element.

'These pictures will be great at her twenty-first, and you can tell her she was at her own baby shower,' Sadhbh laughs.

Obviously Majella was suffering from so much FOMO after missing the second half of her legendary shower she insisted on having another one in lieu of a christening, although the Tenerifian relatives have been told that the child has basically been blessed by the Pope himself. Liz Moran did some muttering about limbo, but Majella silenced her with a tirade about preparing second class for communion for three years in a row and losing any bit of faith she might have had.

'John doesn't mind not being godfather, does he?' Majella worries beside me.

'I don't think you can call them godfather and godmother if you're not doing the church thing.'

'Ah, you know what I mean. I know little Aisling will be in good hands with you and Don watching over her.' She gets distracted by a man at the bar. 'Ais, who is that guy? I swear I know his face but can't place him.'

'Oh, that's Davey, but I think you know him better as Dr Alan Grant.' I hum the *Jurassic Park* music into her ear and she squeals.

'Oh my God! What an icon. I have to buy him a drink.'

She shimmies off in the same black tuxedo dress she wore to the original shower. It's a little oversized on her now, but her boobs are still magnificent, which she's thrilled with, and the dress is great for feeding access.

I wave as Mammy and Dr Trevor arrive, and then repeat 'Trevor, Trevor, Trevor' over and over again in my mind. I have to stop calling him Dr Trevor or Cara and Síomha will be sniggering at me for the next twenty years. ShayMar Eco Farm and Yurt Resort officially went on the market last week, with an auction due in the spring sometime. Mammy was relieved I came to the decision to let it go. And John was right, she did kind of know. She said she wants to help us out with the deposit for the cottage, so we'll be able to keep an eye on the forget-me-nots, roses, peonies and about twelve other perennials we planted on September eighteenth for many more September eighteenths to come. By next summer we'll be giving Diarmuid Gavin a run for his money. Trevor's house in Kerry is for sale too, and is expected to go quickly, given its proximity to Killarney. John, Mammy and I are going down there on St Stephenses Day for a couple of nights, after one last Christmas on the farm. I'm dreading lighting a candle for Daddy at home for the last time, but we'll light one in the cottage too, so he knows where to find us. It's only over the road. Our new home.

I jump as the shock of something freezing cold touches my arm. 'Sorry,' John says, handing me the icy West Coast Cooler, still singing 'Mr Jones'. '*I wanna be just about as happy as I can be –*' He kisses my cheek. 'You looked away with the fairies.'

'Do you think Pablo has slept since August?'

'I doubt it. He stays awake to watch the baby sleep, but then is afraid to sleep when she's awake in case he misses something.'

'He's a medical marvel, I've decided,' Majella interjects. 'Another amazing party, Ais. You should do this for a living.' She nudges me. 'I can't wait to pay you back, though. Since she's making such a song and dance about it, I'll allow Mandy Blumenthal to do the wedding, but the hen party is going to be all me. It's going to be out of this world.'

'Ah, Maj, there's no need for fuss.'

I spin the Pandora ring around my finger, like a little comfort charm. John tried to insist, but I don't want a new ring. This one is perfect. It has a story behind it.

Maj stares at me in mock disgust. 'No fuss? Are you joking me? All the times you've pulled it out of the bag and out of your hole for me and all the girls. We're going to Vegas and Ibiza and Carrick-on-Shannon. You deserve it.'

She scurries off as baby Aisling starts to whimper, already undoing the top button of her dress.

John slings his arm over my shoulder just as the music slows down. He turns to me in delight. 'Our song!' and starts humming along to 'First Day of My Life'. Something tells me he's been in cahoots with the DJ.

Pablo appears in front of us and demands that we 'smile for the camera!' He takes a picture of a generic John, with his brown eyes, hint of a beard and big hands, and beside him, with her natural kink and flushed cheeks, a complete Aisling.

ACKNOWLEDGEMENTS

If you've reached the end of this book, chances are you've read all five instalments of the Aisling series, so míle buíochas for the support. When we pivoted into authoring seven years ago we couldn't have dreamed we'd still be here in 2023. It has been a joy and a privilege to keep Aisling's story going, and we hope you love the ending we gave her.

We are forever grateful to the villages of Kill, Co. Kildare, and Borris, Co. Carlow, for each inspiring Ballygobbard in their own way. The same goes for the pubs, shops and local characters whose spirit is in the pages of these novels. You can take the girls out of the country, but not the country out of the girls.

To our parents and families, thank you for the books, trips to the library and fostering a love of reading in us from a young age. It was one of the first things we bonded over when we met at Ballyfermot College of Further Education all those years ago.

Eoin Matthews, thank you for clearing the kitchen table when we needed to have an extremely professional meeting and for always holding the babies when it was time to work.

We couldn't have done any of this without being able to moan about deadlines to our friends. They are, in no particular order: Louise Keegan, Sheloa Nichols, Imogen Pollard, Unity

Pollard, Breda Gittons, Aine Bambrick, Cliff Barragry, Sophie White, Louise McSharry, Esther O'Moore Donohoe, Deirdre Ball, Fiona Hyde, Ciara Sammon, Conor O'Brien, Richard Toner, Sarah Kisch, the Glossy Posse and the Break Your Face Naas gals. Thanks for listening.

Eternal gratitude to Ciara and Gav Reilly, and love always to the luckiest and loveliest gals, D & B.

We are spoilt by the team at Gill Books, who have gone above and beyond from day one to get Aisling out into the world. Special thanks to Ruth Gill and Nicki Howard.

To Conor Nagle who suggested we write OMGWACA in the first place, we owe you many drinks. Thank you for having faith in us and, with the help of Catherine Gough, helping us to build the Aisling universe.

Our first meeting with Teresa Daly was over a bottle of wine in a pub, and we've since shared many, many, many more bottles over the years. Thank you, T, for your creativity in publicity and marketing and, most recently, your editorial input. And cheers for picking up the tab.

To Aoibheann Molumby, our most patient and understanding editor, thanks for getting it and then letting us run with it. The same goes for our copyeditor, Emma Dunne. We live for your '… or is this just an Aislingism?' comments.

When it comes to publicity, Fiona Murphy reigns supreme. Thank you for your enthusiasm for blowing the budget for Aisling and for occasionally booking us a chauffeur. You know how much those little water bottles thrill us.

Paul Neilan, you are the James Bond of sales. Thank you for the numbers. Also to Linda, we are always pleased to see The Linda popping into our inboxes.

To Chelsea Morgan Hoffmann, Aisling Lenihan and all at Element Pictures, one day when we're watching Aisling on screen, it will all have been worth it. We appreciate your tenacity and you have undoubtedly made us better writers.

Our agent Sheila Crowley is the best in the biz. She never fails to steer us in the right direction, and we live for her tales from the industry. Thanks for always having our backs, Sheila. We feel very safe in your hands.

We are one hundred per cent certain this series wouldn't have been as successful as it was if not for the vociferous support and encouragement from the one and only Marian Keyes. We would make it dark and rainy every day for you if we could, Marian.

And finally, India Matthews, Esme Matthews and Felix Matthews, we did all this to impress you. Why hasn't it worked?